Lizzie's Secret

Rosie Clarke

W F HOWES LTD

This large print edition published in 2016 by
W F Howes Ltd
Unit 5, St George's House, Rearsby Business Park,
Gaddesby Lane, Rearsby, Leicester LE7 4YH

1 3 5 7 9 10 8 6 4 2

First published in the United Kingdom in 2016
by Aria

A CIP catalogue record for this book is available
from the British Library

ISBN 978 1 51005 024 2

Typeset by Palimpsest Book Production Limited,
Falkirk, Stirlingshire

Printed and bound by
Printforce Nederland b.v., Alphen aan den Rijn,
The Netherlands

PROLOGUE

It was dark, so dark and cold. The girl shivered as she heard the footsteps behind her. They were coming closer and the alley seemed endless. She would never reach safety before he caught up with her. The sound of his harsh breathing was close and she gave a cry of fear as she ran faster. She had to get away or he would catch her and then the nightmare would be real. Taking a deep breath, she ran harder and faster, but as fast as she ran he was always there, pursuing her down the dark alley, and she knew that whatever she did he would get her.

'No, please no, don't hurt me . . .' She could smell the stink of foul breath and knew he was too strong for her and she screamed, but it was no good . . . no good . . .

'Wake up,' a strident voice broke into her nightmare. 'It's all right, girl. You're quite safe here. You were just having a bad dream.'

'Where am I?' she asked, aware now of the narrow bed with its hard mattress and the low, shaded light. The woman standing over her was dressed in the uniform of a nurse, her dark hair

1

peeping from beneath a white starched cap. 'What happened to me? Where am I?'

'You don't remember – any of it?' the nurse looked disbelieving.

'No, I only know . . .' She broke off as she realised she didn't even know her own name. Fear scythed through her as she saw the bars on the windows. 'Who am I – and why am I here?'

'Don't play games! You've been brought to this place because your aunt felt it impossible to keep you at home in the circumstances.'

'What circumstances?' The fear was rising in her, because she was gradually becoming aware that this was an institution of some kind and she somehow knew that she was a prisoner here. 'Why am I in this place? What have I done? I want to go home . . .' And yet she did not know where home was. 'Please tell me where I am. What is this place?'

'It's an institution for fallen girls. Don't worry; you're only here until after the event. Your uncle insisted that they want you back – but your aunt wants to hush this up . . .'

'Hush what up? What have I done?'

'From what I gather it's more a case of what someone else did to you,' the nurse said. 'You were attacked . . .'

'Nurse Simpkins!' A sharp voice cut in. 'You know what Doctor said. No talking to this patient until he's seen her.'

'Sorry, Sister, but she was asking questions . . .'

'Well, that's an improvement, young lady,' an older version of the nurse came into her view. 'We'd begun to think you would never come back to us. I'll tell Doctor you're awake. Would you like a drink of water?'

'Could I have a cup of tea please?' She reached out to touch the Sister's arm. 'Please, why am I here? Have I done something wrong? Who am I?'

'So many questions all at once. I think we'll leave it to Doctor to explain – and just water at first. We don't want you being sick all over the place. You've been asleep a long time . . .'

'How long?'

'Doctor will explain. Rest now and my nurse has a glass of water for you.'

'Little sips now,' the nurse held the glass to her lips. She swallowed a few sips, found it more difficult than she'd expected and fell back against the pillows, her eyes closing.

'I think she's fallen asleep again . . .'

'Yes, but it is a proper sleep this time. I daresay she's exhausted . . .'

'Do you think she really can't recall anything?'

The voices seemed to come from a long way off, as if she were shrouded by an impenetrable fog, their words making no sense, as she lost the battle to stay awake.

'I think it's genuine. She was very ill after the miscarriage – sometimes a long illness like that leaves the patient unable to recall, but the amnesia may not be permanent.'

'Perhaps it's best for her if she never remembers exactly what happened. She'll grieve for the babe if she remembers it . . .'

'We're not supposed to get too friendly with these girls. They are here for discipline and because their families are ashamed of them . . .'

'Yes, but she was attacked and raped . . .'

'That's enough, nurse. Perhaps this case is a little different, but the outcome was the same – the uncle and aunt wouldn't have the child had she gone full term . . . at least, the uncle might have done, but *she* was set against it. It's best the girl doesn't know too much . . .'

The darkness was claiming her. She was sinking back into its welcoming arms, shutting out everything, leaving all the pain and the distress behind. She wasn't ready to know, didn't want to remember, because it hurt too much and she wasn't strong enough. If she once looked back and saw his face she would remember and that would be too painful . . .

CHAPTER 1

'**A**re you here for the job too?' Lizzie Larch looked at the girl sitting next to her on the hard wooden chair. She was a pretty girl with soft fair hair and blue eyes. 'I don't reckon we stand much chance, do you?'

It was 1939 and the country was still recovering from the deep depression that had gripped it for most of the thirties.

'It depends how many jobs are going,' the other girl replied. 'I'm Beth Court. I'm after a job in the office . . .'

'Do they want an office girl? I thought they were looking for seamstresses and apprentices to make hats?'

'Well, yes, that's what they advertised,' Beth offered her hand. 'But when I asked about the interview they said there would be a job for a typist too. I'm good at typing, but my shorthand isn't fast enough.'

'I'm not a trained seamstress, but I can sew, so I'm hoping to get the apprentice's job.'

'How old are you? I'm eighteen. I worked for two years in a cardboard factory but then took typing classes and shorthand. Girls in offices get more than a measly thirty-five bob a week . . .'

'Yes, I suppose they do. I was in a canteen on the docks, earning more than two pounds, but I saw these jobs advertised and thought it would be better to learn a trade.'

'Miss Beth Court please,' a woman said and Beth looked nervously at Lizzie, pulling at the blue dress she was wearing under a dark jacket.

'Well, good luck. I hope you get taken on . . .'

'Good luck to you too,' Lizzie glanced around at the opposition: twenty girls after two jobs. It was unlikely that Lizzie would be picked, especially since she had no experience. Aunt Jane had warned her it would be a waste of time, but Uncle Jack had supported her.

'Why shouldn't the girl have a chance of a better life,' he had said. 'If you're thinking of that other business, don't. Lizzie's a good girl, aren't you, love?'

'Yes,' Lizzie had nodded. She knew why her aunt was so strict, of course she did. It was to do with that time she'd been so ill . . . Lizzie couldn't remember much about it, but she knew she'd been in a sanatorium for a long time. She didn't know why and she couldn't remember much from before that time. She'd remembered her name after Doctor Morrison started to treat her, because he'd been kind and gentle, explaining that she'd had a nasty accident and hit her head.

'You were concussed, Lizzie,' he told her. 'Because

of that you've become confused. You were in another hospital before you came to me and they neglected you – but now we're going to make you well. There is nothing to be frightened of now, Lizzie, my dear.'

'Lizzie Larch . . .' she'd repeated the words after him. 'I live with Aunt Jane and her husband Uncle Jack . . .'

'Your parents died years ago of diphtheria and your aunt kindly took you in. You can go home to her and your uncle when you've accepted who you are . . .'

Lizzie had been fifteen then; she knew that because the doctor had told her so and that meant she must have had her accident when she was fourteen. She'd tried so hard to remember what had caused the accident, but all she knew was that she'd had a nasty fall and been very ill for a long time . . .

'Miss Lizzie Larch, please . . .'

A man of about forty was calling her. Wearing a well-worn suit of once-good pinstriped cloth, he didn't strike her as being important at first glance and she thought he might be a clerk or something. Lizzie got to her feet and followed him, not into an office, as she expected, but to a large room where two men and three girls were working at benches. Hats were in various stages of development, piles of them everywhere. The floor was strewn with bits of felt, silk and cottons, and several pins. Girls were machining felt or sewing on feathers and trimmings, but the men were either cutting or shaping the hats with the aid of steamers and moulds.

'This is the workroom. It's where you'll be working if we take you on as our apprentice, Miss Larch. What do you think of it?'

Lizzie was fascinated. 'It's very busy, sir, and it looks interesting.'

'Interesting, eh? Do you think you'd like to work here?'

'Yes, sir, if I were given a chance . . .'

'What can you do?'

'My aunt taught me to use a sewing machine. But I'd like to learn all of it – the cutting and the shaping and the trimming . . .' She hesitated, then, 'I'd like to design hats, sir . . .'

'Would you indeed?' he asked, his bright beady eyes intent on her face. He was a small man, wiry with a thin face, hair that was receding at the temples and faded grey eyes. 'Are you any good?'

'I shouldn't think so,' Lizzie said honestly. 'My aunt says it's a waste of time, but Uncle Jack says my designs look pretty.'

'Humph,' the man grunted. 'Well, we stick to fairly basic shapes here, Miss Larch, but I like a girl with ambition. You know we pay our apprentices twenty-five shillings a week?'

'Yes, sir, I know. But you pay more once I'm trained, don't you?'

'If you finish your six months training, I'll pay you thirty-five shillings, and if you see the year out, I'll pay you two pounds and ten shillings. After that, it depends how talented you are.'

'Are you saying I've got the job?'

'You're the only one who applied for it; the rest of them want to be seamstresses,' he said. 'I'm Bert Oliver – and I own this workshop. We sell to the retail trade. I shall expect you in at eight fifteen each morning. For a start you'll be sweeping up and making tea, but we'll teach you what you need to know – and we'll see if you're any good.'

'Yes, sir – Mr Oliver,' Lizzie felt a tingle of excitement. 'Do I start on Monday?'

'Do you have to give notice?'

'I gave notice last week at the canteen and finished last Saturday.'

'How old are you, Lizzie?'

'I'm twenty next Saturday.'

His brows rose. 'You dress like a schoolgirl, Miss Larch. I thought you no more than seventeen at most.'

Lizzie was too embarrassed to answer, because her aunt made her dresses and was very strict. Aunt Jane insisted that Lizzie should always be modest in her clothes and not attract attention.

'We expect you to wear a plain dark skirt and blouse for work, or a smart black dress, and we provide an overall for in here, but you may serve in the showroom sometimes and for that you must wear black.'

'I've got a grey skirt and some white blouses – if that will do?'

'I prefer black but dark grey will do for now. Very well, Lizzie. Bring all your details of previous work in on Monday and give them to Mrs Moore; she will see to your wages on a Friday.'

'Yes, Mr Oliver.'

'And bring some of your designs in if you want. I might have a look at them when I have time . . .'

Lizzie was still in shock. 'Thank you, sir. I shall look forward to it . . .'

'Off you go then, I'm in need of a trained seamstress and a cutter, though from what I've seen so far in the waiting room that looks like being a hopeless cause . . .'

Lizzie returned to the waiting room still feeling bewildered and unsure whether she was dreaming.

'Lizzie!' Beth Court pounced on her. 'I got my job – what about you?'

'I've been taken on as an apprentice,' Lizzie said. 'My aunt won't be pleased, because the wage is less than I was earning, but it's what I want to do . . .'

'That's all that matters then, isn't it?'

'Yes, perhaps,' Lizzie smiled at her. 'I'm glad you got your job, Beth. It means I'll be seeing you most days, doesn't it?'

'Yes, of course. They don't have a canteen here. We have a staffroom where we can make a cup of tea and eat our sandwiches, if we like – but there's a little café just down the road where we can go for a meal.'

'I shan't be able to afford that,' Lizzie said. 'Aunt

Jane takes a pound of my money – that only leaves me five bob for everything.'

'Surely she won't expect you to pay so much now?' Beth looked surprised. 'I'm getting three pounds in the office for a start. It's mostly invoices for the customers and some bookkeeping, and typing letters to suppliers . . .'

'You must be clever to do that. I didn't take my school certificate, because I was off school for more than a year.'

'You don't sound dumb to me . . .'

'Oh no, I'm not. I read a lot and my uncle helped me with arithmetic and other things . . . but I didn't know the proper work for the exams. My uncle says it's a daft system anyway, and he thinks I'm clever at stuff like drawing . . .'

'He sounds nice?'

'Uncle Jack is lovely . . .' Lizzie broke off with a sigh. 'My aunt has such a sharp tongue and I don't think I could bear to live at home if he wasn't around . . .'

'Sounds rotten for you,' Beth said. 'Look, why don't you come and have lunch with us? Mum always cooks enough for an army . . .'

'Could I really? Won't she mind?'

'Of course you can come,' Beth said. 'Mum always likes to meet my friends and she's a wonderful cook. I know you'll like her, Lizzie, and she will like you . . . and we'll have a look round the market on the way . . .'

⋆　　⋆　　⋆

Lizzie loved the busy market with its colourful canopies and stalls piled high with produce that smelled gorgeous. One was crammed with various kinds of cheese, some of them unknown to her that smelled really strong. She stopped to look and asked the man behind the counter what the different cheeses were. He laughed and explained that the ones that smelled strong were ripe Brie and Stilton.

Beth tugged at her arm and they walked on. The stalls were really busy and the cries of the costers were loud and sometimes shrill, all of them trying to be heard above the next man. The crowds were made up of lots of different peoples: local cockneys with their cheerful grins, greasy caps pulled over their heads; Jews with orthodox ringlets, beards, long black coats and black hats; men with dark complexions, turbans and traditional long gowns, their feet bare of socks and wearing string sandals; women in headscarves tied in a knot, showing just a glimpse of hair, and aprons that crossed over at the front, on their break from the jam factory just down the road.

On one side of the road there was a pawn shop with the sign of the three balls over its door and a few tarnished articles on show; most of the stock was inside, tucked away in the safe, waiting for its owners to reclaim it when they had the money. Next to it was one of the Greenspan trading grocery stores and then a hardware shop and a pub with its sign in black and gold lettering and a picture of a king's head, adjoining it; a tobacconist store with penknives, cigarette cases and signs, and a rack of pipes in its window made up the row of shops. Further on was a Jewish synagogue and next to that a building with the name of a clothing manufacturer over its dirty windows, which were blocked out with grubby blinds. Beth told Lizzie it was a sweatshop and the seamstresses who worked there were made to do impossibly long hours.

'They're all foreign women and I don't think any of them speak English,' Beth told her. 'Come on, we'd better hurry now or Mum will get worried.'

'So what happened?' Aunt Jane attacked as soon as Lizzie entered the kitchen. 'I suppose it was a waste of time. Don't imagine your uncle and I are going to let you sit around doing nothing all day . . .'

'I got the job as an apprentice and I'm going to learn everything.' Lizzie's head rose in defiance. 'My wage is twenty-five bob for the first six months and then it goes up another ten shillings . . .'

'How are you going to manage on that?' her aunt demanded. 'I'll still want my pound a week and that leaves you with hardly enough to get to work . . .'

'Lizzie has done the right thing,' Uncle Jack spoke up for her. 'I've always said that she's wasted in that canteen – and it isn't her fault she missed all that schooling, Jane. She'll give you a pound a week same as usual, but until she's earning more I'll give her ten bob for herself.'

13

'Whose money is that coming out of? Don't think you can cut my money. I work all hours to keep this family decent – and I . . .'

'It's all right, Jane,' he said quietly. 'Lizzie's pocket money will come from mine. I'll share it with her.'

'Uncle Jack,' Lizzie protested, 'you can't give me your beer money. You work hard all week, you deserve something . . .' her eyes stung with tears, because he was always trying to help her, to protect her from Aunt Jane's caustic tongue.

'If he's fool enough to give it to you, it won't hurt him to stay home one night a week . . .' Aunt Jane's eyes narrowed suspiciously. 'So if you got the job where have you been all this time?'

'I met a nice girl at Oliver's workshops. She's got a job in the office and I had lunch at her home and met her mum.'

Lizzie wished she knew more about her own mother, but she had only a tiny silver cross and chain to remember her by. Lizzie sometimes felt upset that almost nothing of her parents' had been kept for her, but then most of her past was shrouded in a hazy mist since her accident.

Sometimes strange pictures flashed into her head and she seemed to recall a nurse bending over her . . . and a room with bars on the windows. All she really remembered was the doctor at the sanatorium telling her that she was Lizzie Larch and she could go home to her aunt and uncle as soon as she was well enough.

14

She'd left school at sixteen, and gone to work in the canteen. At night, her uncle met her from work and walked her home through the dirty and often smelly dock area, which meant he had to shut his workshop early for her sake. He was a busy man and mending shoes didn't bring in a fortune. Lizzie had tried to persuade him that she could walk home alone, because as a self-employed cobbler, Uncle Jack couldn't afford to shut his door half an hour early every night.

He said it was because he didn't want her to have another accident, but when she asked him to tell her more about it, he always shook his head and said the doctor thought it best if she was allowed to remember in her own time.

Lizzie would have liked to know more about her accident. If she remembered, her aunt might stop treating her as if she was still fourteen.

'Have you got to wear a uniform for work?' her aunt asked suddenly, bringing Lizzie's wandering thoughts back to the present.

'Yes, I need a smart black dress. I've seen something in your Butterick patterns . . . if you would let me make it on your machine. I could buy some material on the market.'

'Yes, of course your aunt will let you use the machine,' Uncle Jack took a pound from his pocket. 'Get some good material, Lizzie. Jane has always told you that good cloth makes the clothes, and it lasts.'

'Well, at least someone listens to me sometimes,'

Aunt Jane said. 'If you show me the pattern, I'll cut it out for you.'

'Oh thank you, aunt,' Lizzie smiled shyly at her uncle as he gave her the money. 'If I've got a smart dress I may serve in the showroom sometimes – and that's all good experience.'

'Well, I suppose it's a better job than you had,' her aunt sniffed. 'But don't let it go to your head – and I don't want you staying out late at night.'

'I hardly ever go out . . .'

Lizzie sighed, because it was never any use arguing with Aunt Jane, but at least she had the job she wanted . . .

CHAPTER 2

'Here, put this on, Lizzie,' the girl handed her a dark grey striped overall with a wrap-over front and a tie belt. 'We have to wear these or we get bits all over our clothes.'

'Thanks.' Lizzie tied the belt tightly. 'What's your name?' The girl was fair-skinned with fair hair and bright blue eyes and she wore a pale peach lipstick. Lizzie envied her the modern haircut she'd had done, brushed back off her face into a stylish DA, which resembled the feathers of a duck's tail at the back. Lizzie's own dark hair was scraped back in a bun.

'I'm Tilly Blake,' the girl smiled. 'I do most of the making up, sewing brims into place, sewing on ribbons and trimmings, things like that.'

'I think I saw you trimming a hat when I came for the interview. It looked interesting.'

'I'll show you later.' Tilly thrust a broom at her. 'Best get this place a bit tidy or Mr Oliver will be on the warpath. It's always a shambles by the end of the day, and we were busy on Friday evening so it just got left. He nearly blew a fuse

17

when he saw it this morning. No one wants to clear up after anyone else – that's why Grumble Guts got you . . .'

'Is that what you call Mr Oliver behind his back?'

'His nephew Harry started it,' Tilly said, 'and it just caught on.'

'His nephew – where is he?' Lizzie looked round the workshop.

'He's gone out delivering to the shops. The buyers come here, mostly once a month, and place an order. We make the hats up to their instructions, and then Harry takes the orders out. He fetches our stuff from the manufacturers, makes up orders, checks the stock – and he's a trained cutter too, but he hates working on the shop floor. He'd rather be in the showroom or out in the van, though according to Harry there's going to be a war soon and then he's off. He wants to fly aeroplanes . . .'

'Gossiping again, Tilly?' Mr Oliver's clipped tones interrupted.

Lizzie started to pick up the larger pieces of material that had fallen to the floor, putting them into a large rush basket, which was for reusable scraps. She swept carefully round all the benches and collected all the rubbish, taking it out to the backyard and depositing it in a metal dustbin. Returning to the workshop, she looked round for more jobs.

'Make some tea, Lizzie. You'll find everything in

18

the staff room,' Mr Oliver told her. 'I like mine strong, with three spoons of sugar, but ask all the girls what they want. You can all have a mug before we start the day. It's damned cold out . . .'

Lizzie made a careful note of everyone's orders, her training in the canteen standing her in good stead, but when it came to it, she wasn't quite sure who wanted sugar and who didn't, so she took a tray with a sugar bowl and spoons, letting them help themselves.

'That's an improvement,' one of the men smiled at her. 'You're the new girl, aren't you – Lizzie something?'

'I'm Lizzie Larch,' she balanced her tray on the bench, offering her hand.

He gripped it hard. 'I'm Ed Biggleswick – the head cutter. Everyone calls me Ed, don't bother with Mr Biggleswick, it's a mouthful and made my life a nightmare at school. Just call me Ed and we'll get on all right.'

'Thank you, Ed. Will you teach me to cut out hats one day?'

He smiled at her eagerness. 'If Mr Oliver tells me to. You'll have to wait a bit for that, Lizzie. It takes experience to learn how to shape the hats and the cutting is all important.'

Lizzie took to the friendly man immediately. 'Thank you, Ed. I shall enjoy being taught by you – and I do want to learn everything please.'

'Well, between me and you, there's no magic to it; it's all in the patterns,' Ed winked again. 'But

19

don't let on, because we cutters are the top of the tree and we don't want too many people getting in on the act . . .'

Lizzie started to collect the empty mugs on her tray. She washed them, stacking them back on the gingham oilcloth-covered shelves in the kitchen, and returned to the workshop. Everyone had their heads down, busy at their tasks.

'Ah, there you are, Lizzie,' Mr Oliver boomed at her. 'Come along, I'll show you what I want you to do this morning.' He took her through to a small room at the side of the workshop and showed her the shelves, which were filled with rolls of materials, baskets of ribbons, silk roses, tins of sequins, boxes of feathers and other trimmings. 'You can make an inventory of all the material and trimmings. It's called stocktaking and my lazy nephew was supposed to do it last week, but he's delivering again today and when he gets back he'll find another reason not to do it. If you look at the labels, you'll see whether it's felt, grosgrain, silk or whatever. Make a note of the colour, and whatever amount it says is left.'

'Yes, Mr Oliver. You want me to write it down on this pad?'

'You can write, can't you?' he asked brusquely.

'Yes, sir.' Lizzie took the pen and notebook from the counter, frowning as she looked at the rolls and rolls of material on the shelves. It was going to take ages; at this rate it would take months before she got near a hat . . .

'Get on with it then, girl. By the time you've sorted this lot, you'll know your materials . . .'

Lizzie sighed as she looked at the task ahead of her; it was going to take hours. She saw some steps leaning against the wall and fetched them, climbing to the top shelf. After trying to find the labels unsuccessfully, Lizzie decided that the only way to do this was to take all the rolls down and reorganise the whole stockroom. It looked as if everything was muddled, as if people just shoved a roll into the first available space. It would be a long, slow job, but, as her employer said, at least it would help her to know the materials . . .

'I thought you weren't coming,' Beth said when Lizzie turned up just as she was finishing her lunch. 'Where have you been?'

'I was in the stockroom and no one told me it was time for lunch.'

'Oh well, there's enough in that pot for a cup of tea,' Beth said. 'Have you brought something to eat?'

'I made some cheese sandwiches this morning, but I'm not that hungry . . .'

Beth offered her a sausage roll. 'Mum packed me three; they're lovely but I couldn't eat them all. I was going to give it to the ducks on the river.'

'Oo, yes, I could eat one of those . . .' Lizzie took the sausage roll and bit into the crisp pastry. 'Your mum is a lovely cook. Aunt Jane only makes these for special occasions.'

'I'm glad you like them,' Beth said. 'I was wondering if you'd like to go out one night – to the flicks or something. I go out with Tony at the weekends; he's my boyfriend, but he works late most nights. He's savin' for the future . . .'

'I usually go to the matinee on Saturdays. My aunt doesn't like me to go out at night . . .'

'Not ever? That's pretty rotten for you – and it's not fair. You're older than me. You shouldn't let her boss you about like that, Lizzie.'

'Perhaps you could come to tea on Saturday, and then, when she knows you, she might let me go with you to the flicks.'

'Tony is taking me to a dance that evening, but I can have tea with you first.'

'I've never been to a dance . . .'

Beth stared at her in amazement. 'I've been going since I was fifteen – it was just a church social at first and my elder sisters and brother were with me. I didn't start courting until I was eighteen. Dad wants me to wait until I'm twenty to get married, but I'm hoping to persuade him to let us on my next birthday . . .'

Lizzie looked at Beth's lovely blonde hair, which she wore in a pageboy style clipped back behind her ears at the sides for work. Her eyes were a deep blue and she was so pretty that Lizzie wasn't surprised she had a serious boyfriend. Her own reflection in the mirror was disappointing, for though her features were regular, her eyes were a melting brown and her dark hair was straight, pulled back in the bun she wore at the back of her head.

'You're so lucky, Beth. I wish I could go dancing . . . and have a boyfriend.'

'Well, why can't you? I think you should stand up for yourself more.'

'You don't understand. My aunt is very strict . . . I don't know why exactly, but Uncle Jack says she's only trying to look after me. I suppose it's because I was very ill for a long time . . .'

'Oh, well . . .' Beth shrugged. 'I've got to get back to the office. I'll see you tomorrow if I don't catch you after work. Don't forget your breaks and your lunch period tomorrow – you don't want to let them take advantage of you, Lizzie.'

'No, I won't. I was so busy and the time just went . . .'

Returning to the stockroom, Lizzie looked at what she'd done. All the felt was together on three shelves now. They had mostly red and green and a few half rolls of brown, grey and pink, and just one half roll of a dark blue. She'd found a new place for the tins and reels of cotton and cards of braid, and she'd just started to sort out the grosgrains, silks, velvets and fine straw when the door opened behind her and someone swore loudly.

'What the hell has happened here?'

Lizzie swung round to see a man staring at the shelves in disgust. He had light brown hair that waved back from his forehead, but because it was too long, a bit of it fell forward into his eyes. His eyes were a greenish brown and his mouth was wide, his nose a little long.

'What's wrong? I'm doing the stocktaking and putting everything together so that it's easier to check what we've got . . .'

'You foolish little girl.' He looked so arrogant that Lizzie was angry too. 'We put all the same colour together, regardless of what the material is and then it's easy to find what you need . . . now we'll be searching for ages to find the right match . . .'

'But it will be easy when I finish,' Lizzie argued. 'Everything was all jumbled up . . .'

'It was where I wanted it.' He glared at her. 'Where are the cottons and braids?'

'Over there by the window. They don't need a huge shelf to themselves. This way you can see how much you've got in felts and silks and gros-grains and – you've hardly got any pink felt left and only that bit of blue and no black at all . . .'

'I meant to order all of those last week, but we were too busy,' he said, examining the shelves. 'What would you do if I said I wanted it all back the way it was?'

'I've got no idea how it was, except it was a jumbled-up mess.'

'Oh, was it?' He glared at her for a moment and then suddenly grinned. 'I suppose it may be better when you've finished and we all know where to look . . . I'm Harry Oliver by the way. I presume you're Lizzie Larch?'

24

'Yes. So you're Mr Oliver's nephew,' Lizzie said, still wary. 'He called you lazy and said you were supposed to do the stocktaking last week . . .'

'I never have the time,' Harry said. 'Oh, well, we'll give your system a try, Lizzie. I need some red silk grosgrain and some black veiling . . .'

'That shelf has all the grosgrain – and that one is going to have silk and the straw is going there, and that one is for velvets, and stiffening materials here – and all the veiling and silk ribbons are here on the floor.'

'We haven't got much black veiling left. Are you certain this is all of it?'

'Yes,' Lizzie looked at her list. 'It says there's only a third of a roll left and there are three yards in a roll . . .'

'Damn it! That won't trim six hats.' Harry glared as if it were her fault. 'I'd better go and fetch some from the wholesaler.'

He went out without another glance in her direction. Lizzie looked at her watch. She'd been left to get on all day and no one had brought her a mug of tea through, though she knew they were supposed to stop for one at three o'clock. She'd almost got the shelves to her liking and she would just about finish the materials today. Tomorrow, she would have to start on all those trimmings and lengths of ribbons, to say nothing of the feathers and the silk flowers . . .

CHAPTER 3

'So how did you get on today?' Beth's mother asked when she entered the kitchen. 'Was it all right?'

'Yes.' Beth sniffed appreciatively. 'Something smells good tonight?'

'I hope you're hungry? We're having lamb chops.'

'Everything you cook is lovely, Mum.' She hesitated, then, 'If I gave you an extra couple of bob a week could you put another bun or sausage roll in my lunch packet?'

'Were you still hungry?'

'I'd like to offer Lizzie a bun or something. I don't think she gets very much nice at home – and I'm so lucky . . .'

'You're a lovely girl, our Beth,' her mother gave her a fond smile. 'When I'm baking there's always a few left over now that Dotty and your brother are married, and you can keep your money, love.'

'You spoil me, Mum.'

'Well, once Mary gets married this September I'll only have you at home to spoil.'

'All your chicks will have flown except for me – and I'll get married as soon as Dad lets me.'

'Your dad is only thinking of your future. I was twenty when I married.' She smiled at her daughter. 'My Derek was called up in 1916, nearly two years after the war started. They didn't take married men with children until they began to get desperate. When he left me, he put his barrow in store, kissed me and told me not to worry. I found out I was having the twins a few weeks later, and I would never have managed if it hadn't been for my mother's help. It was two years before your father came back with a wound to his leg that kept him out of the rest of it, and another eighteen months before it healed enough for him to get back to work full time.'

'Is that why he limps sometimes?'

'Arthritis set in when his leg healed. He got a small pension for his war work, which he gave to his mother but we lived on what he earned from the barrow, same as now.'

'I never knew we were hard up,' Beth said. 'All I remember is you smiling and cooking, and Dad coming home with fruit from the stall and laughing as we all scrabbled for an orange or a pear.'

'We managed better than most.'

'You never let on to us if you were worried.'

'I wasn't, because I knew we would get through – and my mother helped us when she could.'

'Granny Shelly? You worry about her, don't you?'

'She doesn't complain but she finds it difficult to get about – and she's getting a bit forgetful.' Beth's mother sighed. 'You wouldn't mind if Granny came here to live, would you?'

'Why should I mind? I love her; we all do . . .'

Beth listened as her mother described how her granny had helped out when she and her brother and sisters were small; teaching her daughter how to manage on the money her husband gave her and sometimes giving her a few shillings extra. Beth loved the feisty old lady and never grew tired of hearing stories about her.

'You mustn't ever let her go in one of those awful old people's homes,' Beth's throat was tight with emotion. 'We need to look after her, love her and cherish her, Mum.'

'Yes, we'll make sure she moves in with us. Where are you going this evening, love?'

'Tony is taking me to the flicks. It's Humphrey Bogart and he likes him – I do too, though I wouldn't mind where we went . . .'

Her mother gave her a long, knowing look. 'I know you don't like having to wait to get married, but promise me you won't be silly, Beth.'

'Tony knows I want to wait, and so does he,' Beth said, smothering a sigh. 'Besides, I wouldn't want to let you and Dad down.'

'Your dad would stand by you and so would I, Beth – but it's not a good way to start a marriage.'

'I'll go up and change,' Beth said, wanting to escape before her mother probed too far.

Mum didn't mean to lecture and Beth hadn't lied when she said she wanted to wait until they were married – but it was getting harder. She could only hope that Tony would go on being content to wait for her.

He'd spoken of what might happen if there was a war before she was twenty. 'I would be sure to be called up, love,' he'd told her. 'I'm just a labourer on the docks, not highly skilled. I earn a decent wage and one day I want my own business. My grandfather had a tobacconist's shop and I'd like to do the same. I reckon I'll look out for a shop with a flat over the top and a garden out back. We could run it together – unless that bloody Hitler spoils things before I can get started.'

The papers had been full of talk about how bad things were getting in Germany for ages; the way they were treating the Jews over there had a lot of people up in arms and even Beth's father talked about it being likely that it would come to a war in the end, but so far the sandbags around important public buildings and the trenches in the public parks up the West End had not been needed; instead the trenches filled with water and were a hazard at night, but everyone prayed that they would never be needed for real . . .

Beth dressed hurriedly and brushed her hair back from her face, fastening it with Kirby grips that didn't show because it frizzed out in soft curls and wisps over her ears and forehead.

When she went back down to the kitchen, her father was washing his hands at the sink, the water turning a muddy brown as it swirled down the plughole.

'You look nice, Beth.' He greeted her with a warm smile. 'Almost as good as those chops your mum has cooked. To what do we owe the honour of such a sumptuous dinner, Mrs Court?'

'It's a celebration of Beth's first job,' she said and smiled back at him. Beth's elder sister had just come in and sat down with them. Mary was a nurse, but she was getting married later in the year and feared that she might lose her job because the Matron did not approve of married nurses, even though they weren't actually barred from being nurses now, as they had been once. 'Had a hard day, Mary love?'

'Yes, very hard,' Mary sighed. 'We lost a patient today. I know he was old but he was a dear man . . .'

'We all have to go one day,' her father said. 'It's a fact of life, Mary.'

'I know, but it still hurts – and there are so many old and sick people needing our help.' She sat opposite him. 'This looks good, Mum. How was your day, Beth?'

'Busy,' Beth said ruefully. 'I was taking dictation for over an hour and then I had to type all my notes up and leave them on Mrs Moore's desk. Harry Oliver is supposed to be in charge of the invoices, but he's so lazy and Mrs Moore has to check everything in case he makes mistakes.'

'Better keep on the right side of her then,' Dad winked at her.

Beth loved her family life and the meals they all took together brought them even closer; it was a

30

time for talking about each other's day and for laughter. She was almost reluctant to leave when the doorbell rang.

'I shan't bother with pudding, Mum. I don't want to keep Tony waiting because we'll miss the start of the big film.'

'You can have your trifle later, if your dad doesn't scoff the lot . . .'

Beth grabbed her coat from behind the door and ran through the hall to greet Tony at the front door, which opened onto the street. He was tall, even taller than her father, and thin, but Beth knew his leanness hid a wiry strength. He worked hard on the docks and was never out of a job, always the one to be picked for overtime because he could be relied on to do a proper job

'We'd best get straight off,' Tony said and kissed her cheek. 'You look lovely, Beth, but you always do. Did you have a good day?'

'Busy but all right,' Beth said and hugged his arm as they walked quickly down the street and arrived at the tram stop just in time to hop on as a tram drew to a halt. 'What about you?'

'Same as always,' he said. 'Trouble is; they want me to work all day Saturday. I was going to look at a little shop in Whitechapel on Saturday afternoon, but I'm going Friday night instead. If it's what I want, I might take it and employ someone to look after the shop until I'm ready to take it over myself.'

Beth didn't say anything, because she knew he'd hoped she wouldn't get the job at Oliver's.

He'd been hoping that she might be content to work in the shop for him, but Beth wanted to use the skills she'd spent a year perfecting, at least for a while, though she'd offered to give him a hand with the accounts at night, and do any typing he needed.

'Are you sure that's a good idea, Tony?'

'What do you mean?'

'Supposing it does come to a war – what will happen to the shop then? Why don't you keep saving your money for the time being and see what happens?'

'I know what you say makes sense, Beth – but I keep thinking a business would give us security, even if I kept on working. I could get a girl to work in the shop and do all the ordering myself.'

'You know I would help with all that, and perhaps help at the shop in the evenings, but I work Saturday mornings . . .'

'And you want the afternoon off, of course you do,' Tony said. 'It wouldn't be fair to ask you, not while you're working in the office at Oliver's – but if we were married you would give all that up and then you could keep an eye on the shop, couldn't you?'

'Yes, of course.' Beth knew it was the answer he wanted. She would be reluctant to leave work immediately when they got married, and it made her wonder if perhaps her father wasn't right in saying she should wait until she was twenty, but when Tony walked her home later and kissed her goodnight in the shadows, all thought of anything but being his wife would fly from her head.

CHAPTER 4

'You've made a good job of the stockroom,' Mr Oliver said. 'I can see what we've got at a glance now and need only refer to the list if something seems wrong.'

'Why don't we have a proper stock book?' Lizzie suggested. 'We could list all the rolls of material as they come in and also have a separate one for the number of hats made and sold.'

'Are you in league with the tax office, Lizzie? If we keep everything as precisely as you suggest it won't give us the chance to fiddle a few bob,' he murmured straight-faced.

Lizzie laughed, not sure whether to believe him. 'I've done all you asked for, sir. When am I going to start learning to make hats?'

'Keen are you?' he looked at her speculatively. 'Well, you can make us all a cup of tea first, Lizzie, and then I'll hand you over to Ed. You're brighter than most of the girls we get here, even if you didn't win any fancy school certificates.'

'I was ill, sir.'

'Something serious?'

'I had an accident, concussion for a long time

and fevers, stuff like that,' Lizzie said wanting to shrug it off. 'I've forgotten it now and I'm fine, perfectly healthy, but I couldn't catch up with the schoolwork I needed for the exams in time. My uncle says I should take them through night school.'

'You don't need them here,' her employer said. 'It's your skills as a milliner I'm interested in, girl. Yes, I've decided you can start with Ed. I need someone who can cut and shape hats, and perhaps finish them – what about those designs you told me o-'

'I didn't think you really wanted to see them, sir.'

'Never say things I don't mean,' he grunted. 'Go on then, make the tea and then report to Ed . . . and you can bring the designs to the office tomorrow.'

'Thank you, sir. I'll leave them in the office for you.'

At last she was going to start learning how to make hats from scratch. Lizzie had attempted one or two at home. She often bought plain hats and trimmed them to her own liking, but they never looked like the beautiful creations she drew with the coloured pencils and crayons her uncle had given her on her last birthday.

After Lizzie had served the tea and washed up, she reported to Ed who looked pleased when she told him she was now his apprentice.

'Oliver listened to me for once,' Ed said. 'I told him it makes sense to train our own cutters. Once

I teach you how to make them and show you how to use the scissors, you'll know all my secrets.'

'I shan't tell anyone else. It's a trade secret, isn't it?'

'Certainly is,' Ed agreed. 'There's machines for all sorts of things these days. Oliver says he does things the old way because it's the best, and I agree with him to a certain extent, but he's a mean old thing and won't spend a penny if an 'a'penny will do . . .'

Lizzie watched avidly as he showed her a book of basic shapes and patterns, which explained how to cut and style various hats. Every word he spoke was a revelation to her and she hung on them, thirsting for the knowledge he could give her.

'You're a good girl,' Ed told her as they took their break for lunch. 'Go and meet your friends. You've only got half an hour.'

'Where do you eat your lunch, Ed?'

'I pop home and get some soup and a cup of tea for my wife. My Madge is a bit of an invalid, see. She was a rare, lovely lass when we married . . .' Ed sighed and shook his head. 'I'll take you to meet her one day, Lizzie. I've got to get off because I'll be late back else . . .'

Lizzie went off to the staffroom to eat her lunch with Beth.

'You're here on time today.'

'Yes, I was helping Ed and he made sure we took our break.'

Beth nodded, then, 'Mum says she'll make one of her Victoria sandwiches for me to bring round on Saturday – if I'm coming?'

'My aunt said you can come to tea,' Lizzie said happily. 'If she thinks you're a sensible girl, I can come to the flicks one night in the week, but I've got to be home before half past nine.'

'You'd miss half the big film,' Beth objected. 'Do you think she'd let you stay with us for the night? I'll get Mum to write the invitation, and I'll promise that my dad will meet us . . .'

'She might let me stay with you if your mum writes to her.' Lizzie sighed as she bit into her sandwich. 'My uncle is lovely, Beth, but Aunt Jane . . . she acts as if I've committed a crime, but Uncle Jack says it's because of my accident.'

'What happened to you?' Beth asked curiously.

'I can't remember anything before I woke up in the sanatorium. The doctor was very kind and told me who I was and that my aunt and uncle wanted me home . . .'

'And you've no idea what happened to you?'

'They said I had a fall but I don't remember anything about it.'

'I suppose that's why your Aunt Jane is so strict. She doesn't want you to have another accident.' Beth offered her half of a pastry. 'It's got apples and sultanas inside.'

'Thanks, that looks delicious,' Lizzie said. 'Aunt Jane spends all her time sewing for other people and hates cooking.'

'I suppose she's too busy,' Beth said and wrinkled her brow. 'I'm not sure, where exactly do you live?'

'My uncle's house is in Wilkes Street,' Lizzie said. 'It once belonged to the Huguenot silk merchants, but it was divided into smaller properties long ago, so we've only got part of it. It's a terraced house now, like yours, but it has three steps up to the front door and an airey in the pavement outside. That means we can have the coal delivered straight into the cellar rather than coming through the house.'

'You said your uncle's rather than your aunt's for once?'

'Yes, his grandfather bought it years ago. Uncle Jack also has a small cobbler's business on the side, which previously belonged to his father and grandfather'

'My dad has a vegetable barrow. It's handy, because we've always got plenty for Mum's stews, but it must be nice to have someone to mend your shoes.'

'Yes, we always have our shoes repaired before they look down at heel.'

'I'm looking forward to meeting him,' Beth said. 'About our trip to the flicks, I think we ought to try and get to see the new film Cary Grant film at the Odeon. I think he's smashing . . .'

'I've seen his picture on the bill posters,' Lizzie agreed, 'but I've never . . .' She broke off as the door opened and Harry Oliver walked in, his eyes bright with mischief as he saw them.

'I thought you two would be down the café with most of the others – Tilly pops home, of course, but Vera and Nancy have gone because the café's doing a cheap meal today . . .'

'I don't want much in the middle of the day,' Lizzie said. 'I would go to sleep all afternoon if I stuffed myself . . .'

'Can't have the new apprentice slacking,' Harry said playfully. 'I want you to become excellent at all things so that I can leave this rotten place and join the RAF . . .'

'Why don't you just go if you feel like that?' Lizzie asked.

'Because Uncle Bert brought me up after my parents died, so I owe him something,' Harry said in a mournful tone. 'He was delighted with your stocktaking, Lizzie, so if you just learn to cut, place the orders and drive a van, old Grumble Guts won't miss me at all . . .'

'I didn't come here to learn to manage the business, just to make hats,' Lizzie retorted with a smile.

'Well, do your best to learn the lot, will you?' Harry pleaded. 'While he needs me I'm stuck here, though once the war comes he won't be able to hold on to me—'

'What makes you so sure there's going to be a war?' Beth asked. 'Tony says it may not happen, and my dad hopes it won't . . .'

'Don't you read the papers, Miss Court? We all know Hitler is determined on war despite that idiot Mr Chamberlain, who thinks he can secure peace in our time.'

'Take your warmongering elsewhere. We're thinking about nicer things . . .'

'Like what?'

'Going to the flicks,' Beth said. 'We're going to the Odeon next week to see Cary Grant.'

'When? I'll come with you – treat you to some toffees . . .'

'If we wanted you, we'd have asked,' Beth said. 'Now, please excuse us, we've ten minutes left of our break and we want some peace.'

Harry shrugged. 'Please yourself, Miss Court. Lizzie, will you come to the flicks with me one evening?'

'I don't think my aunt would agree,' Lizzie said, though she was pleased he'd asked her. 'She won't even let me go out with a girlfriend, unless she approves of her . . .'

'You're twenty not fourteen,' Harry retorted 'Suit yourself. I'll be around if you change your mind – until I join up that is . . .'

'Be a good thing when he goes,' Beth muttered when the door closed behind him.

'Harry isn't that bad, but he did get upset when he saw what I'd done to his stockroom . . .'

'I can imagine.' Beth sighed as she brushed the crumbs from her smart black skirt. 'Oh well, a trip to the loo and then I'm back to work . . .'

'Me too, see you tomorrow,' Lizzie said. She would have liked an evening out with Harry Oliver, but she knew there was no point in asking her aunt who would say she must wait until she was twenty-one and no longer her responsibility.

'You will do as you wish then, but marriage isn't for you and the sooner you accept it the better, Lizzie,' her aunt had said more than once.

Why did her aunt think no one would marry her? Lizzie had puzzled over it a hundred times, but was no wiser.

Lizzie went back to find Ed. He was two minutes late back, but she didn't question him because he obviously had a lot to do in the short break they were given. Instead, she tidied his bench and got out the black felt she knew he intended to cut and shape that afternoon. They had an order for six black felt hats, all the same shape.

'Tilly will trim them differently,' Ed told her when they resumed work 'but this semi-cloche style is popular and easy to wear, so we make it all the time. It can look very different with ribbons or feathers or silk flowers.'

'Yes, I saw an order that Harry was getting ready to go out early this morning,' Lizzie hesitated, then, 'How was your wife when you got home, Ed?'

'Not too bad. She says she'll be able to get her own meal by next week – but I may still go home just to make sure.'

'May I ask what is wrong with her?' Lizzie asked.

'Madge's back went weak after she had our son,' Ed told her. 'The doctors didn't know why, but she ended up in a wheelchair for six months. I had to get someone in to care for her. Couldn't give up work or we would have starved.'

'But she is getting better?' Lizzie asked. 'How does she look after your son?'

Ed's eyes looked away as he replied, 'He lived half an hour or so and then he died. Madge wasn't able to be present at the funeral, which was a great distress to her . . .'

'Oh, Ed, I'm so very sorry.'

'So am I, but sorry doesn't change things,' Ed said and came back to himself. 'We've still got each other and that's all we'll ever have. Madge mustn't ever have another child.'

Lizzie wanted to hug him, to reiterate how sorry she was, but it wouldn't help, because he didn't want sympathy. 'Are you going to show me how to cut out the felt now?'

'Aye, that's the way of it, Lizzie, get on with living; it's the only way.'

CHAPTER 5

'Your mother makes a delicious Victoria sponge, Beth,' Aunt Jane looked at her with approval. 'Lizzie does her best, but she cannot cook as well as your mother. I've never had the time to show her . . .'

Lizzie hid her annoyance, because her aunt had never even tried to show her how to bake, only to cook their basic meals. She'd learned by trial and error and her uncle said she was much better than Aunt Jane had ever been. He'd tucked into his slice of the larger jam tart she'd cooked for them to have at home, but Ed had been thrilled with the four small ones she'd given him for his wife.

'I dare say you've taught Lizzie how to sew . . .' Beth said politely.

'I'm helping Lizzie make a smart black dress for work. I suppose you have to have the same?'

'Yes,' Beth confirmed 'Mr Oliver is very particular about that, especially if the girl is going to serve in the showroom.'

Lizzie silently blessed her. 'Mr Oliver asked me this morning if I had a dress yet and I told him

42

it would be ready for me next week – that's right, isn't it, aunt?'

'It should be – but you'll have to do the finishing touches by hand. I haven't time . . .'

'Of course I shall, it's my dress.' Lizzie felt pleased that she would be able to choose the buttons and trimmings herself.

'And you won't mind if we go to the flicks next Wednesday?' Beth pressed home her advantage. 'My dad will fetch us if you like . . .'

'I think Lizzie will be quite safe with you, Beth – and the idea that she should stay overnight is a good one. I don't have to worry about her missing the bus and walking home.'

'My brother or father always meets me if I ask, but I think Lizzie and I together will be quite safe. Mum would worry if we were late back.'

'Quite right too.' Aunt Jane got up from the table. 'Well, I am glad to have met you, Beth. I can see you've been properly brought up and that is just as it should be.'

'Let me do the washing up,' Beth offered. 'Lizzie can help. You should sit and rest, Mrs Banks. I think you must work awfully hard . . .'

'How kind. You may certainly dry for me and Lizzie can put away . . . but I do like to wash and rinse my best china myself.'

Uncle Jack winked at Lizzie as she made to follow behind them. 'Your Beth has won her over, love. I'm glad you've got a friend. You may need one soon enough . . .'

'What do you mean?'

'I went to see the doc this morning, Lizzie love,' her uncle said. 'I was thinking that if a war came later this year I might be of some service, on fire watch or something, but he told me the old ticker is slowing down, bit of a problem . . .'

'A problem with your heart? What did he say exactly?'

'I've got to have some tests at the hospital, Lizzie – but the doc seems to think I need to take things easy.'

'Yes, I see.' Tears stung her eyes, because she couldn't bear the thought that he might die. It was no wonder that he looked so very tired these days. 'I'm so sorry, uncle. If there's anything I can do . . .'

'Just try to be happy, my love,' he reached for her hand. 'We never had a child of our own. Your aunt had two miscarriages and after that . . . we just gave up. She was so happy when you came to us that I hoped . . . But she's changed over the years. I'm sorry you haven't been more loved, Lizzie.'

'You've loved me. You've been a father to me, Uncle Jack. Please believe me, if ever you need me I'll do whatever you ask.'

'I dare say it is all a storm in a teacup. You'd best help your aunt or we'll both be in trouble – and we don't want that on your birthday.' He smiled and gave her a small package. 'Your aunt might not have remembered, love, but I did . . .'

44

Lizzie opened the little jeweller's box, inside which was a pair of clip-on pearl earrings. 'Oh, these are lovely, Uncle Jack, I love them.'

'That's all right, Lizzie. Go and help your aunt then, before she gets cross . . .'

Close to tears, Lizzie hurried after the others. Uncle Jack needed peace and quiet and Lizzie would do her best to see he got it . . .

Tilly was late into work that Monday morning, and got a telling-off from Mr Oliver. She looked upset, and when Lizzie made tea at the mid-morning break, she asked her what was wrong.

'It's my little Sally. She's got a nasty cough and I was up all night with her. My husband has to be at work at six in the morning, and couldn't help me. Mum was late coming, and she was fussing about Sally, asking if she should take her to the doctor. We're on the panel but we've been with her three times this last month and I know we'll have to pay extra if we take her again.'

'It must be worth it if she's ill.' Lizzie knew how hard it must be to manage on Tilly's wage, even though she was a trained seamstress. Her husband worked as well but was on piecework and didn't always get taken on.

'Mum insisted she was going to take her, even if she had to pay herself, but we couldn't let her do that. Dad died four years ago and she's only got a small pension – but it's hard with a baby . . .'

'Yes, I've heard other people say that. I think most people are in the same boat, Tilly.'

'You'd better get on, Lizzie. We don't want to lose our jobs, even if the pay is miserly.'

'I've heard they're payin' three quid down the munitions factory.' Vera Marsh replaced her empty mug on Lizzie's tray. 'I've a good mind to get a job there.'

'It's a worse atmosphere there than it is here,' Tilly said. 'My neighbour's daughter works there and her skin is goin' yellow . . .'

'Oh, poor thing,' she sympathised and left Tilly to her work.

Lizzie joined Ed at his bench. He was shaping some pink felt into a dome rather like a bowler hat, but it would have a larger brim than the cloches he'd made yesterday, and be trimmed with silk flowers and veiling.

'This is one of our specials,' Ed told her as his hands worked their magic, with a little help from the steamer. 'Mr Winters will be in this afternoon and he ordered six of these hats last time. I'm making it in six different colours. What kind of decoration do you think they need, Lizzie?'

'Well, the pink one could have a silk rose . . . I saw a lovely one in the new stock, Ed. It's purple at the centre and shades out to a pale pink.'

'Perfect, fetch me the rose and the ribbons,' Ed instructed and Lizzie obeyed, pleased that Ed had seemed to like her suggestion.

'Let's have a look' Ed placed the rose against

the hat and then draped the ribbon next to it and nodded approval. 'You've got a good eye for colour, Lizzie. Give these to Tilly.'

Lizzie would have loved the chance to sew the ribbon and rose into place herself but did as she was told and delivered the various pieces to Tilly.

Tilly nodded in approval. 'I like that colour choice. This is one of Mr Winters' specials – he's one of our best customers, but if you serve him be careful, Lizzie. They say he's a womaniser and breaks hearts . . .'

'I'll be careful then,' Lizzie laughed and moved away.

For the rest of the morning Ed had her running back and forth collecting the materials he needed for the hats he was making. She was amazed at how quickly he worked, and thrilled when she saw he'd completed eight beautiful hats, most trimmed to Lizzie's specifications.

At lunchtime, Lizzie met Beth in the staffroom. Nancy, Vera and Harry were there and having a laugh together. Lizzie saw the way that Vera made up to Harry, and looked away; it was embarrassing to watch her flirting, because Harry obviously found it amusing.

'Mum is looking forward to having you stay on Wednesday,' Beth told her. 'You won't mind sharing my room, will you?'

'It will be fun,' Lizzie said and smiled. 'I can't really believe that my aunt allowed it, but you won her round. She spent all day Sunday telling me that I should try to be more like you.'

'Poor you,' Beth sympathised. 'I just wanted to make sure she let you come out with me.'

'I know. I'm so grateful,' Lizzie said. She opened her overall to show off the black dress beneath. 'What do you think? Is it all right?'

'Take the overall off and let me look,' Beth said as Lizzie revealed the simple fitted dress beneath. It had short sleeves, a sweetheart neckline and a straight skirt that finished just beneath her knees. 'Yes, that does suit you; I like it. Why don't . . .'

Beth paused as the door opened and Mr Oliver entered. 'I was looking for . . .' His eyes narrowed in appreciation. 'Much better, Miss Larch. You can serve Mr Winters for me please. Collect the hats Ed made this morning and take them into the showroom please.'

'Yes, sir, of course,' she replied. 'We made eight this morning and Ed said they were all specials.'

'Eight, that's good. Let's hope Winters likes them,' her employer said. 'Get on with it, girl. What are you waiting for?'

'Yes, sir,' Lizzie was galvanised into action, her heart racing with a mixture of fear and excitement.

'Perhaps she wants her lunch,' Harry spoke up as Lizzie rushed back to the workroom.

She collected all the hats, placing them in a large box and carrying it through to the showroom. Lizzie had visited this hallowed place only once before. There was a glass counter and a couple of hat stands, also a mirror on the wall, but it could be so much more attractive with just a small amount of money spent on mirrors, a couple of pretty chairs and elegant stands.

A man was standing near the window, looking at some of what Lizzie termed the basic stock – felt cloches and a couple of straw hats with large brims, which were piled on top of a small square table, and not set off to advantage. His back was towards her and she had time to take all the hats from the cardboard box and place them carefully on the glass counter. She set two of her favourites on the stands, and wished she could make a proper display of the others, but all she could do was set them out on the glass top of the counter.

'And whom do we have here?' a deep male voice asked and Lizzie looked up to see their special customer regarding her with his deep blue eyes. His hair was black and slicked away from his face with some kind of oil. He looked a bit like Clark Gable as Rhett Butler in *Gone with the Wind,* which was one of the few films Lizzie had managed to see, his skin rather pale and his eyebrows thick and dark.

Lizzie's cheeks warmed as his gaze went over her, taking in every detail of her appearance. 'I'm Miss Larch,' she said in a formal tone. 'I work with Ed as his apprentice and I've been asked to help in the showroom as everyone else is busy.'

'Ah, I see. I wonder why they've been hiding you from me. Or do I?' His eyes gleamed with mischief. 'Has my reputation gone before me, Miss Larch?'

49

'I'm sure I don't know what you mean, sir.' Lizzie gave him a straight, no-nonsense look, and he laughed, picking up one of the hats to examine it.

'So these are the latest designs, are they?' He transferred his gaze to the show of hats. 'Yes, well, I can see a little originality in these . . .' He picked out one of the hats for which Ed had asked Lizzie's advice. 'I love that colour combination and this hat is elegant . . . are they the usual price?'

No one had told her the prices. Lizzie hesitated, because she didn't want to make a mistake, and yet to run back to the workshop and ask would make her appear foolish.

Clearing her throat, she said, 'Not quite, sir. The pink one is five shillings more and the others have all gone up by half a crown . . .'

His eyes narrowed for a moment, and then he nodded, the faint flicker of a smile on his mouth. 'Oliver's making hay while the sun shines, I suppose. I can't say as I blame him, because once this war starts, we none of us know where we'll be . . .'

He took out his wallet and began to take out some money. He counted out eight pounds and then added another one pound two shillings and sixpence.

'There you are then, Miss Larch,' he said. 'I normally pay cash. If you'd like to make out my invoice – Sebastian Winters of Bond Street . . .'

Lizzie looked round for something to make out his invoice on. He nodded towards the small table with the basic hats on top. 'I think you'll find the invoice pad is in that drawer.'

Feeling stupid Lizzie went to the drawer and took out the invoice book. There, on the first page, was an invoice made out to this same customer. All the hats were priced at twenty shillings, except for a basic cloche, which was twelve shillings. Relieved that she hadn't made a mistake, Lizzie made out the invoice, adding the extra she'd charged on top and totalling the amount. She marked it as paid with a rubber stamp she'd found in the drawer.

'Did you want to take your order or is it usually delivered?'

'You could deliver it if you like? I would be happy to take delivery in person . . .' he arched one eyebrow and laughed at her dismay. 'No, no, I'm joking, Miss Larch. If you would replace the hats in that cardboard box, I'll take them with me. I came in because I was running low on this particular style. I think my customers are stocking up in case they can't get what they want once the war starts . . .'

'Do you think it will really come to a war?'

'We'll be fighting the Germans within the year,' Mr Winters said. He hesitated, then, 'Whose idea it was to trim these hats? I can recognise fresh talent when I see it.'

'I'm working under Ed; he's our head cutter . . . and he asked my opinion on most of them.'

'Ah, yes, now I begin to see. Well, you've got a

good eye for colour and style. Send my congratulations to your employer, Miss Larch.'

Lizzie was just wondering what to reply when Mr Oliver entered the room.

'Everything all right, Mr Winters – Lizzie looked after you properly?'

'Yes, very well. I was just saying she has talent. You're lucky to have found her, Oliver – you should make sure you don't lose her to the competition. I could do with a girl like Miss Larch in my shop . . .'

Mr Winters picked up his box and went out without waiting for Mr Oliver's reply, but just before he left, he turned back and winked at Lizzie. She felt hot all over, especially as her employer was frowning over the copy of the invoice.

'What's this, Lizzie? I see you sold Mr Winters all eight of the specials . . . but what else did he buy?'

'We trimmed the hats differently, sir, so I charged a little extra for them. I charged five shillings for the one with that lovely pink silk rose, and half a crown extra for all the rest, because we used the best trimmings. I believe the normal price is a pound?' She crossed her fingers in case she'd got it all wrong.

'Mr Winters pays a pound for each of the specials,' he said. 'And who told you to put the price up?'

'It was my idea, sir. Mr Winters was very complimentary about the new styles so . . . I didn't want to charge too little, because we'd used the best trimmings, and no one told me.'

'We always use the best for the specials,' Mr Oliver

said, frowning. 'Did he complain or say he might buy fewer in future?'

'No – he said that his customers were stocking up in case there was a war and they couldn't find anything they liked once it started . . . and he said he didn't blame you for making hay while the sun shone . . .'

'Did he indeed?' Mr Oliver's frown cleared. 'You used your initiative, Lizzie. I've been thinking of charging a bit extra for the better hats . . .' He considered for a moment. 'Any other bright ideas in that head of yours?'

'Well, I think if the showroom was made a little smarter we might attract more passing trade, bring customers in off the street . . .'

He shook his head emphatically. 'We're wholesale, Lizzie. It wouldn't work, trying to mix the two. Most of my customers have regular orders; they just ask for variations in colour and trimmings and leave it to us. Winters is the exception. His customers are the top end; he buys a lot of his stuff from our competitors and they employ a designer to think up new styles for him . . .'

'Couldn't we do that?' Lizzie asked. 'Mr Winters sells our hats in the West End – I bet he gets more than twice what you charge for them . . .'

'Too much outlay for me,' her employer told her. 'Right, get back to Ed. We've got a larger than normal order for the basic hats this month . . .'

CHAPTER 6

'Oh, I did enjoy that film,' Lizzie said as she and Beth joined the bus queue. 'Cary Grant was lovely, and I liked the actress too . . . What was her name?'

'Katharine Hepburn,' Beth said. '*Bringing up Baby*! I never realised it meant a leopard cub, did you?'

'No, I hadn't seen anything about it, didn't even know it was on until you said. It was such fun tonight, Beth. I really enjoyed myself.'

'Me too.' Beth hugged her arm. 'We shall have to see if we can get you to a dance next Saturday . . .'

'I don't think my aunt would agree . . .' Lizzie was doubtful. 'You should have heard the lecture I got this morning, telling me to behave tonight . . .'

'Why does she treat you as if you're about twelve? I shouldn't put up with it if I were you.'

'I've thought of telling her I'm old enough to please myself, but she did bring me up when my parents died. Anyway, I don't want to upset her at the moment. Uncle Jack isn't too well and I don't want to make things uncomfortable for him.'

'Up to you, of course. Here's our bus . . .'

She exclaimed in disbelief as the bus swept on past them without stopping. 'That's the last bus home . . .'

'I think it was full up,' Lizzie said. 'They might have let us get on, even if we had to stand . . .'

Beth was silent for a moment, then, 'We could walk to the tram stop. It's in the next street and I think it runs a bit later than the bus . . .'

'We'll have to try or we'll be walking all the way home.' Lizzie tucked her arm through Beth's. 'Good thing I'm not going home . . .'

'Mum may worry but she'll understand. We didn't miss the bus because we messed about; it just went straight by as if we weren't there . . .'

Lizzie would've felt nervous if she'd been alone, and she dreaded to think what her aunt would say if she could see them walking through the streets at this time of night.

They had to turn off the busy street into a narrow lane to reach the tram stop in the street further up and it was dark. A shiver of apprehension went down Lizzie's back, and then she heard the heavy footsteps behind them. Her heart began to pound as the steps came nearer and nearer and she longed to turn round to see if they were being followed but resisted.

They'd almost got to the tram stop when a large dark-coloured car drew into the kerb just ahead of them. A man jumped out and walked back to them and Lizzie's stomach cramped with sudden fear; this was what her aunt was always going on about, strange men accosting her at night.

'Ah, I thought I was right – Miss Larch, isn't it?' Sebastian Winters tipped his hat to them. 'I don't like to see two young ladies walking alone at this hour, especially around here. May I give you a lift in my car? My driver won't mind if I sit up front with him for once . . .'

Lizzie caught the smell of wine on his breath. 'It's kind of you, Mr Winters, but I'm not sure . . .' she began, but Beth cut in swiftly.

'You're the customer Lizzie served with those hats,' she said and smiled up at him. 'We'd love a lift. Our bus just went straight past the stop – so if you don't mind, thank you for the offer. Lizzie is staying with me and I live in the East India Docks area. I'll give you instructions on the way . . .'

Sebastian Winters' driver had got out and opened the back door for her and she slid inside on the back seat. Lizzie had no option but to follow. She wasn't sure why she was so nervous; she hadn't been in the least nervous of Mr Winters in the showroom, but it might have been something to do with the dark street and the absence of other people – and those heavy footsteps. Something had made the back of her neck tingle, something that hovered just beyond that curtain in her mind. Glancing out of the window as she slid onto the back seat, she saw the dark shape of a man staring after them – a man wearing a long trench coat such as soldiers had worn in the last war . . .

'I don't bite, Lizzie Larch,' Sebastian Winters said and smiled at her, over his shoulder. 'Your friend trusts me – surely you can?'

'Yes, of course. It's just . . .' Lizzie felt coldness at her nape. There was something about this lane – something that made her nervous. She was suddenly glad to be inside the luxurious car, her fear gone as swiftly as it had come. 'Thank you, it's very kind of you to stop for us.'

'The least I could do,' Mr Winters assured her. 'I've been thinking about you, Lizzie Larch. Perhaps we could meet for a coffee or a drink one evening . . .'

'Perhaps,' Lizzie agreed, because she couldn't confess to this man that her aunt expected her home at the same time every night.

Lizzie took her place beside Ed at his workbench the next morning. She was feeling happy. Beth's parents had welcomed her the previous night as if she was one of them and she'd enjoyed sharing a room with her friend and talking about their visit to the pictures. After Beth had fallen asleep, Lizzie had lain wakeful for a while, remembering the irrational fear she'd had in that dark lane before Mr Winters had stopped for them. If he hadn't come along when he did, would that man in the trench coat have attacked them? Something about his manner as she'd looked back at him had been menacing.

Lost in her thoughts, she wasn't immediately

aware that Ed was very silent, working away at cutting some silk grosgrain and the stiffening needed to make it hold its shape, but then she noticed his frown.

'Is something wrong, Ed?' she asked, and he nodded once, but still didn't speak. 'I haven't upset you?'

'Lord no, Lizzie. It's my wife. Yesterday evening, she was in a lot of pain. I didn't want to leave her but we've got some big orders to fulfil and if I'm not here . . .'

'Surely Mr Oliver would understand if you needed an extra hour or so off?'

'He says margins are tight and he needs us all to put in maximum effort,' Ed told her. 'I'm sorry, Lizzie, I should have explained that this brim needs to be cut on the bias like this . . .'

'Yes, I saw what you were doing,' Lizzie said. 'Is that so that you can get the floppy look?'

'Yes, clever girl,' Ed said approvingly. 'Look, I've got all the hats I need from this roll and there's only enough for one small cloche left . . . why don't you try cutting out the shape?'

Lizzie stretched her shoulders at the end of what had seemed a long but exciting day. Ed had shown her exactly what to do and she'd seen her first cloche take shape. Using the steamer and the clamps and the moulds was frightening at first, but she'd soon got the hang of it and Ed had placed her finished hat with his to be trimmed by Tilly.

'Ed, is there anything I can do to help you?' she said as he began to put away his tools for the night. 'If you needed any help at home . . .'

'Well . . .' he hesitated, then inclined his head. 'I wouldn't have asked, Lizzie, but there's a pile of ironing waiting for me this evening, and I was going to cook a shepherd's pie with the rest of the mince we had yesterday. If you could do the cooking, I'll catch up on my chores. With Madge so ill these last couple of days . . .'

'Don't say any more,' Lizzie smiled at him. 'I'd love to help out, Ed, truly I would. You've been so kind to me, teaching me so much.'

'You're the one that's helping me,' Ed said with his sad, gentle smile. 'Don't you realise how much more work I can get through now, Lizzie? If I made six or seven good hats in a morning and a half dozen of the basic shapes, I considered I'd done well – but with you here we're making at least two dozen basics and a dozen of the specials a day. I know that's far more than Vera makes, and she doesn't cut.'

'You work so hard, Ed,' Lizzie said. 'It must be tiring and then you have all the work to do when you get home . . .'

'All I care about is that I keep this job and my Madge gets better. With my skills I could get a job anywhere, but this place suits me . . . but if you could help me, Lizzie, I'd be grateful.'

Lizzie said goodnight to Beth and the others and then went off with Ed. His house was only just round the corner, an end of terrace with two up and two down, and a lean-to with a small yard at the back, leading straight into the kitchen. The kitchen was untidy, with washing on lines at one end and a basket piled with clean clothes that needed ironing and the furniture was old, dark oak and dull from lack of polish. Everywhere smelled slightly of sickness, despite the bowl of dried rose petals in the hall.

Ed took Lizzie into the sitting room because his wife's bed had been put in there so that she was close to the kitchen and did not have to be helped up and down the stairs. Ed had told Lizzie that the toilet was in the backyard, but his wife had a commode next to her bed and Lizzie's nose told her that it had been used recently, but she resolutely ignored it, because it must be embarrassing for Madge to have a stranger in her home at such a time.

'Madge, my love,' Ed said and bent to kiss her pale cheek, 'Lizzie offered to come and cook our tea for us while I get on with some other jobs . . . you remember she made us those jam tarts.'

'They were so lovely,' Madge said and held her hands out, clasping Lizzie's hands in a moist grip that told of her slight fever. 'You're such a kind girl. My Ed told me you were lovely and you help him ever so much at work.'

'Your husband is teaching me to make hats,' Lizzie said and bent to kiss her pale cheek. 'I'm so sorry you're unwell again, Mrs Biggles—'

'Oh no, you must call me Madge,' she cried before Lizzie could finish. 'You're a friend, Lizzie. My Ed says he couldn't have managed recently with all the extra work if you hadn't been there . . .'

'How kind,' Lizzie said. 'Is there anything I can do for you before I start cooking?'

'Oh no, Ed will do all that,' Madge said, looking shy. 'Cooking will help him with the rest of it . . .'

'I'll show you round the kitchen and where the food is,' Ed said and led the way. One look told Lizzie that he hadn't had time to wash the dishes from his lunch and she made up her mind that as soon as she had the pie in the oven and the vegetables ready, she would do as much as she could before she went home. Rolling up her long sleeves, she set to with a will as Ed returned to his wife.

She'd finished most of her chores by the time Ed brought his wife's chair through. He saw what she was doing and shook his head.

'You've done enough, Lizzie. I can manage now.'

'Would you like me to give the bedroom a little polish before I go, Madge?,' Lizzie asked.

'I'd be very grateful,' Madge said. 'Ed has far too much to do and that polish smells lovely.'

'I'll come again another time,' Lizzie promised and went into the downstairs bedroom. She would do this one last job before she went home, because the time had fled and her aunt was going to wonder where she was . . .

★   ★   ★

61

'Where on earth have you been?' her aunt started as soon as she entered the kitchen. 'We've been going frantic. Your uncle was about to go to the police . . .'

'I'm sorry if you worried about me.' Lizzie apologised. 'I went to Ed's house and helped his wife, because she's ill. He has so much to do and so I cooked their supper . . .'

'You selfish, careless girl!' Aunt Jane said and slapped her face.

Lizzie recoiled, putting her hand to her cheek. 'I was just doing a good turn for a friend . . .'

'Jane, that wasn't necessary. Lizzie has explained why she's late. She didn't do anything wrong. It was good of her to help a friend who needed her,' her uncle exclaimed.

'If she has time to clean for someone else she can do more here . . .'

'Lizzie does her share. Besides, I fetched a pie and chips for us so we didn't starve. I didn't bring any for you, Lizzie, because I thought you might have eaten out.'

'No, but a piece of toast will do for me,' Lizzie said. 'If we've got some cheese or jam that will be fine'

Aunt Jane sighed with exasperation and went off into the sitting room, where her sewing machine was kept, and they heard the treadle going as she started work. Uncle Jack sighed and looked at her sadly.

'She works too hard and it makes her tired, Lizzie. I'm sorry she hit you . . .'

'It's all right. I didn't mean to worry you, but Ed is good to me and he needed some help,' Lizzie said.

No need to apologise to me.'

'Shall I make you a cup of tea, Uncle Jack?'

'Get your supper first, love. You'll be worn out . . .'

He sat back in his rocking chair by the fire, eyes closed. Lizzie felt a pang of fear as she looked at his face. His skin looked a putty colour and he looked so tired. She wondered what the doctors had told him, whether he'd had the results of his tests yet, but didn't want to ask, because he would tell her if he wanted her to know.

'I'll make us a cup of tea first,' Lizzie said. 'I can sit and eat my bread and jam with you – and then I'll make apple turnovers for tomorrow . . .'

Her uncle had his eyes closed. He looked exhausted and she knew the small argument had upset him. Had her aunt not noticed how tired he looked or didn't she care? Tears stung behind her eyes, but she mustn't let him know it upset her to see him this way. He needed her to be strong for him and she would for as long as he needed her.

Ed and his wife had their troubles and Lizzie would help them all she could, but in future she would make sure her aunt knew she would be late. She didn't want Uncle Jack being upset for no good reason . . . because she was afraid that his heart wouldn't stand the strain, and if she lost him – Lizzie couldn't even think about that . . .

She touched his shoulder, handing him his cup of tea and he smiled up at her.

'You know I love you, Lizzie,' he said. 'My life would've been hell without you, love. When I go, there will be something for you.'

'Please don't,' she said. 'I want you to stay here with me . . .'

'I shall for as long as I can,' he said. 'I'm sorry, Lizzie. It won't be much longer. When I'm gone, you should leave this house – make a new life for yourself elsewhere. I should have liked to see you wed, but I suppose . . .' He shook his head and sipped his tea.

'Perhaps I might get wed if I could go out with friends,' Lizzie said. 'There's a man where I work – Mr Oliver's nephew – Harry has asked me to the flicks twice but I had to say no. He seems to like me. And Beth wants me to go to a dance with her and her boyfriend. If I went I might find someone . . . but Aunt Jane makes it so difficult.'

'It isn't fair to you. I know Jane must seem unreasonable, but she believes she is protecting you,' he sighed. 'Why don't you just tell her you're going to dinner at Beth's house and want to stay the night so that you can spend the evening with your friend?'

'It would be lying . . .'

'Only a little white lie,' her uncle patted her

hand. 'If it keeps the peace why not tell a few white lies, my love? I should be happier if I knew you were secure before I go . . .'

'I'll just tell her I'm going to Beth's on Saturday then . . .'

CHAPTER 7

The narrow alley seemed endless and it was so dark. She ran as fast as she could, the sound of her footsteps echoing in her ears as her breath came in short pants and her chest hurt. She couldn't run any faster and she knew he would catch her. The fear was almost suffocating and she could hardly breathe. He was just behind her now. Glancing back, she saw the dark outline of a man – a man in a long trench coat – but it was too dark to see his face. Fear swept through her and she renewed her efforts to escape, but it was no good; he was catching her. She could hear the ragged sound of his breathing and then she felt his strong hands on her shoulders, dragging her down . . .

Lizzie woke with a start, sitting bolt upright in bed. She was cold, covered in a fine sweat, and shaking. Her head was filled with such vivid pictures of herself running down a dark alley. The fog was curling in from the river, filling the streets, filling her lungs with its foul taste. She could still hear those footsteps pounding after her and in the distance the hoot of a ship's horn and a tram rattling by. The fear was still with her as she struggled to shake off the awful dream.

It was the first time she'd looked back in her dream; the first time she'd seen him . . . a man in a long trench coat similar to those worn in the Great War. Was her dream a memory or was it just a nightmare? Everyone said that she'd had an accident when she was fourteen, but what had caused it?

It was just because of that man she'd seen following her the night that Sebastian Winters picked her and Beth up in his car. Just a silly dream! She wouldn't think about it any more.

It was six o'clock. Lizzie's little alarm clock beside her bed was set to go off at half past, but she moved the lever so that it wouldn't ring. Pulling on her dressing gown, she went down the hall to the toilet, thinking how much luckier they were than most people who still had to go out to the backyard or use a chamber pot under the bed.

She had a strip wash in the basin; because Aunt Jane said a bath more than twice a week was a luxury they couldn't afford, shivering a little in the cool air. It was June now but still not really warm enough to be called summer. Or was it just that the house always seemed cold? Aunt Jane kept the range going in the kitchen, but she seldom lit a fire elsewhere, except in the worst of the winter.

Lizzie went downstairs to finish the ironing she hadn't got done the previous night because she didn't want Aunt Jane nagging her today. She worked from eight until twelve on Saturday mornings, and then she was going home with Ed to help him with a few chores. She'd made up her mind to wash the kitchen floor and then go upstairs and clean the bedrooms.

Ed had told her that he was using the single bed in the back room because Madge had been too ill for him to share their double bed. Lizzie knew that the large front bedroom did not have a bed, but she would sweep and perhaps clean the floors, polish the furniture and, if Ed wanted, change the sheets on his bed.

As they worked at their bench that morning, Ed told her that Madge was looking forward to having a chat to her, and the hours went so quickly that it seemed hardly any time at all before they were getting ready to leave. It was just as they were tidying up the bench that Mr Oliver came up to them. Lizzie got a little shock as she saw he was carrying the sketchbook she'd given him days ago when he'd asked for examples of her designs.

'I shan't keep you long, Lizzie,' he said and opened the book. 'This hat – it looks good on paper, but how would you make it up?'

Lizzie hadn't known how to make the hat when she'd drawn it, but two weeks of Ed's tuition had taught her enough to describe exactly how she would like to see the hat made up.

'The shaping is similar to a boater,' she said and he nodded, because that much was obvious. 'But the hat is made from two layers of stiffening and covered with silk grosgrain. The brim material is pleated and goes right over the stiffening, sewn inside and finished with a ribbon to cover the stitches, and the brim is puffed and soft, apart from the stiffening that forms the crown beneath. It is trimmed with silk roses at the front.'

'Sounds complicated and expensive,' Mr Oliver said. 'I want it costed properly and the details on my desk first thing Monday morning.'

'Yes, sir,' Lizzie felt a twist of excitement inside.

'Well, that's a feather in your cap, Lizzie.' Ed took the book from her, scrutinising it for a moment. He questioned her on the size of the brim, and Lizzie showed him the pattern she would use in his book. He did a couple of sums on his pad and nodded. 'If you use the best silk it would cost thirty shillings to make up, which means it would have to sell for nearly two pounds five shillings . . . too much to be practical, Lizzie, at least that's what he'll say.'

Lizzie thanked him, but kept puzzling over it in her own mind. Perhaps there was another way to make the hat a bit cheaper, because she knew none of their regulars would pay over two pounds for a hat. Their own customers probably couldn't afford to pay nearly four pounds, which it would have to be in a retail shop – but she had more important things to think of today.

Firstly, she was going to help Ed clean house and then she would go home and change before meeting Beth. Her tummy was filled with butterflies at the thought of the evening to come. It was the first time she'd been to a dance and she could hardly keep her excitement inside . . .

'You've got the house looking much better,' Madge said when they sat down to have a cup of tea and a slice of the seed cake Lizzie had made. 'Everywhere smells so nice and I know it was getting bad, but I couldn't ask Ed to do any more. He works so hard.'

'Yes, he does,' Lizzie said. 'Yesterday we had a huge order and Ed said it would have taken him three days alone. We finished it this morning – and Mr Oliver was pleased, even if he didn't say much.'

'Bert Oliver is a slave driver.' Madge broke a piece of the cake to pop in her mouth. 'This is so delicious, Lizzie. You're a girl to be proud of . . .'

Lizzie blushed with pleasure. 'It's nothing. I like coming here and I'll come one evening a week and sometimes on a Saturday too. It seems a shame to have that lovely big bedroom upstairs empty though . . .'

'Yes, it is a lovely room, and I'd rather have my sitting room for sitting in, but I can't manage the stairs with my back.' Madge sighed. 'Perhaps one day I will, but until then . . .'

'Yes, I know,' Lizzie said. She'd wondered if Madge and Ed could earn a little extra money by taking in a lodger, but she didn't say anything because it wasn't practical. They couldn't manage to look after themselves, let alone have a lodger – unless of course the person they took in was willing to do a bit about the house . . .

'I've so enjoyed having you here,' Madge told her. 'I'm feeling a little better again. I think it was just a chill . . . and sometimes things seem so hopeless. I've watched my Ed get more and more tired . . . but since you started helping us, well, it's given us both some hope again.'

'It's been lovely for me too,' Lizzie assured her. 'I like doing what I can to help – you won't think I'm rude, but you're just the sort of person I've imagined my mum would have been.'

'Don't you remember your mother, Lizzie?'

'Not well,' Lizzie said. 'I think I was quite small when my parents died – and then, when I was fourteen, I was ill and lost quite a chunk of time. The doctor said it was amnesia due to a bang on the head . . .'

'Oh, my poor Lizzie.' Madge reached across the table to squeeze her hands. 'I'd love to have you as my adopted daughter.'

'I feel as if you and Ed are family.' Lizzie kissed Madge's cheek. 'I'm just going to wash up these cups and then I have to leave. I'm going to stay with my friend Beth this evening – we're going to a dance . . .'

'You'll enjoy that, Lizzie. I remember when my Ed first took me to the Pally. I was really excited and I had a new dress for it. It was pale blue silk – artificial silk, of course – and the sleeves were short and puffed. I still have it in the wardrobe upstairs.'

'That sounds lovely. I don't have a special dress for dancing. I'll just wear my Sunday one.'

71

Lizzie washed the cups but Ed came in and took the drying cloth. 'You've done more than enough, Lizzie,' he said. 'I don't know what we can do to thank you.'

'I don't need thanks,' Lizzie said, feeling a little shy. 'I don't have much family, and I'd like to think of you as my very good friends.'

'Of course we are,' he said. 'But I was feeling low when you offered to help, Lizzie, and I'm truly grateful.'

'Think nothing of it. I'll see you on Monday morning,' Lizzie said. 'Bye for now – have a nice evening.'

Lizzie's dress that evening was pale grey silky rayon. Her aunt had made it for her some months earlier but Lizzie had removed the little white collar that had made it look so school-girlish and altered the front so that it dipped in a sweetheart neckline. She'd taken the bodice in with darts that made it fit into her waist rather than blousing out and being caught in with a belt; it looked almost as smart as the black dress she wore for work. Lizzie would've liked something in a bright colour, perhaps pale blue, but she couldn't afford to buy a new dress.

She wished she'd got a locket or a necklace of some kind, but she'd never had one, and her mother's silver cross was too precious to be worn in case she lost it, but she had got her pearl earrings that Uncle Jack had bought her for her birthday.

Her shoes were the good black suede ones she'd bought when she was still earning reasonable wages, and her uncle had kept them in good repair so that they looked nearly new.

Slipping on the jacket she used for work, Lizzie packed her nightdress and toothbrush and went out to catch the tram that would take her to Beth's home. She sat next to a window, looking out at the busy roads as the tram moved off, its bell making a clanging sound.

Getting off at the nearest stop to Beth's street, Lizzie walked past several grimy buildings, small manufacturers and a small corner shop, before turning into the rows of terraced houses. On warm days she fancied you could smell the docks from here, the stink of diesel oil and fumes lay heavy in the air and you could just see the tops of tall cranes on the dockside. A dog was hunting hopefully in the gutters, its tail wagging. A young girl was playing with hoops in the street and a man with a barrow was transporting a folded-up mattress and some bits and pieces from one of the houses, trundling down the cobbled street.

Lizzie smiled as she reached Beth's front door, which looked cleaner than any of the others in the street. Beth's mother welcomed her warmly, taking her upstairs to deposit her things and telling her that Beth had just popped out to the corner shop to get something for her.

'She won't be five minutes,' Mrs Court said, leading Lizzie back down into the kitchen. 'I'm just pressing Beth's dress for her. What are you wearing this evening?'

'This dress,' Lizzie said, feeling a little uneasy as she saw the lovely yellow and white spotted voile dress Mrs Court had been pressing. Lizzie could imagine what Beth would look like wearing it and suddenly felt dowdy. 'I don't have anything like Beth's dress . . .'

'Beth is a lucky girl, because her father gave her some money towards this,' Mrs Court said, looking Lizzie over. 'Your dress fits you nicely, Lizzie – but perhaps it could do with a brooch or a little necklace.'

'I don't have anything . . .' Lizzie half wished she'd worn her mother's silver cross, but it meant too much to her to risk losing it.

'Well, I'm sure I can find something you can borrow,' Mrs Court said. 'I know! I've got a lovely blue silk rose; it would just give a touch of colour to that dress, Lizzie . . .'

'Yes, it would,' Lizzie agreed. 'If you don't mind lending it to me.'

'I'll just fetch it . . .'

Within minutes she was back and she pinned the little arrangement of a blue silk rose, some veiling and a soft feather to the shoulder of Lizzie's dress.

'Take a look in the mirror, dear . . .'

Lizzie did so and smiled. The flower arrangement made her plain dress look stylish and pretty.

'It's lovely, thank you. I'll take good care of it for you.'

'Nonsense, it's a little present,' Mrs Court said. 'I never go anywhere to wear it and it suits your dress.'

Just then, Beth returned with some shopping for her mother. She smiled to see Lizzie, told her she looked nice and swooped on her own dress, carrying it off upstairs to change. Lizzie fastened the little buttons at the back for her and Beth sat down to fluff up her hair at the mirror. She sprayed some light perfume on her wrists and behind her ears and handed the atomiser to Lizzie.

'Have a little if you like,' she offered. 'Tony gave it to me for Christmas.'

'Are you sure?'

'Of course I'm sure,' Beth said. 'We're friends and we share what we have, Lizzie.' Lizzie used a tiny drop of the perfume from the pretty atomiser. 'Tony is paying for the tickets tonight. He can afford it; he's worked overtime every night this week and he's jolly well going to give us a good time this evening.'

'He is very kind and generous, but I'm happy to pay for myself.'

'Next time, but this is Tony's treat,' Beth said. 'I love your shoes. Are they new?'

'No, they just look new because my uncle repairs them and brushes them to keep them nice,' Lizzie said and looked at her hair. 'Should I wear it down this evening, Beth?'

'Sit down and let me see what we can do.'

Lizzie obeyed and Beth wielded the brush. Lizzie's hair was shoulder-length and had a little wave when it was loose, but the ends were uneven, because her aunt usually trimmed it when it got too long. She watched wide-eyed as Beth brandished the scissors and started loping bits off. As a nicer shape emerged, Lizzie smiled in the mirror. 'I like it, Beth. Cut a bit more off so it looks like a bob . . .'

'Are you sure?'

'Yes please.' Lizzie felt reckless; her aunt might grumble but suddenly she didn't care. She looked more attractive as her hair got shorter, more of a modern girl than the old-fashioned schoolmarm her aunt seemed to want her to be. When Beth had finished, Lizzie swung her head and her hair moved enticingly. She patted it with her hand. 'I love it. It makes me feel different.'

'You certainly look different,' Beth said. 'Here, use a little of this powder on your cheeks – and this pink lipstick.'

Lizzie did as she was told and laughed when Beth exclaimed 'Wow'. 'I feel wonderful. Even my dress looks better now.'

'Your dress suits you,' Beth said a bit doubtfully. 'Next time buy blue or green or something brighter if you can.'

'Next time is a long way off,' Lizzie said, 'but I do like blue. Your dress is gorgeous, Beth.'

'Dad gave me the money to buy it' Beth said. 'It was for my birthday but I haven't worn it many times.' She glanced at the little watch she was wearing. 'Tony will be here shortly. Come on, we don't want to miss anything . . .'

CHAPTER 8

The big room was crowded; a sparkling ball hanging from the ceiling sent showers of pinkish light over the polished wood floor. Lizzie had never been in a proper ballroom and she was impressed. The band was seated on a stage at one end and there was a room next door where a bar was open and some couples were already drinking wine.

'We don't want anything yet,' Beth said when Tony offered to buy them drinks. 'Later, after we've danced a few times.' She looked at Lizzie and smiled naughtily as Tony took her off to dance. 'I'm not deserting you, love – look who's here waiting for you . . .'

Lizzie glanced round and saw Harry Oliver. He was wearing a smart navy suit with a little stripe in the material and a pale blue shirt with a navy tie; his black shoes were shiny patent and he looked so smart that she would have felt dowdy without her new hairstyle and the corsage pinned to her dress.

'Lizzie, you look gorgeous,' Harry said, his eyes moving over her with approval. 'You ought to wear blue. That flower is your colour . . . and your hair is wonderful. I never realised just how pretty you were.'

'I'm not pretty,' Lizzie said, her cheeks warming.

'Wrong word. You're bloody beautiful!'

'Harry Oliver! There's no need to swear at me.'

'I'm just stunned. You must admit you do look a bit stuffy at work – but that new style brings out the colour of your eyes. I never realised that your hair has red lights in it before, and your eyes aren't brown . . . they're hazel . . .'

'Were you going to ask me to dance?' Lizzie said, embarrassed. 'I've no idea how to do this one. Beth showed me a few steps, but I'm not sure . . .'

Harry grinned and took her hand possessively. 'I'm a great dancer, Lizzie. All you have to do is follow me . . .'

Lizzie shook her head at his arrogance, but as he led her into the dance she discovered that he wasn't bragging. She relaxed, letting him direct her around the floor, sometimes by a whispered word and sometimes just by a flexing of his body. Harry told her the band was playing a Bing Crosby song.

'The singer isn't a patch on Bing,' Harry said, 'but he's the world's best crooner in my opinion. I love to listen to Bing on my gramophone.'

'We don't have one, but I have heard this song on the radio.'

'I'll show you my collection of records one day,' he promised, and pulled her in closer. 'You smell wonderful, Lizzie. How about being my girl? We can go out for meals and to the flicks . . . and I'll take you on the Serpentine.'

'We don't really know one another . . .' Dancing with Harry was like a dream for Lizzie. She'd never expected to feel like this but she wasn't sure whether it was the thrill of being here or being held in his arms.

'If you don't say yes we never shall. I'm leaving at the end of next month to join up. Things are warming up and everyone in the know says there'll be a war by the autumn. If I'm away flying kites for the RAF, I'll want someone to write to . . . and I really do like you, Lizzie.'

Harry could be so persuasive. She knew he was lazy at work, arrogant and sometimes careless of others, but deep down she rather liked him – and, like her uncle said, it was time she went out and had fun . . .

'All right, I'll come out with you on Saturdays, and we can have a coffee on Wednesday nights. I visit Ed and his wife then and you can meet me afterwards and walk me home – if you want.'

'Well, that will do for starters,' Harry nuzzled her neck. 'I'm falling for you, Lizzie Larch, and one day you'll know we were made for each other.'

'Your friend's all right,' Tony said as he led Beth into the waltz. 'She's loosened up a bit as the evening's gone on. I think that chap of hers has been buying her gin and orange all night.'

79

'I doubt if Lizzie would drink gin. It's just that she was nervous at first. I think she was afraid she was going to sit around and watch us all the time – but when I told Harry she was coming he jumped at the chance. I think he's sweet on her, though he's a bit arrogant; boss's nephew and set to inherit the business.'

'Lizzie should grab him while she has the chance then,' Tony said. 'I've seen another shop I like. The other one was useless because the rooms were so tiny, and I want it to be our home until I can afford a nice house with a garden.'

'I still think you would be better to leave it for a while. Everyone thinks a war is coming despite what Mr Chamberlain says . . .'

'I know I'll be called up, and that's why I want to get a place of my own. If your father sees me as a serious businessman he'll let us get married sooner, Beth. We've got to make him see sense, because if there is a war, I could be killed and we would never have . . .'

Beth was silent, because a part of her agreed with every word. She'd heard her parents talking about the war and the fact that her brother would have to go and Dottie would lose her husband to the war too, Mary as well if she was married by then. They'd spoken of heartbreak and the pain they'd experienced in the last war – and Beth didn't know what she'd do if Tony was killed.

'At least we can save Beth from that,' her father had said. 'Dotty and Mary will be married, we

can't change that, and the lad will have to go –
but Beth is too young to go through it. If Tony
comes back and she feels the same, fine, but if he
doesn't . . .'

'You don't think it's a little unfair to deny them
a chance of happiness?' Beth's mother replied.

'A brief happiness that could lead to Beth being
a widow, with a child before she's hardly married?
No, that's not my idea of happiness, love.'

'Well, you can ask,' Beth said to Tony now,
remembering that conversation, 'but I don't think
Dad is going to change his mind.' Her father was
trying to protect her but didn't seem to care how
she felt or that she was unhappy.

Their dance ended and Beth went off to the
cloakroom to freshen up and get her emotions
under control. When she returned, she looked for
Tony. He was standing at the entrance to the bar
talking to a flashy blonde – Sylvia Butcher. Beth's
nails curled into her palms as she saw the way the
other girl fluttered her long lashes at him. Sylvia
was wearing far too much make-up in Beth's
opinion, and her hair wasn't natural blonde – and
that dress revealed too much of her bosom. If he
was taken in by that cheap tart . . . she felt her
temper rising but controlled it as she made her
way to join Harry and Lizzie. They were watching
as the next dance began. It was a military two-step
and more complicated than some of the others.

'This is one of my favourites,' Beth said as she
joined them.

'Mine too,' Harry said. 'Lizzie didn't fancy trying – how about you, Beth? You don't mind, Lizzie?'

'Of course not. Go on, Beth. I'll watch you and memorise the steps so I can have a go next time.'

Beth let herself be swept away into the lively dance. Harry was a marvellous dancer, much better than Tony, and she was soon enjoying herself. Towards the end of the dance they passed Lizzie, who was now standing with Tony. 'I'm really glad you asked me to come this evening,' Harry said as their dance ended. 'Lizzie looks great, doesn't she?'

'She's always been pretty,' Beth said. 'It's the awful clothes her aunt makes her wear and the way she scraped back her hair. Anyone would think she wanted to look plain, but I know Lizzie longs to have fun – her aunt's so strict . . .'

'Thanks for telling me,' Harry said a gleam of mischief in his eyes. 'I'll have to think of a way of getting round her . . .'

They walked to join their partners. Tony turned to Beth, a flash of annoyance in his eyes. 'I got you a glass of lemonade but gave it to Lizzie as you were dancing. Would you like one now?'

'Yes, please,' Beth said, and Harry said he could do with a beer and offered to fetch a round of drinks for them all.

Tony looked at Beth a bit oddly. 'You looked as if you were enjoying yourself?'

'Harry's a good dancer. I told you he's sweet on Lizzie – besides, you were busy, and Lizzie didn't fancy trying that one . . .'

'What do you mean busy?' Tony demanded. 'Oh, you mean Sylvia? She came up to me, Beth. I could hardly ignore her, could I? I've known her for years.'

'You went out with her at school.'

'We weren't together then . . .' He grinned. 'You're not jealous, are you? Surely you know Sylvia's reputation. You don't think I'd want someone like her as my wife? It's you I love, Beth.'

Beth nodded, her annoyance fading away. Tony was in love with her. It was foolish to think he might be interested in Sylvia. She was known to be fast, and if the whispers were true she'd been with a lot of men. Tony wouldn't marry a girl like that . . .

They'd got home at fifteen minutes past eleven. Beth's father had looked pointedly at the clock but he hadn't said anything as the two girls came in. Beth knew she might get a lecture the next day after Lizzie had gone home, but she was so much luckier than Lizzie, who would be in awful trouble if her aunt knew where she'd been that night. Her friend had confided in her that Harry wanted her to be his girlfriend.

'I don't know how I'm going to get away with it,' Lizzie said. 'I hate lying to my aunt, but I don't think she would let me out of the house if she thought I was going out with a man on my own.'

'Just tell her you'll be with me. It will be true some of the time, because we can go out as a foursome. I think it's safer for both of us if we do that, Lizzie. Tony wants to get married and Dad won't hear of it yet. Tony's getting impatient, if you know what I mean . . .'

'I suppose it wouldn't be a lie if we go as a foursome. At least for a start . . . and then I can find a way to break it to her. I would say straight out, but I don't want to upset my uncle'

'Well then,' Beth said, 'a few small lies never hurt anyone. It isn't as if you're doing anything wrong, Lizzie. Your aunt is the one that's wrong, giving you no freedom . . .'

CHAPTER 9

'Well, Lizzie,' Mr Oliver said on Monday morning. 'What is the damage? Have you worked it out properly?'

'Yes, sir,' Lizzie said. 'Ed helped me cost the hat I'd drawn, and it is rather expensive. If you use the best material, it would need to sell for two pounds five shillings . . .'

'Far too much,' he said. 'Disappointing . . .'

'I wondered if it might be worth making one up,' Lizzie suggested. 'Mr Winters has a shop in Bond Street and it follows that he has some rich customers. Also, I have come up with a compromise – a hat made of felt but with some soft pleating on the brim . . . that would sell for twenty-two shillings and sixpence.'

'You've given this some thought,' Mr Oliver said, eyes still narrowed. 'Could you make up a sample of each by tomorrow morning?'

'Yes, with a little help from Ed and Tilly – but I'd like to do most of the work myself, sir.'

'I haven't got money to throw away if you make mistakes, Lizzie Larch.'

'I shan't go wrong if Ed helps me cut the pieces

first,' Lizzie said. 'If I can show Tilly how I want it to be sewn and then finish it myself . . .'

'All right, get on with it, but I want decent merchandise I can sell.'

Ed turned to her as he walked off. 'You'd better show me what you need, Lizzie.'

'I made sketches of the hats in various stages,' she told him with a smile and opened her pad. 'The felt one looks almost as expensive as the all-silk hat, but it will cost less.'

'Less than you estimated, I should think,' Ed agreed and smiled. 'I like your hats, Lizzie. I'll do the cutting first and then you can talk to Tilly while I get on with the orders.'

Lizzie went off to the stockroom. She'd just collected all she needed when Harry entered carrying several rolls of material, some fine straw and a parcel. He dumped them on the floor and winked at her.

'You can enter these up for me when you're ready, Lizzie.'

'I'm busy for the moment,' she said. 'Don't be so lazy, Harry. They won't let you get away with careless behaviour in the RAF and I don't see why I should do your work.'

'Lizzie, I thought you liked me,' he said and looked reproachful. 'I've got an appointment elsewhere . . .'

'I do like you, Harry,' she said. 'I'll do them later if you like, but for now I'm busy.'

'Give me a kiss,' Harry said, grinning. 'I love it when you're bossy, Lizzie Larch.'

'Behave yourself,' she said and avoided him as he tried to catch her.

'Yes, well, this blue silk is very attractive, Lizzie,' Mr Oliver said and turned the expensive hat all ways, searching for any small mistakes, but couldn't find any. 'Who did the pleating?'

'I showed Tilly how I wanted it and she did it,' Lizzie told him. 'I chose the colours and finished it by hand, but Ed cut the shapes and Tilly did her job too.'

'What about this pink and cream felt?' he asked, looking at it critically. 'It's almost as stylish as the blue one but I don't think it costed out at anywhere near the price?'

'No, it was quite a bit cheaper. You could sell it for a pound if you wanted . . .'

'No, I'll charge twenty-five shillings,' he said decisively. 'This is different, Lizzie. We've got swathes of the silk tulle rather than pleats, so it took less time to do. You're a clever girl.'

'I have good ideas sometimes,' Lizzie said, 'but I couldn't have made these hats alone . . . at least I couldn't yet.'

'Give yourself time,' he said and looked pleased. 'Mr Winters will be here in the morning for his order. We shall just have to see what he says to these . . .'

Lizzie went back to Ed as he was packing up for the evening. She told him what their employer had said, thanking him for his help.

'It was all your idea. We haven't had anything new for ages. Tilly changes the colours and uses different silk flowers, but that pleated hat was different, really stylish – the way it went right under the brim, too – that is classy, Lizzie. I bet Sebastian Winters buys it like a shot and orders more.'

'I hope so,' Lizzie said. 'I've always wanted to design hats . . . it started after I was ill, for something to do . . .'

'Madge wondered if you were coming on Wednesday evening.'

'Yes, please, if you will have me?'

'Bless you, Lizzie, of course we'll have you. My Madge has taken to you. She would be disappointed if you didn't come.'

'Good, I like her so much, Ed. It makes a lovely change for me to be with friends.'

'We haven't had much time to talk today,' Ed said. 'Your hair looks nice, Lizzie. Did you cut it for the dance?'

'Yes, to smarten myself up a bit,' Lizzie said.

'It suits you.'

'Thanks, Ed. My aunt was horrified but Uncle Jack told me he liked it – and I've decided I'm old enough to wear what I like and have my hair cut if I want. I'm not a schoolgirl even if Aunt Jane thinks I am.'

Ed nodded his approval and left her to get her coat and join Beth. The two girls walked to the bus stop together, laughing over their day and making plans for the weekend.

'Tony says he doesn't mind meeting up at the pictures. He's taking me up West for tea and he's going to buy me a present . . . so we'll meet at the Odeon at half past six . . .'

'Yes, fine. I'm not sure when I'll be meeting Harry. We didn't have time to talk today, but I'll let you know tomorrow . . .'

Beth's bus came first and she jumped on. Lizzie's seemed a bit late and she was beginning to wonder if she'd missed one. She looked about her, feeling slightly anxious. A tramp loitered in the doorway of a nearby shop. Unshaven, with long greasy hair and filthy clothes, he was leering at her in a way that made her feel uncomfortable and a shiver of fear trickled down her spine. Suddenly, he grinned horribly and opened his coat, showing her his naked arousal through his open trousers. She averted her gaze in disgust and was about to turn and run when a car pulled into the kerb and Sebastian Winters got out.

'I hoped I might catch you. May I take you home, Lizzie?'

Lizzie was overcome with relief. She thanked his driver as he opened the back door for them and they both got in. For a moment Lizzie felt odd sitting there beside Sebastian Winters, but he kept a distance between them and she began to relax. The tramp had frightened her, reminding her strangely of her dream, but she was safe with Sebastian.

'You wanted to talk to me, sir?'

'Sebastian please,' he said, turning to look at her. 'How are you getting on at Oliver's?'

'I'm enjoying my work. We made two special hats this morning . . . but I chose the materials and the designs.'

'So you're progressing then,' he nodded, his expression serious. 'Just what is it that you want from life, Lizzie? Surely you won't be content to stay at Oliver's forever?'

'I want to design and make hats . . . be a fashionable milliner with my own label . . .' The words tumbled out of her, words she hadn't even known were in her head. 'Of course that's ridiculous. A girl like me doesn't stand a chance . . .'

'Why ever not? You have good ideas. Oliver showed me your sketchbook. I picked out a design I'd like to see made up . . . the pleated brim. Is that what you've been making this morning?'

'Yes, it is, in a deep midnight blue, as I showed it in my sketch.'

'Are you pleased with it?'

'Yes, but I also like the other . . . it's a variation on the idea but cheaper to produce.'

'I suppose that was Oliver's idea?'

'No, mine, because not every woman can afford the kind of prices your customers can, Mr Winters. I wanted something similar for more ordinary women like me.'

'You intrigue me, Lizzie Larch,' he said and his eyes were intensely blue. 'I don't know why you imagine you are ordinary . . . and I like the new hairstyle.'

'Thank you.' Lizzie caught her breath as he leaned closer and picked up a strand of her hair, letting it fall through his fingers. The action was sensual, the scent of him appealing to her instinctively.

'Chestnut brown. You can see the colour now it isn't all tied back in that horrible bun. All you need is pretty clothes and hats and you could mix with the best . . .' There was something in his eyes that made her heart race, something that made her think he wanted much more than a discussion about stylish hats.

Lizzie sat up straighter, unsure how to react. 'I'm not that sort of girl, sir. If you were thinking of asking me to be . . . to be . . .' it was just too embarrassing. 'Well, I'm just not that kind of person.'

Sebastian laughed in delight and flicked her cheek with his fingers. 'What a foolish girl you can be,' he said and sat back. 'Believe me, Lizzie; if I wanted a girl to seduce, I could have a vast choice. No, I think you have talent and I can use that kind of talent . . . I have some very rich ladies in my clientele and they often ask me for original designs. I do not buy all my stock from Oliver's, far from it. I've been looking for something – or should I say someone who could produce original work for a while, and I'm hoping I've found her.'

Lizzie stared in disbelief. She couldn't be hearing

this; things like this didn't happen except perhaps in dreams . . .

'I-I'm not sure . . .' she said. 'I'm not clever and I've only just started to learn my trade. I don't think you really mean what you said . . .' He had to be flirting with her, and there was only one reason a man like Sebastian Winters would flirt with a girl like her.

'You don't know me, Lizzie. One day you'll know that I never say what I don't mean – and I usually get what I want, but I'm not going to bully you. After I've seen those hats we'll talk again.' He waited for her reply but Lizzie was lost for words. 'My driver is slowing down. I think we must have reached Wilkes Street . . . I think that's where you live, isn't it?'

'Yes, but how . . . Oh, I suppose Beth told you the other night . . .,' Lizzie got her breath back. 'Thank you for the lift – and I hope you like the hats . . .'

She jumped out of the car before he could get out and open the door for her. Her heart was racing and she was still shocked. A man like Sebastian Winters could open the way for her to achieve her dream . . . but could she trust him?

'Did I hear a car door just now?' Aunt Jane said as Lizzie entered the kitchen.

'I was given a lift home, because my bus didn't come,' she said. 'Mr Winters is a customer and he saw me waiting.'

'You could have been abducted, murdered or sold to the white slave trade,' her aunt cried and struck her on the side of the head. 'You stupid, stupid, girl!'

'Jane, don't,' Uncle Jack warned.

'Mr Winters is perfectly respectable. He asked me about my work at Oliver's and said he might have a job for me designing and making special hats for his wealthy clients,' Lizzie said resentfully, holding the side of her face.

'Oh yes, and I'm the Queen of Sheba.' Her aunt looked furious. 'I should have thought you would have learned, Lizzie. You of all girls ought to know how dangerous it is . . .'

'Jane, no,' Uncle Jack said sharply. 'I dare say the gentleman is perfectly decent. She's home and none the worse. Besides, she is old enough to go out when she likes and come home how and when she likes . . .'

'And who is going to pick up the pieces next time? It's taken all this time to pay off the bill at the . . .'

'Jane, be quiet!' Uncle Jack spoke in a tone Lizzie had never heard from him. 'I won't have you nagging her over a silly thing like a lift from a gentleman she knows – I'm sure Lizzie would never get into a car with a man she didn't know.'

'Of course not,' Lizzie said. 'Please don't argue over me – and please don't worry about me. I'm not a child.'

'Have it your own way,' her aunt muttered. 'Get

on with the supper, Lizzie. I'll be working. Call me when it's ready . . .'

Lizzie looked at her uncle as the door closed behind Aunt Jane. 'Uncle Jack – what was she going to say? Something about a bill . . . was it for the sanatorium? Has it taken years to pay it off?'

He sighed heavily. 'I didn't want you to know – but it cost me quite a bit of money. I had to take out a loan and there was interest on that, so I've only just managed to pay the last instalment.'

'I'm so sorry. I would pay it back if I could . . .'

'Nonsense, my love; I shouldn't dream of it. You are my niece. I couldn't leave you in that institution any longer, Lizzie. You were slipping away from us; they told us you would never recover. The doctor at the sanatorium brought you back from the brink and I would've paid any price . . .'

'Oh uncle,' Lizzie said. She knelt by his chair and put her arms about him, resting her cheek against his. 'I do love you. You've been so good to me.'

'You have become my life,' he told her simply. 'Just be happy, my love.'

'You mustn't quarrel with Aunt Jane on my behalf . . .'

'It was time I told her what's what, Lizzie. I know she resented my paying that money, but it was mine. I earned it and she always had her share.'

Lizzie felt the sting of tears as she got up to make the tea. She'd wondered why her aunt was so careful with money, always nagging Lizzie about every penny she spent, and now she understood. It must have been difficult for her uncle to pay that bill and he'd never uttered one word of reproach to her – never even let her know that it had cost him to send her to that private sanatorium.

She tried to remember where she'd been before that, but although she felt cold all over, as if a dark cloud had descended, she still couldn't recall anything before the doctor in the sanatorium had spoken to her about going home.

'I'm sorry I've caused so much trouble for you both,' she said as she brought her uncle a cup of tea.

'No, Lizzie,' he said firmly. 'I sent you out that evening to buy my cigarettes. If I'd gone myself, it would never have happened . . .'

'My accident,' Lizzie said. 'I've never known exactly what happened. Did I fall and hurt myself . . . or was I attacked . . .?'

Uncle Jack's face was very pale. 'What makes you ask, Lizzie? You haven't remembered that night?'

'No – but sometimes I've wondered . . .'

'The doctor told us that it was best if we didn't tell you, Lizzie. He says that if you want to remember it will come back in time, and if your mind doesn't want to let it in it won't. I think he knew what he was doing, love. Until he started to treat you, you didn't know us. I thought you were lost to us forever . . .'

'Please, do not distress yourself, uncle. I just wish I could repay you for all you've done for me.'

'You do that every day with your smile and your caring,' he said and shook his head. 'No more questions, Lizzie. You'd best get the supper on before your aunt goes on the rampage.'

CHAPTER 10

Lizzie noticed Tilly's red eyes when she took the trays round with everyone's tea. She served all the others and then took her mug back to the girl's bench, perching on one corner.

'What's wrong, Tilly? You've been crying . . .'

Tilly swallowed hard. 'My husband had an accident at work yesterday. They took him to hospital and I was allowed to visit for ten minutes last night . . . but he was asleep and didn't know I was there . . .'

'I'm so sorry. What happened?'

'He slipped as he was moving some heavy crates and one fell on him. He could have been killed . . .'

'I'm so sorry,' Lizzie said. 'If there's anything I can do to help just tell me.'

Tilly hesitated, then, 'There is, if you mean it?'

'Yes, of course. What can I do?'

'I can only visit for a few minutes at night, because Mum looks after my little one all day and she won't stay longer than half past seven. On Saturday I could have an hour visit with him, but Mum's going to a friend's wedding. I can't ask her to take care of Sally . . .'

'What time is visiting Saturday afternoon?'

'From three thirty to four thirty . . .'

'I could have your little girl,' Lizzie said. 'I go to Ed's house and do a few jobs, but I could take the child with me. I think Madge would love to see her, and if you're home by five I can meet my friends as arranged for the evening.'

'Oh, Lizzie, you are a darlin',' Tilly said and hugged her. 'You'd best clear it with Ed and his wife first . . .'

'I'm going there tonight,' Lizzie said. 'I'll ask Madge, but I'm sure she would love it.'

Ed was a little uncertain when Lizzie mentioned the idea later but he said he had no objection if his wife agreed. They worked in harmony until midday and then, just as Lizzie was going to lunch, Mr Oliver came up to them.

'Sebastian took both the hats you made as well as his usual order,' he said. 'and he's ordered three of the pleated variety, one in black, pale blue, and emerald green, and he wants six of the cheaper one in whatever colours you think will look stylish . . .'

'He must have liked them,' Lizzie said, feeling a little shocked. 'When does he need them by?'

'Like everyone else, he wants them yesterday,' Mr Oliver grunted. 'I told him Saturday morning – but I still want the other orders on time, so you'll have to work in your break if necessary, Lizzie.'

'I don't mind, but what do I get out of it?' she

asked, holding her breath as he glared at her. 'Well, they were my designs and if I have to work extra hours.' Lizzie held her breath but after all they were her designs and she didn't see why she shouldn't get something out of it.

'I'll give you five bob if you get them done on time, and Ed still gets his orders out,' her employer told her. 'It's up to you how you work it between you . . .'

'That told him, Lizzie girl,' Ed whispered. 'Good for you, standing up for yourself. You should be paid for new designs. He would have to pay anyone else – and designers charge the earth for their services; that's why we stick to the same styles. Bert Oliver won't waste money if he can help it . . . but you took a risk, lass. You got away with it this time, but you might not be so lucky next.'

'Of course you can bring Tilly's little girl on Saturday,' Madge said when Lizzie asked her. 'It will be a treat for me. She can sit on my lap while you're busy and perhaps she'll just go to sleep.'

'Well, we'll have the pram so she can go in that if she's trouble,' Lizzie said. 'As long as it isn't too much for you?'

'I'm feeling a bit better in myself again,' Madge said. 'I've told Ed that he needn't come home midday if he's busy at work because I can make a cup of tea and a sandwich now. I feel a bit awkward about letting you do so much, but I don't want to stop you coming, even if we only have a chat . . .'

'You're not fit to polish or scrub floors,' Lizzie said. 'All Ed wants is to see you well again – and I like coming . . .'

'Well, I've got something for you, a surprise,' Madge said. 'I couldn't give you money and I know you wouldn't take it if we tried – but I do have something you might like.'

'You don't have to give me anything,' Lizzie said. 'Honestly, I just want to help Ed and see you . . .'

'Well, this isn't any good to me now, but it might be of use to you.' Milly pointed to something hung over the back of a chair. 'Bring it here, Lizzie, and hold it up against you.'

Lizzie picked up what she immediately saw was a pale blue dress. It had short fitted sleeves, a shaped neckline, narrow waist and a gored skirt. The material was silky but not real silk, of course, and the buttons at the front were pearly and very pretty.

'It's much too long,' Madge said, 'but you could shorten it, Lizzie, and I think it looks as if it will fit?'

'It's my size,' Lizzie said, 'and I can easily make any adjustments – but this is such a lovely dress, Madge. It's the one you told me about – for your first dance . . . you can't want to give it away?'

'I'd love you to have it,' Madge said. 'I think it will suit you and I shall never wear it again. Please take it with my love. It isn't payment, it's a gift from me to you . . .'

'It's lovely and I can't wait to wear it,' she said

and kissed Madge's cheek. 'Now, I'm going to finish that ironing before I leave and your meal will be ready in five minutes . . .'

Aunt Jane looked at the dress as Lizzie placed it carefully on the old daybed in the kitchen, smoothing the skirts out reverently. It must have been expensive new.

'Where did you get that? It isn't new?'

'It belonged to Madge. I shall have to cut the length, because it's too long, but I don't think it needs much else doing.'

'Are you sure it's clean? I don't want fleas in my house.'

'It is perfectly clean. Madge told me she had it cleaned before she put it away.'

'Well, I dare say it smells of mothballs. I should steam it and hang it in the scullery until the smell goes, if I were you. If you really want charity . . .'

'It smells of lavender,' Lizzie said, hurt that her aunt should make stinging remarks about the gift. 'I'll cut the skirt to my length and hem it and then I'll steam and iron it. I shall wear it this weekend.'

'Going out with your friend again I suppose?'

'First of all, I'm going to collect Tilly's little girl so that she can visit her husband in hospital, and I'm going to take her to Madge's house. Afterwards, I'll get changed and go to Beth's house . . .'

'And what is Beth doing all afternoon?'

'Her boyfriend is taking her up West for tea and he is going to buy her a present . . .'

'And what happens this evening – do you play gooseberry or do you have another friend?'

Lizzie took a deep breath, then, 'Harry Oliver is coming too. We're going as a foursome.'

A flash of annoyance showed in Aunt Jane's eyes. 'You are being very foolish. It can't come to anything, Lizzie. No matter what your uncle says, about you being old enough to know your own mind, you will end up with a broken heart and you will have only yourself to blame.'

'Why? Why shouldn't I be happy? I'm not saying I shall marry Harry but I might if I like him enough and he asks . . .'

'He wouldn't if . . .'

'Jane, no,' her uncle intervened from the doorway. 'I've told you before . . .'

'I shall leave you to get the cocoa,' Aunt Jane said looking angrily at her husband. 'I have some work to finish.'

Lizzie was puzzled. Why was her aunt so certain that no one would ever want to marry her? She'd thought it was because she was plain, but Harry said she was pretty . . . so why did her aunt say such things?

CHAPTER 11

'I've been looking forward to this all week,' Harry said when they met outside Ed's house. Lizzie handed him her little overnight bag and he put it in the back of his van. 'Let's go to the Italian cafe, Lizzie. We can have coffee and cream cakes – they're delicious at Luigi's.'

'Shall we get back in time to see the first big film? We've got to meet the others at half past six.'

'We'll get there, though we might miss the cartoons,' he said. 'But the Pathé News and the big film won't start before a quarter to seven. I'll take you and Beth home in the van afterwards, Lizzie.'

'Yes, all right,' she said, taking his arm. 'But we mustn't be late.'

They finally arrived at the cinema just ten minutes later than promised. Beth smiled and greeted them, but Lizzie could see that Tony wasn't too pleased. So Lizzie felt a bit guilty as she queued with the others for the one and ninepenny seats. They had just got to the head of the queue when the manager announced that the seating had all gone and there was only standing room, unless you paid two shillings and sixpence for the circle.

'Damn,' Tony muttered, fishing in his pocket for the extra. 'If we'd gone in earlier it would have saved us money.'

'It's my fault so I'll pay,' Harry said cheerfully and pulled a ten bob note out of his pocket.

Harry paid for their tickets and then bought some sweets at the kiosk near the entrance to the darkened cinema. The usherette showed them to their seats just as the newsreel began, and they sat down to watch. The modulated voice of the Pathé News commentator told of Britain's first military conscripts, and showed how they were settling in at their camps; the King and Queen had visited the World Fair in New York, and in Germany several hundred Jews had been deported to Poland. There were also pictures of the sinking of the Thetis submarine during trials in Liverpool Bay and pictures of post-boxes blown up by what were thought to be IRA bombs all around the country.

Lizzie was glad when the news was over, because not much of it was good, and it seemed there was unrest everywhere. She relaxed when the big film started. It was the *Bishop's Wife,* a romantic comedy, and starred Loretta Young, Cary Grant and David Niven. She'd wondered what kind of film they were going to see and relaxed as she heard her friends laughing at the poor Bishop's tangled troubles.

Harry gave her the box of Fry's chocolates he'd bought and munched a nutty toffee beside her. She liked it that he didn't try to put his hand on her knee or even around her shoulders. It would certainly have spoiled the evening for her if he had, but as it was she was able to enjoy the whole experience and thanked him warmly as, at the end of the evening, they all piled into the little van he used for delivering hats.

The two girls were able to squeeze into the front seat with him, but Tony had to go in the back and she heard him muttering to Beth. Lizzie was afraid the evening had been spoiled for her friend and squeezed her hand, but Beth shook her head. She was annoyed with the way Tony was behaving.

'I really enjoyed myself this evening,' Lizzie told Harry. 'Thank you so much for taking me to see that film. I loved David Niven . . .'

'Yes, I've always like him. I talked to Tony last week and we thought you girls would rather see that than a dark thriller?'

'Yes, very much so. I like the Odeon too; it's much more luxurious than any other cinema in Bethnal Green.'

'Most of the others are what my uncle calls fleapits, though the Regal isn't too bad.'

'I went there once with my uncle, but the seats were a bit hard. It's not that bad, but the Odeon is much better.'

'We'll go up the West End one day,' he said smiling at her, 'but you really need the whole afternoon for that.'

'Perhaps one day. I help Madge on Saturdays and then I have to spend some time with my aunt and uncle. I've promised to go to church with Aunt Jane tomorrow.'

'You won't come with me for a walk in the afternoon?'

'I can't, not yet,' Lizzie said. 'Perhaps, if you still want to, another week . . .'

'What about a dance next week?'

'I'm not sure,' Lizzie said. 'Unless Beth is going, I would have to go home afterwards and . . . my aunt might not like it if I'm out late . . .'

'You've got to grow up and live your own life. You can't let her dictate to you forever.' Harry raised his brows as if to challenge her.

'That's what Beth says. I'll see what she says.' Then, to change the subject, 'I've enjoyed making those new hats this week . . .'

'My uncle has decided to sell more of the better hats,' he said. 'You've started something, Lizzie Larch. He says if you can produce hats like that from start to finish he can get rid of one of the girls who do the trimming. He says he doesn't need three of them if you're able to do the work yourself . . .'

'Oh, I hadn't thought of that . . .' Lizzie felt sorry for the girl who would lose her job. 'It won't be Tilly will it? I wish I hadn't said anything about finishing them myself now.'

'You've probably done the girls a favour,' Harry said. 'They're little better than slaves those girls. He's getting you at half price and knows it.'

'Tilly just looked up and smiled at me this

morning – and she was told quite sharply to get on with her work.'

'She'll probably get the push one of these days,' Harry shrugged carelessly. 'Most of the girls don't last more than eighteen months. They get fed up with the work and go elsewhere, but it isn't easy, so a lot of them just get pregnant and mostly their blokes marry them.'

'That's cynical,' Lizzie said with a frown. 'Besides, Tilly's married and she needs the work with her husband in hospital. Anyway, I couldn't have done it all on my own.'

'Perhaps I'm wrong, but Tilly takes longer to do her work than either Nancy or Meggie.'

'Tilly takes more trouble over her hats.'

'I've told my uncle that many times,' he said and looked thoughtful. 'He never listens to me. I'm just the delivery boy.'

'You're more than that, you know you are.'

'I would have left long ago, but he was good to my mother after Father died. She died last year; they said it was her heart.'

'I'm so sorry.' Lizzie looked at him curiously as they drew up outside Beth's house and the others got out. Tony hadn't spoken a word the whole journey and looked sulky as Lizzie bid him goodnight. Beth looked fed up, as if she'd sensed Tony's black mood. 'Does your uncle know you intend to leave soon?'

'No, but we'll all have to go once the war starts, and I may as well get in early.'

'The RAF not the Army?'

'I like the uniform,' he said and laughed. 'I suppose I'm mad to risk upsetting him. Uncle Bert doesn't have any children. He may leave the business to me.'

'But if you don't like working for him . . .' She shook her head. 'It's not my business, of course.'

'It might be one day,' he said, making her look at him intently. 'It's too soon to talk of the future, but I really like you, Lizzie . . .'

Her cheeks were burning and she couldn't meet his gaze as she said, 'I like you too, Harry. I'd better go in. Beth and Tony are already at the door.'

'They look as if they're having a row. Besides, it's not that late . . .' He leaned forward to give her a chaste kiss on the cheek. 'Goodnight, Lizzie. I shall look forward to seeing you again soon.'

'Yes, perhaps we should go to the flicks on our own next time, but I'll talk to Beth. I had a lovely time, Harry. Thank you so much for taking me.'

'Thank you for coming, Lizzie. I want to go out as much as we can before I join up because I don't want to waste a minute . . .'

Lizzie smiled uncertainly and joined Beth at the front door. Tony had stalked off and she guessed he was in a temper; she hadn't seen him kiss Beth goodnight and realised her friend looked unhappy.

'Is Tony angry?' she whispered. 'I'm sorry if it upset him because we were late.'

'It's not just that,' Beth said and forced a smile.

'He doesn't want to go out in a foursome. Says we can meet up at the dance if you like, but he wants to be on his own with me when we walk home.'

'I'm sorry, Beth. I know you did this for me, but you mustn't fall out with him over me.'

'Tony wants more than I can give,' Beth said and looked as if she might burst into tears. 'It's not your fault, Lizzie – it's us. Tony wants to get married and I can't, and I won't do what he wants . . . I'm not giving in and doing it until we're married.'

Beth lay awake long after Lizzie had fallen asleep. She'd held the tears back with difficulty because she didn't want Lizzie to feel guilty. Tony had complained because she and Harry were late, and he'd been in a bad mood all evening.

'I look forward to the walk home,' he'd said as they lingered outside her door. 'I don't see you often enough, Beth, and when we do – I want to kiss and touch you. We can't do that with those friends of yours hanging around.'

'Lizzie can't get away from her aunt unless she comes with me . . .'

'Tell her to grow up – and that goes for you, too, Beth. Unless you're going to be a bit friend-lier, I'm not going to bother coming round . . .'

'What do you mean?' she asked, feeling a pang of fear mixed with disbelief. 'You know I can't . . . suppose I fall for a baby? My father would kill me.'

'No, he wouldn't, he'd see sense and let us get married. It would be his fault anyway for making us wait.'

'I won't let my family down,' Beth said and turned her shoulder on him. 'You know how I feel.'

'Well, you know how I feel now,' Tony said and walked off. Beth had wanted to call him back but pride wouldn't let her. If he couldn't wait, he would have to suit himself – but there Beth's determination started to crumble. She knew that Sylvia Butcher wouldn't turn him down.

Tears on her cheeks, she turned her face to the pillow. Sometimes, Beth almost hated him, because she didn't want to shame her family and she didn't want a baby just yet either, especially out of wedlock. It had taken a long time to learn the skills she had and she wanted to work a bit longer and save her money so that she could have a lovely white wedding – although at the moment she was sure there would be a wedding at all.

CHAPTER 12

Lizzie saw the look on her aunt's face as she walked into the kitchen that Sunday morning. She'd had been crying and that was so rare that Lizzie's heart caught with fright.

'Uncle Jack . . .?' she said, her throat tight with emotion. 'Is he . . . worse?'

'Oh yes, of course he told you he was ill, didn't he?' her aunt said bitterly. 'Never mind him telling me, his wife . . . Now, he's dying and I'm going to be left alone to cope with everything . . .'

'Dying . . .?' Lizzie's heart pounded and her throat was tight with tears. 'Where is he?'

'Upstairs in our room. He was taken ill last night. Fortunately, I had a client with me and she went to phone for a doctor.' Aunt Jane looked at her with something resembling loathing. 'He asked for you over and over but I didn't know how to reach you and then the doctor gave him something to make him drowsy.'

'May I go up and see him please?'

'Please yourself. I'm not sure if he will know you . . .'

Lizzie ran from the room, taking the stairs two

at a time. Her aunt's words had stung her, making her feel so guilty, because she ought to have been here when he needed her and she couldn't bear it if it was too late.

Opening the door of his room, Lizzie peeped in, her heart beating rapidly. She walked softly towards the bed, hardly daring to speak for fear of disturbing him. Yet as she approached, his eyes opened and lit with love, his hand moving on the bedclothes as if reaching for hers. She sat down next to him and took his hand in hers, running a finger over it as if to comfort him, or perhaps it was she that needed comfort, because he seemed at peace.

'I waited for you,' he said and the love in his eyes broke her heart. 'I wanted you to know, Lizzie. Your aunt must have the house for her lifetime; it's her right and I couldn't do otherwise, but the shop and the goodwill is yours. I've arranged it with the lawyer, made a proper will . . .'

'Please, don't,' Lizzie was crying silently. 'I love you. Please don't leave me, Uncle Jack . . .'

'It's my time, love. I want you to be independent and happy. You can sell the business and keep the property; that will bring you in a little rent. It's all I can do for you, Lizzie. I ruined your life and I can never make it right . . . please forgive me . . .'

'There's nothing to forgive. You've given me so much.'

'I owed you more, but your aunt must have her home while she lives, and I dare say she'll go on for a long time, but then it will be yours.'

'Please . . .' Lizzie held his hand to her cheek. His eyes closed and he whispered something more. She couldn't hear it all but knew he was telling her he loved her.

Watching the colour fade from his cheeks, Lizzie knew that he'd gone. He'd hung on to say goodbye and then he'd given up. Tears were streaming from her eyes now and she felt devastated.

She would stay until the funeral was over and then she would go. Aunt Jane might call her selfish and ungrateful, and perhaps she was, but she couldn't live with a woman that hated her – and she'd seen real hatred in her aunt's eyes this morning.

Lizzie sat for a while just holding her uncle's hand, and then she got up and went downstairs. The doctor would have to be told and someone would come to do what was necessary. Perhaps her aunt would want his body to remain here or she might have it taken to a chapel of rest; it wasn't Lizzie's choice. She'd loved her uncle, but Aunt Jane was his wife. Lizzie could only do what she was told . . .

Aunt Jane just looked through Lizzie when she told her that he was dead. She didn't speak to Lizzie but went upstairs to look for herself.

Lizzie went down the road to the corner shop and asked to use the phone. Joe Bent looked at her sadly as she told him the reason for needing to make the call.

'He was a good man your uncle,' he said. 'Why

he stayed married to her I'll never know, but he'll be at peace now. She'll be using the funeral parlour down the road, because he's the cheapest. If I were you I should pop down there, after you've phoned the doc, and ask them to call.'

Having spoken to the doctor, Lizzie smiled, thanked Joe and returned to the house. Her aunt had come downstairs. She listened when Lizzie told her she'd sent for the doctor.

'You could have saved your steps if you'd waited. You'd best go down the road and tell them to come and fetch him when the doctor has been. I'm not having the stink of death in my house.'

'Is there anything else you need while I'm out?' Lizzie's nails curled into her hands because she hated her aunt for talking like that, as if Uncle Jack was a piece of dead meat, but held her tongue out of respect to her uncle.

'If there is I'll tell you . . .'

Lizzie didn't mind how often she went out, because she could hardly bear to be in the house and know that her dear uncle was lying dead up in his room. It seemed Aunt Jane could hardly wait to get rid of him, and Lizzie knew that as soon as he had gone, she would be burning his death sheets and airing the room, as if he had never existed.

It was unbearably painful to know that a kind and gentle man had not been truly loved by his wife. Lizzie's eyes burned with tears, but she went

114

through the motions, holding back her tears until she lay in bed at night.

The next day it was easier because her uncle had been taken to a place of calm and peace and Lizzie was back at work. Ed listened to her and then just put his arms about her and held her clasped to his chest. Tears fell, but Lizzie brushed them away. They had a lot of work to do and she knew that crying would not bring back the man she'd loved.

'I shall be at the funeral with you,' Harry said when she told him some of what had happened during their lunch break. 'Don't worry, Lizzie, I shan't let that old dragon get her claws into you any more than I can help. What are you going to do afterwards?'

'She can come and stay with me,' Beth said. She'd listened in silence but now she put an arm about Lizzie's waist. 'I'll ask Mum tonight, but I know what she'll say. You can share my room, Lizzie.'

'Thanks, both of you,' Lizzie said. 'I'm glad I've got friends. I'm not sure I could have got through without you.'

Living with her aunt was not an option. Aunt Jane had barely spoken to Lizzie since Uncle Jack died, and then only when she had to; her aunt had never cared for her, but now they were like two strangers forced to share the same living space, and after the funeral it could only get worse.

★   ★   ★

'Well, if you don't mind sharing your room until after Mary's wedding, Lizzie can come as soon as the funeral is over. I shall want fifteen shillings for her food and washing, same as your sister and you pay, Beth – but if she's happy with that I shall be glad of the money.'

'Lizzie gives her aunt a pound a week,' Beth said. 'She was pleased when I told her she'd be welcome here. I think she dreaded moving into lodgings.'

'Well, she can move some of her things here when she's ready. We don't have much room, but we'll store them somewhere until Mary's room is empty.'

'I don't think Lizzie has much of her own, apart from a few clothes and some drawing things. Her aunt is so mean to her . . .'

'Well, we'll look after her when she comes to us,' her mother said.

'I think Mr Oliver is trying to take advantage of her too. Lizzie is so clever, Mum. You should see the designs she draws – and she makes hats look really special. She should have her own hat shop.'

'Perhaps she will one day, but we'll look after her in the meantime.' Mrs Court finished setting the table. 'What are you doing this evening, Beth? Is Tony taking you out?'

'No, he's working late again,' Beth said. 'I saw him at the bus-stop this morning. He went to look at a shop in Whitechapel but it wasn't what he wants so he didn't take the lease. He was disappointed, but, it's probably better to wait for a while.

If there is a war – well, he would have to leave everything to his staff and that wouldn't work.'

'It might, if you were there to look after things – don't you think that's what Tony wants?'

'Yes, I know it is. He thinks if he had the shop, Dad would let us get married at Christmas, instead of making us wait until after I'm twenty – but I don't want to give my job up yet, Mum.'

'Perhaps your dad isn't so wrong, love. After all, it's only eighteen months or so now. It's surprising how time flies, isn't it?'

'Yes, I know.' Beth felt anxious. 'Supposing it does come to a war, Mum, what happens then? What happens if Tony is called up and he wants to get married quickly?'

'I don't know, Beth. If it happens you will have to ask your dad. I think he will still say you should wait until you're twenty – but if there's a war and you really want to marry Tony, he might relent. That nice Mr Chamberlain keeps saying it isn't going to happen and Germany would never declare war on us. And perhaps he is right . . .'

CHAPTER 13

Lizzie didn't cry in church or even as she stood by the grave and threw a rose into the open ground. She'd cried all her tears and now felt empty and numb. She was glad that both Harry and Beth had got a few hours off to be with her. Ed had wanted to come but Mr Oliver couldn't spare him.

'I'll be thinking of you, Lizzie,' he'd told her. 'Madge says you're to come to us whenever you like . . . we're your family now.'

Lizzie had thanked him but she'd decided that she would stay with Beth's family once she'd settled things with her aunt. Mrs Court had come to the funeral and told her she was welcome to stay with them for as long as she liked, which was a relief since her aunt was still ignoring her and Lizzie knew she wanted her out of the house.

'Come on,' Harry said, squeezing her hand as they left the churchyard. 'I'll take you home and then I can cart your stuff round to Beth's house.'

'Yes, please stay until everyone else has gone,' Lizzie said. 'I have to talk to my aunt and I'm not looking forward to it. If you're there, we shan't come to blows . . .'

'She'd better not touch you.' Harry looked so fierce that for the first time in days Lizzie felt like smiling.

She'd been cleaning and baking every spare moment she'd got since her uncle's death. A spread of ham sandwiches, home-made biscuits, small cakes and sausage rolls was waiting for the guests at her uncle's house. Lizzie had thought it might only be her and her friends that went back, but instead about twenty other people piled into their tiny sitting room and overflowed into the kitchen. Uncle Jack had been a popular man, and a lot of his friends had turned up to see him off.

Aunt Jane wore the face of a suffering martyr all the time the guests were there, but gradually they drifted away, leaving a mountain of washing up behind them.

'We'll help with this before we go,' Mrs Court said and gave Lizzie a hug. 'Come to us whenever you like, love.'

'I'm going to talk to my aunt when you've gone, and Harry will bring my stuff over. I don't have that much, a suitcase and a couple of cardboard boxes . . .'

'Just as well or we'd have nowhere to put them,' Beth's mother said and wiped up a delicate china cup.

'I'll see you later.' Beth hugged her. 'We'll go now, because the sooner you leave here the better.'

Lizzie nodded. Harry had taken no part in the washing up, watching the others and saying nothing, but after they'd left, he took her hand and held it firmly.

'Come on, let's get it over with . . .'

They were about to walk into the sitting room when Aunt Jane entered the kitchen. Lizzie saw by her face she was angry, and then she noticed that her aunt was holding something that looked like a will.

'Do you know what this is?' she asked in the bitter tone she'd used of late towards Lizzie. 'It was delivered by hand a few minutes ago. It's your Uncle Jack's will. As usual, I'm the last to know, because I can see by your face that you know the terms of it . . .'

'He told me something before he died . . .' Lizzie faltered, feeling glad that Harry was standing at her shoulder.

'He left everything to you, apart from the insurance policy . . . about fifty pounds they told me when I telephoned and asked yesterday. Everything else – this house and the business is yours . . .' If a look could kill, it was aimed at Lizzie now. 'Twenty-five years of marriage and I get a paltry fifty pounds . . .'

'The house is yours rent-free for your lifetime . . .' Lizzie stopped as her aunt moved towards her threateningly. 'I didn't know until he said . . .'

'Oh no, of course not.' Aunt Jane hit out, but Harry moved too quickly for her and all she contacted with was his arm. 'Yes, she's got you running after her, hasn't she, but just you wait until you know what she really is . . .'

'You'd better shut your foul mouth, madam,' Harry said, glaring at her. 'You're speaking of the girl I love, and one day she's going to be my wife.'

Aunt Jane stared at him and then started laughing. Her laughter got wilder and wilder until she was clearly hysterical and Harry took her by the shoulders and shook her.

'I don't know what's so funny, but we're going to fetch Lizzie's things now and we're leaving.'

'Mrs Court has asked me to stay with her,' Lizzie said, delaying him for a moment with a touch of her hand. 'I'm sorry we had to part like this, Aunt Jane, but I don't think you'd want me here even if I said I'd stay . . .'

Her aunt had stopped laughing. 'I shan't be here that long myself, but don't think you're getting the house that easily. I'm going to consult a solicitor about my rights, and if I can't actually get what belongs to me, I'll see you don't have it for as long as I live. You can't stop me letting it to a tenant and having the money.'

'I'm not so sure about that,' Harry said, but Lizzie placed a gentle hand on his arm.

'I don't want to stop you renting the house,' she said. 'It should have been yours. I know that and so did Uncle Jack, but he chose to leave things the way he did. I could speak to the solicitor, because the house should be yours.'

'No,' Harry said. 'Don't give into her, Lizzie. Think about it before you make any promises. Your uncle wanted you to have it and you owe it to his memory to believe he knew what he was doing . . .'

Lizzie looked at him uncertainly. She felt uncomfortable about inheriting most of her uncle's property, because it really ought to be his wife's, despite the way she'd treated him.

'I doubt the solicitor would let you,' Aunt Jane said bitterly. 'Jack will have it all sewn up tight enough. I always knew it might come to this . . . he was a damned fool and it was his fault . . .'

'You mean the accident,' Lizzie said, staring at her intently. 'Just because he sent me out for a packet of cigarettes and I fell and hurt my head . . .'

Her aunt smiled strangely, a cold cruel glint in her eyes as she said, 'A fall – is that what you believe Oh, no, Lizzie, that wasn't what happened. Believe me.'

'What did happen then? You've never told me . . .'

'Don't give her the chance to hurt you.' Harry took Lizzie's arm, steering her from the room. 'Don't listen to her, Lizzie darling. She's a vindictive old witch and she'll tell you a pack of lies. We'll get your things and leave.'

Lizzie looked back and the smile on her aunt's mouth chilled her. Harry was right. Aunt Jane wanted to hurt her. It was a good thing she was leaving right now . . .

★   ★   ★

'I'm really happy you're going to stay with us,' Beth said when Lizzie hung her things in the wardrobe and put her undies in the drawer Beth had emptied for her. 'You'll be like another sister, Lizzie – and we can go everywhere together . . .'

'Yes, we can,' Lizzie said and hugged her. 'I always wanted a sister and now I've got you. Things are going to be so much easier for us both now, Beth.'

Beth agreed and they went down to have the tasty snack Beth's mother had prepared for their supper: a slice of toast and dripping and a mug of sweet cocoa made with condensed milk. It was yummy sitting by the fire tucking into the treat and Lizzie realised what she'd been missing all these years as she listened to the Court family bickering and laughing, teasing each other, especially when Mary came home after seeing her fiancé and Beth's other sister Dotty and her husband popped in with their baby for a few minutes on their way home from visiting his family. The small kitchen was crowded and Lizzie felt a part of the family, surrounded by friends and the love and kindness of people she knew she could trust. At last she was free to enjoy life, meet her friends and do what she wanted, just as her uncle had wanted for her . . .

Uncle Jack's death was going to hurt for a while longer, made worse by the bitter accusations and the hatred she'd seen in her aunt's eyes, but it was over . . . Now she could put the past behind her and move on.

CHAPTER 14

'Well, Lizzie, I don't do this for all my girls,' Mr Oliver said that day in early August. 'I always make them serve their full term as an apprentice, but you've proved quick and clever – and neither Ed nor Harry will give me a moment's peace if I don't put you on full wages.'

'That's very kind of you, Mr Oliver.' Harry had hounded his uncle these past few weeks, telling him that Lizzie was a marvel and if she didn't stay he would regret it. 'I'm glad you're pleased with my work.'

'Well, don't take advantage of my good nature,' her employer said. 'Get on with your work. I need that order fulfilled by tomorrow – but Ed is right, you do make a good team.'

Lizzie laughed softly, delighted with the news, as Mr Oliver moved on. 'Thanks, Ed,' she said. 'I know you warned him that you'd never cope if I left, and after both Nancy and Meggie went to work in the munitions factory it put the wind up him.'

'Don't compare their work with yours,' Ed said.

'You've learned to cut and shape the hats in record time, Lizzie, and you can sew the pieces together and then trim them if you want, though you tell Oliver that you need Tilly to help you.'

'I didn't want him giving her the sack,' Lizzie said. 'Brian, that's her husband, is just about hobbling around now, but he won't get his old job back at the docks. All he will be able to do is the job of a caretaker or something that doesn't involve heavy lifting.'

'Do you know if he can drive?' Ed asked. 'I reckon Oliver would take him on to replace Harry. He has only waited this long for your sake, because he wanted to be off weeks ago, Lizzie . . . When is the big day to be?'

Lizzie blushed and shook her head. 'Not yet,' she said. 'He has asked me to marry him, but I said we've got to wait for a while. I'm not twenty-one until January and I don't think Aunt Jane would sign the consent form if I asked her.'

'Do you know where she's living?'

'Some kind of apartments . . .' Lizzie wrinkled her brow. 'I'm not sure, but I think it's a home for people who need help and can't manage alone. I suppose she found herself a little job helping the warden or something . . .'

'You haven't written to her?'

'No, not yet. We parted on bad terms and I would rather leave it for a while.'

Ed arched his eyebrows. 'Do you want to get married, Lizzie?'

'I might,' she said, her cheeks warm. 'I'm fond of Harry . . . I might love him, but I'd rather wait until next year and not ask Aunt Jane.'

'Well, Oliver won't be keen on losing you . . .'

'I shan't leave even if we get married. I've got lots to learn yet,' Lizzie said. 'I love my job; especially now you let me make up my orders and I do the final touches . . . it's almost what I wanted to do . . .'

'You should work for a top-class milliner,' Ed said. 'Some of the designs you draw are wonderful. Oliver will never let you make them up here – you do know that?'

'Oh yes, I know, but I shan't be here forever. Besides, he lets me buy materials and I've been making hats for Beth's sister's wedding. None of them know yet, but I shall finish them this week and I'll take them home and surprise them all . . .' She'd rented her uncle's shop out for a few shillings a week and the solicitor had got her fifty pounds for the lease, which she'd put safely in the bank, but she could afford to spend a little on hats for her friends, especially after all they'd done for her.

'Well, that hat you've been making for yourself is very different,' Ed said and chuckled. 'I don't think our customers would touch it with a barge-pole, far too impractical as well as expensive, but I love the originality. Will you let me come and work for you when you're a famous designer?'

'Oh, Ed,' Lizzie giggled. 'I do love working with

you; if ever I have my own shop – or workshops, I'll be sure to ask for you.'

'Well, we'd best get on or Grumble Guts will be after us,' Ed said. 'He doesn't give extra wages for nothing. Let's get that order ready for tomorrow, or we'll be in trouble . . .'

'Are we going to the dance this week?' Harry asked when Lizzie went into the restroom for her lunch break. 'Beth says she's going with Tony. Apparently, they've made it up for the moment . . .'

'It's a bit on and off with them. Tony wants to get married, and he wants Beth to leave Oliver's and work in a shop he's bought, but I don't think she's sure how she feels . . .'

'Well, she'll have to make up her mind soon, because once the war starts he'll be called up, same as the rest of us . . .' Harry hesitated, then, 'I'd like us to get married soon, Lizzie. You know I love you – and I want you to be my wife. I've told my uncle he should let you take over as much of my work as you can . . .'

'Oh thanks; like I don't have enough to do!' she teased.

'I didn't mean you should do more. Good grief, I don't do that much, especially now I order the stock in advance by phone – which was your idea, Lizzie. It's just deliveries . . .'

'We had an idea about that. Could you teach Tilly's husband to drive the van? Tilly was telling me he's worried about getting a job that will pay the rent . . .'

'I'll go round this evening and see if he wants to try. With his leg in plaster, he might have a bit of a job with the pedals at the moment, but if he's game I am . . .' Harry said, grabbing her and kissing her. 'What a clever girl I've got!'

'This is for you, Mrs Court,' Lizzie said, taking out a white felt hat trimmed with pink tulle and a deep pink rose. 'And this blue one is yours, Beth, with my love. This navy one is for Mary to go away in, and this is mine . . .' She took out a pale lemon, fine straw hat with a curving brim and a frill of pleated tulle that swirled over the brim and right round the dome. 'Ed loved it when it was finished, but he didn't think it would sell.'

'Of course it would,' Beth said, looking at it admiringly. She tried on her own hat, which was a small pillbox shape that perched on the back of her head and was decorated with veiling and a small silk bow at the back. 'This is lovely, Lizzie. It will go with my costume perfectly . . . and a lot of other things too.'

'Well, blue is your favourite colour,' Lizzie said and smiled as Beth ran to try it on in front of the mirror.

'These must have cost such a lot of money,' Mrs Court said. 'I'm very grateful, Lizzie, because I couldn't find a pretty hat I could afford – but you must let me pay for mine.'

'Certainly not,' Lizzie said. 'I made them all as presents, and I've just had a big rise at work. Mr Oliver let me buy the materials at cost, providing I didn't work on them in his time, so I've been working on them in my lunch break – and at Ed's. Madge is so much better and she loved seeing them. Ed made her a pretty hat for her birthday, but she doesn't get out much to wear it.'

'Bring her to Mary's wedding if you like,' Mrs Court said. 'One more won't make any difference, and it will be nice for you to have another friend there – because Beth may be busy with her sisters sometimes.'

'Are you bringing Harry to the wedding?' Beth asked as they put the hats away and sat down to a supper of cold ham and big ripe tomatoes with some fresh bread and butter.

'I asked if he wanted to come but he wasn't sure. He's going to enquire about joining the RAF tomorrow and they might want him to report straight away . . .'

'I doubt it,' Mrs Court said. 'It will be a few weeks before they want him . . .'

'I wouldn't be so sure about that,' Mr Court said, coming into the kitchen from the backyard and washing his hands at the sink. 'With war looming, he'll likely be sent straight off to join a training unit . . .'

'I hope not,' Lizzie said, her heart catching with fright at the thought of what might happen to him. 'We were going to the dance this Saturday.'

'Well, he may not have to go just yet,' Mrs Court said and shook her head at her husband. 'Sit and eat your tea, all of you. I've got loads of ironing to do this evening.'

'I'll do some of it for you,' Lizzie offered.

'You're a good girl, Lizzie, but there's no need for you to bother. You and Beth can wash up though, and give the kitchen a bit of a clean.'

The girls nodded their willingness to perform the tasks asked of them. They chattered throughout the meal and then as they washed up afterwards, and did whatever tidying was necessary.

'You're not seeing Tony this evening?'

'He's viewing property again, though I keep telling him it's a waste of time.'

'Harry had to see someone,' Lizzie said. 'We could go for a walk if you like, or just sit and listen to the radio.'

'Let's walk down to that pub near the river and have a drink,' Beth said. 'We don't have to go inside, because they have tables outside in the summer and a lot of girls from the factories go there. I don't feel like staying in all evening and I don't see why we shouldn't go to a pub without Tony and Harry, do you?'

'No,' Lizzie said with a dreamy smile. 'We can do what we like . . . can't we?'

The pub had put up some fairy lights on poles set around the yard, which looked out over the river. There wasn't much of a view, because of the cranes and warehouses that crowded the water-side, but there was a tiny gap through to the river and the water looked dark and mysterious. Every now and then they caught sight of a riverboat moving downstream, lights twinkling from its decks.

Hearing a scream of laughter from the girls at a nearby table, Lizzie glanced towards them and saw that Nancy was one of the party. She waved to her and Nancy waved back enthusiastically, then jumped to her feet and came over, drawing up a spare chair and exchanging greetings and surprise at meeting them here.

'We come here once a week if it's nice. It's good to get some fresh air after being in the factory all day.'

'What is it like there?' Beth asked.

'We ain't supposed to talk about it much, but some bits are all right and some are a bit scary . . .' Nancy lowered her voice. 'Did you hear about the accident last week?'

'No, what happened?' Beth asked.

'One silly cow went and blew herself up,' Nancy said. 'They tried to hush it all up and they closed that department for a few days, but it's open again now, but we ain't supposed to talk about it, so don't say nuthin'.'

'Of course not,' Beth assured her. 'Why don't you come back to us, Nancy?'

'Not on your nelly. I get a pound a week more and they don't nag like Oliver when he's on the

131

warpath.' Nancy laughed coarsely. 'We work hard down the factory but we 'ave a laugh. I'm not in that department anyway, so I'm not worried . . . 'Sides, the silly cow was careless or it wouldn't have 'appened.'

Nancy stopped to have a drink with them and then a girl from the factory crowd beckoned her and she rejoined her friends. Beth and Lizzie finished their drinks and got up to leave. They were walking home through the gathering dusk when the car pulled to a halt just ahead of them. Recognising it, they paused and waited for Sebastian Winters to get out and walk back to them.

'Hello, you two,' he said. 'Been gadding out again?'

'Just for a glass of lemonade in the Willows Pub,' Beth gave him a flirtatious smile. 'You been waitin' for us then?.'

'What makes you think that, Miss Court?' he asked, a mocking smile on his lips as he turned to Lizzie. 'Have you made any new hats recently . . . anything different?'

'You should see the hats she made for my family and herself for the wedding . . . They're wonderful, much better than Oliver's sell . . .' Beth answered before Lizzie had the chance.

'Wedding? Someone I know?'

'My sister Mary – next week,' Beth said, and then, recklessly, 'you can come if you want. It's at St Peter's at two o'clock and we're having a reception at the church hall afterwards. Mum decided on a buffet and there will be plenty of food . . .'

'I might, if I have time,' Sebastian said. 'I should like to see those hats – but I meant is there anything new for me?'

'Nothing new,' Lizzie said, 'but if you like, I'll show you some designs Mr Oliver is considering.'

'Can I see them now?' he asked. 'Shall I walk with you – or may I take you in the car?'

'Tell your driver to follow us and Lizzie can bring the book out to the car. My parents won't want visitors at this hour.'

'Of course not,' he said. 'I was thinking of asking if you'd both like to come to a party next Saturday, but obviously you have the wedding. Perhaps another time?'

'Yes, please, next time,' Beth said. Lizzie walked silently at her side as she chatted away to Sebastian Winters, laughing and giving him flirtatious looks.

Beth stood outside talking to him while Lizzie went in and fetched her sketchbook. She thrust it at him, slightly piqued because he was responding to Beth's flirting. 'This book is full so I shan't need it for a while. Take it away and then bring it back to me at work. If there's anything that appeals, we can cost it up and let you know how much it would be.'

'Goodnight, Mr Winters. It was nice seeing you – don't forget to ask us to your next party, will you?' Beth said.

'You will be the first to hear about it,' he promised and Beth fluttered her eyelids at him, before going into the house.

'Have you thought about me or the offer I made you?' he asked Lizzie as they were briefly alone. 'I meant every word – you're wasted at Oliver's.'

'I wasn't sure you meant it. I think you say a lot of things you don't mean. See if you like anything in my book and let me know.'

'Thank you,' he hesitated again, then took hold of Lizzie's arm and held it, bringing her round so that he gazed into her eyes. For a moment she was close enough to inhale the scent of his body and whatever he used on his hair; it had a pleasant woody smell, not the sickly violets scented oil that a lot of men used. 'I may flirt around, but I really do like you, Lizzie Larch – don't forget that . . .' Lizzie thought that if they'd been somewhere more private he would have kissed her and she wasn't sure whether she wanted it to happen or not. 'You're something special. Remember my offer, Lizzie, please?'

'How could I forget?' Then, giving him a tantalising smile, she went inside while Beth lingered.

'Be careful of him, Beth,' Lizzie said as she joined her in the hall. 'He's a flirt and I wouldn't trust him if I were you.'

Beth laughed softly, her eyes full of mischief. 'It's you Sebastian Winters wants, not me – worse luck . . .'

'He's interested in stylish hats that's all . . .'

Beth's brows went up. 'I think he wants more than that and I'd warn you to be careful, but I know I don't have to.'

'Good.' Lizzie wondered at her own feelings of jealousy because Sebastian had enjoyed Beth's flirting. After all, he meant nothing to her other than as a customer . . . did he?

CHAPTER 15

'I'll call for you at five this evening, and we'll have tea somewhere before we go to the dance,' Harry said that Saturday morning. 'I want to celebrate because I'm off next Tuesday. I've been told to report to somewhere in Norfolk, so this may be our last outing for a while . . .'

'You've actually done it then.' Lizzie's stomach contracted with fear, because once the war started Harry would be in danger. 'Oh, Harry, I'm going to miss you . . .' She didn't want him to go but she knew it was what he'd set his heart on.

'I'll miss you too, but if I wait any longer I'll get called up into the Army and I'd hate that, the RAF is far more civilised, Lizzie.'

'Does your uncle know?'

'He'd expected it before this and he's going to take Brian on as a replacement driver . . .'

'He's picked the driving up all right then?'

'The first time I took him out his plaster cast got stuck on the accelerator and we nearly went through a shop window,' Harry chuckled, 'but after that he was fine. I've told my uncle to give him a chance, because Brian won't be one of the first to be called up – if he ever is with that leg.'

'Don't,' Lizzie begged. 'It's too awful to think about . . .'

'We'll talk tonight,' Harry promised, gave her a quick kiss and sent her on her way.

She was dressed and ready when Harry came to call for her that evening. He looked very smart in his dark grey suit and white shirt with blue spotted tie. His shoes were shining, proper patent dance shoes, and she was glad she'd bought herself a new pair of shoes with her extra wages.

'You look beautiful,' Harry said. 'Come on, I want to make the most of this evening. My uncle told me to take the van, and it's better than queuing for a bus when we come out.' He bowed to her mockingly. 'Your chariot awaits, my lady.'

Glancing at Harry as he drove through streets alive with people, going out for the evening, Lizzie felt a tingle of excitement. The bright lights of the shops and theatres gave the city a special atmosphere at night, because it came alive in a different way. People threw off the cares of everyday life and looked forward to a couple of hours down the pub or the working men's social clubs, unless they could afford the upmarket restaurants and theatres in the West End. Harry was making the most of the time before he joined his unit and taking Lizzie to one of his favourite places. Somehow she knew that the evening would turn out to be special.

Harry had something on his mind and Lizzie was almost certain she knew what it was.

They went to Luigi's, the little Italian café that Harry had taken her to previously

'This is lovely,' she said as they sipped their second cup of cappuccino. 'You spoil me, Harry. I know it's expensive here and then the dance . . .'

'I'd give you the earth if I could.' Harry reached across to take her hand in his. 'I've asked you if you'd marry me before, Lizzie, but this time I'm serious. I want to get engaged now and married next time I have leave.'

'Harry, are you sure?' Lizzie's stomach was tying itself in knots and her heart raced. She'd sensed this was coming and she knew she was going to say yes, but she had to ask. 'You don't know much about me . . .'

'I know all I need to know,' Harry said, his smile caressing her. 'You're lovely inside and out and I adore you – so will you say yes?'

Lizzie drew a deep breath, then formed the word he wanted to hear. She saw his face light up with pleasure and her own doubts faded into insignificance. She couldn't question that he wanted her, loved her, and she responded with all the needy love that had waited for an outlet.

'We'll have to write to my aunt and get her permission,' she said. 'I'm not sure what she'll say, but I hope she just signs and ignores me. I'm twenty-one next January. Surely she can't refuse me now?'

'Why should she?' Harry said. 'If she makes trouble, I'll sort her out.' He reached into his jacket pocket and took out a little black leather box; from that he produced a gold ring with three small garnets and two pearls in a bar and Lizzie held out her left hand, a little gasp of delight on her lips as she saw the expensive ring. 'There, you're mine now,' he smiled triumphantly. 'Ask your aunt to send her permission in writing, Lizzie – and then we can arrange the wedding as soon as I come home on leave.'

'Yes, I will . . .' Lizzie couldn't stop smiling. She was going to marry Harry and continue to work at his uncle's workshop. What more could she ask of the future? If a little voice reminded her of another man who'd had plans for her future, she shut it out. Sebastian Winters was just a flirt and, if she let him, he would break her heart. 'Where shall we live afterwards?'

'Oh, I'll find us a little flat, somewhere in the area so that you can walk to work,' he promised. 'Leave all that to me, Lizzie. I told you I'd look after you when we left your aunt's house that day, and I shall . . .'

The reminder of that day sent a little shiver down Lizzie's spine, making her feel cold, but she shrugged the irrational fear off. Her aunt couldn't hurt her now. She'd made a new life for herself and she was going to marry the man she loved and be happy.

★   ★   ★

Beth was thrilled for her when Lizzie showed her the ring at the dance that evening, but she was a bit quiet after that and Lizzie thought she saw shadows in her eyes. Was she upset because her father wouldn't let her get married for another year?

'Maybe if Tony were to ask your dad at Christmas,' she suggested as the men went off to fetch them some drinks, 'perhaps he'll see the sense of it, especially once the war starts.'

'Dad thinks I might be widowed before I'm hardly a wife and he doesn't care what we think.'

'Would you marry Tony if you could?'

'Yes, I think so, but sometimes . . .' Beth shook her head. 'Take no notice of me, Lizzie. This is your night and we're celebrating your happiness.'

In bed that night Lizzie heard Beth shed a few tears. Harry had brought Lizzie home in the van and they'd sat outside talking until Beth and Tony arrived, taking the chance to kiss and plan their future together. Beth and Tony had taken ages to walk home, and by the look on Beth's face when they arrived, they'd had another row. Lizzie didn't let on that she'd noticed, because she didn't want to make Beth even more upset.

In the morning, Beth looked glum and told Lizzie in confidence that she thought it was over with Tony. 'I've told him that I'm not interested in having sex until we're married and he says he'll find someone who is.'

'No, he couldn't have said that, Beth. He doesn't mean it.'

'He sounded as if he did . . .'

'Surely if he loves you he'll wait?'

'Oh, he'll sulk for a while and then come back with his tail between his legs,' Beth agreed, 'but I'm not sure I want that. I've been thinking about what happens when the war starts, Lizzie. Tony won't go until they make him, but when he does he'll be away for ages – months or years. I'm thinking about joining some sort of military unit . . .'

'You wouldn't leave Oliver's?' Lizzie was shocked.

'I might,' Beth said. 'I'm not going yet and I'll tell you first – but I don't want to sit around doing invoices when there's more important work to do . . .'

'You won't go to the munitions factory? You know how dangerous it can be – and some of the girls go yellow . . .'

'No, I don't fancy that but . . . the Wrens or the nursing aid service . . . they called them VADs in the last war, so my father said . . .'

'It's a worthwhile thing to do,' Lizzie said. 'I couldn't leave Oliver's. I love my work – besides, he's going to need all of us in the workshops . . .'

'What if the supply of materials runs out?'

'I'd better remind him to stock up well just in case things get difficult. I respect you for wanting to do something to help the war, Beth, but I want to stay where I am for now anyway.'

'The nursing detachment might not take you if you're married,' Beth said and smiled. 'Anyway, it hasn't happened yet . . .'

'But it's going to.' Lizzie said. She would miss Beth's company if she joined a military unit, but then, if Lizzie married, she wouldn't be living here either.

'Will you serve Mr Winters this morning?' her employer stopped by Lizzie's bench as she was cutting out some patterns on the Tuesday morning. 'He particularly asked for you. His order is ready, isn't it?'

'Yes, he ordered ten hats, all of them priced from twenty-five to thirty-five shillings.' Lizzie looked at the cheap watch she'd bought for herself. 'What time is he expected?'

'In half an hour,' he said. 'You can take a break, make tea for everyone and then tidy yourself up.'

Lizzie put her scissors down. 'I wanted to get those patterns done this morning . . .'

'Don't worry, Lizzie. I'll do them for you,' Ed said cheerfully. 'You are coming tomorrow evening? Madge missed you on Saturday afternoon. We bought a nice dress though. It will go with the hat I made for her and she's going to wear it to the wedding this week. She's really looking forward to coming with you.'

'You're not coming?'

'No, lass, weddings are not for me. Madge will be all right with you.'

'Yes, of course she will,' Lizzie said and went off to make the tea and tidy herself up. She collected all the hats they'd made for Mr Winters and took them into the showroom, making certain she had an invoice book to write down his order.

She had everything set out as best she could when the doorbell jangled and he entered. He gave her a reassuring look and then turned to a young woman he'd brought with him.

'This is Miss Mabel Hennessy and I've asked her to come in and tell you what she wants herself.'

'Oh . . .' Lizzie was lost for words as she saw the smart young woman, dressed in a navy two-piece suit and a cream silk blouse, with a cream straw hat that Lizzie remembered trimming herself. 'How do you do, Miss Hennessy – what can I do for you?'

'Hello, Lizzie,' the girl said and smiled brilliantly. 'I wondered if you would be an angel and make me some of these wonderful hats. I spotted your drawing book in Sebastian's office and made him tell me all about you – and then I twisted his arm to bring me to meet you.'

'I see . . .' Lizzie hesitated, then, 'Did Mr Winters tell you that these designs are not our regular stock? I would have to clear it with Mr Oliver and cost out the materials and the time . . . because these hats are individual and different . . .'

'Yes, of course, and that is why I want them,' Miss Hennessy told her. 'I'd like to order twelve for my wedding at the end of September – and

I'll show you the three designs. I want them in different colour schemes and I thought we might discuss that . . .'

'Well, I'm not sure . . .' Lizzie began, but then the door from the workshop opened and Mr Oliver entered.

'Ah, Oliver,' Sebastian Winters said. 'We were just discussing the possibility of Miss Larch making some hats for a special customer of mine. Miss Hennessy understands that they will be quite expensive, but she wants Lizzie to make her wedding hats . . . and I was quite unable to dissuade her from coming here.'

'What's this, Lizzie?' Mr Oliver asked and looked at the sketchbook. 'Did you offer to make some hats for this lady?'

'No, sir. Mr Winters asked about some different styles and I gave him the sketchbook. I was going to consult you about any new styles if anything appealed . . .'

'Quite a few appeal actually,' Sebastian said before her employer could answer. 'I should like six of the designs, which I've marked with a tick, and if Lizzie could cost them and then give me an idea of the colours she intends to use I should like to order three dozen – five of each.'

'I see . . .' The size of the order had got Mr Oliver thinking. 'I should have to put Lizzie full-time on an order like that – and these other hats the young lady wants, will they come through you?'

144

'Yes, of course. I've promised Miss Hennessy she can have a discount from me, but they will be retail at my end, as usual.'

Mr Oliver nodded, then looked at Lizzie. 'Can you make these yourself without help from Ed?'

Lizzie had been looking through the book, noting the styles Mr Winters wanted and also the more extreme styles Miss Hennessy had chosen. 'Yes, sir, I believe so. I will consult Ed in our own time over one or two of them, though I think I know what to do, but I'm sure he can put me right . . . and he will help me cost them up for you over the weekend.'

'All right then,' her employer said, surprising her. 'I've been considering putting you on the specials full-time, Lizzie, and it looks like this is the time to do it. We've got to make hay while the sun shines . . . don't know how long I'll be able to get all the materials we need. Local stuffs are OK, but some of our best stock comes in from abroad, a lot of the silk from Italy . . .'

'I was going to suggest we doubled or trebled our next order, just in case,' Lizzie said and he nodded in agreement.

'All right, we'll make them all – but if Miss Hennessy doesn't want the hats when they're ready, you'll buy them, Mr Winters?'

'I assure you I shall want them,' Miss Hennessy said, but Sebastian smiled and nodded.

'These are just what I need for my shop,' he said. 'I shall be able to purchase more from you

145

in future, Oliver, if you're going to let Lizzie loose . . .'

'Not sure about that,' Mr Oliver said. 'We'll see how this works out . . .'

He grunted and went back into the workshop. Lizzie finished writing down the details for Miss Hennessy's hats and then wrote up the invoice for Sebastian Winter's order. He paid for them, asked Miss Hennessy to wait in the car for him and turned to Lizzie with a serious expression.

'Don't forget, if you get bored working for Oliver I can offer you a better job, Lizzie Larch.'

'Oh?' Lizzie's spine tingled. 'I'm not sure what you mean, sir? You've never said exactly what you mean by my working for you . . .'

'I'll give you five pounds a week to come and design and make hats for me. Depending on what happens once the war starts, I'm thinking of opening a small workroom at the back of the shop. You would be the designer and have others working under you – and in time you would receive a share of the profits and a range with your own label . . .'

Lizzie caught her breath because the offer made her head spin. To have her own label and work for a prestigious shop in the West End was beyond her dreams . . . and yet the voice of caution was telling her not to believe in fairy tales.

'I don't think I could do that, Mr Winters. It would be disloyal to Mr Oliver.'

His eyes seemed to snap with annoyance, as if

he'd been sure she would jump at his offer once it was made.

'You won't get a better offer.'

'No, I'm sure I shan't,' Lizzie said and felt regretful. 'At this moment I cannot give you the answer you want, sir.'

'Well, I'm sorry about that,' he hesitated, then, 'I didn't tell you, but there is a small flat that goes with the job. It's part of the deal and you only have to pay for your electricity.'

Lizzie's cheeks burned, because she was now, more than ever, certain that there were strings attached to this offer. All this was too good to be true, which meant there had to be more to it, an ulterior motive.

'And what else would you consider my duties for this favour?'

He stared at her in bewilderment for a long moment and then gave a shout of laughter. Shaking his head, he said, 'Oh no, Lizzie Larch, I'm not after your body, lovely as it is.' As Lizzie remained silent, his smile faded, 'Well, I've given you two chances and that's more than I do most people. Stay where you are in your safe little world, Lizzie. I shan't bother you again, believe me. The one thing I don't do is beg.'

CHAPTER 16

Lizzie forgot about Sebastian Winters and his offer in the excitement of Mary's wedding. It was lovely being part of a family and preparing for the big day. She and Beth had tried clothes on together and Beth helped Lizzie choose a simple white dress with a yellow bolero that complimented the hat she'd made for herself.

On the day of the wedding, Madge came round to Beth's home an hour before they all left for the church. She, Beth, Mary and Lizzie had all made bits and pieces for the big day. Mrs Court had left the sandwiches until the last minute, but everything else had been packed into big tins to be taken round to the hall just before they left for the wedding. One of their neighbours and her daughter was going to set it all out on the tables for them.

It was all a bit of a rush, and Mrs Court was still fussing over her hat and the pretty corsage of roses and fern pinned to her suit when they finally got her out of the house. Lizzie and Madge went with Mrs Court in the car hired for the wedding party, because they'd both been giving her a helping hand; Mary and Beth stayed behind with Mr Court to follow in the second car. Two cars were a luxury, but Mr Court had insisted on paying the extra money so that Mary's pretty white lace dress wasn't squashed by crowding too many into one vehicle.

'You'll only get married once, Mary,' he'd told her. 'We'll splash out a bit and start saving again for Beth's day – but she has a way to go yet, so there's plenty of time.'

Lizzie had seen her friend's face when her father spoke of her wedding as being a long way off and felt sympathy for her, not least because, as yet, Tony hadn't been round after their last quarrel.

After the ceremony, everyone gathered outside the church and threw confetti over the bride and groom; photographs were taken and then the guests trooped into the church hall, which was just round the corner.

The food was good, plain home-prepared fare and seemed popular, judging by the jostling round the long table. Beer, sherry and orangeade had been provided. Beth's mother had made a two-tier cake with frosted white icing and a tiny bride and groom on top. To Lizzie, who had never been invited to a wedding before, it seemed a lavish affair and she thought Mary was lucky. Her parents were far from being comfortably off, but somehow they'd found the money to give Mary a wonderful wedding. Lizzie couldn't imagine her aunt giving her a send-off like this if she married Harry.

She looked lovely in her pretty dress and so happy. Catching a look of envy in Beth's eyes, Lizzie put an arm round her waist.

'It will be your turn next,' she whispered, but Beth shook her head. Tony had been invited but he hadn't turned up and Beth seemed to think that it was over between them.

'I'm not sure I'm bothered,' Beth said but Lizzie knew she loved Tony and was hurting inside.

The bride and groom were going for a short honeymoon at Southend. Mary's husband was working on the railways, which meant he could probably get out of signing-up if there was a war, but Lizzie had heard Mary telling Mrs Court that Andy was going to join up when war came.

After the young couple had left, Lizzie and Beth helped clear up the plates and glasses and cups. Most of it was hired for the day and would be collected by the firm who had rented the crockery out. Hardly any food was left over, and Mrs Court said it wasn't worth taking home, because it would be dry after being on the table for hours, except for the remains of the cake.

'Mary was lucky,' Mrs Court said when they were all home. She'd taken off her wedding finery and was busy making a fresh cup of tea for them all. 'She got a proper fruit cake with white icing, but if there's a war, newly-weds won't be so lucky in future. In the last war we couldn't get dried fruit for love nor money. I'd been buying what I needed for ages . . .'

'I'm going out for a walk, are you coming, Lizzie?' Beth had clearly had enough of hearing about weddings. 'We'll walk home with you, Madge – and leave you and Gran in peace for a while, Mum.'

'Your grandmother is lovely,' Lizzie said as they returned home after leaving Madge to tell Ed all about the lovely reception and give him the piece of cake Mrs Court had sent wrapped in a paper serviette. 'I'd only seen her twice before but I had time to chat to her this afternoon.'

'Mum is going to ask her to move in,' Beth said. 'Mary's room is free now and you'll be leaving to get married . . .'

'If my aunt agrees,' Lizzie said. 'She might make me wait until my birthday just to be awkward . . .'

'Surely not,' Beth said and then looked gloomy. 'I think Tony has started going out with that girl . . .'

'What girl?'

'Sylvia Butcher. I saw her this morning when I took some food round to the hall. She gave me such a look – gloating, like the cat that's got the cream. I know she wants Tony and now I think she's got him – and it's all my father's fault. If he'd let us get married this Christmas, Tony wouldn't have minded waiting . . .'

'Perhaps your father just needs time to save up for another wedding . . .' Lizzie suggested.

'I know it wouldn't have been easy for Dad, but I wouldn't mind having just family and going without all the fuss and bother . . . but that cat's got Tony now . . .'

'Perhaps it's just a fling and Tony will come back,' Lizzie said but Beth shook her head.

'If I know he's been with her I shan't have him.'

The letter from Lizzie's aunt when it came was brief. She did not approve of Lizzie's decision to marry and advised her to think carefully but she'd signed the necessary permission. Lizzie showed the letter to Harry when he came home on leave that weekend and he was thrilled, seizing her about the waist and swinging her round in exuberance.

'I knew when they gave me that thirty-six-hour pass something good would happen,' he told her. 'I'll buy a special licence and as soon as I get another leave, we'll be married, Lizzie.'

'Yes . . .' Harry's excitement was catching and she responded willingly when he grabbed her, holding her close and kissing her with a passion that took her breath and left her trembling. 'I do love you, Harry.'

Harry insisted on taking Lizzie round to his uncle's house. She'd only met his Aunt Miriam a couple of times previously, but now she was welcomed as part of the family and his Uncle Bert insisted on getting out a bottle of sweet sherry.

'Well, that's good news,' he said as Harry told him that they were planning to get married as soon as he got another leave. 'Just let me know and I'll arrange a reception for you – but you'll need somewhere to live . . .'

'Yes, I know. I rang someone last night. A friend of mine told me about a flat coming up for rent. It's not far away from here, so Lizzie will be able to walk to work. She intends to keep working for you until we start a family, but that won't be just yet. It wouldn't be fair on her, with me away all the time . . .'

He didn't need to elaborate. Everyone knew that the future was going to be difficult for young men at the front. Every day the papers carried dire stories, and it was only a matter of time, despite Hitler's denials that he had no intention of going into Poland. All the signs were there and most people expected it daily.

Lizzie made the most of the time she had before Harry went back to start his training. He didn't expect to get home for a few weeks, which would give her time to find a pretty dress of some kind. They would marry in church, but it wouldn't be a white wedding with all the usual trimmings. She couldn't afford a lace dress and a veil, but Harry said it didn't matter. All he wanted was to make Lizzie his wife.

The morning after he'd announced his intentions to his uncle, Harry went out and found them somewhere to live. He paid the rent in advance, before taking Lizzie to see it, because, as he told her, someone else was after it and he'd had to get in quick. It was over a small workshop that made men's shirts and was part of the rag trade area. When he took Lizzie later that evening, she saw that most of the buildings were small manufacturers with offices over the top. Some of them were still open and she saw a rail of ladies' coats being transferred from one side of the road to the other. It was a hot August night, but winter coats were being made now ready for sale in a few weeks when the weather turned colder.

Lizzie thought the rooms were very small, but the rent of fifteen shillings was reasonable, and it actually had electricity, a fireplace in the sitting room and a gas cooker in the kitchen. The landlord had renovated the whole place and it smelled of fresh paint. She'd never lived in anything this modern-looking before and looked in wonder at clean plasterwork on the ceilings and walls, and wooden floors that were painted with clear varnish. All it needed was a few rugs, pretty curtains and furniture, and she would enjoy choosing something modern and bright.

'It's lovely,' she said. 'I never expected anything like this . . .'

'Only the best for my Lizzie,' he said and kissed her. 'We shan't be able to afford all the furniture we want to start with, love, but my aunt says I can have my bedroom furniture and we can have a look in the second-hand shops for the rest.'

Since there was only the kitchen, the sitting room, one decent bedroom and what Lizzie would call a box room, she didn't think it would take much to make the place look nice.

'I haven't spent the money the lawyer got me for the lease of Uncle Jack's shop. I can make some nice curtains and we only need a small table and two chairs in the kitchen, perhaps a cabinet for the bits and pieces . . . I could get a couple of armchairs in here and . . . oh, it will be fun looking . . .' Lizzie felt excited as she planned how to make things nice for them.

'It may be six weeks or more before I get leave,' Harry pulled her into another passionate embrace. 'I love you so much, Lizzie. I want to make love to you . . .'

Lizzie hesitated, on the verge of saying she was ready, because his kisses made her want more, to know what loving a man was all about.

'Don't worry, love, I'm not going to,' Harry said as she was silent. 'Much as I want you, I know it wouldn't be right, just in case something happens to me. Some chaps have been hurt during training and I would hate people to point the finger at you. You're my Lizzie and I'm going to look after you. I don't intend to have an eight-month-old baby or worse . . . I'm proud of you, Lizzie and I won't have anyone whispering behind your back.'

The look he gave her made Lizzie smile and yet she felt coldness at the nape of her neck. Harry was so intense, so sure of himself . . . supposing she let him down in some way . . . would he still love her then?

CHAPTER 17

After Harry had returned to his training camp, Lizzie worked all hours to finish the orders. The hats Sebastian Winters had ordered costed out at between thirty-five shillings and two pounds each to make, which wasn't much more than he'd paid before, but Miss Hennessy's order was more expensive to make. She'd mainly chosen hats with large brims and lots of veiling, although apart from one of them they were easy enough to shape.

The hat that caused Lizzie the most trouble was a beautiful creation of silk velvet and tulle. It was a soft design with a V-shape at the front that looked rather like opened birds' wings and was sewn with feathers and a jewelled motif.

'It looked lovely on paper,' Lizzie said, after unpicking her first attempt and remodelling it so that it was slightly more shaped and stiffened. 'I never thought Oliver would accept it and I hadn't given a thought to how I would make it.'

'Just as well, we worked it out together,' Ed told her. 'Soft hats are fine, but not if you're going to have that fancy structure at the front . . . that needs support.'

'I've learned my lesson now,' Lizzie said humbly. 'I don't know what I would have done if you hadn't sorted me out, Ed.'

He chuckled softly. 'You've still got a way to go, Lizzie love,' he told her. 'Oliver threw you in at the deep end, didn't he?'

'I told him I could do it,' Lizzie said, because she wanted to be fair. 'I hadn't worked that one out properly though.'

'Next time do several drawings so that you can see how you're going to make it up, Lizzie. I know you like drawing these fanciful things, but most women want a practical hat.'

'Yes, I know,' Lizzie agreed. 'I have to make them in a certain time and that means they need to be simple in structure.'

Ed inclined his head. 'Save your flights of fancy until you're a famous designer.'

Lizzie shook her head, because that wasn't going to happen. She'd turned down Sebastian Winters' offer and remembered it wistfully – but it wouldn't have worked. She would soon be married to Harry, and he wouldn't have wanted her to work for anyone but his uncle.

The declaration of war took no one by surprise, but it was awful just the same. Lizzie heard it on the radio with Beth and her family. Outside the sun was shining but Lizzie felt cold all over as she heard the Prime Minister tell the British people that they were now at war. Germany had broken all her promises and invaded Poland, wreaking havoc on a people too weak to stand up to the might of the German machine.

'God help us,' Mr Court said. 'I'd hoped my son and my daughters' husbands would never have to go through what we did, but it looks as if we're in for it now.'

'It will be worse than last time,' Mrs Court said, close to tears. 'The papers say it will be war in the air . . . we'll be bombed, much worse than what happened in the first war. Things have moved on . . .'

'Yes, I'm afraid you're right,' her husband said. 'I feel sorry for the poor buggers that have to fight. I had enough of it last time. I shall offer my services of course, but I doubt they will take me.'

'Don't be a fool, Derek,' Mrs Court cried. 'Let the young men go. You've done your bit . . .'

'Even if they won't take me in the forces, I'll be useful somehow . . .'

Over the next few days the recruiting offices were choked with men wanting to sign up. It seemed that people had forgotten the pain and horror of the war that was supposed to end all wars and were now carried high on a wave of national pride and ready to fight for king and country.

Beth was very quiet for a couple of days and then she told Lizzie that she'd made enquiries about training to be a nurse.

'Oh, Beth, what does your mum say?'

'I'll tell her once I've been accepted,' Beth

shrugged. 'I'm not going to stay home and do nothing now our men are going to be fighting'

Lizzie nodded, feeling a little guilty because the idea didn't appeal to her. For the moment she wanted to stay where she was – and once she was married the women's services probably wouldn't want her anyway, because although it wasn't absolutely forbidden as it had been once, those in charge often thought married women were too much of a liability to take on important jobs. Married women had children and they took time off if their children were ill, and in times of war, people had to keep their mind on the job . . . at least that was the way some officials saw it. They thought the WVS was fine, but when it came to the dangerous and vital work it should be reserved for men, but women were capable of a lot more than some men gave them credit for and by the time this war was over they were going to need them.

Harry's letter came through five weeks after Mary's wedding. He was coming home on leave the following week for eight days. Time for them to marry and go on a short honeymoon.

Lizzie's spine tingled as she read the letter. It was going to happen at last and she could hardly wait. She told her friends and wrote a card out for all of them, including Aunt Jane. Lizzie didn't particularly want her aunt at the wedding, but she thought she ought to invite her.

'Are you sure it's what you want to do?' Mrs Court asked her twice. 'You know we are happy to have you here for as long as you wish?'

'Yes, I do know and I've been happy with you, but Harry wants us to be married and settled . . .'

'You're so young,' Mrs Court said.

'I'll be twenty-one, next year, and I feel older,' Lizzie replied. 'Harry's done everything, sorted it all out. We're just having a civil ceremony and a little reception at a small hotel – and you will all be invited. We'd thought of a church, but it's easier to arrange at the Registrar's Office when you don't know the exact date beforehand.'

'Beth is going to say she wants to be married too,' Mrs Court said, looking anxiously at her daughter's back. 'I know it isn't up to me, Lizzie – but I do wonder if you're rushing things.'

'No, I don't think so,' Lizzie assured her. 'Harry loves me and I love him . . .' as she said it, Lizzie felt sure it was true. 'I know we've only known each other a few months, but Harry said he loved me from the first minute he saw me and . . .'

'Well, if you're sure, love,' Mrs Court gave her a hug. 'I'm always here if you ever need me.'

'Thank you, I'll remember that . . .'

Harry met her from work the evening before their wedding, which was the 19th September and a Tuesday. Lizzie hadn't been sure when he would get home and flung herself into his arms, kissing him until she was breathless. He leaned forward, opening the door of the van for her to get in.

'We'll go to the flat, Lizzie,' he said. 'The bedroom stuff is being delivered in the morning, first thing. Have you done anything about the other furniture?'

'The rooms aren't big, so I've bought small neat things – a nice oak table that folds back against the wall when you don't need it, and two chairs in the kitchen and a chintz-covered suite in the sitting room I think you'll love it; it's quite modern.'

'The bedroom stuff is Edwardian, but really pretty, Lizzie. I thought we could have a new modern mattress . . . if that's all right?'

'It sounds good to me. We don't need too much for a start, because we can buy things as we go along, when we find out what we like – choose it together.'

'You will be doing most of the choosing,' Harry said. 'I've got a week after the wedding and then I'm off to finish my training. After that I could be sent anywhere . . .'

'Oh, Harry . . .' Lizzie felt a sinking sensation inside. 'I wish you didn't have to go back . . .'

'We all have to now, love. I'm not going too far for a start,' Harry told her. 'I'll be based just outside London this time and I shall be able to come home on regular two-day passes until I've finished my training . . .'

Lizzie nodded and kissed him, but she had a

strange feeling of foreboding hanging over her. However, she told herself she was being a fool. Harry was doing what he'd wanted to do and it was surely better than his being called up to the Army. Every woman in the country would be feeling as she was, worried about husbands, brothers, sons and even fathers. Beth's father had found himself an evening job fire-watching, and checking that no one was showing a light from their blackout curtains. It seemed that the whole country had war fever and were all bent on doing their bit.

CHAPTER 18

Lizzie stretched and yawned, wondering why she felt so good and then her eye fell on the simple white dress she'd bought for her wedding. It was the first time she'd ever purchased a dress from a good shop, and she'd wanted it to be special.

'I'll bring you a cup of tea up and some toast.' Beth smiled at her. 'We've got to make a fuss of you today, Lizzie.'

'Thanks.' Lizzie touched her hand. 'It was my lucky day when I met you, Beth.'

Beth went off and Lizzie lay back against the pillows. It was nice not to have to get up and rush off to work. For a whole week she would be with Harry and they could do whatever they wanted. Lizzie had never been away to the seaside for a whole week before and she could hardly control her excitement.

Beth brought a tray of tea and toast up and the two girls sat together on the bed and ate their breakfast. It was a lovely way to spend the hours before her wedding and Lizzie could not remember feeling this happy in her life.

After breakfast, Lizzie had a bath and washed her hair. Beth pinned it up for her with Kirby grips and Lizzie sat on the bed waiting for it to dry. Mrs Court came upstairs when Beth took the tray down and brought her some cards that had come through the door, mostly by hand, and the posy of flowers that Harry had sent.

'I thought you would want to see them,' she said smiling and then pulled a face as she heard the front doorbell ring. She went to the head of the stairs and called down, 'Beth answer the door please.'

'All right, Mum.'

'So, are you excited?' Mrs Court said and bent to kiss Lizzie's cheek. 'Derek was really pleased you asked him to be one of the witnesses . . .' They heard footsteps coming up the stairs and then Beth entered, looking uncertain. 'Who was it, love?'

'It's your aunt, Lizzie. She says she has to see you – that it's important . . .'

'Of all the days to come,' Mrs Court said, looking cross. 'Do you want to see her, Lizzie?'

'I suppose I shall have to. Where is she?'

'I asked her to wait in the front room,' Beth said. 'If I were you I'd send her away. I'm sure she's here to make trouble . . .'

'She always said I should never marry. I have no idea why and I don't care what she says. She can't hurt me now . . .' Lizzie shrugged on her bathrobe over her petticoat and went down to Mrs Court's parlour. Her aunt was wearing a grey coat and black hat; it was obvious that she hadn't come dressed for a wedding. 'You wanted to see me, Aunt Jane?'

'I've been ill or I would have come sooner,' her aunt said. 'I want you to reconsider this foolish idea of yours, Lizzie. It will end in tears for you . . .'

'Why should marriage to Harry make me unhappy? We love each other – besides, we're getting married today . . .'

'I know. It was a shock when your letter came. I wasn't well and signed the papers but I should've told you years ago, but Jack forbade it . . .'

'Told me what?' Lizzie asked and felt chilled at the look in her aunt's eyes. She had a tingling sensation at her nape and was suddenly nervous. 'What should I know, Aunt Jane?'

'You've never remembered what happened to you?' Aunt Jane shook her head. 'Of course not or you would realise how foolish it is to think of marriage.'

'Why? Is it impossible for me to have children or something?'

'I've no idea about that, though it may be . . .' Aunt Jane took a deep breath. 'I never agreed with that doctor. I thought you should face up to what happened . . . to the shame of it . . .'

'Shame?' Lizzie's stomach was tying itself in knots now and she felt shivery. 'What shame, aunt? What did I do?'

'It wasn't what you did . . . at least, as far as I know. It was what someone did to you, Lizzie.' Her eyes were cold, unforgiving. 'You went running out of the house that night. I called you back but you wouldn't listen. You brought it on yourself.'

'Please tell me what happened.' Lizzie had to know the truth now.

'You were viciously attacked and abused physically,' her aunt said, the words so harsh that Lizzie felt as if she'd struck her. 'In the struggle you were knocked unconscious.' Her aunt went on relentlessly, 'You were ill for a long time afterwards and when you lost the child, you developed a fever and you never recovered your senses properly, though you drifted in and out for months and then you went into . . . a state of shock the doctors called it.'

Lizzie was stunned, unable to credit what she was hearing. 'I was raped . . . I had a child . . .'

'An unpleasant word, but I suppose that is the truth of it, though we can never know what happened that night . . . but you were left unconscious and bleeding. If you hadn't been found by a nurse coming off a late night shift, I dare say you would have been dead by morning. Perhaps that would have been for the best . . .'

Lizzie recoiled from the shock, unable to take in what her aunt was saying. 'You would rather I had died . . .'

'I did not want your shame to rebound on us, but of course your uncle moved Heaven and Earth to get the right treatment for you, especially after the child miscarried and they told us you would die. It cost him a fortune to send you to a private sanatorium . . .'

'My God, you are a cruel witch,' Lizzie said, staring at her with new-born hatred. 'All these years you let me believe it was an accident . . . you never told me a word and now on my wedding day . . .'

'Well, you had to know, because there's still time to stop it . . .'

Bile rose in Lizzie's throat. 'Get out, I never want to see you again,' she said and then rushed from the room and out to the toilet in the backyard.

As she vomited into the toilet pan, Lizzie was struggling to come to terms with what her aunt had told her. How could all those things have happened to her and she couldn't remember any of it? Raped, battered and left to die . . . she couldn't take it in, couldn't accept it was true.

She'd been carrying a child but it had been lost. Had her body rejected it and how long had she carried it . . .? So many questions unanswered. Her mind whirled with them, reeling from the shock, still unable to take any of it in.

As the first shock started to recede, Lizzie began to think for herself. She couldn't remember any of it, and because of that she began to reject what she'd been told. Surely if she'd been beaten and raped, carried and lost a child, she would remember something. No! It was a lie, a cruel lie to prevent her marriage. Aunt Jane had simply wanted to hurt her, so she'd invented this story. It couldn't be the truth . . . surely she would remember something. She must know if she'd carried a child and given birth to it! So it had to be a lie – it had to be, because if it was true . . .

'Lizzie, are you all right?' Beth's anxious voice was outside the door. 'Did that old witch upset you?'

'Yes,' Lizzie said, making up her mind in that moment to ignore her aunt's wicked lies. 'She hates me and always has . . .'

'I wish I'd slammed the door in her face,' Beth said. 'I can't understand anyone who would come all this way just to be nasty on your wedding day . . .'

Lizzie went out to her friend. 'It was her revenge because my uncle left everything to me. I think she's always hated me.'

'Come on back upstairs and I'll brush your hair,' Beth said. 'She's a vicious old witch and if I were you I should never speak to her again.'

'I don't intend to.' Lizzie felt numb as she followed Beth back upstairs, the shadows her aunt's bitter words had left behind flooding into her mind once more.

Supposing it was all true? Harry loved her because he thought her perfect, untouched . . . if he thought she'd been tarnished . . .

Sitting down on the edge of the bed as her legs suddenly felt weak, Lizzie was frightened. 'I'm not

168

sure I can go through with it . . . if she was telling the truth . . .'

'What are you talking about' Beth asked but Lizzie just shook her head.

'I can't talk about it . . . it was lies, it had to be . . .'

'Lizzie love, look at me,' Beth took her by the shoulders. 'Harry adores you and you love him, don't you?' Lizzie nodded, her throat so tight with tears that she couldn't speak. 'Well, then, don't let her win, Lizzie. You've found a new life for yourself. You can't throw it away because of her nasty tongue.'

'No . . .' Lizzie raised her head, pride asserting itself. Harry loved her. She would tell him what her aunt said and they would laugh over it, because it was the most ridiculous tale. 'No, it's just nerves, Beth. All brides have them, don't they?'

Beth looked at the simple white dress Lizzie had chosen for her wedding and felt a little envious. It fitted her as if it had been made for her, even though she'd bought it off the peg at a shop in the West End. She had made herself a hat of fine straw with tulle and veiling that had the sparkle of silver in it, and her shoes were white satin, her gloves lace and around her throat she wore a silver locket on a chain, which had belonged to Harry's mother.

'You look gorgeous,' she said. 'I do envy you, Lizzie, but it's too late for me now. I've finished with Tony.'

'I'm sorry, Beth. It's unfair that I should meet Harry and marry him within a few months and you have to wait ages.'

'Not your fault,' Beth hugged her. 'Are you all right now, love? She hasn't ruined your big day?'

'No, I'm over it now,' Lizzie replied, though Beth wasn't sure she was telling the truth. 'Is my dress all right?'

'That dress is lovely, but I wish you'd had your wedding in church.'

'It was easier and quicker this way. Besides, the church wanted three weeks' notice and Harry couldn't give it,' Lizzie replied, though Beth thought she looked a little disappointed. 'Harry wanted us to be settled in before he goes off for his final months of training – and we're having a few days at Torquay, in a posh hotel on the front.'

'Yes, you are very lucky. I'm going to miss you, though. I was just getting used to having you with us and it was nice.'

'You will have your bedroom back and you must admit it is better with all my stuff gone.'

'I shall still miss you.'

'I shall visit often and you must visit me when you can.'

'I shall,' Beth promised, but felt a bit miserable. 'As long as you're happy, Lizzie. That's all I care about – besides, I shall have to go away if they take me on as a trainee nurse.'

'I know I shall be happy with Harry. I hope you'll be happy too. I know you'll find someone you like soon . . .'

Beth nodded, but Lizzie didn't really know how it felt to be let down by a man she loved. Despite knowing that he wasn't worth her tears if he would throw her over for a peroxide blonde who was anyone's after she'd had a few drinks, she'd wept night after night, but now she'd made up her mind to put him out of her life and forget him.

Beth watched Lizzie take her marriage vows. It wasn't anywhere near as nice as a church service in her opinion, yet if Tony hadn't walked out on her the way he had, she would have taken it.

Beth made herself forget her own troubles as she saw that the wedding ceremony was over. It had taken no more than a few minutes before they were back out into the sunshine and piling into the cars Harry had hired to take them to the hotel for the reception. He looked so handsome and the way he touched Lizzie's hand, the expression in his eyes was so tender and caring that Beth felt her heart tighten with pain. It was a long time – if ever – since Tony had looked at Beth that way.

Beth wanted to be truly loved, the way her father loved her mother – and the way Harry obviously adored Lizzie. If Tony truly cared for her he would have waited until she was ready, and if he couldn't . . . then perhaps he wasn't the one for her.

'Oh, Beth,' Lizzie said, her eyes shining as they kissed at the reception. 'I'm so happy. Look at that lovely buffet Harry arranged for us – and that cake: three tiers. I'm sure we'll be eating it for months. I shall bring some round for your mum when . . .' the happiness died from her eyes. 'I mustn't think about Harry going off so soon. He'll be back for short breaks and I'll soon get used to it . . .'

'You'll be too busy to feel lonely,' Beth said. 'Can I visit on Saturday afternoons and evenings – until I leave for my training anyway?'

'I should love that,' Lizzie kissed her cheek. 'I'm so excited. I've never been further than Southend for a day trip. We've got five whole days to spend in Torquay.'

'You're so lucky. I wish I was in your shoes. Oh, I don't mean married to Harry . . . but you know.'

'Yes,' Lizzie smiled softly. 'I know I'm lucky, but I'm nervous too. It's all so new and strange – it feels as if I've leapt off the edge of a cliff and I'm not sure where I'll land.'

'You've no need to worry,' Beth told her, sensing that she was anxious about what her aunt had said to her. 'Forget that old witch, love. Harry worships you. It's in his eyes every time he looks at you, Lizzie. You'll be looked after and loved all your life.'

'Yes, I think I shall,' Lizzie said. 'I'd better talk to Harry's uncle and cousins. I've got a big family all of a sudden . . .'

Beth watched as she moved off to welcome a rather odd-looking man, his wife, her tall plain sister and her two daughters, and some other people Harry had vaguely said were cousins on his mother's side. His own parents were dead, but he still had quite a large family and they all made a fuss of Lizzie and gave her exciting-looking parcels for their wedding gifts.

She kissed Lizzie on the cheek when the time came for Harry to take her away on their honeymoon. Lizzie had made her choice, and Beth had made hers. As soon as she could, she would leave Oliver's to become a nurse, because they were going to be needed. She would forget Tony and find happiness with her work and her friends . . .

CHAPTER 19

Lizzie looked round the comfortable hotel room. It wasn't the biggest or the poshest hotel in Torquay but it was clean and smelled of fresh lavender and, set up on the cliffs, it had a lovely view out over the sea. She knew it must have cost Harry quite a bit to pay for this as well as the flowers, cars, and her lovely 22ct gold wedding ring, of course.

She'd paid for her clothes herself out of the money that had come to her from her uncle, and most of her small legacy had gone now on things for the flat and presents, for Harry and her friends. Harry had spent most of his savings on getting things nice for them and he wouldn't be earning much while he was training in the RAF. His wages would depend on how well he qualified at the end of his trial period – just as the success of her job at Oliver's depended on Lizzie's talent.

Lizzie was deliberately dwelling on thoughts of the wedding and the good wishes of her friends, because at the back of her mind a tiny dark cloud was hovering. She'd had a moment of doubt when she'd thought she couldn't go through with the wedding, but Beth had told her to stand firm and forget her aunt's cruel words. Lizzie had managed to do that for large chunks of the time because the wedding was so lovely and everyone was kind . . . but always the thought that perhaps she didn't deserve all this was there at the back of her mind. Her aunt had spoken of shame and Lizzie suspected that if those same people who kissed her and wished her happiness knew of her shame they would turn their noses up at her . . . but it wasn't true. It couldn't be true! Her aunt had been lying, with the purpose of making her call off the wedding, to punish her . . .

Harry came to put his arms about her as she stood looking out of the window at the sea. It was dark now because the hour was late, but the moon was bright and the waves moved restlessly, dashing themselves against a rocky outcrop that looked shiny black in the silvery light.

'Are you happy, Mrs Oliver?' he whispered against her ear. 'How does it feel to be an old married lady?'

'I don't know.' She turned in his arms, looking up at him with love. 'I'm a very new married lady and I feel nervous. I don't know anything about being a wife, Harry.'

He would be so disappointed if he wasn't the first . . . the thought popped into her mind and her throat went tight with emotion. Tears stung her eyes but she banished them.

It was lies, just lies. There was nothing to worry

about. Her body was responding to Harry's, to the touch of his mouth on her neck, and his hand moving over her bottom and pushing her against him. She gasped as a wave of sensual pleasure went through her and dismissed her fears. She couldn't feel like this if her aunt's story was true . . .

'I do love you, Harry. Please don't stop loving me, will you? Don't be disappointed in me . . .'

Harry burst out laughing and bent his head to kiss her softly on the lips. 'You could never let me down,' he said and gathered her into his arms, carrying her to the bed and kissing her again before he dropped her unceremoniously on the turned-back sheets. 'You are the most beautiful thing in my life, Lizzie. I'm the one who is afraid of letting you down.'

'Oh, Harry, you daft thing,' she said and giggled. 'Are you about to have your wicked way with me?'

'Silence, wench,' Harry teased. 'I am your lord and master now and you will obey me.'

Lizzie smiled, looking up at him confidently, because something inside her told her that Harry's unceremonious dumping of her and his teasing covered the fact that he too was nervous. She believed, without being told, that he would never hurt her and she opened her arms to him as he lay down beside her and pressed his lips to hers in a passionate kiss that spoke of how much he loved and wanted her. She loved him and she could trust him, nothing else mattered. She would forget all those wicked lies and give herself to her husband with all the love that she felt for him.

It was some time later that they lay together, all clothes abandoned in a heap, bodies slick with sweat and satiated with the sweetest loving that ever a bride had – at least that was the way Lizzie would always remember it. Harry's touch thrilled her; his kisses were light and lingering, drawing a response from her that she might have compared to a master musician coaxing music from violin strings if she'd thought about it, but of course it never occurred to her. All she knew was that something inside her sang with joy as she gave herself to him with wondrous abandon. She wanted this night to go on forever, wished that it might never end and finished by weeping softly in his arms.

Harry lay beside her for some minutes afterwards, and then he sat up, and got out of bed, pulling on a striped silk dressing robe. He stood looking at her for several minutes and Lizzie's glow of pleasure left her, because the look in his eyes was so cold that she was frightened.

'What's wrong?' she asked. 'Was it something I did?'

'Who was he?' Harry asked and ice shot down her spine. 'Who was the filthy rotten bastard who had you first?'

'What do you mean? Harry, no . . .' Lizzie shuddered as she saw the anger and bitterness in his face and it suddenly struck home. Harry was asking her who had been her first lover, but it hadn't been that way at all. She'd been raped and beaten and the horror of knowing the truth at last left her shaken and humiliated. It was all true. Everything her aunt had told her was true, and Harry knew – and he was disappointed and angry. 'It wasn't like that, believe me . . . I didn't know . . .'

A harsh disbelieving laugh burst from him. 'What the hell are you talking about? Even the most innocent girl knows she's been making love with a chap . . . whether she's willing or not.'

'I didn't,' Lizzie said in a voice that hardly resembled hers. 'It was a part of my illness . . . you remember I told you that I had lost a chunk of time?'

Harry's eyes narrowed. She could see by his expression that he was too hurt, too shocked and disappointed to believe her. She swallowed hard as she tried to find the words to explain, knowing that whatever she said he was going to think she was lying . . . and in that moment she understood what her aunt had been telling her. This could ruin her marriage before it had truly begun.

'Yes, I remember that but you never said anything . . .' An odd look entered his eyes. 'Are you saying you were raped?'

'Yes, I was – attacked, battered, raped and left for dead,' she said in a whisper. 'I was ill for months, and then, when I started to get better, I had lost months of time. I never knew what happened until this morning . . .'

'Why this morning?' Harry asked and something had softened slightly in his tone. 'Tell me the truth, Lizzie.'

'Aunt Jane came and told me, brutally, coldly – she said I shouldn't marry you because it would make my life miserable, and she said I had no right to be your wife, because of my shame . . . but I didn't know. I thought she was lying. Even after she told me, I thought she was lying. She hates me, Harry. I didn't think it could be true . . . how could I be hurt like that and miscarry a child . . . and not know?'

Harry's face had gone cold again. 'There was a child . . . did you carry it to full term?'

'She said I miscarried in hospital and it led to my long illness. I didn't ask any questions, because I didn't want to know, because if it was true I knew it would spoil everything . . .' His eyes were like black ice. 'It has, hasn't it? You hate me now don't you, Harry?'

'Hate? I'm not sure what I feel about you – but you've destroyed me . . .' He swung away from her and picked up a packet of cigarettes, lighting one and drawing on it deeply. 'I thought you were so lovely, so sweet and innocent – my little Lizzie.' His back towards her, she saw the tension in him as he drew on the cigarette again, and then he turned to face her. 'I'm not sure how I feel, Lizzie. You're not who I thought you were. I feel cheated, tricked . . .'

The love and adoration had all gone and he was

like a stranger. 'I'm still me, Harry. I don't even remember what happened – please don't punish me. I'm not a wanton. I didn't have a lover . . . I was raped, beaten and left to die in a deserted alley . . .'

'I'm not punishing you, of course I'm not. I'm just not sure how I feel yet, Lizzie. I'm sorry. I'm sorry for what happened to you . . . your aunt and uncle should've told you the truth. If I'd known before, perhaps I could have accepted it – but it feels as if I've been deceived, as if I've been trapped . . .'

'No, please, don't think that of me. I'm sorry I didn't tell you, but I couldn't accept it – and there wasn't time to think. I couldn't just walk away from everything we'd planned.'

'Didn't you think I would know?'

'I had no idea about any of it. Harry, please believe me, I'm just the same . . . I don't remember anything . . .'

'That sounds incredible,' he said, but she could see he was puzzled, hurt and angry. 'If I thought you were lying – that you'd had a lover . . .'

Lizzie's distress and shock was turning to anger now. 'If you don't believe me, we shall have to part,' she said in a troubled voice. 'I'm sorry, Harry, but I don't think I deserve this – and I don't see why you should accuse me of lying. I've never lied to you. I'm the one that was lied to all those years. If I'd known, I wouldn't have married you . . .'

'What do you mean?' he asked defensively.

'I'm not decent. It's what my aunt said; she told me that no decent man would want me if he knew the truth, and now I know she was right. The way you look at me – as if I were something the cat brought in . . .'

Lizzie got out of bed and dressed, then she took her case from the rack the hotel provided and began to take her clothes from the wardrobe and throw them into the case.

Harry moved swiftly to stop her. 'What the hell do you think you're doing?'

'I'm going home, back to London – to Beth's house, if they'll have me, and if not . . .' She stopped as he grabbed her arm, pulling her away from the wardrobe.

'You're not leaving me,' he said furiously. 'What do you think people would think?'

'I don't care what anyone says or thinks,' Lizzie's voice rose sharply. 'I can't stay here and have you look at me like that, Harry. I'd rather be dead . . .' Lizzie hit at his chest with bunched fists, tears streaming down her face, angry and miserable at the same time. 'I hate you for thinking I'd do something like that . . . I wouldn't cheat you, but you hate me now and you won't believe me. She was right, I shouldn't have married . . .'

She threw herself back on the bed and curled into a ball of wretched misery. Harry touched her shoulder. 'Please, Lizzie, don't cry. I can't bear to see you like this – and I don't hate you. I just feel so disappointed . . .'

Lizzie shrugged his hand off. 'How do you think I feel? To know that I've been violated by someone I don't know – abused and beaten – and no one ever told me . . . I had a right to know.' She sat up suddenly, anger blazing out of her. 'I had a right to know years ago.'

'I'm so sorry for what happened to you . . .' Harry looked at her and then sat on the bed beside her. She saw that he was crying too. 'I'm sorry for what you suffered and for the way you've been treated – and I'm sorry that I feel this way, but . . . I can't help it.'

He was hurt and bewildered. He didn't know what to do or say to her. She wished that she'd stopped the wedding and explained to him, but she'd been so mixed up, so hurt and distressed, refusing to believe that her aunt's words could be true.

She touched his hand, sadness replacing the anger which had died with his tears. Harry moved his hand away, as if he didn't want to be touched by her, and she drew back, hunching her knees to her chest.

'What are we going to do?' she asked after a few moments of silence. 'You don't want me now. I know you feel cheated because I'm not what you thought me . . .'

'We can't split up just like that. No one would understand. My uncle would think I was a feckless idiot unless I told him the reason, and I couldn't do that – it wouldn't be fair to you, Lizzie.'

'Thank you,' she said in a small voice. 'I would rather people didn't know – I feel dirty, ashamed . . .'

'No!' Harry's head came up at that and he took her hand in his, holding it. 'You mustn't feel that way, Lizzie. You were not to blame. I don't blame you for what happened – but I worshipped my innocent lovely girl and now . . . I don't know how I feel.'

Lizzie still couldn't remember what had happened to her . . . why did it matter so much to him? Yet she could see that it did and her heart wept for his disappointment. Harry had thought her perfect and put her on a pedestal in his mind, and now she'd tumbled off.

'I'll do what you want,' she said, humble now. 'I wouldn't have hurt you for the world, but I don't think I can live with you if you look at me as if I were dirty.'

'I'm sorry. It was just the shock. I think we have to see this week out and then I'll be back at my training and – we'll talk about the future next time I come home on leave. When I've had time to think.'

'If that's what you want.' she said dully.

'It will be all right. We're still friends, Lizzie. I know you didn't mean to cheat me. I could kill that witch for not telling you the truth long ago. What she did to you was unspeakable.'

'I think it was the doctor's idea that I shouldn't be told until I remembered of my own accord and

I never have. I see now that my aunt wanted to tell me long ago – she sometimes hinted things, but Uncle Jack always stopped her.'

'Then he was as bad. Couldn't they see what might happen one day?'

'Aunt Jane always said I shouldn't marry. I suppose she knew that no decent man would want me if he knew . . .'

'Oh Lizzie,' Harry said and his hand crushed hers. 'Please don't – that isn't true.'

'Isn't it?' she asked, looking at him as the pain of the betrayal swept through him. 'I thought you loved me, Harry – not some picture in your head. I didn't know that I'd been ruined, but surely if . . .' She shook her head. 'I'll try to do what you want but it's impossible . . .'

He reached for his clothes and began to dress.

'Where are you going?'

'Out for a walk. I'm not sure what to do, Lizzie. I have to think about this carefully . . .' He hesitated, then, 'You stay here until I get back and then we'll think of something.'

Lizzie sat staring at the door for hours, wondering where Harry was and whether he would return. She thought about packing her clothes and leaving, but there wasn't a train until the morning and she didn't feel like sitting on the station all night. Besides, what would Beth and her family think if Lizzie walked in when she was supposed to be on honeymoon?

It was about three in the morning when Harry came back. She could see by his face that he was tired and strained, and her heart felt as if it were breaking. Lizzie hated herself for causing him this pain.

'I've been thinking,' Harry said. 'You were right when you said it would be impossible to carry on here as if nothing had happened. Perhaps one day I'll be able to accept it – but not yet. I'm going back to base, Lizzie. I suggest you stay here and go home at the end of the week as planned . . .'

'Stay here alone?' Lizzie stared at him in shock. How could he think she'd want to stay here now?

'The room is paid for and I'll give you some money. You can enjoy the walks and the views. I know it's not great, but it's better than trying to go on with our honeymoon . . . isn't it?'

'Yes, I suppose so,' Lizzie agreed, feeling torn apart by his manner. He was just throwing away all they had, as if it didn't matter. 'What do I do then? Just go home as if we had a wonderful time?'

'Yes. You can tell everyone I had to go straight off and return to work. No one has to know anything . . .'

'And we just go on like that forever?'

'Not forever,' Harry said. 'Just until I've had time to come to terms with this – it will be all right in time, Lizzie. I'll get over it . . . enough to be friends anyway.'

'You want to just be friends?' Lizzie felt as if

she'd been run over by a steam roller. Nothing made sense to her anymore.

'Surely you can manage that?' he said. 'Perhaps one day I'll feel differently.'

'You expect me to just sit at home and wait to be forgiven – as if I'd committed a crime?' Lizzie didn't know whether to weep for the pity of it or throw something at him and tell him to get out of her sight.

'No, you haven't done anything wrong. I'm at fault. I should be able to forgive – but for the moment I can't . . .'

Lizzie watched as he collected his things from the wardrobe and drawers. She felt sick and empty and couldn't think of anything to say to stop him leaving her here in this place. The last thing she wanted to do was stay here alone.

Harry paused at the door with his suitcase in his hand and looked back.

'I'm sorry, Lizzie,' he said. She didn't answer because there was nothing she could say.

After Harry had gone, Lizzie felt the coldness enter her heart. She was hurt and angry, her heart damaged by his behaviour. Yet she knew they could never have gone through a charade of a honeymoon. It was all so miserable – just as her aunt had said, but it needn't have been this way. If Lizzie had been told the truth sooner, she could have made her choice – either to stay single or to tell Harry her story.

Crying wasn't going to help her, but she'd made

up her mind about one thing. She wasn't going for long walks on the cliffs alone. She was going back to London and the flat. She wouldn't go into work, but if anyone saw her she'd tell them Harry had been called back to his base . . .

In the end Lizzie spent two days at the hotel because, when she enquired at the station, there wasn't a train she could use her ticket for until the Thursday morning. It would be too expensive to buy another, so she stayed on until she could use her regular return ticket.

In London once more, she let herself into the flat and looked round, the pleasure she'd felt in making this into a home gone. Lizzie felt empty of any emotion. What had it all been about? Harry had been so sure that he loved her and then . . . But perhaps what she'd done was unforgivable?

She ought to have called off the wedding and told him what her aunt had blurted out that day – but it would've caused so much upset and she'd been so sure it was lies. Now her marriage was in ruins and Harry no longer loved her . . .

What was she going to do for the next few days? Lizzie didn't want to go straight back to work, because she knew everyone would look at her, and the more discerning would know she was lying. Ed would be certain to ask what was wrong and she didn't want to lie – and yet to tell the truth would shock him and shame her.

Lizzie picked up her sketchbook and looked at

some of the more original hats she'd drawn. Perhaps now was the time to have a go at a few of them. She could pay a visit to a wholesaler and buy some materials and then amuse herself with her flights of fancy, as Ed called them.

She would visit the wholesaler and buy the materials she wanted, and she would get enough food to last her for another few days. The last thing she wanted was to bump into one of her friends in the market before she felt calm enough to go back to work – and she did want to work on some ideas of her own.

There was one in particular, a little hat made of fine straw, silk and lace that looked a bit like a witch's hat. She knew Bert Oliver would never let her make it on his time, but now she had time to spare she could experiment – at least it would fill a few empty hours . . . and she had to do something or she would go mad, because she couldn't forget that look of disappointment in Harry's eyes . . .

CHAPTER 20

Beth caught the bus home after spending some time window shopping. She didn't want to buy anything because all her money would be needed for her nursing training. She'd been told that she would be accepted and given a list of things she needed to buy for herself. Her first uniforms would be provided free, but her shoes had to be bought out of her own money, and she'd been advised to buy good comfortable ones. She would also need books and money for her own use; though her accommodation would be free.

'We make that restriction, because so many girls simply waltz in and out without giving notice. So we do not pay you until you've proved your worth – and the pay is one pound and fifteen shillings a week for the first six months . . .'

Beth had groaned as she heard that, because it meant a pay cut for her. Yet she'd signed the paper put in front of her and felt proud of herself, but now she was feeling uneasy, because her mother and father would not be pleased.

It was nearly dark when Beth reached home.

Her parents and her sister Mary were sitting in the kitchen drinking tea, and they all looked at her when she entered.

'Nice to see you,' Beth said to her sister. 'Is everything all right at home?'

'I came to tell Mum that Andy has signed up,' Mary said, looking fed up.

'Well, you knew he was going to, didn't you?'

'I kept hoping he would change his mind.'

'Sorry, Mary love. It must be upsetting for you . . .'

'Yes, it is. Tony was here earlier,' Mary told her.

'What did he want?'

'He came to see you, of course, Beth.'

'He hasn't bothered for ages.'

'He's busy, setting his business up at nights,' Beth's father looked at her oddly. 'I should have thought you would want to help him with that, Beth. It's a lot of work for a man to do when he's been at work all day.'

'He didn't tell me he'd gone ahead with it,' Beth said, feeling cross that her family seemed to be on Tony's side. 'I knew he'd found somewhere but I didn't know he was setting it up.'

'You didn't tell us you'd had a quarrel with him?'

'Tony wanted me to work for him and get married at Christmas. I told him we couldn't and, besides, I have plans of my own.'

'I give him credit for wanting to better himself, Beth. He's got more in him than I thought.' Her father stared hard at her. 'And what plans have you got, young lady?'

Beth took a deep breath, then, 'I've applied to become a nurse. They've put me on the list and I was told I've been accepted subjected to my details being checked . . .'

'You want to be a nurse like Mary?' Her father stared at her in surprise.

'Yes, well not quite like Mary. It's a voluntary unit they've set up because of the war. I'll take a shorter course than Mary took and I'll train on the wards; there is no college training . . .'

'Why don't you do it the right way if you're going to?' her father asked. 'Get your State Registration the way Mary did . . .'

'Because I want to be of use sooner rather than later,' Beth said. 'I'm doing this for the duration. I don't want to do it for life . . .'

'I thought you wanted to work in an office,' her mother said. 'Why the sudden change of mind, Beth?'

'I need to do something worthwhile. Working at Oliver's when young men are being killed isn't my idea of worthwhile . . .'

'No one is being killed yet . . .'

'Beth is right,' Mary spoke up for her sister. 'We're going to need all the trained girls we can get, Mum. The hospital is building temporary accommodation; because once it does start the casualties will be so large they will overwhelm us.'

Her father nodded, 'It's a pity to give up the job you trained for, Beth – but it's the right thing to do. You can always find a typist's job when it's over – but what will Tony have to say if you have to go away?'

'We're finished,' Beth told them, wanting it out in the open. 'He's been messing around with another girl and I shan't put up with that.'

'You didn't tell me,' her mother said, looking upset. 'So that's why he hasn't been round much – but perhaps he wants to come back, love . . .'

'I don't want to see him. I'm going to the bathroom. I don't want to talk about Tony anymore, right?'

Beth heard the buzz after she went into the hall and knew they were discussing her break-up with Tony. Well, her mother might think she should give Tony another chance but Beth had had enough . . .

Beth's indignation lasted for the next few hours, but then she started wishing that she'd been home when Tony came round. At least he had come, which seemed to indicate that he wanted to see her. Perhaps he'd just been too busy to take her out for the past couple of weeks, but he ought to have found time to tell her . . . Maybe she'd been wrong about him seeing Sylvia Butcher . . .

Beth had been very hurt at the start, but now she was just fed up. All Tony seemed to think about was work and his new business. She wanted to go out, to have fun. Tony seemed to think she ought to be sitting around waiting for him when he chose to come round, but she wasn't on a string to be pulled back and forth as he thought fit.

Beth's mood lasted for most of the night and

she lay tossing and turning in bed, feeling miserable. At work she was kept busy all day, making up invoices and writing up various accounts, typing letters. When her lunch break came, she decided she wasn't going to sit in the staffroom and brood. She'd go down to the café at the end of the road and buy herself a cheap meal.

She was sitting drinking a glass of orange squash when a man came and sat down at her table. She was startled and looked up, recognising Sebastian Winters.

'May I speak with you, Miss Court?'

'Yes, of course, Mr Winters.'

'I wanted to contact Lizzie – I was told she wasn't at work when I asked for her. Do you know where she is?'

'She got married,' Beth said and saw his face change colour and a little nerve flick at the corner of his eye. 'Her husband has joined the RAF and they are on honeymoon . . .'

'I see . . .' He tapped the table with his gloves, a look somewhere between anger and shock in his eyes. 'Do you know when she returns home?'

'Yes, on Friday night, because Harry has to return to base on Saturday morning.'

'Of course . . . perhaps you will tell her I should like to see her one day?'

'Yes, but she'll be back at work next week if you wanted to see her. I happen to know there's a big order for her specials . . . she makes such beautiful hats.' Beth sighed.

'Yes, she is talented. I dare say you enjoy wearing her hats?'

'Unfortunately, I don't go out anywhere I can wear pretty hats very often.'

'I'm sure a young lady as pretty as you must get lots of invitations?'

'Thank you for the compliment but I assure you, I never go anywhere interesting these days.'

'You intrigue me,' he said. 'One favour deserves another – I'm giving a garden party on Sunday afternoon, the week after next, at least we'll be in the garden if it's fine and in the house if it rains. Would you like to come?'

'Only if I can bring Lizzie – and that's if she wants to come.'

'Here is my card. I live in Hampstead, as you can see. Please feel free to arrive at any time between three and five in the afternoon.' He rose and tipped his hat to her. 'Thank you for the information, Miss Court. I am much obliged to you.'

Beth watched him go. She wasn't sure Lizzie would wish to go to the garden party, but she certainly did. It was her chance to see how the other half lived.

'I'm glad you brought this to show me,' Ed said, on Lizzie's return to work the following week. He turned the witch's hat over to look at the silk lining and the way it was formed. 'This is a fine piece of work, Lizzie – but it must have taken ages?'

194

'Yes, it did, too long. I would need to sell it for three pounds – and that doesn't show much of a profit if I count my time.'

'You must count your time,' Ed warned. 'I like it very much as a fun hat, but I fear the straw may fray because of the way you've cut it. I know you have over-sewn the edges with the lace, but it may still give after a little wear – and if it was expensive . . .'

'Yes, I see. It is very delicate but that is what gives it its appeal, I think.'

Ed agreed with her but he didn't think it was worth showing it to Oliver because he would think it a waste of time. Lizzie knew he was right but felt disappointed because she'd really liked it.

'Shall I show you how to form a cone that will be less likely to disintegrate?'

'Yes, please,' Lizzie said eagerly and watched as he measured and cut a piece of fine straw, twisting it deftly so that it became the basic shape Lizzie had wanted. He gave it to her to seam inside on the sewing machine, and then cut some silk lining and stiffening, which she inserted in the point and then lined with the contrast silk. This hat was fashioned of maroon and lined with a faded rose pink, and Ed suggested Lizzie finish it, as she thought fit. She edged it with black satin ribbon and sewed a frill of black lace inside so that it cascaded over the face to form a fine veil and looked like the brim of a witch's hat.

'Yes, simpler and elegant,' Ed approved. 'You

can use the basic pattern for other materials of course, but it isn't a shape that will sell in large numbers.'

'No, of course not. Thank you for showing me. How much did it cost out at?'

'A lot less than yours,' he said. 'I know you think our range is limited, Lizzie, but that comes from experience. The people who buy from us want constant sellers, the kind of thing their customers buy over and over again.'

'The customers I'm thinking of will want something different.'

'Yes, I know what you would like,' he said and shook his head. 'You're ambitious and you have flair. I understand that you want to create something very stylish and new – but much of that comes with the trimming.'

'How much do I owe you for the materials?' Lizzie asked, picking up the hat she'd made under his direction.

'Call it fifteen shillings,' he said. 'But why don't we show it to Oliver and let him try it in the stock? If the customers don't like it, you can buy it then if you like.'

Lizzie got on with her work until Mr Oliver came round. He asked her if she'd had a good time, how Harry was, and looked through the pile of stock they'd made. To her surprise he didn't mention the cone-shaped hat and Lizzie thought she'd seen a faint smile on his mouth.

Beth pounced on her the minute she entered the

staffroom at break time, giving her a hug. 'I've missed you so much,' she said. 'I expect you had a wonderful time?'

'It was a nice hotel and a lovely place.'

'Is something the matter?' Beth asked and Lizzie nodded.

'I can't tell you here – come round this evening?'

'Yes, of course.' Beth stared at her. 'Is it to do with what your aunt said on your wedding day?'

'Yes,' Lizzie managed. 'I'll tell you tonight.'

'All right,' Beth squeezed her round the waist. 'You shouldn't let her upset you, love.'

'It isn't her, it's Harry,' Lizzie said. 'I really can't say now . . .'

She wasn't sure how much she could tell her friend but knew she had to say something, because she'd almost gone mad sitting in the flat alone. Beth was her best friend; Lizzie needed to talk and she was the only one who would understand.

'All right, love, I can wait,' Beth said. 'I met Sebastian Winters on Friday. He wants to talk to you – and he invited us to a party not this Sunday but the next . . .'

'I don't want to go,' Lizzie said. 'You should go if you want . . .'

'Not without you,' Beth said. 'Look, Vera is coming in now. Eat your lunch and we'll talk this evening . . .'

Beth arrived bearing a bottle of sweet sherry. 'I thought you might need a drink by the sound of

197

you,' she said. 'What happened, Lizzie? I know that old witch said something awful to you, but you wouldn't say and I didn't like to ask too many questions . . .'

'I couldn't have told you then, besides, I thought she was lying, but I have to tell you now, Beth . . .'

Lizzie spilled out the whole story, skirting over what happened between her and Harry, but leaving her in no doubt that he'd been shocked and angry.

'I don't think he loves me any longer,' Lizzie said. 'We couldn't have stayed there together like that for a week. I came back as soon as I could and I've made a couple of hats . . .' She stopped as she saw the look of anger in Beth's eyes. 'I can't blame him; I'm not the sweet innocent virgin he thought I was . . .'

'The self-satisfied little prig!' Beth burst out furiously. 'Is he so perfect? Don't tell me he's never been to bed with a woman before, because I wouldn't believe it. Couldn't he see what it meant to you – couldn't he understand how you suffered? I should like to horsewhip the pair of them – your rotten aunt and Harry . . .'

A little sob broke from her as she hugged Beth. Her friend held her so tight that she had to break free because she could hardly breathe, but she was feeling better.

'Thank you. I knew I could tell you – but I don't know what to do, Beth. What am I going to do if he's left me? His uncle will want to know why and I can't tell him. I should be too embarrassed . . .'

'Why should you have to? It's not your fault – none of it is your fault, Lizzie. Someone hurt you badly and your aunt and uncle kept the truth from you . . .' Her gaze narrowed. 'You still don't remember, do you?'

'No, nothing at all. I wondered if I might, once I was alone with plenty of time to think, but it's still all a blank.'

'Your aunt should have told you all this ages ago.'

'I might not even have thought of marriage if she or my uncle had told me the truth and I certainly would have explained to Harry if I'd known. I do understand why Uncle Jack tried to spare me, but he was wrong. It would have been much better had I told Harry the truth at the start.'

'Yes much better,' Beth agreed. 'I would say come back to live with us, but I'm leaving home when my appointment comes through – but Mum would have you if she understood your situation . . .'

'I'm going to stay here for a while. I'm not sure I can afford to live here alone – but I have to wait until I hear from Harry. Some of the furniture is mine, but some is his . . .' Lizzie swallowed hard, fighting a wave of emotion. 'We were going to be so happy here . . .'

'Perhaps he will get over it and come back to you.'

'Perhaps, but it can't be the same,' Lizzie said. 'I've been wondering what to do but I can't see my way clear. I suppose I could join a voluntary organisation like you – but . . .' She shook her head. 'I just don't know what to do . . .'

'Carry on at work until I leave anyway,' Beth said. 'And come to that party with me next week. You've done nothing wrong. Harry is the one that should apologise.'

'I was upset for him – I am still sorry I didn't tell him, but he married me and he was supposed to love me. Surely it isn't too much to try and understand how I feel?'

'If he was a proper man he would,' Beth said and Lizzie shook her head.

'I can't blame him, Beth. He'd put me on a pedestal. I was his perfect Lizzie and it hurt when he realised that I wasn't perfect . . .'

'That isn't love,' Beth said with disgust. 'Oh, I've gone off men altogether. Tony wanted me to do exactly what he wanted; he didn't care how I felt – they're all the same . . .'

She picked up the sherry bottle and poured them both a large glass. 'Come on, have a drink and drown your sorrows, love. We'll find a way through, Lizzie. You've still got your friends – and I'm not the only one that cares about you. Ed and Tilly would be up in arms if they knew – and Madge would murder him.'

'I couldn't tell Ed,' Lizzie said, but she was smiling now. 'Oh, I've got something to show you . . .' She ran into the bedroom and brought the witch's hat back. 'What do you think of that?'

'It's beautiful! May I try it on?'

'Yes, of course you can,' Lizzie said and laughed as Beth ran to the mirror and tried on the delicate hat. It suited her and she preened herself, obviously in love with it. 'You look lovely in it, Beth. I'll give it to you as a present.'

'You can't afford to do that,' Beth said. 'You might be able to sell it for a profit. I would buy it if I didn't need all my savings for my training . . .'

'Poor you,' Lizzie said. 'I'll let you wear it one day if you like, when you're going somewhere nice . . .'

'For that party at Mr Winters' house . . .' Beth gave her a meaningful look. 'We could both do with some cheering up. I'd really love to go and I'd feel much better if you came with me – admit it, you're feeling right down in the dumps, aren't you?'

'Well, perhaps,' Lizzie said. 'Yes, I'll give it some thought, because I don't see why I should just sit in the house and mope all the time. If Harry wants to divorce me, he should let me know.'

'He'll turn up out of the blue one day,' Beth said and gave her another hug. 'You wait and see. I'm sure he'll be back and with his tail between his legs . . .'

CHAPTER 21

'Harry . . .' Lizzie said when she returned to the flat that Friday evening and found him lounging on the sofa. 'You didn't let me know you were coming . . .'

'I wasn't sure I was,' Harry said. 'I didn't expect to get a twenty-four-hour pass until they told us this morning, and even then I wasn't sure what to do.'

'I've been wondering if you would come,' Lizzie said, her throat tight with emotion. 'I didn't know what to do – should I give notice here or . . .?'

'This is our home. I shall be paying the rent through my bank and I'll send you some money every now and then, though you get your wages and that should be enough when I'm not here.' His tone was cool but not harsh.

'Yes, it would be if you pay the rent – but do you want me here? If I left you, you could divorce me and . . .'

'No,' he said sharply. 'I don't want a divorce, Lizzie.' The look in his eyes puzzled her. 'Look, I'm sorry for the way I behaved. I came back for you three days later but they told me at the hotel you'd gone. I got angry again because you'd left, but I should have come here.'

'Why did you come back? I don't understand?' Lizzie's heart raced, because he'd given her no clue as to his feelings. He didn't seem angry but he wasn't loving either.

'After I left you, I went to see your aunt . . .'

'Why – didn't you believe me?'

'Yes, and no – it seemed so strange. I got the whole story out of her, Lizzie. I'm so sorry for what you had to suffer. She's an awful woman – she was so nasty that I knew she'd meant to destroy us . . .'

'I think she's punishing me because my uncle was fond of me and left me his property – even though she has the house for her lifetime.'

'That may not be as long as you'd think,' Harry said. 'She got herself in such a passion that she had a fit while I was there. The doctor told me she has some sort of tumour in her head and it's slowly killing her.'

'Oh no, how terrible for her,' Lizzie said. 'I had no idea . . .'

'You're not sorry for her – after what she's done to you?'

'Of course I'm sorry for her. No one deserves that sort of illness – whatever she did to me . . .'

'Well, I think she deserves all she gets,' Harry said. 'She almost finished us . . .'

'Almost?' Lizzie swallowed hard. 'Are you saying . . .?' she couldn't go on, because his eyes seemed to be pleading with her.

'I want to try again – if you'll have me, Liz?' Harry moved towards her, his hand outstretched. 'I know I was a selfish bastard that night. All I could think of was my disappointment. I couldn't bear to imagine anyone else touching you, loving you – but it wasn't like that at all. You were abused and you didn't even know much about it . . .'

Lizzie felt the tears on her cheeks. She'd been so hurt, so angry, that she'd almost decided to leave the flat and her job and join up as Beth had, but now Harry's words and his looks were drawing her back, spinning a web about her.

'But I'm not what you thought I was, Harry,' she whispered and her damaged heart ached. 'Can you bear it – can you still love me as your wife?'

'I know one thing,' he said. 'I know I can't bear my life without you. I thought when I left that I couldn't live with that knowledge but now I know there are worse things. To face a life that didn't include you would be infinitely worse . . . it doesn't bear thinking of, Lizzie darling.'

'Oh, Harry . . .' she moved towards him, needing and wanting to feel his arms about her. 'I thought you must hate me – that you'd never want me again . . .'

'I've thought of nothing else but holding you and loving you,' he said. 'Please forgive me, Lizzie. Don't leave me – don't hate me because I'm weak and selfish and I didn't know how to behave that night.'

Lizzie felt a shiver of longing and need as their

lips met and she knew that even though things could not be the same, she still felt love for this man. She wanted him in her life, because the alternative was an empty wasteland.

'Take me to bed, Harry. Please make love to me, let me forget all the wicked things she said – tell me that you don't think I'm shameful or disgusting . . . please love me . . .'

'I'll always love you,' Harry said and swept her into his arms, carrying her into their little bedroom and falling with her to the bed.

Afterwards, Lizzie lay beside her husband as he slept. She looked down at him and saw how young he seemed and she felt so much older. The act of making love had seemed enough for him, and he'd come quickly inside her, crying out that he loved her.

Lizzie had found it harder to give herself than the first time. She was scarred, still hurting inside, even though she'd promised all was forgiven. Something within her had held back from him and she hadn't experienced that same flow of pleasure. Harry said that he wanted only to forget, but she knew he would not; he would carry what had happened inside him and so would she.

She lay for a while with tears on her cheeks and then at last she slept until he woke her and made love to her again. She let him kiss her and take her as he would, but some part of her could not respond; it was as if her innocent joy in loving had died.

'I love you so much, Lizzie,' he'd told her again in the heat of lovemaking. 'You'll be true to me, darling? You'll never leave me for another man?'

'I love you,' she'd whispered. 'I'll never leave you.' But the fact that he'd felt it necessary to ask made the pain twist inside her.

Harry had come back to her because he claimed to love her and need her love, but she knew there was doubt in his mind. Lizzie sensed that Harry still wondered if he could trust her, even though he knew she'd been taken down without her consent. Lizzie's heart wept as she lay beside him, unable to sleep.

Loving Harry, having him back, was a bittersweet thing. She was not sure that such a fragile love would survive the trials of life and she understood why her aunt had warned her not to marry. Only a very special man would bear the knowledge of what had happened to Lizzie and let it make no difference. Despite his promises of love, she knew that the knowledge was like a canker inside Harry.

After Harry went back to his unit, Lizzie slipped into the life she'd known before she married him. She worked with Ed in harmony, went home with him to visit his wife, and now she stopped to share the supper she cooked for them once a week. Beth insisted she visit her home often until she was sent away on her nursing course, and Lizzie ate Sunday lunch with Mrs Court and her large family.

It was a busy life, too busy to be lonely, though there was a place inside Lizzie's heart and head that was always alone. She wrote to Harry, cheerful letters about her work and her friends, but he sent her brief postcards about nothing in particular. She knew she'd made a mistake and wished that she had not married so swiftly, but she wouldn't let herself cry over it. Lizzie had made her bed and she must lie in it.

'Go to a garden party in Hampstead on Saturday?' Lizzie said doubtfully. 'I know I said I might, but that was before Harry . . .'

'You promised . . .' Beth pleaded. 'It's the chance of a lifetime, Lizzie. He must live in one of those big houses near the Heath. There will be lots of posh people there – fashionable ladies, I expect. We could both wear one of your hats – they might ask who made them and then we could tell them you made them . . . besides, Harry isn't likely to get another leave yet, is he?'

'No, I shouldn't think so.' Beth's idea was tempting. If people liked the hats they might make new customers for the workshop. She looked at Beth's face and realised that her friend was excited by the idea of a party in Hampstead.

'Which of my hats would you choose to wear if I agreed?'

'Could I wear the green straw? That witch's hat is such fun. I could never wear it anywhere else, but for a garden party – it would be a real lark.'

'Yes, it does suit you,' Lizzie agreed. 'Go on then. I'll wear the hat I made for my wedding with my white dress – what dress will you wear?'

'I've got my black tailored costume.'

'The hat will look lovely with that . . . I suppose we could . . .'

'Yes, let's,' Beth giggled. 'I'll take good care of your hat, Lizzie. I won't spoil it, so you can sell it afterwards.'

'No, Ed warned me that the straw may fray so I shall not be able to sell it, but I want people to see it. When it's been shown to a few people, I'll give it to you.'

'We'll have a good time on Saturday, because I'm leaving soon and I don't know when I'll see you again . . .'

CHAPTER 22

Lizzie looked at Beth as they arrived in front of the big house set back in its own grounds. Neither of them had expected anything like this, and she could see from her friend's face that she was wondering if her decision to come had been the right one.

'Shall we go for a walk and then go home?'

'Dressed like this?' Beth shook her head. 'Mr Winters invited us, so we shall go through with it now we've come – besides, you look great, Lizzie.'

'So do you,' Lizzie said. 'That outfit makes you look as if you're a model out of a glossy magazine.'

'I feel different, exciting,' she confessed. 'Come on, let's go in and see what people make of my hat . . .'

They rang the front doorbell. It was answered by a pretty young woman wearing a pale blue full-skirted dress and a large white hat. She stared at Beth's hat and giggled.

'Gosh, I've never seen anything like that,' she said. 'It's mad but really fun. Come on in. My name is Sandra. Everyone is out the back enjoying themselves. I came in for a moment or I wouldn't have heard you – we all just go round the back . . .'

Lizzie and Beth followed her through a large sitting room to a pair of open French windows. Outside there were lots of people milling around, mostly pretty girls, but also a few gentlemen. Small tables were set out at intervals and had umbrellas over them to protect people from the sun. There was a large buffet spread under a yellow striped awning and two men wearing white aprons stood behind it to serve the guests with food, of which there was a bewildering variety. Lizzie was impressed by everything she saw, as was Beth. They looked at each other, knowing that they were way out of their depth amongst these people but determined to enjoy themselves nonetheless.

'Ah, Miss Court and Lizzie Larch . . .' Sebastian Winters came up to them, smiling. 'I'm so glad you came. Please, let me get you a drink and help yourself to some food.'

'Thank you.' Beth beamed at him. 'I'll have a white wine please – and some of that delicious food. Everything looks wonderful . . .'

'I'm glad you like it. You look charming yourself, Miss Court – and I love that wonderful hat. I think you made that, Lizzie?'

'It's just a bit of fun. I don't imagine anyone would actually buy something like that . . .'

'I know of more than one young woman who would buy it just for the fun of wearing something so different – and outrageous.' His eyes seemed warm and caressing on her face. 'I always knew you had talent. I suspect you made this in your own time – are there any more?'

'A few . . . I can't afford to make hats just for fun, even though I'd like to.'

'Make a few of your madder ideas up for me and I'll pay for them . . .'

'I would have to ask Mr Oliver . . .'

'Do them in your own time. He doesn't need to know . . .'

'I don't think I could do that, but if I tell him you'll buy them . . .'

'I shall. I give you my word. Will you make a few flights of fancy for me, Lizzie Larch?'

'Of course, but you do know I'm Lizzie Oliver now?'

'To me you'll always be Lizzie Larch – it looks better on a label than Lizzie Oliver, don't you think?'

'Yes . . .' she breathed in sharply. 'But . . .'

'Make those hats for me, Lizzie, and we'll talk about the future – yes?' His eyes were challenging her, daring her to accept, and she felt something inside responding. Lizzie saw that Beth was already being served with a drink and some food at the buffet. 'Perhaps I should join Beth . . .'

'Yes, of course. I must circulate, but I wanted to tell you that I'm pleased you came – and I do love both your hat and Beth's.' Sebastian's hand touched hers for a moment; she felt a tingle shoot through her and pulled it back with a gasp. She was Harry's wife and this wasn't right!

Lizzie thanked him, her cheeks pink as she moved to join Beth and take her choice of the delicious food. Their plates filled with tempting little tarts, miniature sausage rolls, a couple of fancy fingers of something on toast, and various other bits, they found an empty table and sat down.

Lizzie had followed Beth's lead and chosen a medium white wine, which she sipped warily.

They had been sitting alone for a few minutes when a very handsome man in a light-coloured blazer and cream flannels came up to them, hovering before asking if he could sit with them.

'Yes, if you wish,' Beth said, before Lizzie could answer. 'This food is awfully good. I don't know what's in these little canapés but they taste delicious.'

'I think that must be the lobster. Unfortunately, it brings me out in spots, but don't be alarmed, most people love it – I'm just subject to a few allergies.' He offered his hand. 'My name is Mark Allen, by the way. I'm fascinated by your hat, Miss . . .'

'Beth Court. Lizzie made it, she's so clever with hats,' Beth said. 'I'm just a secretary, I'm afraid.'

'I think that's awfully clever too,' he replied seriously. 'I don't do anything much – son and heir to the estate. Father lets me think I'm helping out now and then, but to tell you the truth I feel pretty useless . . . but that is going to end. Next week I intend to join the Merchant Navy . . . that's if they'll take me.'

'Lizzie's husband is in the RAF,' Beth informed him. 'You haven't got much to eat. I could eat twice as much of these things. I've never tasted anything so delicious.'

'You must try the cakes and the syllabubs; my sister loves sweet trifles. I tell her she will get fat but she never does . . .' He looked almost shy, then, 'Why don't I come with you and tell you what everything is?'

'Oh yes, thanks,' Beth said and got up with alacrity.

Lizzie watched as her friend went to the buffet with Mark Allen. It was obvious that she was enjoying herself, but Lizzie preferred to sit and watch all the pretty girls. Sebastian Winters had invited more girls than men; they were dressed in gorgeous clothes and their hats were obviously expensive. Lizzie looked at the designs and realised that Harry's uncle was right; one or two of them were wearing unusual designs but most were basic shapes and it was the trimming that made them different.

Sebastian sat down in Beth's vacant chair. 'Did that hat your friend is wearing take a long time to do?'

'Too long,' Lizzie said. 'To earn anything on it, I would need to sell it for four pounds. It was just a whim . . .'

'Beautiful though, like its creator,' he said. 'I always knew you had talent, Lizzie, which is why I should have liked you to work for me.'

'Perhaps I should have done,' she said. 'I've learned so much working with Ed – but sometimes I do want to make more exotic hats.'

'I could sell a hat like the one your friend is wearing for more than seven pounds,' Sebastian said reflectively. 'Of course it would be a special customer and you couldn't sell more than one. If it could be done in less time and retailed cheaper – but I suppose individual designs will always be more expensive.'

'Yes, perhaps.'

'May I get you another drink – perhaps something different?'

'I'm fine, thank you,' Lizzie replied. 'I don't drink much wine . . . I'm afraid, I'm not used to the high life.'

'My friends enjoy these parties, so I give them. I'm just as happy with a quiet dinner for two.' There was something in his eyes at that moment, something reflective and sad that made her wonder about the real man – the man beneath the successful and polished façade.

'Yes, that's what my husband likes,' Lizzie said and his eyes met hers. 'He is in the RAF and I miss him, but next week he'll be home on leave.'

'Why did you get married so suddenly?' Sebastian asked, a brooding expression in his eyes. 'It was rather sudden, wasn't it?'

'It wasn't because I was pregnant, if that's what you're thinking. My uncle died and I had to leave my home and . . .' the words deserted her, because

214

she didn't know why she'd rushed into marriage with a man she was no longer sure she loved.

'Why didn't you have a little patience?' he asked, his expression somewhere between exasperation and disappointment. 'You'll wake up and discover you made a mistake one of these days, Lizzie.'

'Why should I? I love Harry . . .' She raised her eyebrows in teasing mockery. 'Would you rather I'd been one of your many girlfriends?' She let her gaze wander over the garden and all the lovely ladies wandering about in their beautiful clothes. 'I think I'd get lost in this crowd.'

'You would never be lost in any crowd.'

'I'm not that special, Sebastian, and you know it. It's only because I said no that you're interested.'

'Why don't you trust me? I could help you even now – if you would let me . . .' Again, there was that challenge in his eyes, making her aware of him on so many levels, not least the attractive man who liked to flirt with any woman that came within his orbit.

'You're very kind, but I have to try to make a success of things myself.'

'I admire your independent spirit, Lizzie. I hope it works out for you, and I mean that sincerely – whatever you think of me.' For a moment longer his intense gaze seemed to dwell on her and once again she felt that tightness in her throat, a needy wanting that she knew she must crush now, before it caused harm. 'Well, I shall have to love you and leave you for now – but remember you have a friend in me if you need me, Lizzie Larch.'

Lizzie understood passion now as she had not before her marriage, at least Harry had done that for her – and it had made her realise how attractive Sebastian was, and what that look in his eyes really meant.

He rose and went off to speak to some of the other young women milling around his large garden. Lizzie stood up and wandered off, taking the chance to explore some of the more secluded areas. She needed a little time to think about her reaction to Sebastian, because it was unexpected and unwanted.

There were several shaded walks, because the garden was huge, and she wandered past an ornamental pool with a fancy bridge over it and found a seat on the other side, sitting in the shade of a tree to watch the party from afar. Beth was circulating and a lot of the women were talking to her, clearly intrigued by her hat; she took it off and let one of them try it on, and the young woman giggled and preened herself to her companions.

Lizzie wasn't sure what to think. Most of them seemed to find the hat amusing, but she wasn't sure they would want one of their own. After a while, a man came strolling over the bridge to her and smiled.

'May I sit down?' he asked. 'I'm John Saunders and my girlfriend has fallen in love with your witch's hat. Your friend told her where you work and she wants to come and see you – we're getting married at the end of October and she would like something different, though I'm not sure she would be brave enough to wear a hat like that . . .'

'I could probably trim some hats to suit her if she wanted.'

'I'll tell her then. Wendy is a little shy and didn't want to ask you herself. Why don't you come and circulate? I'm sure they are all dying to meet you.'

'Thank you, Mr Saunders, I will.'

He stood up and they walked back together to the lawn where the other guests were still enjoying themselves. She'd been feeling a bit out of it, as if she didn't belong, but now she began to enjoy herself.

Even if the witch's hat was not saleable, it had certainly aroused people's interest and that was what she needed. If only a few of those who had promised to visit the workshops kept their word, she might get Mr Oliver to listen to her idea about bespoke orders. God knew, she needed something to fill her empty life . . .

It was past seven when they left the party. Mark Allen had offered to drive them both home and Beth accepted without consulting Lizzie. She was a little dubious about it and would have preferred to catch the underground, but Beth had been drinking more than her and was flushed with triumph.

'Everyone was fantastic over your hat,' she gushed 'You should set up a shop of your own.'

'I don't think I'm quite ready for that, Beth.'

Lizzie wasn't quite as convinced that the women Beth had talked to would actually seek her out.

Mark dropped her outside her flat and Beth refused to come in with her.

'I'll see you soon,' she said and handed Lizzie the hat. 'You'd better have this back. I don't want it to get spoiled.'

Lizzie was going to tell her that she could keep it, but decided to hang on to it for the moment

Walking upstairs to her little flat, Lizzie smelled something, her nose wrinkling at the unpleasant odour. Was that something burning?

She went into the kitchen first and saw that the remains of beans on toast were on the table and dirty saucepans in the sink. Her heart caught and she rushed into the sitting room to discover it was empty, but she could smell cigarette smoke.

'Harry . . .' she called and then saw the note propped against the plant pot on the sideboard.

Where the hell are you, Lizzie? I know you didn't expect me, but I got a twelve-hour pass. I waited as long as I could . . . I thought you would be home. Harry.

Her throat tightened as she realised she'd missed him. If only she'd known; she would much rather have had a few hours with Harry than spend them at that garden party.

Brushing away foolish tears, Lizzie sat down and concentrated on looking through her most recent drawings. It would be silly to cry just because she'd missed Harry.

Yet even as she worked on the design, her mind kept turning to Harry and the few precious hours she'd missed with him. He would wonder where she'd been and when he knew she'd been to a party at Sebastian Winters' house . . . he was going to be angry.

CHAPTER 23

Tony was waiting for Beth the next evening. He looked serious and her heart caught. She'd loved him once, at least she was almost sure she had, though after the way she'd responded to Mark Allen's kisses the previous evening she wasn't certain how she felt now. For a few minutes in Mark's car she'd been swept away on a wave of a feeling that was new to her. It was different to anything she'd felt for Tony and she'd almost given into her need, but just in time he'd pulled away.

'It wouldn't be fair to take advantage, Beth,' he'd said apologetically. 'I like you an awful lot, dear girl, but we don't know each other – and I don't want to make trouble for you.'

'No, I don't want that either. Thanks for being honest . . .'

'I should like to get to know you,' Mark said earnestly. 'Look, I'm going to be honest with you. We're from different worlds, Beth, and my father expects and all that . . . but I'm taking the first step to breaking out of the traces by joining the Merchant Navy, and I'd like to see you again – if you're willing to take a chance on an idiot like me . . .'

'You're not an idiot,' Beth said quickly. 'You've been honest, Mark, so I'll be the same. Something happened just now between us that I don't understand. I've been courting regularly, but I've never felt like that with him, even though I thought I wanted to marry him. We fell out recently and I'm not sure how I feel – but I should like to meet you again . . .'

'What about the flicks one night – and a drink afterwards? We should get to know one another, Beth – do it slowly and not rush things.'

'Yes,' she agreed and kissed his cheek. 'When shall we meet?'

'Not tomorrow – Tuesday? Do you want me to pick you up?'

'No, we'll meet somewhere. My parents would be on Tony's side – and they'd say you were only after one thing, because you belong to a different class.'

Mark laughed. 'You're a breath of fresh air to me, Beth. I feel as if I've been running and accidentally fallen down a ravine. The view is beautiful but I'm not sure of the landing . . .'

His fanciful words made Beth giggle. She was breathless and nervous of seeing him again and yet it made her feel wonderful to know that he wanted to see her.

Tony was glowering now as she reached him. 'I thought you were never coming. Where have you been?'

'I was asked to work later to finish a report.'

'It's time you gave notice and came to work for me – for us. You could work at your own pace, Beth. Once we're married . . .'

'I don't know how you dare ask me. You haven't been near me for ages and I know you've been seeing Sylvia Butcher . . .' she flung the accusation at him even though she wasn't sure.

'She isn't important, just a little fling. You know I love you, Beth. I want to get married and be together properly . . .'

'Dad won't give us permission yet. Besides, I'm not certain it's what I want . . .' Beth broke off as she saw the flash of anger in Tony's eyes. 'I'm sorry, but you haven't bothered to take me out or visit for ages.'

'When I come, you're never there. I had to tell you, Beth. I've got my call-up papers and I leave in three weeks . . .'

'Oh, Tony, I'm sorry. Do you really have to go – can't you get out of it somehow?'

'Why should I? There's not much for me round here, is there?'

'What do you mean?'

'You've been seeing someone else, Beth. I saw you get out of his car last night. Your mother said you would be home soon, but it got later and later and then I left to wait by the stop.'

'If you'd let me know you were coming, I'd have been at home – but you gave me the impression we were over.'

'I'd almost decided to finish it ages ago,' he muttered, looking sullen. 'I came round to sort it out last night – but then I saw you get out of his car . . .'

He couldn't have seen her kissing Mark, because they hadn't kissed outside her house but in a dark spot a few streets away, where she wasn't likely to be seen and recognised. Besides, Tony had no right to expect her to just sit around waiting for him.

'Are you going to deny it?'

'No, I shan't deny it, Tony. Mark gave me a lift back from the party we went to last night – and he's asked me out tomorrow.'

Tony grabbed her wrist. 'I forbid you to go. You're my girl and I don't want you messin' with blokes like that – do you hear me? That sort only wants a girl like you for one thing.'

'So now I'm a cheap tart am I?'

'I didn't mean that – but you should stay where you belong, with blokes like me.' He tightened his grip on her arm.

'I don't belong to you,' Beth told him coldly. 'Take your hand off me, Tony. You're hurting me.'

'You deserve me to really hurt you . . .' he was angrier than she'd ever seen him.

'If you hit me I shall never speak to you again.' Beth faced him, angry herself now. 'I mean what I say. I certainly shan't marry a bully – and I'm not sure marriage is what I want now. I've signed up for a nursing course . . .'

'You're going away?'

'They haven't told me yet, but probably. I have to report next week . . .'

'You can leave your bloody job when you want, but you wouldn't do it for me.'

'I'm not interested in shop work . . .'

'You're an ungrateful bitch, Beth Court. I wanted us to be married and you would have had a home and a living if there's a war and . . . I didn't come back. It was as much for you as me – but I see you've had your head turned. Meet your bleedin' rich bloke. Just don't come running to me when he leaves you with a bun in the oven . . .'

'I shan't!' she cried angrily, but as he walked away she felt a crushing pain in her chest. This time he was really angry: this time he wouldn't come back. 'Tony, I'm sorry . . .' she cried but the words were only a whisper and he didn't turn his head. Beth felt the tears on her cheeks as she watched him run and catch a bus.

'Tony, I do love you . . . I did love you so much,' she said into the empty street.

Oh, she didn't know how she felt anymore. She'd loved the man she'd thought Tony was but he seemed to have changed – and now there was Mark Allen . . .

CHAPTER 24

'If you've got a minute, Lizzie,' Mr Oliver said that morning as she was about to take her lunch break. 'I'd like to talk to you about the future . . .'

'Yes, of course, sir . . .'

'Come into my office, Lizzie,' he said, giving her a friendly look 'I think you should call me Uncle Bertie, at least in private. You're married to Harry now and part of our family – and Aunt Miriam would like you to come to lunch on Sundays now and then . . .'

'That is very kind of her.' Lizzie followed him into the office and sat in the chair he indicated, waiting expectantly.

'Well, Lizzie, I've been thinking about what I can do to make your work here more rewarding. I've been told that you are a treasure and I should take care that you do not run off to the competition . . .'

'I wouldn't do that,' Lizzie said feeling uneasy. 'I don't know what people have been saying . . .'

'Compliments, Lizzie, compliments.' He folded his hands and looked at her over the desk. 'You suggested once that we should smarten the show-room and perhaps take in passing trade. I explained that I couldn't afford a girl to be there standing around all day – told Winters the same thing when he rang me with his idea . . .'

'His idea?'

'Yes, but I'd been thinking along the same lines . . .' he cleared his throat. 'I am going to take on a big government contract, Lizzie. I shall put Vera in charge of that and Ed will give her a hand, but he'll also work with you – but I'm going to smarten that showroom up in readiness for our new bespoke business. I understand that one or two young women want you to make hats for them – special designs that would not be viable as our regular lines . . .'

'Bespoke hats?' Lizzie questioned. 'You want me to do the same as I did for Miss Hennessy?'

'Yes, but instead of showing them sketches I want you to make up individual hats that we can show. You can then change colour schemes and trimmings but you'll know what is feasible and what isn't – I can't have you wasting your time, Lizzie. Especially if I'm going to give you another rise . . .'

'And this idea came from Mr Winters?'

'He says he can put special customers our way and we'll give him a concessionary price – they will be his customers and he will send them to us but guarantee the sale, as he did before.'

Mr Oliver was willing to invest a little in the

showroom, give her an increase in her wage and allow her to work on the bespoke hats, but only because Sebastian Winters had guaranteed it. It would mean a chance for Lizzie to show what she could do and the prospect excited her, but she knew that she had Sebastian Winters to thank for her good fortune. He hadn't been able to get her to leave Oliver's so now he'd come up with a new suggestion. It meant that his part in Oliver's investment was key and would bring her into constant contact with him.

'We can try it,' she said, a tingle of excitement low in her abdomen. Yet a part of her urged caution. What did Sebastian want in return? 'But if they are going to be all my designs I want a label in them – Lizzie Larch Hats . . .'

'Why not Lizzie Oliver?' he asked.

'Because it sounds better,' she said without hesitation and blocked out the thought that she might not always be Lizzie Oliver.

'Yes, perhaps we should have a label in them, because we're going to be charging retail prices. I shall leave that side of the business to you, Lizzie – and you'll be in charge of the normal hats too. I'm going to be overseeing my government contract . . .'

'Are you allowed to tell me what it is for?'

'We'll be making berets and caps for the armed forces,' he said. 'It's steady work and will bring in good money. I'm not sure how long we'll be able to continue with our normal stock. We may not

227

get some of the materials we need – silks and some of the feathers come from overseas, and they won't risk men's lives bringing them in now. The Germans are bombing anything that moves on the sea with a British flag and men are dying. We shall have to make do with stuffs we can source locally . . .'

'Yes, I do see that,' Lizzie said, 'but I need Tilly. You should get another girl to help Vera – you always told me seamstresses were two a penny, but Tilly's work is outstanding.'

'You drive a hard bargain. Oh, all right, I dare say I can find someone – though there's plenty of work in the factories now, and it isn't easy to get anyone any good.'

'I'm sure you could pay a little more if you have a good contract . . .'

Lizzie saw him scowl because he'd been used to paying low wages for long hours. He didn't like having to agree to Lizzie's terms, but whatever Sebastian Winters had said to him had made him aware that, if she chose, she had another job waiting for her.

'Well, as it happens I know someone who might come back to work. She retired a couple of years back, but she's a widow now and I dare say she might do a few hours a week . . . Tilly can work for you three days and for me the other two and a half.'

Thank you, Uncle Bertie.'

Lizzie smiled at the concession and knew it was the best she was going to get.

★   ★   ★

228

If it hadn't been for the pressure at work, Lizzie wasn't sure what she would have done with herself, especially after Beth left to start her nursing training. They had supper together the evening before she left and Beth was full of her news.

'The first few months of my training will be at Addenbrooke's in Cambridge,' she told Lizzie, 'but they will be bringing me back to the Royal London after that. So it looks like I'll be able to see you more often then . . .'

'I shall miss you while you're away, but it's good news that you will be coming back in a few months.'

'I couldn't believe my luck when they told me,' Beth said. 'So far they've only had the casualties from the Merchant Navy to deal with, but they think the hospitals will start to overflow with wounded soon. Apparently, they think I'm the sort that will stay – and they think it's a good thing to have London girls working locally if they can . . .'

'I'm so pleased, and I'll bet your mum is too . . .'

'She's happy at the moment anyway,' Beth said. 'My granny has moved in with her – and Mary is pregnant . . .'

'That's lovely,' Lizzie said.

They'd enjoyed themselves that evening, but Lizzie began to miss her best friend almost at once. She loved working with Tilly and Ed, and visited Madge at least twice a week, but Beth had been special.

Harry didn't write to Lizzie even after she wrote to him and explained her absence. One brief postcard came and then, three weeks later, he turned up at the weekend, coming into the stockroom just as she was finishing for the day.

'Harry, I've missed you so much,' she said and flung herself into his arms. He gave her a brief hug and kissed her, but she felt restraint in him and knew he was angry. 'What is it?'

'What did you go to that bloke Winters' garden party for?'

'I didn't know you were coming home, Harry.'

'That isn't the point. He was after you before we married. You're my wife now.'

'Oh, Harry. Please don't be jealous. He invited Beth and me and she thought it would be a chance to show off my hats. A lot of women admired them, especially the hat Beth wore. I hardly spoke to Mr Winters . . .'

'I don't want you going out with other men while I'm away . . .'

'That's a horrid thing to say.' Tears stung her eyes. 'I'm not like that – I wouldn't let you down, Harry. I only went because Beth wanted to . . .'

Lizzie moved away from him, turning her back to hide her distress. Then she felt his arms go about her and his face was pressed against her hair, his lips moving on her cheek as she turned towards him.

'Forgive me, I'm a brute,' he said. 'I didn't mean to make you cry but I was worried when you weren't there – and then when your letter said . . . I was so jealous. I know Winters wants you, Lizzie. I've heard him talking to my uncle about how talented you are . . .'

'He just sees me as a milliner – the one that got away,' Lizzie said and lifted her face for his kiss. 'If I'd wanted, I could have taken his job ages ago, but I didn't trust him, Harry. I love you . . .'

'I'm a damned fool,' he said, 'but some of the chaps talk about their wives or girlfriends having it off with other men while they're away, and once I get posted it may be ages before I see you, Lizzie . . .'

'Don't,' she begged. 'I can't bear to think of you far away from me. It was long enough this time.'

'I'm lucky I'm still getting leave. Some of the men are being transferred to secret bases and they aren't even allowed to go home or tell anyone. Once the war really starts . . .'

'I keep hoping it won't,' Lizzie said, sniffing and rubbing at her eyes with the hanky he offered. 'The papers seem to say one thing one day and something else the next. Everyone says it's never going to happen . . .'

'That's how much they know,' Harry said. 'Our boys are flying on missions I can't tell you about – and they're damned dangerous. We've lost a few pilots already. It won't be long before it starts in earnest, believe me.'

'Oh, Harry . . .' Talk of pilots being killed frightened her. 'Do you think Germany will invade us?'

'It's our job to stop them,' he said grimly. 'We've

got the Channel between us, and our boys will shoot them out of the sky and sink them in the water – at least, we'll have a damned good try.'

Lizzie was shivering despite the warmth of the workshop. Reaching for his hand, her fingers curled about his and she looked up at him imploringly. 'Let's go home, Harry. I don't want to think about the future or what might happen. I just want to enjoy being with you while you're here . . .'

'Lizzie, I love you so much. Never forget that will you? And if anything does happen to me, remember me. I don't expect you to mourn me forever, but don't forget me.'

'Harry, I don't want to lose you and I could certainly never forget you . . .'

They hurried through streets that were already dark because of the blackout, wanting to be at home together. Once inside their tiny flat, Harry drew her hard against him and kissed her so fiercely that he bruised her lips, but she didn't complain, because she sensed the need in him.

She led him through to their bedroom and towards their bed. Somehow they discarded their clothes and then they were tumbling on to the clean sheets, inhaling the scent of lavender as they went into each other's arms. Harry's kisses had never been sweeter or more passionate as they caressed and touched, exploring each other's bodies, carried away on the tide of need and desire that overwhelmed them. His urgency helped Lizzie to abandon the reserve she'd felt the last time they made love and she blocked everything out but her love for him and his need of her.

This time, Lizzie gave all of herself, revelling in the touch of his hands and his long legs pressing her down into the feather mattress; his lean body covered hers and she felt the smooth hardness of him, sensing that his training was making him fitter and stronger. In those few moments she was his in a way she'd never been and it seemed to her that they became one whole person – a person who could never be complete again unless the other was there. With him inside her, filling her, she became the woman she hadn't truly been until this moment, understanding something women had understood since time began. Before this she'd still been an unsure, romantic girl but now she belonged to Harry as never before: she was his woman, his flesh, his soul – and he was all her world. He had to be, because it was too late for regrets and she wouldn't let herself think about the look in another man's eyes.

Afterwards they lay for a long while without talking, without needing to talk, just inhaling the scent of each other and the feel of sweat-slicked skin cooling. Harry lit a cigarette and they shared it. When it was finished he drew her to him again and she tasted the tobacco on his lips, but then he began to kiss her throat and her breasts, working his way down her body with tongue and lips, making her tingle and tremble as he aroused her to new heights of desire. When his mouth reached the most secret central part of her and began to lavish her with a sweet caress of tongue and lips she began to writhe and buck as the feeling swept through her like a brush fire and she was consumed in its flames.

It must have been long afterwards, when they had slept, that Lizzie woke again to discover the bed was empty.

'Harry . . .' She slid her hand across the sheets and felt them cold. 'Harry, where are you?' Lizzie jumped out of bed and ran naked through the flat to find Harry in their tiny kitchen. He turned and looked at her, hungry eyes going over her body, and she blushed, because it was the first time she'd walked naked in front of him and it felt somehow odd out of the bedroom.

'I thought you'd gone . . .'

'I have tonight and all day tomorrow,' he said and smiled at her. 'I was going to bring you tea in bed . . .'

'Lovely, we'll take a tray back. Are you hungry? I made some cake and sausage rolls . . .'

'I've already started on them,' he grinned at her. 'I was starving, Lizzie – but I don't want to get up. I want to make the most of our time together – because I don't know when I'll get another leave.'

'We'll stay in the whole time,' Lizzie promised. 'I've got plenty of food to cook for us when you're ready.'

'I saw the chops and the bacon and eggs. We can have that later.'

'They've already started rationing some foods, but your uncle says it will get much worse. He told me weeks ago to stock up on sugar, treacle and tinned foods, so I did.'

'Well, he's been through a big war,' Harry said and picked up the tray. 'I'll follow you through . . . you've got a beautiful bum, Lizzie. I've never had a good look before this . . .'

'Harry!' Lizzie said, feeling herself go hot all over. She was very conscious of being naked and made a rush for the bed, covering herself quickly. Harry laughed, leaned in and kissed her.

'You're adorable, Lizzie. You can't be shy after last night.'

'It was dark or almost,' she said. 'Aunt Jane told me to undress in the dark and never look at myself naked – it was as if she thought the body was something shameful.'

'Your aunt was a dried-up old biddy,' Harry said and laughed. 'You look beautiful like that and I want to look at you in daylight so that I can think of you like this when I'm flying up there in the clouds.'

Lizzie sat cross-legged in the bed, letting the covers fall away from her as she took her tea and the plate of crispy, flaky sausages rolls and the delicious butter cream sponge she'd prepared earlier. This was how she loved Harry, the way he'd been before he discovered she wasn't the virgin he'd expected; he'd come back to her and she was so relieved and happy. Please God, let them have another chance, let everything be as she'd hoped it would when she married him. She bit into the sausage roll, enjoying the taste and licking the flakes of pastry from her lips. Harry reached toward her and licked a tiny crumb from the corner of her mouth.

'Tastes even better on your lips,' he murmured. 'I must admit you're not a bad cook, Lizzie.'

'Thank you kindly, sir,' she said, quirking a smile at him.

'You should ask my Aunt Miriam to teach you to make chicken soup – it's economical and will come in handy if food goes on the ration. We shan't get luxuries like this then . . .'

'No, we shan't.' Lizzie's smile dimmed and a shiver went down her spine. A lot of men were going to be killed trying to bring food to them here in England – and a lot more would be killed defending them and the country they loved. Something told her that the men flying flimsy aircraft would suffer some of the worst losses and the thought frightened her.

'Perhaps Hitler won't want to fight us when it comes to it – why should he? I don't see why we have to fight over foreign countries.'

'Because he's power-crazy and he knows we shan't let him ride roughshod over the rest of Europe if we can stop him . . .'

'Will we be able to stop him? Lizzie's eyes widened in fear and she shivered. What would happen to Harry once he started flying missions over Germany? Would he come through it all or would he be lost to her?

'Yes, of course we shall,' Harry told her confidently. 'Our planes are fast and our pilots are brave. Hitler won't know what's hit him if he dares to look our way.'

Harry was laughing, but Lizzie thought it bravado. She knew people had promised the last war with the Germans would be over in a few months and that had dragged on for years; the bloodiest, terrible conflict they'd ever known. It was supposed to be the war to end all wars, but another one had begun. She suspected it would be as bad in its way, if not worse than the last one.

'I'm frightened . . .'

'Come here,' Harry commanded and took her plate away. He drew her to him, wrapping his strong arms around her. 'You're thinking too much, Lizzie. Wait and see what happens before you start fretting . . .'

'Yes.' She reached up for his kiss. 'I shouldn't cast shadows, not while you're here – not while I have you home. We'll be all right, it will work out somehow. I know it's all going to be fine.'

'Of course it will,' Harry said and kissed her full on the lips. 'I love you, Lizzie. You're mine and I'm not going to give you up that easily . . .'

CHAPTER 25

Lizzie felt miserable after Harry left. She mooched about the flat for a couple of days and then started making her special hats. It stopped her feeling sorry for herself and took her mind off her loneliness. Even Beth's letters, which came regularly twice a week and were full of her news, only helped for a short time. She was bored and a little resentful. Harry was enjoying his life in the RAF, because it was what he'd wanted, but she hated him being away and she was terrified that she would lose him – that one of these days he wouldn't come back to her.

It was a week after Harry left her that she was called to the showroom and told that she was needed urgently. Lizzie discovered that Sebastian Winters had brought two ladies with him; Wendy, a girl she'd seen at his party and an older lady Lizzie guessed was her mother because they looked a little alike, both with the same soft brown hair.

'Oh, it is the right place,' Wendy said in a gush and looked relieved. 'Mother wasn't sure, because this is more a wholesale area . . . at least it looks . . .' the girl broke off, a flush in her cheeks.

She glanced around, as if slightly embarrassed. 'You have some lovely hats here . . . Oh, I love that pink straw with all the tulle and the rose.'

'Mrs Harrison, this is Lizzie – Lizzie, this young lady is desperate for something different and I assured her she would find it here.' Sebastian shook hands with Wendy's mother. 'I shall leave you in Lizzie's capable hands – and I'll return to speak with you later, Lizzie.' He smiled at each of them and then went out.

'Mrs Oliver?' the older woman offered her hand to Lizzie. She took it and smiled as she felt the firm no-nonsense handshake. 'Good, I'm glad we've found you. Wendy adored your hat the other week at the party and has talked of nothing else since. Now, we shall need at least a dozen hats for Wendy and I would like a special hat for the wedding – though there are others I think I might like to purchase from your shelves. They are all for sale?'

'Yes, Mrs Harrison. Please feel free to try on what you wish.'

Lizzie saw that Wendy had already snatched off her own hat and was busy trying on the pink straw she'd seen from across the room in front of one of the wall mirrors Lizzie had persuaded Uncle Bertie to invest in, and her mother had taken a red felt with a black ribbon and a curling feather from the stands and was trying it on in front of the full-length mirror. It suited her well, but the pink hat was very big on Wendy and she saw doubt in the girl's eyes, but she'd already anticipated something of the sort and was carrying a smaller version of the hat.

'That one is a little over the top for you,' Lizzie said, offering the alternative, which was just that bit smaller but even prettier because the net veiling was very fine and the pale pinky-mauve rose set it off to advantage. 'Try it and see, Miss Harrison.'

Wendy took off the larger hat, handing it to Lizzie, trying the smaller one in front of the mirror. She gave a cry of delight at the way it set off her quiet beauty and turned towards them, her face glowing.

'Isn't she clever, Mama?' she cried. 'It looks as if it were made for me.'

'As a matter of fact it was,' Lizzie said. 'I had you in mind when I trimmed it. I was hoping you would come.'

'It is quite remarkable,' Mrs Harrison said and smiled. 'You may put that one aside for my daughter. Why don't you two talk about other hats you think suitable while I browse.'

'Would you like to come into the workroom?' Lizzie asked hesitantly. 'I could show you some designs I've been working on, also trimmings and ribbons . . . and then we'll discuss colours and go on from there . . .'

'Oh, yes, please. Please reserve this hat for me and I'd like to try the white straw when we come back . . .'

Almost two hours later, Lizzie's first bespoke

customers left carrying four hatboxes and she had a firm order for another eight hats, one for Mrs Harrison and the other seven for Wendy. She would be busy day and night for the next week. Luckily, she had all the materials and trimmings in stock, and she blessed Uncle Bertie for buying in enough of the basic stuffs. Both Wendy and her mother had chosen mostly conventional shapes with different trimmings, but though the cone shapes had amused them, Wendy didn't buy one. However, she did love the way Lizzie had shaped the brims of other models so that they had the look of a buccaneer's hat, softened by ribbons or the occasional cute feather.

'I haven't seen this style anywhere else,' she said, and ordered a cream version with a brown feather and a red version with a black feather and ribbon. 'I've bought most of my clothes but I wasn't happy with the hats the shops showed me – but yours are so well finished.'

Lizzie started on Wendy's hats immediately and worked steadily all day. Just as she was thinking of leaving that evening, she was called into the showroom. Sebastian had returned as promised. The intimate smile he gave her made her breath catch and she recalled how jealous Harry had been over his garden party.

'Mr Winters,' she said uncertainly. 'How are you?'

'Very well, thank you, Lizzie,' he said, an amused look in his eyes. 'I hope you got a decent order from Wendy and her mother?'

'Yes, they seemed delighted, even with the prices we charged. I can hardly believe that customers like that are prepared to come all this way just for a few hats . . .'

'Don't you believe it,' he said, looking at the neat price tags. 'Even at the prices we agreed, they are less than they would pay in some of the top West End milliners. Besides, you have something special, Lizzie Larch. I've told you that before . . .'

'Mr Oliver is giving me more freedom to design as I please now, which I know is because you asked him to . . .' she said with a little frown, because it still rankled slightly that Bert had only agreed because of Sebastian's request.

'So he should. You're wasted here, Lizzie, though the training you received was invaluable. If things don't go quite as you hope you could come to me – we could still launch your exclusive line through my shop in the West End.'

'I'm sorry, but I couldn't leave my job here,' she said. 'I like what I'm doing – but I am grateful for all you've done to help me, and I hope we can be friends?'

'Friendship?' he said and smiled oddly. 'Well, I'll take what you're offering, even though it's not what I want. As far as my order for the shop goes, I'd like the large pink hat and the black and green cone . . . not the one your friend wore to my party, the more substantial one. I'd also like that white one with the tulle and the black rose.'

'Thank you,' Lizzie said. She brought out some

hatboxes from under the counter, wrapping her creations tenderly in tissue before placing them in the boxes. Sebastian Winters had his wallet out and paid her in cash and she handed him his receipt. 'I hope you sell the hats well.'

'I expect I shall,' he said, 'but the cone is just for a talking point really. I'm going to make it a part of a fantasy display in my window. Your hat gave me a great idea of my own, Lizzie. I'll come again soon – and I'll want mainly the big hats you make so stylish.'

'Thank you . . .' she felt an odd pang of regret as he turned away from her.

Lizzie went back to the showrooms after he'd left. Why did Sebastian Winters keep coming back to make her offers? He'd vowed he wouldn't, but it almost seemed as if he couldn't stay away.

Uncle Bertie was hesitant as she showed him a new design. He studied it for several minutes, and then nodded.

'You'll need Ed to help you cut that one,' he said. 'Even I'm not certain how you're going to shape that brim, Lizzie. Are you sure it will sell?'

'I think Mr Winters will love it,' she told him and he shrugged.

'Well, it's up to you, but Ed has a lot do this month – and Vera is working flat out on the Government orders. Ed is going to have to divide his time between you. But if you think it's the way to go . . .'

'We need to come up with something different if we want our bespoke customers coming in regularly for their hats.'

'Get on with it then. No time to waste in talking.'

Lizzie sighed, because it seemed as if there was no pleasing him, even when she finished the hats for Wendy by the end of the week. Sometimes she wondered what might have happened if she'd accepted Sebastian's offer to work for him, but she was Harry's wife and though things would never be quite as she'd hoped at the start, there was no going back.

CHAPTER 26

Beth sighed and eased her aching back. She'd been working a twelve-hour shift and she was so tired. All she wanted to do was to go home and relax in a warm bath . . . if there was any warm water left at the Nurses' Home.

Living in the official accommodation was all right. Beth got on with most of the other girls and she didn't mind sharing her room with Rose Brown, but there was never enough hot water for everyone. It was pot luck, and you could never be sure if you would manage to get enough for a bath. No one was supposed to fill the bath above a certain line, but some of the girls broke the rules, caring only for their own comfort. Beth had done it herself before now, but sometimes she wished she could live somewhere that had running hot water all the time.

She was reflective as she walked through the dark streets, pulling her coat collar up around her neck and shivering because the weather had turned bitter. It would soon be Christmas and Beth wasn't sure if she would get home for leave on the day. She hadn't taken home leave yet, content to stay

245

in Cambridge and go out with friends. Several weeks had passed since she'd got Mark's last letter, and like every other girl with a boyfriend in the forces, she was starting to worry.

It was so different here in Cambridge from the grime and bustle of the East End of London. There were lots of nice shops, green spaces, cinemas and cafés to visit, as well as the magnificent colleges, and also the river, although she hadn't been on the punts yet because the weather had turned cold by the time she'd arrived in Cambridge. Most of her life revolved around the hard and very menial work she was required to do at the hospital and the studies that took up most of her evenings. Learning to be a nurse was turning out to be exhausting.

'Beth . . . is it you?' the man's voice made her jump, but she turned round in delight to see Mark before her. It was more than two months since she'd seen him, though he'd written to her several times. 'The other girls told me you would have finished your shift at the hospital and be home about now. So I waited here rather than come round and miss you . . .'

'Oh, Mark, it's so lovely to see you,' Beth said and let him draw her close and kiss her. 'I'm filthy after a hard day's work. I was just hoping I could get a bath, but the water will probably be cold.'

'Don't bother about a bath,' he said. 'You can come back to my hotel. I've got a bath of my own and lashings of hot water.'

'Lucky you,' Beth said and kissed him. 'I shall need some clean clothes . . .'

'You can nip in and grab them,' he said, 'but I came to tell you I'll be away for months after this leave so we have to make the most of tonight and the next couple of days . . .'

'All right,' Beth said and laughed, catching his urgency. 'Don't move an inch. I'll be back before you know it . . .'

Mark promised he wouldn't even breathe, and Beth was feeling excited and thrilled as she hurried to collect some clothes from her room. She thrust them into a large shopping bag and ran back to Mark, ignoring one of the other nursing students when she called to her.

'I adore you, Beth,' Mark said. 'I've been thinking about this for weeks, planning what we'd do and where we'd go – do you think you could get a couple of days off?'

'It's difficult because I would miss lectures,' Beth said, 'but I'll try. Perhaps one of the girls would let me copy her notes . . .'

'You mustn't miss important lectures,' Mark said. 'I'll be waiting for you each night and we'll spend as much time as we can together.'

'Yes, we will,' she promised. 'It was such a lovely surprise you being there this evening, Mark. I was feeling fed up and lonely, and now you're here . . .'

Relaxing in a bath of hot water scented with pleasant-smelling crystals, Beth felt her tiredness seep away. She'd ached all over, but the prospect of being with Mark soon had her out of the bath and dressed in the skirt and jumper she'd hurriedly grabbed from her room at the nurse's home. The rules said that she had to be in by eleven in the evening, unless she was working, but in reality no one checked and some of the girls ignored what they thought of as an outdated stricture.

Beth knew she dare not have done this if she were still living at home, because her parents would have been up in arms if they'd known she was planning on spending most of the night with a man she hardly knew – except that Beth felt she'd known Mark all her life. It was true they'd only met and gone out together a handful of times, but she felt she'd got to know the real Mark through his letters. He might come from another class to Beth, but underneath he was a warm, loving man and she knew he liked her a lot; he might even love her, as she was almost certain she loved him. She'd thought she loved Tony only a few months previously, but after their quarrel she'd put him out of her mind; she was with Mark now and his letters were loving and caring, giving her something to look forward to after a hard day on the wards.

Dressed in her comfortable clothes, she emerged from the bathroom and discovered that Mark had had a meal delivered to the room.

'I thought it would be nice to be alone for a while,' he said as she stared at the array of dishes set out on a trolley. 'You don't mind, do you?'

'This is lovely,' Beth said, taking in the tempting green salad and the variety of seafood; prawns and something else in a pink dressing, and white rice with hardboiled egg in it. 'I've never had food like this, Mark. What is in the pink sauce?'

'Lobster tails . . . I recall you liked it at Sebastian's party.'

'Oh yes, it was wonderful – but how on earth did you get it these days?'

'Well, this hotel prides itself on providing good food,' he said. 'At the moment, they're having difficulty in getting hold of enough decent meat, but they had a delivery of fresh seafood today and I grabbed our order before they ran out. The manager told me they only had enough to serve the first ten people that asked. I hope there's something you like, Beth?'

'To be honest I've never had much of this sort of stuff,' Beth said. 'Dad eats cockles and whelks when he gets the chance, but Mum never cared for seafood. But the salad and rice look wonderful – and I'm dying to try the rest.'

'Here, help yourself,' Mark said, offering her a plate and looking anxious.

Beth took some of the delicious-looking rice and the salad and then the tiniest amount of seafood in pink dressing. She forked a minute piece into her mouth and tasted and a smile broke out.

'Oh, that is delicious,' she said. 'I should like some more of that . . .'

'You can have it all, because I don't eat it; I got

249

it just for you,' Mark said but she laughed and shook her head.

'You spoil me . . .' She took two large spoonsful, whilst Mark helped himself to the salads and rice. 'I shan't want to go back to the hospital canteen fare of watery mash and soggy chicken pie.'

'That sounds even worse than the food they serve us in our canteen. They say the menu on the ships is better than we get at the base, but I've yet to experience it . . .'

Beth paused with a forkful of food halfway to her mouth. 'You haven't been to sea yet?'

'Only for training and coastal work . . .' Mark told her, before adding, 'I'm on the Atlantic run after this leave, Beth.'

'Oh, Mark . . .' Beth had been sipping the delicious wine he'd ordered. 'That's so dangerous . . .'

'Yes, but it has to be done . . .'

They looked at each other in silence, because ships on that run were being sunk by German U-boats; the Germans believed that if they could stop food getting through to Britain they could starve the people into submission without a prolonged war and were concentrating all their efforts on the merchant ships for the moment.

Tears caught at her throat, because everyone knew how the ships on the Atlantic run were suffering, and now that Mark was one of the men risking his life to bring supplies to Britain, she was even more aware of the danger.

'I didn't order a pudding,' Mark said, 'but if you wanted we could ring down and they'll bring it up.'

'I shan't need it after this . . .' Beth said, relishing the delicious food

Between them they cleared all the dishes and Mark patted his stomach in content. 'I was looking forward to a decent meal on leave, which is why I chose this place. Come here, Beth . . .' He patted the side of the bed where he'd perched to eat, leaving Beth the comfort of the single armchair. 'Sit here and talk to me, tell me how you're getting on . . . Are you enjoying your nursing?'

'At the moment I'm just skivvying,' she said mournfully. 'I enjoy the lectures and helping with the patients, but we VADs don't get much of that – it's all bedpans and scrubbing.'

'Poor Beth,' Mark said and put his arms about her. She turned to face him and her heart did a giddy somersault as she saw the look in his eyes. 'This damned war. I love you. You must know that, Beth?'

'I've felt it reading your letters,' she said her voice no more than a whisper. Although she hadn't spent much time with him, his warm and wonderful letters had made her realise how very much she liked him. No, her feelings went deeper and were much stronger than mere liking. 'I love you too . . .'

Mark pulled her closer, kissing her first on the lips and then her throat, her earlobes and nose. 'I think of you all the time, Beth,' he said. 'Look,

251

why don't we get married while I'm here? I could get a special licence . . .'

'I'm not old enough,' Beth said regretfully. 'I wish I could, Mark – but my father wouldn't consent, even if you asked him . . .'

'Hell . . .' Mark ran his fingers through his thick hair. 'I thought if we could have a quick wedding . . . I dream of us being together, Beth – you know . . .'

Beth nodded, his tone of voice and the look in his eyes arousing feelings inside her. Suddenly, she knew that she couldn't bear to lose him as she'd lost Tony. She pressed closer, initiating their kiss which was unlike any other kiss she'd ever known and in a reckless mood, said, 'We don't have to be married, Mark. We can be careful. You may be away ages and . . .'

Mark looked down at her in concern. 'Supposing something happened, Beth? Supposing I couldn't get back . . .'

'Don't – please don't,' she whispered. 'I love you and you love me – we can't think about anything else. Making babies isn't that easy. I know of women who have tried for years . . .'

'Oh, Beth my darling,' he said and drew her tight against him. 'I do love you so very much . . .'

'I love you . . .'

'I want you so much,' Mark said against her hair, his hand stroking her thigh over her skirt. 'It wouldn't be fair to you, Beth, but I wish . . .'

'Why shouldn't we?' Beth said, her need making

her speak her thoughts aloud. 'We love each other and we shall marry one day, shan't we?'

'Of course we shall. You're the only one for me, Beth. Whatever happens, I shall never marry anyone else.'

'Then love me. I want you to, Mark. We can be careful – I've heard that there are ways . . .'

'Yes,' he said doubtfully. 'I could pull away at the last, but that isn't always fail-safe. I didn't bring anything – I never thought you would want to before we marry.'

'Does it make you think ill of me? It was just that you're leaving . . .' she said, looking worried. 'I'm not easy, Mark . . .'

'I know that,' he said and stood up, pulling her hard against him. 'I want this more than you'll ever know and I'll still love and want to marry you – but you have to be sure, just in case . . .'

'It can't happen the first time,' Beth said. 'Not if we're careful . . .'

'If anything happens let me know. I'll get leave and marry you as soon as I get back . . .'

'I love you,' she whispered. 'If you love me nothing else matters.'

Mark kissed her so sweetly that the last of Beth's doubts fled. She wanted to experience the fullness of love before he left, to know they belonged to each other – perhaps then she could be sure he would come back to her.

In that moment Beth didn't care if she did fall for a baby. All she wanted was to show Mark how much she cared so he would take the memory with him and never forget her.

Of course it wasn't just once, because once could never be enough for either of them. Beth wasn't going to worry about what she'd done yet. Their loving was tender and sweet and she felt truly loved, cherished and wanted. She knew she ought to call a halt but she couldn't bring herself to leave the warmth of their bed; it was just so lovely to be held close and stroked. Mark's hands were so gentle and they made her shiver with delight when he touched and caressed her. His kisses thrilled her, and when he reached for her again she went to him willing and eager. Several times they loved, dozed, talked of getting up and then made love again. Beth never wanted to leave him.

In the end she slept and it was getting light when a knock at the door woke her. Mark was up and dressed and he brought a tray of tea to the bed. She sat up, only now aware of her nakedness and slightly embarrassed to remember their night of unbridled passion.

'We must have fallen asleep,' she said, slightly shocked to realise she'd spent the whole night in his hotel room.

'Don't mind me looking at you,' he said. 'You're beautiful, Beth, and you are mine – and I was the first. I shall never forget that and I promise I'll marry you as soon as I get a long enough leave to come back . . .'

'My father might not allow it . . .' Beth glanced at her watch and shot out of bed. 'I'm on duty in just over an hour. I have to get back and change into my uniform or Sister will murder me . . .'

'Drink your tea and I'll order a taxi . . .'

'That's so wasteful,' Beth said. 'I can walk it in half an hour.'

'You're already in trouble for being out all night,' Mark said ruefully and kissed her. 'Get dressed quickly and I'll take you back in my car . . .'

CHAPTER 27

Wendy and her mother came on the Tuesday of that week to collect and pay for the hats they'd ordered, and they both bought another simple straw hat from the collection Lizzie had taken through to the show-room just that morning. They lingered for a while, talking about Wendy's wedding, which was now imminent, and Lizzie began to understand what Uncle Bertie had meant when he said selling to the public was time-consuming. At last the two ladies took their leave and she was just preparing to return to the workroom when the door opened. She turned and saw that it was Mabel Hennessy, looking very smart in a black suit with a large straw hat.

'Hello,' she said. 'I didn't know you were coming today?'

'Oh, I didn't make an appointment, just popped in to see what you have new. I have to tell you that I'm very cross with you, Lizzie Larch. I've just seen some of the hats you made for Wendy and I'm jealous.'

'Since your last visit, I've been allowed to try

my wings a little – but most of Wendy's hats were fairly conventional, apart from the trimmings.'

'Well, I loved the hats you made for me and now I want something special.'

'Please try anything on you like,' Lizzie said. 'Of course, I can make the designs in different colours with different trimmings . . .'

'I love that black and green pointed hat in the window . . . May I try that please?'

'Yes, of course, if you wish – but I should tell you that it is really just a bit of fun for display. It was a first go at that idea and may be a bit flimsy . . . it probably wouldn't last long.'

'That hardly matters,' Mabel said airily. 'I don't want my hats to last forever; it would be so boring.'

Lizzie handed Mabel the hat and she tried it on in front of the mirrors. As soon as she put it on, Lizzie knew it was right. It had looked well on Beth but it was perfect for Mabel. She must have had her in mind when she was making it.

'How much is it?'

Lizzie hesitated. She could make something for Beth in a slightly different way and knew her friend wouldn't mind.

'If you're interested in buying other hats I will give you that one,' Lizzie said. 'I couldn't sell it because it may fray after you've worn it a couple of times . . .'

'Really? You will give it to me?' Mabel gave a cry of delight and hugged Lizzie impulsively. 'You are a darling. Of course I'll buy all my hats from you – they are a lot less than Sebastian charges for them. Now, there are two more in the window I want to try – and I love that yellow straw with the big wavy brim; it's so different. I want to try that red cone-shaped hat – and the black pillbox and that white felt with all the tulle . . . and then you can show me some of your designs. I want something exclusively for me . . .'

Lizzie brought her all the hats she'd asked for and there was soon a large pile of them on the counter, all of which Mabel declared she wanted to buy. When Lizzie showed her some of the designs she was working on, she went into raptures over two styles: the buccaneer felts, which were easy for Lizzie to shape and trim, and a new one which she was just trying to work out in her mind.

'I should like that one in brown, black and red,' Mabel said, 'and this one is gorgeous in the colours you've shown . . . that sort of pinkish mauve with a soft brim over the face and that veiling.'

'I've just started to think about that one,' Lizzie told her. 'I can do have the felts ready in two days – but the other may take longer.'

'Will you make it for me by the end of next week? That's when we leave for America, you see, just after Wendy's wedding. My husband has a new appointment and we shall be away for months . . .'

'I shall do my best,' Lizzie promised, 'but if the style doesn't quite work I'll have a similar one in that colour ready for you.'

Mabel paid for the hats with a cheque. Lizzie hadn't been asked to take a cheque before but because she knew Mabel she accepted it.

After she'd gone, Lizzie returned to the workshop and showed Ed the large order she'd just taken and the cheque. He nodded, but looked concerned as he worked on cutting the order he was preparing.

'Something wrong?'

'She came on her own without an appointment, you say?'

'I know what you're thinking, Ed. Customers for the bespoke hats are supposed to telephone first – but I think she's a law unto herself. She wouldn't think it necessary to make an appointment.'

'Well, she should. You mustn't encourage customers to call out of the blue, Lizzie. You'll get behind with your work when we're busy and you know what Oliver will have to say about that – and be careful about taking cheques, because sometimes they bounce . . . Our boss wouldn't be too happy then, Lizzie.'

Lizzie could imagine it, but it was done now and she didn't think they could afford to simply send customers away if they didn't have an appointment. If they wanted the bespoke service to be a success, they had to do whatever the ladies wanted . . .

She was pleased as she thought of Mabel's excitement over the witch's hat. It had really suited her and she could wear that sort of quirky hat. Of course, she had promised it to Beth, but she would

259

just have to make her something else – something in the same colours but more practical.

Sighing, Lizzie thought how much she missed her friend now that she was away in Cambridge. She had other friends but Beth had been more like family. She would make the hat for her at home and tell her about it in her next letter . . .

Beth came to see Lizzie at the weekend. She'd got an unexpected leave and had taken the chance to come home for a few days. Lizzie knew nothing about it until she answered her door at half past eight that night.

'Beth . . . you're home.'

'Yes, they gave me leave out of the blue, so I jumped on the train and came home for three days.'

'Why? You haven't done something awful and been given the push?'

'No, of course not,' Beth denied but Lizzie saw the faint flush in her cheeks. 'We're taking some preliminary tests next week and so they gave us a few days off to do some revision.'

'So you came home instead?'

'I can revise wherever I like,' Beth said. 'Are you going to invite me in or leave me to freeze out here?'

'Come in,' Lizzie said. 'Have you eaten? I can get you some toast and marmalade, but I haven't any eggs or bacon – or cheese either . . .'

'What do you live on, fresh air?'

'I ate it all earlier,' Lizzie explained as she led the way upstairs. 'I usually shop on Saturday and just buy bread for toast on my way home. Sometimes I eat with Madge and Ed – and I've been to lunch at Aunt Miriam's a few times at the weekends . . .'

'Aunt Miriam now is it?' Beth teased and then suddenly turned and hugged her. 'I've missed you so much, Lizzie . . .'

'What's wrong, Beth. I know something is, so tell me . . .'

'Mark came to see me in Cambridge – he's on the Atlantic run now,' Beth said in a choking voice. 'I've been reading about the attacks on that shipping . . . I don't think I could bear it if anything happened to him, Lizzie. I love him so much.'

'You hardly know him, Beth – and he's . . . well, his people are different from ours.'

'You can't help who you fall in love with,' Beth said and flung herself down in a chair. 'I thought I loved Tony – but I didn't know what love was. I was so naïve . . .'

'And now you're not?' Lizzie saw the faint flush in her friend's cheeks and fear clutched at her. Beth was different and she had an awful feeling she knew what had caused the difference. 'So are you going to marry him or what?'

'As soon as we can arrange it. Mark would have married me on his leave by special licence, but I'm not old enough . . .'

'Well, you knew what your parents would say,

don't you? If they wouldn't let you marry Tony until you were twenty . . .'

'I can't bear it,' Beth said and there was a sob in her voice. 'It seems like ages since he left and it's only been two weeks.'

'It's more than a month since Harry got a twenty-four-hour pass . . .'

'A month – but Mark may be away for years,' Beth said and her mouth trembled. 'I can't bear it, Lizzie. I know he'll forget all about me . . .' She flung herself down in a chair. 'What am I going to do?'

'You'll be able to write to him and he will write to you – but if he's away for months, well, you might have changed your mind by then . . .'

'No, I shan't. It was different with Tony. I didn't know anything then – Mark is so much more . . . oh, I don't know. He has more to say about things; he knows about history and politics and art – everything. We just sit and talk for ages, and he treats me as if I were bone china. When he kisses me I melt . . .'

'Beth, I'm so sorry. Really, I am, but everyone is in the same boat now. All the young men are signing up to one of the forces – and most of them will serve overseas. Mark will be safer in one of those huge ships.'

'Ships can sink,' Beth said gloomily. 'It's all right for you, you're married to Harry.'

'If Mark loves you he'll keep in touch somehow – and you will marry one day.'

'That's what he says. He says he'll buy me a ring but we have to keep it to ourselves for a while. He will speak to Dad on his next leave and then we'll get married . . .'

'What are you upset for then?'

'You know my father,' Beth's gloom increased. 'He'll make me wait for years . . .'

Lizzie nodded, feeling sympathy for her. 'I know you feel unsure now, Beth, but if you love each other it will work out. Look, I made this hat for you instead of the witch's hat . . .' She produced a beautiful straw boater in fine green straw trimmed with black lace and an exotic flower.

Beth pounced on it with glee, trying it on in front of the mirror and exclaiming, 'I like it more. It really suits me. Did you sell the other one?'

'Well, sort of. Mabel Hennessy – well, Carmichael now. She wanted it and she bought several others. I know I said it was yours, but I thought you wouldn't mind?'

'No, of course not. I'd rather have this, because I can wear it more often . . .' Beth turned and hugged her. 'Mum said to ask you to lunch on Sunday. She misses seeing you now that you're so busy.'

'Tell her I'd love to,' Lizzie said. 'And now I'm going to make us both a lovely hot cup of cocoa . . .'

CHAPTER 28

Lizzie was just tidying the showroom when Sebastian Winters entered that morning. He was carrying a single pink rose, which he placed on the counter.

'I saw this lovely thing and thought of you, Lizzie Larch – and then I decided to see what you have new in stock . . .'

'Well, there are these . . .' Lizzie said, her cheeks heating a little at the exquisite compliment, and directed him to a display of large hats with extravagantly shaped brims, trimmed in various ways, either simply with an exotic flower or with masses of veiling, and one rather striking emerald hat with a long wide black ribbon draped round the brim that finished in tassels and would bounce when the wearer walked. She tried the emerald hat on and turned her head so that he could see the effect.

'That one is fun,' he said and smiled with his eyes. 'How much is it?'

'I'm afraid it is three pounds . . . expensive, I know.'

'Very expensive, but I love it: in fact, I should like to take the complete collection – all . . . five, six, no, eight – unless there's any more?'

'No, I had ten similar hats; the wavy brim has turned out to be popular. I sold two the first day I put them out.'

'I'm not surprised. I'll give you my cheque now – if you trust me?'

'Yes, I think I can trust you to honour it,' Lizzie said and smiled.

She packed his hats carefully, took his cheque and thanked him for the custom.

'Oliver should have some labels printed with your name on,' he said as he prepared to leave. 'Lizzie Larch Hats . . . it sounds good and would make them even more exclusive.' Lizzie hesitated, because Uncle Bertie had promised he would see to it, but so far she hadn't heard anything more about it.

'I'm not sure . . . where would I get something like that done?'

He took out one of his personal cards and wrote a name on the back, handing it to her. Lizzie placed it in her pocket. She would have to speak to her employer about keeping his word.

'Thank you. I'll talk to Mr Oliver.'

'Well, if he lets you down, you know where to come . . .' he said and grinned at her, then picked up his purchases and started towards the door; there he paused and glanced back at her, a twinkle in his eyes. 'Remember where I live, Lizzie – my door is always open to you.'

'I think you are an incorrigible flirt, Mr Winters – and I'm Lizzie Oliver now.'

'You'll always be Lizzie Larch to me.'

'You're being foolish . . .' she said accusingly.

'What I am is stubborn. I never give up on something I want.'

Lizzie saw the gleam in his eyes and decided not to answer. He was most definitely flirting and she ought not to flirt back. 'Thank you for your order, Mr Winters.'

He nodded, looking thoughtful, then, 'I may not get in myself for a while. If I send my manager along, will you make sure he sees all the new stuff?'

'Are you going away?' Lizzie experienced an odd pang of regret, but she smothered it almost at once. She had no right to feel a sense of loss. Sebastian was a customer, nothing more.

'Yes, I think I may be, for quite a long time.' Suddenly, his eyes sparkled with mischief. 'Will you miss me, Lizzie Larch?'

'What about your shop?'

'Oh, that will carry on, I hope.' He looked rueful. 'Everyone has to make a few sacrifices. I dare say the shop will survive until it's over; if any of us does . . .'

Lizzie's heart caught at his words. She couldn't think of anything to say, because she felt shivery all over. The finality in Sebastian's words as he closed the door was frightening. She picked up the rose he'd brought her and sniffed it, wondering at the gorgeous perfume and why Sebastian had bought her such a thing.

She was about to go into the workroom when

the shop door opened again and a young lad wearing a dark uniform entered. She realised he was delivering a telegram and her heart caught with fright as he held it out to her.

'Telegram for Mrs Harry Oliver,' he said. 'Does she work here?'

'That's me . . .' Lizzie said, feeling breathless, almost too afraid to take it from him. 'What is it?'

'It's all right, missus,' he grinned cheerfully. 'It's a greeting telegram not one of them others . . .'

'Oh . . . that's all right then.' She took it and tore the envelope open, reading the brief message. Harry would be home that evening; he had six days' leave.

'Any reply, missus?'

'No, thank you. It's wonderful news; my husband is coming home on leave.' She saw his hopeful look and took sixpence from the purse in her pocket. 'Here you are. Thank you for bringing me good news.'

Harry was coming home for a long leave and Lizzie was aware of mixed feelings. She wanted to see him, felt lonely when he was away for long periods, but what had happened on their honeymoon had somehow spoiled things for her and she knew that even though they were lovers again. things would never be quite the same.

Going through to the workroom, she saw that Uncle Bertie was standing at her workbench and looking very annoyed.

'Come into the office, Lizzie.'

She followed with a sinking heart, wondering what she'd done wrong. Her work was up to standard, wasn't it? And her orders were all on schedule.

'Have I done something wrong?'

'It's not you – but that customer of yours.' He picked up a small piece of paper marked with red ink. 'That woman's cheque bounced . . .'

'Oh no, I can't believe it . . .' Lizzie felt a sinking sensation inside. 'I was so sure she wouldn't let us down.'

'Well the bank says to get in touch with her if I want my money.'

'Oh . . .' Lizzie bit her lip. 'She and her husband have gone to America. I think they will be away for some months . . .'

He cursed and pondered over the cheque. 'Well, I'll send a letter to her address, but it looks like that's a loss – and no business can stand many of them, especially in times like these.'

'I'm sorry . . .' Lizzie produced the cheque Sebastian had just given her. 'This one is all right, isn't it?'

'Of course it is. Mr Winters is our best customer – especially since you started working here. I'm not blaming you, Lizzie, but let this be a lesson to you. Be careful who you take cheques from – and make sure account customers don't have a black mark against them in the book.'

'I'm sure Mabel didn't mean to let us down. Something must have gone wrong . . .'

He nodded, but she could see he was still annoyed. 'I am sorry . . .'

'Get on with your work. I don't want those orders to be late . . .'

Lizzie left the office without telling him the good news about Harry. He would be pleased when he knew, but for the moment he was too annoyed with her over that cheque. She returned to her work, shaking her head when Ed looked at her. He had warned her about the consequences and she felt too much of a fool to talk about it.

Instead, she concentrated on the design she was creating, making a mental note to go shopping before she went home. She must try to get some decent pork chops for Harry's supper and whatever else she could find in shops that had less and less to offer. It meant queuing for ages, because wherever you looked these days there were long queues outside the shops, and as soon as any fresh produce came in it was snapped up by eager customers . . .

'It's so wonderful to be back,' Harry said later that evening after they'd eaten their meal. 'We've been training so hard, Lizzie. I was beginning to think I should never get leave again.'

'And now you have six days – it's the best leave you've had since you started.'

'I know,' he said and kissed her hard on the lips. 'Come to bed, darling. I've missed you so much, my love.'

'I've missed you too,' she said and went into his arms. 'It's lonely when you're not here . . .'

It was some time later that they lay side by side in bed, their bodies sweat-slicked and satiated, brought close by the sweetness of their loving.

'Lizzie, can you get a few days off?' Harry asked as he trailed his fingers down her spine. 'I would like to go away, to the country for a while, so that we can be together every minute.'

'I would have to ask your uncle,' Lizzie said doubtfully. 'I've no special orders to make at the moment, but . . .'

'I'll go and telephone him now,' Harry said and reached for his jacket. 'Have you got any change for the phone box, Lizzie?'

'In my purse on the sideboard,' Lizzie said, carrying the dirty plates through to the kitchen. 'Take what you want . . .'

'I'll be back in a few minutes,' Harry called from the sitting room. 'You can pack some things for us as soon as you've done that because I'm not taking no for an answer . . .'

Lizzie washed the plates and put everything away and then went into the bedroom and got out the small cardboard case she'd bought for her honeymoon. She packed a warm skirt and two jumpers, underwear, also her prettiest dress and a couple of cardigans. Then she took some of Harry's shirts and slacks from the wardrobe. She added socks and underwear and was about to add sponge bags and towels when he walked back into the bedroom.

'What did he say?'

'He didn't like it much, but he gave in when I told him a few things . . .'

'What things?' Lizzie asked, feeling anxious.

'Nothing important . . .'

'I know Uncle Bertie; he wouldn't give in unless you had a good reason.'

'I told him what I've been doing and when he understood he said it was all right.'

'Harry, please tell me.'

'Well, I've been flying missions over Germany, taking low-level pictures of factories, ships, troop movements – and sometimes we get shot at, either while we're there or on the way back . . .'

Lizzie swallowed hard. It was dangerous work and it brought home to her that her husband could die on one of the missions, making regret and fear surge through her.

'Oh, Harry,' she said and slipped her arms about his waist. 'I thought you were still training . . .'

'Yes, I am but they're so short of trained observers that I've been training on the job, rather like nurses that train on the wards. It's not as if I'm flying the damned kite. They've put me in the Observer corps, Lizzie – it's what this badge is for.' He pointed to an unusual badge with a circle in gold braid and one wing. 'To be honest, they lost three observers in one week, so I sort of got thrown in at the deep end, but it turns out I'm rather good at it . . .'

'I thought you were a navigator?'

'It's what I do on the way there and back,' Harry gave her a lopsided grin, 'but then I have to get the pictures they need, and my pilot takes us in damned low. Not many of them are as good at it as Robbie is – but we have a high risk of being shot down in the flak once they know we're about . . .'

'I wish you didn't have to do such dangerous work . . .'

'It's war, Lizzie,' he said. 'Forget it. I'm on leave now and I want us to have a good time . . .'

Lizzie thought she noticed a change in his manner, he seemed less happy to be home than he had at first and she thought there was a new coldness in his manner, but she couldn't see any reason for it and thought it was probably just in her mind – because she couldn't forget the way he'd behaved on their honeymoon . . .

The days of Harry's leave went quickly and Lizzie sensed a reserve in him even when they were having fun, walking down leafy country lanes, sitting by the fire in country inns and lying in bed. The only time that Harry really seemed to come to life was when he made love to her and he did so with an urgent passion that did not always leave her feeling either happy or satisfied. Harry seemed in a hurry, on edge, nervous, springing up for a cigarette as soon as it was over.

Lizzie had hoped that as time passed they would talk more, get to know one another properly, find common ground to meet, but instead, she felt that Harry was drawing away from her. The sex was still good between them, but she sometimes felt that was all it was – just sex without love or tenderness, as if he were putting his mark of ownership on her. Or perhaps the change was in her, because there was a tiny part of her that couldn't forgive the way he'd acted on their honeymoon.

'Is anything wrong?' she asked once when he got up and went to stand looking out at the night sky.

'Should there be? Is there anything you want to tell me?'

'Nothing I haven't already. I'm busy at work and I miss you – that's pretty much my life now, Harry. Beth came home for a couple of days. We went to the pictures once and I had lunch with her family. I see Madge and Tilly and that's about all . . .'

'No men?' Harry turned to look at her and she gasped as she saw accusation in his eyes. 'What about Sebastian Winters?'

'He comes to buy hats but you know that . . .'

'What was his card doing in your purse then?'

'Harry! You can't think . . .' she said, feeling hurt that he should be so suspicious. 'He wrote a phone number on it for me – a place where I could get labels to sew into my special designs. Your uncle promised I should have my own label but he's never done anything about it . . .' She moved towards him. 'Surely you must know I wouldn't . . . Harry, I love you. I thought you loved me?'

'Of course I do . . .' Harry stepped towards her, pulling her into his arms. 'I'm a jealous idiot, Lizzie. I'm sorry, really sorry. It's just that when I'm away, I can't help wondering if you're with someone else . . .'

'I wouldn't,' Lizzie said desperate to make him believe her. 'I would never cheat on you . . .'

'Forgive me – it's just being away and the pressure of what we're doing . . .'

'Yes, it must be awful for you.'

'Worse for the chaps who go home and find their wives in bed with other men,' Harry said, and there was a look of desolation in his eyes. 'If it happened to me – I wouldn't want to live . . .'

'Harry, no! Don't say that,' Lizzie cried. 'I love you – you know I do . . .'

And yet even as she said it, she wondered. His moods and suspicion hurt her and little by little she was becoming more resentful and each time he hurt her she withdrew a little.

'I'm sorry,' he apologised. 'I'm being ridiculous. Take no notice, Lizzie. A lot of the chaps in my unit are morbid – it's because we know the odds are against us.'

'Couldn't you ask for a transfer?'

'No!' His voice was sharp. 'I'm not a coward, Lizzie . . .'

'Of course you're not . . .' He swung away from her and she watched as he dressed. 'Are you going out?'

'I need a walk in the fresh air.'

'It's bitterly cold out . . .'

'Go back to bed, Lizzie – and forget everything I said. I'm just a fool . . .'

Lizzie went back to bed after he'd gone but it was a long time before she slept. She must have fallen into an uneasy dose though, because when she woke Harry was shaking her shoulder.

'Wake up, Lizzie. It's just a dream. I'm here, my love. You're all right.'

Lizzie was aware that she was shivering, trembling in his arms. She'd been dreaming, a dream so vivid and dreadful that it had made her call out.

'I was dreaming . . .' she said. 'I could hear his footsteps and then his hand was on my shoulder, pulling me down. I could smell his foul breath and then . . .'

'Then what happened, Lizzie? Have you remembered?'

'The dream always ends there.' Lizzie looked at him with tears on her cheeks. 'I don't remember anything but the dream reflects what my aunt told me.'

'It's probably best you don't remember,' he said and drew her against him, holding her close. 'It's my fault for doubting you, telling you about the missions. I never meant to upset you.'

'If you're in danger and under pressure you should be able to tell me. I'm your wife. We should share everything. I do love you. I know you were hurt because of . . .' She got no further because Harry kissed her hard on the lips.

Afterwards, he drew back and looked at her. 'I'm sorry I'm a jealous idiot, but it's because I love you. I wanted you to be perfect that first time – but it wasn't your fault, Lizzie darling. I have accepted it and I want you to forgive me for hurting you. I didn't know you had these dreams . . .'

'I don't have them often,' she said. 'I haven't had one for ages . . .'

'Let's forget about it and enjoy ourselves,' Harry said and kissed her again, softly and with tenderness. 'I shan't get a decent leave again for ages so we mustn't spoil what we have.'

'No, we mustn't,' Lizzie said. 'Please don't stop loving me . . .'

'Hey, no more tears,' he said and wiped her cheeks with his fingertips. 'I'm the one who should be saying that – I'm just a stupid man who doesn't know how lucky he is . . .'

CHAPTER 29

'You must miss Harry now that he's gone back to his base,' Tilly said to Lizzie that morning as they stopped for their morning tea. 'With the way things are going it's such a worry for all our men. I know we haven't felt the effects of it much here yet, apart from some shortages – but the Merchant Navy is catching it out on the Atlantic and the RAF must be involved in all that stuff.'

'Yes, of course I worry about him. Doesn't every woman with a husband, brother or son in the forces?' Lizzie didn't tell Tilly about what Harry had said about low flying over German factories and aerodromes. Harry wasn't supposed to talk about what he was doing and they were always being warned of spies . . . *careless talk risks lives* was a popular slogan. The posters were on walls everywhere, just as there were the posters exhorting women to work.

Lizzie mustn't even tell her best friends how worried she was that he might be shot down on a routine sortie over the German coast. In those light planes with no firepower as protection, the pilots and crew were in danger every time they flew across the Channel. Lizzie could only pray that her new telephone wouldn't ring with bad news.

Harry had had the phone put in for her while they were on holiday, telling her that he wanted to be able to keep in touch even if he couldn't visit as often as he liked in future.

'I shan't feel so cut off from you if you're connected,' he'd told her. 'I should hate to think of you alone at the flat if anything were to happen – I mean you might be pregnant. If you have fallen for a child and I'm not around, you could ring Uncle Bertie and he would send Aunt Miriam to visit you; she's very good with babies . . . she delivered me because the midwife was late.'

'Then I'll be sure to ring her if it happens, but we don't even know if it has happened yet.'

'Well, we haven't been bothering to take precautions,' Harry said. 'I want to be a father, naturally, but like the selfish man I am, I hope it won't be yet because I shall miss all his first times – his first steps . . .'

'I don't see why it should happen yet,' Lizzie said. 'I would rather not be pregnant just yet, because I want to get the bespoke line up and running first.'

Lizzie didn't think it was likely. After all, they'd only been married a few months and Harry hadn't been home that often – besides, Lizzie was young and she wasn't sure she was ready.

She'd had a faint warning tummy ache that morning. If her guess was right, she would start her monthlies in a few hours . . .

'I know several women with sons or fathers in the army,' Tilly was saying. 'I know they're all worried to death – but what I was trying to say was if you're in bother, Lizzie . . . well, you can come to us. We're grateful that you asked Harry to teach my husband . . .'

'Gossiping again?' Mr Oliver glared at Tilly. 'You're not irreplaceable, girl. Get on with your work and let Lizzie get on with hers . . .'

'I swear I'll go down the munitions factory one of these days,' Tilly muttered as Lizzie collected their mugs.

'It's a necessary job,' Lizzie said. 'I feel a bit guilty at times because I ought to do something worthwhile. Something to help now that the war is on . . .'

'You can't join the forces,' Tilly said. 'You're married and you'd be away when Harry came home, and he wouldn't like that . . .'

'No,' Lizzie agreed. 'Yet I feel I ought to find something . . .'

'I expect there are voluntary things you can do at night.'

'Yes. I'll speak to Mr Oliver and see if he's heard of anything. He usually knows what's going on . . .'

Lizzie took the chance to speak to her husband's uncle that evening. He nodded, looking thoughtful, then said, 'As a matter of fact, if you really want to help the war effort, I know of a canteen opening up and they need voluntary helpers two or three nights a week. Your Aunt Miriam is helping to run it – and she asked if I thought you might like to go along, Lizzie. It will be a sort of social place for servicemen on leave. The committee is hoping to get the use of a church hall, and if they do they can have music on the gramophone and perhaps a spot of dancing – or singing round the piano.'

'That sounds interesting, tell Aunt Miriam that I'd love to help her.'

'Right, she'll come round one of these days and have a chat to you,' he said, beaming at her. 'Now, Lizzie, I've got some news for you . . .'

Lizzie knew that look. 'What are you up to now?'

'I've got another Government contract to make hats, caps and berets for the forces,' he said. 'The ladies' services this time, and they want a bit of style about their hats. I shall be turning over a large part of my workrooms to the production, but I want to keep the bespoke hats going. That's where you come in . . .'

'A Government contract will keep you busy even if there is a turndown in trade for the usual stuff,' Lizzie said, appreciating his astute move. 'What do you want of me?'

'We obviously cannot produce anything like the quantity of hats we've been turning over once we start this extra work for the Government, but Ed told me he enjoyed making those special hats for you and I have to admit that the ones we had in stock sold well.'

'I was going to ask you if I could make some new designs,' Lizzie said, 'but you won't have time now.'

'I've talked this over with Ed and we've decided that we'll go for the more stylish hats during this period, Lizzie. I've stocked up on materials as much as I could, because I knew that government orders would be priority once a war started. As a government contractor I'll get all the material I need for their work, but buying for my own use may not be viable for a long; the time might come when the workers would be on short hours . . . So here's what I thought – I'll oversee the bread and butter stuff but Ed will work with you on your designs . . . and I'll give you five per cent of the profits we make, on top of your wage.'

'The profits on the bespoke hats? Not the Government contracts?'

'You think you're entitled to a share of the business?'

'No, I don't,' Lizzie said. 'I just wanted to be sure what you were offering me. I think it's very generous of you – but for how long will you be able to carry on with the special hats?'

'I have a stockroom full of materials and trimmings, and I've got more in the house ready to bring out when we need it,' Uncle Bertie said and grinned. 'I know how my father struggled to keep going when I was away in the Army in the last war. At the end he had to look for work elsewhere but he left it too late to get much of a contract. I've been putting every spare penny into stock for months.'

'I'm grateful for the five per cent on the profits from the special hats. It will make a big difference to us.'

'It's like this, Lizzie. Ed will probably leave if I don't let him work with you, and it keeps me ticking over until this war ends . . . God knows how long that will be. Besides, I promised Harry I would look out for you and this could be the start of a long working relationship. After all, you and he are all I have to come after me . . .'

Lizzie knew that Uncle Bertie had no one but Harry to hand his business over to when he died. He and Aunt Miriam had had two children, both girls, and both had died of diphtheria when they were still children. He was fond of Harry, and after the first shock of their marriage, he'd become fond of Lizzie too – and she of him.

'Then of course I am delighted to agree,' she told him and gave him a quick hug.

'I'm glad,' he told her gruffly. 'I'm not getting any younger, Lizzie. I could have done with Harry around, but I knew he'd go once the war started and at least he got his training done before the rush.'

'Yes,' Lizzie said. 'He told you he's in the Observer corps now?'

'Well, that's a responsible job. He always had a good eye for things – that's why he picked you,

Lizzie girl – and I'm going to need you. Some of my best girls have already gone to work in the factories.'

'Yes, I know, but I think Tilly will stay, because she doesn't fancy working there even though the money is good.'

'It goes against the grain to give up any of our basic work, but by catering for the better end of sales and conserving our stocks it should keep us going for a while – and you never know what I may be able to wangle. Once you're in with the right people you can sometimes get in on anything that's going cheap . . .'

'Uncle Bertie!' Lizzie cried. 'I think we shall do very well, because there will always be a woman looking for a pretty hat – and the shops won't have so many to sell once the materials become hard to find, will they?'

'No, that is the problem, not just for us but for everyone in the manufacturing and the retail business. Materials will soon be in short supply and overseas orders will be almost impossible to get.' He shook his head over it and then looked at her. 'What other styles do you want to introduce, Lizzie?'

'I need to sit down and draw a few shapes before I say – but I've been thinking that women are doing men's jobs now and I rather like the idea of them wearing men's styles. Some of the ladies I know are brave enough to wear them without much change, but if the shape were slightly softer at the front and then some could be trimmed to make them more feminine . . .'

Uncle Bertie nodded. 'Yes, I think you may be on to something, Lizzie. I saw a design for women's forces uniform the other day, and I noticed that styles were becoming less feminine. You work something out and I'll tell Ed to talk to you about the detail.'

After work that evening, Lizzie got out her sketch-book and let her imagination soar; the designs she created were magical and she knew that she'd moved on to a new level. These were the kind of hats that Sebastian admired and would want in his showroom – but he hadn't been in since that last time and she didn't want to show them to anyone else. Perhaps one day . . .

Coming out of her dream, Lizzie laughed and put some of the designs into her folder, leaving just four she wanted to show Ed, including a design for a woman's trilby and also a rather fetching bowler that was worn to the side of the head and adorned with a ribbon bow.

It was late and Lizzie put away her sketch pad. She had to get up for work in the morning, but at least for a while she'd forgotten the loneliness of knowing Harry wouldn't get another leave for ages. He'd been sent off somewhere for extra training on some new equipment and expected to be away some months.

'I shan't be able to get home for ages, perhaps

not until after Christmas,' he'd told her when he rang. 'Take care, Lizzie darling. I love you and I'll be in touch as much as I can.'

At least she was luckier than Beth, Lizzie thought just before she went to sleep. Beth had heard nothing from Mark Allen since he went off to sea. They could only keep their fingers crossed and hope all was well . . .

CHAPTER 30

Beth stared at her white face in the mirror. She was now three weeks late and her period still hadn't come. She couldn't believe that she could be so unlucky. Her own mother had told her that sometimes children didn't come for ages, and, until she became pregnant, Beth's elder sister had complained all the time that she hadn't fallen for a child although she'd been married several years – and Mark had tried to be careful . . .

It just wasn't fair! Beth knew that her parents would be disappointed in her and angry that she'd let them down, and in her heart she didn't blame them. It was just so stupid – if she was pregnant she would lose her job. She would have to return home in disgrace and the thought made Beth feel like curling into a ball and hiding herself away. She knew Mark was at sea and that his job was dangerous – supposing he didn't get back . . .

Beth's spine crawled with fear. A wave of shame and remorse swept over her as she remembered that she'd initiated their lovemaking. Had Mark thought she was cheap and easy because she'd given herself to him so willingly? Her flesh cringed at the thought and she thought she might die of the shame, but then she remembered what he'd said to her about her being the only one and that he loved her and wanted to marry her. Surely he'd meant those words? The reason she hadn't had a letter recently was just that he hadn't been at sea and unable to send anything; he wouldn't just desert her.

At least she didn't feel sick yet, Beth reflected, pulling herself together. She must just carry on as usual and hope for a letter from Mark. It was probably just her guilty conscience, she decided as she got dressed and went down to breakfast in the nurses' home.

She couldn't be sure she was pregnant just because she was a bit late with her period. Beth didn't have leave for Christmas, but she would get a few days leave the week after. Perhaps by then her period would have come and she would have nothing to worry about . . .

'Oh, Beth,' Lizzie said when she saw Beth waiting for her when she left the workshop that evening a week after Christmas. She'd spent Christmas Day with Beth's family and the day after with Aunt Miriam, because both families had refused to take no for an answer. 'I was just thinking about you.'

'And here I am like the bad penny.'

'Your mother told me you'd got a week off and would be home today.' Lizzie smiled at her. 'I was going to ask if you wanted to come with me to the social club Harry's aunt has started with some other ladies. It is for servicemen on leave . . . and a lot of them will be injured . . .'

The Germans had torpedoed British ships, beginning the day war was declared and the casualties had continued, although as yet the only air raid warnings had been trials or false alarms, but as the fighting intensified overseas and in the air, there was bound to be many casualties. All kinds of regulations had come in, from every household having to have a stirrup pump in case of incendiary bombs to the blackouts in the streets. It was impossible to buy the material for blackout curtains, because the shops had sold out and the government was advising people to paint their windows black; fines for those who showed a light could be swingeing.

'What would I have to do – at the club?'

'Help me cut sandwiches, set out plates, serve cups of tea and wash up – but in between we get to talk to the men and that's nice. Last night one of the men played the piano and some of the girls were dancing with the others . . . it's a nice atmosphere, Beth, and we can do with more volunteers.'

'Yes, all right, I'll come. Why not? I haven't got anything better in sight.'

'I go on Monday, Thursday and Friday evening. We don't open on a Sunday at the moment, because most women have children and a home to look after. I suppose it would be fun if we're together . . .'

She hesitated, then, 'Do you think I could stay over the nights we go to the club? It's not easy getting home late at night in the blackout and Mum would let me if you came round and asked . . .'

'Of course I will,' Lizzie said. 'I often feel lonely at night and there's nothing to do but draw my hats or listen to the radio. You can sleep with me – unless Harry comes home on leave . . .'

'Then I'll go home,' Beth said and laughed softly. 'I wouldn't want to cramp his style, Lizzie.'

'No, he does rather like to spread himself around.' Lizzie's eyes lit up with amusement. 'He is in the habit of walking around in the middle of the night with nothing on . . .'

'I'll definitely go home in that case,' Beth said and giggled. 'Have you heard from him recently?'

'I get five minutes on the phone every so often and the occasional letter, but he doesn't say much because he isn't supposed to – you know how it is now. He didn't even get home at Christmas, which didn't please him . . .'

'I know how that feels,' Beth nodded her agreement. 'I just wish I could hear something of Mark.'

'Can't you just write care of the Merchant Navy Portsmouth?' Lizzie asked. 'It might get to him in time . . . if it's important?'

'No, not yet – but I'm worried about him, Lizzie. I know several ships have been torpedoed.'

'He'll contact you as soon as he can, Beth.'

'He promised to let me know when he got back . . .'

'I am sure he will, love.'

Beth nodded and sighed. 'It's just that he's been away for weeks, but I suppose I just have to be patient, as we all do . . .'

'It isn't easy, I know.' Lizzie put her coat on. 'Let's go back to mine for a cup of tea. I'll lend you something to wear, and then we can go to the club together.'

'I like some of the new hats in the showroom, Lizzie. They're very different, aren't they?'

'Yes,' Lizzie said. 'I told you Uncle Bertie had put me in charge of production as far as the ladies' hats are concerned?'

'Yes, it's made more work for you, hasn't it?'

'Yes, but I design in the evenings when I'm not at the club. It means I'm busy with trimming but I'd rather have something to do than sit and twiddle my thumbs.'

'How is the bespoke business doing?'

'It must be doing all right, because Uncle Bertie would soon let me know if things weren't right.'

Beth cast an eye over her slim figure. 'You haven't fallen for a baby yet, have you?'

'No, though I thought I might after that holiday we had together. It's early days yet and I'm glad really. Having a baby while there's a war on and my husband is away – it's not ideal . . .'

'No, especially when you have a business to run . . .' Beth hesitated, then, 'It must be difficult living here alone, Lizzie?'

'I'm used to it now, though as I said, I do feel

lonely at night sometimes – but even when I lived with Aunt Jane it was never like having a family. You must feel it living in Cambridge after having your family round you. I know Mary is married now, but I dare say she and Dotty still pop round sometimes and your brother and his wife?'

'Oh, Dotty is always there now she's getting near her time. She kept moaning when she wasn't pregnant, but now she's always got a bad back or swollen ankles or something.'

'I suppose having a baby is like that,' Lizzie said. 'Shall we go now? We can get some fish and chips for supper on the way home if you like.'

'Mum will have a meal ready. She's always got enough to feed an army, or so Dad says – though it isn't going to be as easy once the rationing really gets underway. The prices food was getting to was awful but the government have brought in regulations now so the profiteers can't make fortunes out of us.'

'Don't you believe it,' Lizzie said. 'If they can't do it legally, they'll do it another way – the black market, Uncle Bertie calls it. He bought some tinned stuff the other day and gave me some for my store cupboard. Says we have to look after ourselves because you can't trust the government to see we don't starve.'

'Mum will go back to endless stews,' Beth said. 'Sometimes there might not be much more than veg in them, but they always taste good with her fresh bread. Thankfully, Dad has always kept accounts, so he will still have a licence to buy and sell food – some of the lads on the barrows aren't so lucky. They can't get a licence and that means they can't buy wholesale from the markets, well, not legally. Dad says it's their own fault for fiddling on their income tax, but he's sorry for them really.'

'What will they do?'

'Most of them are joining up,' Beth said. 'The older ones will have to go into the factories, I suppose.'

Hurrying through the blackout, the girls laughed as vague shapes loomed up out of the gloom. It was becoming commonplace to bump into people and apologise but everyone was in the same boat and all they could do was smile and carry on.

Back at work, Beth became increasingly anxious during the next two weeks, when her period still refused to materialise. She was almost certain now that she was having Mark's child and there was still no word from him.

If she hadn't loved Mark, she might have tried drinking hot gin sitting in a hot bath, though she'd heard other girls talk about it as an old wife's tale as a way of getting rid of unwanted babies. However, Beth's love for the father of her baby made her feel it would be wicked to try and miscarry it, even though she was terrified of the consequences.

She was just going to have to carry on as best she could for as long as was possible.

CHAPTER 31

Lizzie looked about the crowded room and smiled. In the weeks she'd been coming here so much had changed, because what had started out as just a small gathering had grown, and since Christmas the place had been packed and the noise of the laughter and music made it difficult to hear what people were asking for.

'I'm sorry,' Lizzie said, leaning nearer to the young soldier. 'Did you ask for two sausage rolls?'

'Yes, please, if that's all right?'

'Of course it is,' Lizzie said and smiled at him. 'The food is given by various friends. Everyone has been generous, sharing what they can, and we get extra coupons because it's for our boys. After all, you deserve it . . .'

'I'm not sure I do,' the young soldier grinned awkwardly. 'I've only just finished my training.'

'Don't worry, you'll be needed soon enough,' Lizzie said. 'Besides, the rationing is getting worse all the time, so enjoy it while you can.'

He nodded cheerfully and moved off to join the group around the piano, who were belting out some of the more popular songs. As yet they hadn't experienced much of the war here and some people were calling it the false war, but at sea the merchant ships were being attacked, and, before Christmas, British ships had trapped one of Germany's large battleships – the Graf Spee – in the River Plate, but instead of surrendering, the captain had chosen to scuttle his ship and take his own life.

Lizzie knew that British planes were also flying into the danger zone on a daily basis, but so far Harry seemed to be surviving, thank God! He phoned at least twice a week and sent postcards now and then, but as yet there was no mention of him getting leave and Lizzie felt increasingly lonely in the evenings, which meant her time helping out at the club was a welcome change.

Aunt Miriam had been collecting glasses on a tray. She brought them back to the counter where Lizzie stood, looking at her enquiringly.

'You look a bit down, Lizzie.'

'Oh no, I'm all right – just thinking, you know.'

'You haven't heard from Harry if he's coming home?'

'No, he hasn't phoned for a while and it's nearly two weeks since he wrote,' Lizzie felt an icy tingle at her nape. 'I'd be worried if I thought . . .' she shook her head. 'No, if anything were wrong I should have heard by now.'

'Yes, of course you would. He will probably turn up and surprise you.'

Aunt Miriam took the tray into the kitchen and Lizzie took a cloth and went to wipe some tables down, clearing away the empty plates. She went to the kitchen and brought out two platters of fresh cut sandwiches, thinking that ham would be in short supply next month; it was a favourite with the men but getting more difficult to buy and next month it would be rationed.

'Hello, Lizzie Larch . . .' the voice caused Lizzie to start and almost knock over a jug of milk she'd just filled. 'I didn't expect to find you here. I nearly didn't come . . .'

Lizzie looked at the man she hadn't seen for months. He was wearing the uniform of an army officer and she thought his rank was that of a captain. The uniform suited him more than the severe suits he'd worn for business and there was a slight tan to his skin, as if he'd been in the sun. She knew better than to ask, because he probably couldn't tell her.

'Sebastian, how pleasant to see you again. Are you home on leave?' Lizzie felt a little breathless. It was just such a shock seeing him here – and in uniform.

'Just for a couple of days that's all,' he replied, smiling at her in a way that made Lizzie feel rather warm and a little uncomfortable. 'How are you, Lizzie? Business doing well? I've seen your designs in Oliver's window and I thought they were really stylish.'

'I'm doing well enough,' Lizzie said cautiously.

'It's a good thing Oliver thought to buy up so much stock while he could. You won't find it easy to get supplies soon. Most of the factories are turning over to war production for the troops or essentials – and the special trimmings and silks from overseas will not be available. Shipping costs lives these days and other goods are more important.'

'Yes, I know,' Lizzie said. 'Uncle Bertie is constantly complaining about deliveries. He's on the priority list for his government contracts, of course, but even the essentials will become more difficult to source.'

'The war has hardly got going yet,' Sebastian replied. 'Wait until the shortages really start to bite. I'm not certain of my shop's future at the moment – but we'll try to keep things going for as long as we can.'

'Yes, you must,' Lizzie said. 'Can I get you a cup of tea – or something to eat?'

'I'd rather you came out with me for a drink so that we can sit and talk'

'I don't think I can do that,' Lizzie said. 'I shall be here until nearly eleven and then . . . well, I am married you know.'

'I still want you to work with me one day, Lizzie. Even if I have to slow things down for a few years at the shop, I'll have plans for the future. Oliver isn't the only one to get in on government contracts, you know. I've taken over a boot and shoe factory. It's army contracts, of course, but it means I'll have a business to come back to when it is all over.'

'Aren't you in the army?'

'In a manner of speaking,' he told her and smiled. 'You know what they say, Lizzie – careless talk. I find time to look after my own affairs, and I have people I trust in charge. Has my manager been buying from you as I instructed?'

'Yes, a few hats each month,' she said. 'Not as many as you bought, but I may not have the right hats in stock when he comes. My customers take as many as they can in case stocks run out . . .'

'Well, if you won't come out with me this evening, I'll call on you at the showroom tomorrow and have a look at what you have in stock. Take care of yourself, Lizzie . . .'

Miriam came up to her as Sebastian wandered over to the piano to listen to the exuberant delivery of one of Vera Lynn's popular songs. She was fast becoming a favourite with the forces and the public, perhaps because she was pretty and her songs gave people hope.

'Who was that?' Miriam asked. 'I thought it was one of Bert's customers . . . Sebastian Winters, but he's in uniform . . .'

'Yes, he was,' Lizzie said and shrugged. 'I don't think he's on active service though; he was talking about his new factory – makes boots for the army.'

'Oh, one of those honorary commissions,' Harry's aunt said. 'I suppose it gets him out of being thought a conchie or something.'

'Yes, probably,' Lizzie said, because she wasn't sure about Sebastian Winters. She'd thought he was doing war work for the Government, but now he was talking about boot factories and special contracts and she wasn't sure what to think.

Seeing him had given her a bit of a jolt. She'd been very tempted to go for a drink with him, but of course it was out of the question. If Harry ever discovered that she'd been out with another man, especially Sebastian Winters . . . she dared not think what he would do or say. His jealousy made it impossible for her to have a friendship with another man – and yet Lizzie's feeling on seeing Sebastian was one of pleasure and, after all, what was wrong with having a friend?

It was ridiculous, but sometimes she felt trapped. Uncle Bertie had absorbed her into his business, making her responsible for his whole production of ladies' hats, and while she appreciated the extra money she made, sometimes she felt that he took her for granted. Because she was Harry's wife, she was family and finding herself drawn more and more into their circle. Aunt Miriam had brought her into the social club and often walked home with her. It seemed to Lizzie that they were watching over her for Harry's sake and although she appreciated their kindness, sometimes she would have liked a little freedom.

It was mid-morning the next day and Lizzie was just admiring a red cap she'd designed, which was rather like a soldier's but with an embroidered design to represent the badge and a jaunty feather, when she heard the showroom bell behind her.

'Very unusual,' a voice said and Lizzie jerked round to see that Sebastian was standing watching her. This morning he was wearing his greatcoat over his uniform and he'd removed his cap. The light caught his dark hair and it looked almost blue-black for a moment. 'Does it sell?'

'We don't know yet; it is a part of our new range of mannish hats for ladies. The trilby hat over there is already popular and the little bowler has sold a few, but this is a new idea. I thought it might appeal to someone . . .'

'It appeals to me,' Sebastian said. 'Would you let me try it in my shop?'

'Yes, why not?'

'Thank you . . .' He glanced around at the various stands. Lizzie had several of them now and they set the hats off so much more than the old way Oliver had of just piling them on the counter. 'I like that white straw at the back.'

'It's an order for a wedding,' Lizzie said. 'All those over that side of the counter are orders. Everything in front of you is for sale.'

'The pink one is rather nice – and that emerald green. I'll take all of these felts, Lizzie, if that's all right?'

'Of course. Do you want to take them with you?'

'I'll ask someone to fetch them next week,' he said, and then as Lizzie turned he caught her arm.

'I think of you all the time . . . can't get you out of my mind, Lizzie. Surely, you know how I feel about you?'

Lizzie felt a spasm in her stomach and caught her breath. She'd always laughed his approaches off, but his tone told her that he was serious and there was something in his eyes, a need or longing, that touched her heart – but it was much too late.

'No, Sebastian, I don't know,' she said and turned to face him. 'I can't know. I'm married to Harry and I love him. It's too late for anything even if . . .' the words caught in her throat. 'I'm grateful for your friendship. I always have been, but I can't offer you more.'

'I don't want gratitude,' Sebastian said and looked angry. 'Why don't you trust me, Lizzie?'

'I do trust you,' Lizzie said awkwardly. 'Perhaps at the start I didn't, but that was ages ago – and I do like you. If I'd known you better, I . . . should probably have taken your offer to work for you. I'm sorry, Sebastian, but don't you see . . . it's too late now?'

'You made a mistake marrying Harry Oliver,' he said harshly. 'You should have gone into partnership with me – and married me when you were ready. You were too young, Lizzie. I wanted to give you time. Oh, Lizzie Larch, I love you more than you could ever imagine . . .'

'No, don't say it . . . you can't mean it . . .' She'd always assumed he was just flirting that he was interested in having her work for him and perhaps

300

a flirtation or seduction – but love and marriage? For a moment the suggestion just took her breath; he couldn't mean it surely – but he wasn't teasing her now.

The appeal in his eyes, the way he seemed to catch his breath and the sheer need she sensed in him filled Lizzie with a longing to be in his arms, to be held and kissed. She was tempted almost to the point of giving in but then she realised where her thoughts were going and was horrified. No! She couldn't betray Harry. She loved him and he was her husband. This was stupid, wrong and she was just feeling lonely – lonely and resentful of this war that had taken Harry away from her. Yet the thought that he might truly care for her somehow tore at her heart, causing her pain and regret.

Why had he always seemed to be teasing and now suddenly sincere and urgent?

'You know this isn't right,' she said gently, because something in her knew she was hurting him and she could feel his pain, echo it in her heart, and knew she was guilty of wanting what he was offering her. 'I'm married, Sebastian. You mustn't say these things to me.'

'I know.' He looked rueful, and just for a moment vulnerable, and then the old confidence was back and she thought she'd imagined that moment when he'd seemed to need her so much. 'It was worth a try. One of these days I'll get you, Lizzie Larch, so don't expect me to stop trying.'

Lizzie laughed and leaned forward, giving him a gentle kiss on the cheek and retreating swiftly before he could grab her and kiss her properly. She was still smiling as he left the showroom, understanding that she liked him far more than she would have believed possible when he first approached her to work for him months ago. Then she'd thought him a shallow flirt and the kind of man a girl ought to be careful of, but now she knew Sebastian went much deeper than she'd believed – and she would have liked to know more of him, but she mustn't think that way. It was wrong and much too late.

CHAPTER 32

Lizzie checked her store cupboard and realised she needed to do some shopping. She'd hardly bothered recently, grabbing some chips on the way home or making do with toast and tomatoes, or cheese if she could get it. Spam and corned beef were usually available and Lizzie liked both, cooking a few mashed potatoes when she wanted a proper meal, and of course she ate with her friends once or twice a week. She knew Aunt Miriam had been hoarding sugar and tinned foods, and when she saw in the paper that one woman had been prosecuted for buying a huge amount of sugar before rationing started, she dropped a word of warning in Miriam's ear.

'Oh, she was foolish, buying all that from one supplier. I go to lots of shops, Lizzie. You should listen to Bertie, because there will come a time when you may not be able to get what you want in the shops.'

Lizzie had bought a few extra things, storing them away for when Harry came home, but when he was away she didn't use that much anyway.

'It's no good,' Lizzie said aloud. 'I need to go shopping . . .'

Picking up her purse and her ration card, Lizzie saw that her meat ration hadn't been used for two weeks. She decided that she would treat herself to a joint and do a nice roast. Perhaps she would ask Madge and Ed to come and share it on Sunday. She reached for her coat and scarf, because it was cold, picked up her basket and went out. She would pop round to Ed's later that evening and extend her invitation . . .

It was late afternoon when Lizzie returned home to the flat. As soon as she let herself in, she sensed something and, as she got to the landing, she saw the light on in the living room. She gave a little scream of delight and rushed into the room.

'Harry! Why didn't you let me know? I had no idea you were coming home . . .'

'I wasn't sure until the last minute,' Harry said. 'I thought you would be pleased with the surprise . . .'

'I am, of course I am,' Lizzie said and put her arms around him, hugging him. He didn't respond immediately, and then he pulled her in so tight that she struggled to breathe. 'I'm so pleased I went shopping. I can get you something to eat – you can have bacon and egg or a cheese sandwich . . .'

'A sandwich will do. I ate on the train coming down from . . .' Harry broke off and shook his head. 'Not supposed to say where I am based or what I'm doing . . . damned ridiculous but best not . . .'

Lizzie went into the kitchen and put the kettle on, then got out the fresh bread, butter and the small slab of Cheddar cheese she'd bought. It was carefully wrapped in greaseproof paper and, sliced thin, would normally last her a week for sandwiches, because she didn't eat much in the middle of the day, especially when she was busy.

'I must have known you were coming,' Lizzie said as Harry came through and picked up the first round she cut. 'I bought a small joint of brisket and I haven't done that in ages. I was going to invite Ed and Madge, but of course I shan't now.'

'You sound disappointed. Perhaps you would prefer I hadn't come and you could have a cosy evening with your friends?'

'Harry, don't be ridiculous! I was just saying. It seemed a good idea, and if I didn't invite my friends sometimes, I'd go mad sitting here alone every night.'

'Well don't look so bloody miserable about it,' Harry said, clearly angry. 'If this is what coming home is like after all this sodding time I'm not sure I'll bother again.'

'Harry!' Lizzie cried, shocked by his sudden attack. He didn't often swear and she didn't like it. 'What have I done wrong? Why are you so angry with me? Of course I'm glad you're home – it's just that I thought it would be nice to have friends round, because you haven't written for ages and I didn't think you were coming . . .'

For a moment his face was filled with fury and

then it disappeared and he slumped down in the chair. 'I'm sorry. It's been hell recently and I never expected to get this pass – and then you seemed as if you preferred to be with your friends . . .'

'Not if I can be with you,' Lizzie said and knelt by his side. He looked tired and drained and she didn't understand – but he was obviously under strain.

'I'm sorry, Lizzie, but it felt as if you'd forgotten me – shut me out. You're obviously coping well and don't need me . . .'

'Of course I need you. I love you, Harry. You've given me everything. If you and Uncle Bertie hadn't helped me, I should probably have been working in the munitions factory now.'

'Sebastian Winters would take you like a shot.'

'I turned him down. I'm your wife, Harry.'

'I love you, Lizzie. You won't run away and leave me will you?'

'Where would I go?' She laughed up at him. 'You know I love you, darling. I expect you're tired and hungry, aren't you?'

'Not particularly hungry . . . Why don't we go out somewhere?'

'There's a good film on at the Odeon . . .'

'No, I feel like company. A pub somewhere: one that has a piano. I want to see people enjoying themselves and having a few drinks.'

Lizzie hesitated, because she didn't like pubs much and some of them in the district seemed to get rowdy.

'You wouldn't rather just stay in and have a few drinks – or visit your uncle?'

'No, I want to go to a pub,' Harry said. 'Get changed into something smart, Lizzie. I want everyone to see what a pretty wife I've got . . .'

Lizzie was annoyed as the drunken soldier brushed past her as she made her way back from the cloakroom, because the soldier had managed to spill a few drops of his beer on her best red dress. She noticed that Harry had invited a man in RAF uniform to sit down at their table and, as she approached, another RAF officer arrived with a loaded tray and placed it on the table. Harry was laughing, clearly more at ease with his friends than her, and she had a feeling he'd arranged this even before he'd told her of his intention to visit a pub.

The two officers stood up as she came up to them.

'Robbie and Jeff,' Harry said, nodding at the two men. 'This is my Lizzie – I told you, she designs hats . . .'

'Pleased to meet you, Mrs Oliver,' the officers said and offered their hands. Lizzie shook hands and sat down opposite the one called Robbie. 'Harry said you were beautiful,' he said. 'We all thought he was bragging, but he failed to do you justice.'

'Watch him, Harry,' Jeff joked. 'Robbie has all the ladies swooning when he starts sweet-talking them.'

Harry laughed and lifted his glass to his friend, seeming not to take any notice of Jeff's ribbing, but a little later when Lizzie was laughing at one of Robbie's jokes, she noticed the dark look her husband was giving her.

Feeling slightly annoyed, Lizzie carried on talking to his friends in the manner she always spoke to everyone, polite, friendly, but nothing more. If Harry didn't like the attention his friends were giving her then he shouldn't have arranged to meet them. Lizzie hadn't wanted to come. She would have preferred to stay home or go out for a quiet meal in a nice restaurant, but Harry wanted to be with his friends and it seemed that he enjoyed their company; it was Lizzie he was angry with and that was just stupid.

Harry was quiet as they walked home late that night. He'd had several drinks, more than she'd ever known him to have before, but he didn't seem merry or drunk – just quiet and sullen. When they let themselves into the flat, Lizzie went through to the kitchen to make some cocoa. Harry was sitting in the chair when she returned with two mugs, his head back and his eyes closed.

'Are you asleep?' she asked.

Harry didn't answer. She put his mug on the table beside him and then took hers through to the bedroom. She drank it while sitting on the edge of the bed, then went to the bathroom to clean her teeth. Harry hadn't come through, so she peeped in the sitting room. He hadn't touched his cocoa and was still sitting with his eyes shut.

'Are you coming to bed, Harry?'

No answer. Lizzie hesitated for a moment and then went and climbed into bed. If he'd fallen asleep where he was, he must be tired and she didn't want to wake him.

It must have been early morning when she felt the covers pulled back and then Harry's weight as he crawled in beside her. The next moment his arms went round her and he was nuzzling her neck, murmuring endearments as he pulled at her nightgown, inching it up with one hand. She was still sleepy, and a little cross with him for his behaviour that evening, and not in the mood for lovemaking.

'No, Harry,' she muttered, still half asleep. 'Tomorrow; I'm tired . . .'

'You can't refuse me,' Harry muttered and then his body was lying on hers, crushing her into the mattress as he fumbled between her legs, forcing them open and pushing his fingers inside her. 'Why aren't you wet?' he grumbled as she resisted what felt like an invasion. 'Damn you, you don't love me anymore . . .'

Lizzie tried to protest but his lips ground on hers in a punishing kiss and then he was thrusting into her with such ferocity that she felt a wild beast was tearing at her and she cried out in pain. Her mind refused to believe what was happening, because Harry had always been such a caring, tender lover. He couldn't be doing this – it was little short of rape. She felt cold all over and a little sick. Harry must know how this would affect her – after what had happened when she was fourteen! How could he subject her to such rough treatment?

Lizzie tried to push him off but Harry was in the grip of some wild fit and he just pounded into her until he collapsed in a heap, groaned and then rolled off her, immediately falling into a deep sleep. He was snoring. Harry never snored; it either had to be the drink or he was feigning it.

Lizzie pushed away from him, got out of bed and went into the bathroom, locking the door behind her. She ran a hot bath and got in, letting the tears stream down her cheeks. How could he do that to her? He wasn't like the man she loved – he wasn't her Harry. Something had happened to him and Lizzie didn't like it.

She stayed in the bath until the water felt cold and then dried herself, wrapping her bathrobe round her and going through to the kitchen to put the kettle on. There was no way she was going to get back into that bed while Harry was in it – not while he was in the grip of whatever madness had taken him over.

She drank her tea alone, refusing to take him one; he didn't deserve any kindness. Lizzie was very angry. Some women might put up with their husbands treating them like that but she wasn't one of them. Unable to return to bed, she finally curled up in the sitting room with her coat over her and drifted into a cramped and uneasy sleep.

Church bells were ringing when Lizzie woke to see Harry standing there with a cup of tea in one hand and a bacon sandwich on a plate in the other.

'It was all I knew how to make,' he said, looking like a naughty schoolboy as he set both the cup and plate down on the table beside her. 'I'm so sorry for the way I behaved last night, Lizzie. I expect you hate me now – I deserve it. I could beg you to forgive me, but if I were you I wouldn't – what I did . . .' he broke down, his face working with distress. 'I can't believe I did it – I was just so damned jealous. Robbie was making a play for you all evening . . .'

Lizzie stared up at him, feeling cold and unforgiving. 'That doesn't give you the right to rape me, Harry.'

'Rape . . .' he blenched as she said it. 'I didn't mean – I just wanted you so much and you said no – wouldn't let me love you . . .'

'So you took what you wanted regardless of my feelings? When you know what happened to me – what it did to me the last time?' Lizzie stood up, looking him in the eyes. 'I don't take that from anyone, Harry. I'm not a doormat and I've got too much pride to live with a man who thinks he can use me like that . . .'

'Lizzie don't,' Harry begged. The tears were streaming down his cheeks now and then he was on his knees, catching at her robe, hugging her

311

around the legs like an abject child. 'If you leave me I'll go to pieces. I can't go on without you – you're all that keeps me sane. You don't know . . .' he broke off shaking his head. 'I'm so ashamed.'

Lizzie resisted for a moment longer, and then reached down to touch his hair as a feeling of love, or pity, overwhelmed her. 'What's wrong, Harry? What has happened to you? I don't understand?'

He looked up at her. 'I'm a coward, Lizzie – a miserable rotten little coward and I want to run away and hide.'

Lizzie sat down and looked into his face. 'What makes you say that? What has happened to make you feel that way?'

'We've been flying almost non-stop missions over enemy territory, taking aerial photo surveys and the flak is bad, Lizzie. Three of the squadron have been shot down this month and both pilot and navigator were killed – or burned beyond recognition . . .'

Harry's hands were shaking as Lizzie reached out to take them. Everyone moaned about all the fuss and petty restrictions when nothing was happening, and it didn't really seem as if there was a war at all, but what they didn't realise was that some of the men were facing danger every day of their lives; men at sea and young flyers risking everything to find out more about the enemy's installations and ships.

'I'm sorry if you've lost some of your friends, Harry.'

His hands stilled as she caught and held them. 'We've been lucky so far, Robbie and me – but I'm terrified every time I go up, Lizzie. I wanted to fly, wanted to do my bit for my country – but I'm a coward. I get the shakes sometimes and the only thing that keeps me going is the memory of you – of your sweet face.'

'Harry, dearest,' she said, her throat tight as she struggled to hold back her tears. 'I don't know what to say . . . I'm sure you're not the only one who's frightened of getting shot down.'

'Robbie laughs at danger; he loves the thrill of it, and we always get the best pictures because he takes us in closer than anyone else dare fly. So far we've had the devil's own luck, but I know it can't last. We've done more than sixty missions, Lizzie, and a lot of the chaps only manage a handful. I think I could stand the idea of death but it's getting burned . . .' He shuddered and bent his head. 'I'm so ashamed. What I did last night – and now you know I'm a coward. You won't want me around, Lizzie. I'll go to a hotel for the rest of my leave. It's only until Monday night . . .'

'Of course you won't go to a hotel. This is your home, Harry. I got you a present for Christmas, even though you didn't get home . . .'

'I bought you something too,' he said and looked up at her, hope in his eyes. 'You don't hate me?'

'No – but you hurt me, Harry. Not just physically but mentally. I'm not going to leave you, but if you ever do anything like that again, I shall . . .'

'I shan't! I promise on my life. I wish I'd thrown myself under a train rather than hurt you like that, Lizzie. Can you forgive me?'

'Yes, I think so, but it's going to be a while before I feel I can trust you again,' she said. 'I don't think you're a coward, Harry. What you're doing takes guts and even if you do feel terrified you do it – don't you?' He was still her husband, still a brave man doing a dangerous job, even if he had made her wish she'd never married him.

'I have no choice. I couldn't ask for a transfer – and it wouldn't happen if I did. I chose to train as a navigator and observer and I'm stuck with it. If I wasn't flying reconnaissance missions, it would be bombers or some such thing – and they will be in the thick of it once it really starts.'

'You don't think your commanding officer would put you on groundwork?'

'I can't ask, Lizzie.' He looked rueful. 'I can just imagine the looks I'd get – that's the worst bit. I have to laugh and joke and pretend like the others – I'm even more afraid of being thought a coward than of dying. I couldn't face the other chaps if . . .' He shook his head and looked miserable.

'Don't you see, Harry?' Lizzie said earnestly. 'They probably feel just the same as you do – that's why they brag and play ridiculous jokes, as they did last night. Robbie wasn't after me; he was just showing off like a little boy . . .'

Harry arched his brows at her, before getting

to his feet. 'When did you get to be so grown-up and wise?'

'Perhaps last night had something to do with it,' Lizzie said, though she knew she'd been changing for a while. It had begun at that garden party, when she'd seen something in Sebastian's eyes – a feeling of need and wanting . . . She'd refused to acknowledge it then, but a more recent memory was haunting her. Why that sudden urgency when he came to the workshop the last time? Was it because he was going away – perhaps into danger? The thought caught at her heart, giving her pain and she had to force herself back to the present, back to what Harry was saying.

'Will you ever forgive me?'

'Let's forget about it for now,' she said turning to hide her tears. 'I'll give you my presents and you can give me yours . . .'

Uncle Bertie came round later when Lizzie was cooking dinner. He caught the delicious smell of roast beef and looked envious as she took it out of the tin and turned it before returning it to the oven.

'My favourite,' he said. 'Your aunt has a chicken whenever she can, but I'd choose beef every time – have you made puddings?'

'Lizzie makes lovely crisp Yorkshires,' Harry said and grinned. 'You can have some if you like.'

'I wouldn't dare,' his uncle said and chuckled. 'Your aunt would be offended if I didn't do justice

315

to her Sunday dinner. I only came round to see you, Harry. I couldn't believe it when Lizzie rang and said you were home. She didn't tell us you were coming . . .'

'It was a surprise,' Harry said. 'I didn't know until half an hour before I caught the train.'

'Come round for tea or supper if you like,' Uncle Bertie invited. 'Now, if we could have a word on our own, Harry lad. It's just man-to-man stuff, nothing Lizzie would be interested in . . .'

Lizzie didn't even turn her head. She wanted the dinner to be perfect. It was difficult making things seem normal after the previous evening and Harry's confession. She felt guilty for not having realised what a strain he was under. How he would cope with the next months, and perhaps years, she didn't know – because he was clearly cracking under the pressure and Sebastian said it had hardly started yet. Perhaps he didn't know about the reconnaissance missions like Lizzie he was waiting to see what would happen when the two countries really came to blows.

No, she was sure he knew much more, was mixed up in things she knew nothing of – and perhaps that explained the way he'd been in her workroom when he'd seemed to plead with her to love him. Safe at home in her own little world, how could Lizzie understand what men exposed to danger were thinking? Some inner sense told her that Sebastian would be exposed to danger soon, even if he hadn't been already. Most things to do with the war were kept secret until after they happened, because the Government suspected there were German spies or sympathisers everywhere. Lizzie and Beth had laughed at the idea, but perhaps there was a lot more going on behind the scenes than most people guessed.

She had just finished beating the mixture for the Yorkshire when Uncle Bertie came back into the kitchen, followed by Harry. He shook his head at her as she offered him a glass of sweet sherry.

'The only thing that's good for is a trifle,' he said. 'I was wondering if you finished that new design, Lizzie – the cap with the embroidered badge.'

'Yes, I did finish it but I sold it immediately. I'm making more but they aren't finished.'

'You sold it before showing it to me?' Uncle Bertie looked annoyed. 'Who bought it?'

'Oh . . .' Lizzie glanced at Harry but he didn't seem interested and was investigating the trifle Lizzie had made the previous day and just finished with a decoration of cream and nuts. 'Mr Winters called in to buy a few hats and saw it. He wanted it, so I let him buy it. I'm sorry if you're disappointed . . .'

'Doesn't matter,' Uncle Bertie said, preparing to leave. 'I hope you will be pleased with what I've done, Lizzie . . .'

Harry went to the door with him, returning just as Lizzie poured the pudding mixture into small bun tins. 'Do you know what he just told me?'

Lizzie shook her head, pushing the tray into the oven before turning to look at him. He seemed abstracted, a little displeased.

'He's giving you half the business . . . well, leaving it to you in his will, apparently. Aunt Miriam will get the other half for her lifetime and then it comes to me – if I survive the war. If not, you will get the lot . . .'

Lizzie thought she heard resentment in his voice. Obviously, he'd thought his uncle would leave the business to him, as everyone had assumed, Lizzie included.

'He shouldn't have done that,' Lizzie said at once. 'I'll tell him I don't want it. I expect it's just a precaution, because of the war . . .'

'Because he thinks I may not make it?' Harry said harshly. 'It's more than likely that I won't. Pilots and their navigators will be some of the highest casualties in the future. He's being sensible . . .'

'Harry don't – please, I didn't mean it that way . . .'

'No, but it's what he's thinking . . . what happens to the business when he goes if I've been killed . . .'

'Your uncle isn't going to die for years. He'll probably change his mind once the war is over and you start working in the business again.'

'He thinks you're a huge asset to the business, told me he needs you. Apparently, there are other government contracts he could take on if you would oblige him.'

'What kind of things?'

'Clothing mostly, I think, but you should ask him if you're interested.' His brows rose, seeming to mock her.

'I'm not really,' Lizzie said. 'I'm happy with the arrangement we have – and I think the business should come to you, Harry.'

'Give his ideas some thought, Lizzie. It would mean security for your future – especially if I'm not around . . .'

'Don't – please don't say anything.'

'You have to face the facts, Lizzie. It's more likely that I shall die than survive . . . Uncle Bertie is hoping we'll have a son so that he can pass the business on. Oh, he didn't say it but his hints were clear enough.'

'I'm not sure I'll be able to have a child,' Lizzie said, 'after what happened to me – the miscarriage and my long illness. I'm sorry, Harry. I thought it might happen after our holiday but it didn't and I've wondered since if I was damaged inside.'

'You should see a doctor and ask his opinion . . .'

'Perhaps . . .'

Harry took her by her upper arms, his fingers pressing into her flesh. 'I mean it, Lizzie. I think you should find out if you are able to have a child.'

'If you insist . . .'

'I do,' he said and his eyes looked cold, angry. Lizzie felt a sinking sensation inside. If she couldn't have children Harry would resent her more than he already did. She knew that despite all his declarations of love, he still felt cheated because she hadn't come to him as a virgin bride.

'I'd better set the table,' she said, feeling empty inside. Her marriage had been doomed from the moment Harry discovered her secret; it seemed Aunt Jane was right when she said that Lizzie should never marry. 'Dinner will not be long.'

'I'll do it,' Harry said. 'I might as well make myself useful.'

She nodded and turned away to start the vegetables cooking. Her eyes stung with tears and it was difficult to pretend that she was happy that her husband was home when she felt miserable. She'd promised to forgive him and she would try, but something inside her had gone out, like a candle in a storm; the confident love she'd felt had faded to a small knot in her chest and she thought it felt more like pity than love. He needed her and she couldn't shut him out, but the joyous loving affection she'd felt for him had gone.

CHAPTER 33

Beth hung over the toilet, feeling wretched. She'd been sick twice that morning and she could no longer hope that her period would come and rescue her from the certain shame carrying a bastard child would bring on her and her family.

She pulled the long chain and went to wash her hands; the water was only a trickle and brownish again, because the icy weather had caused another pipe burst. Shivering in the cold toilets, she rubbed her arms and wondered why she'd wanted to take up her present job away from home. At the moment she longed for nothing more than to be home with her mother – although she would be furious when she found out Beth was pregnant.

Her frantic prayers had been unanswered. She was having Mark's baby and she'd received no word from him in three months. Surely he must have returned from the Atlantic run before this?

She considered the possibility that Mark had merely been toying with her affections, but dismissed it at once. Her heart told her that he'd loved her and she couldn't – didn't want to believe otherwise.

Something must have happened to him. If Mark had been killed, she would not know what to do, because she knew her father would throw her out once he learned of her shame. He might have tolerated it had it been Tony's child, but not the child of a man he'd never met. Her father wouldn't be the only one to turn her back on her when he found out the truth, everyone would. No, not everyone; Lizzie would still be her friend.

Beth's eyes stung with tears, because she felt so very low. She wanted Mark to be waiting for her when she left work. She longed for him to put his arms about her and tell her they would get married. There would be no problem with getting permission now, because Mum would sign when she knew the truth, even if her father still refused . . .

Beth went down to the hall and checked to see if there were any messages for her in the pigeon-holes that held their post, but as usual there was nothing.

'Hi, Beth,' one of the other nursing assistants caught up with her. 'Our first exams are coming up next month. How are you getting on with your studies?'

'Oh, not too bad, I think – what about you, Meg?'

'I'm fairly confident, but I'd like someone to test me. Would you test me if I do the same for you?'

'Yes, of course,' Beth agreed, though she knew it no longer mattered whether or not she passed her exams.

Feeling tired, her back aching after a hard day scrubbing bedpans, running errands and assisting Sister Ross with a feverish patient, Beth was looking forward to a bath and supper.

'Miss Court . . .' Beth froze as she saw the imposing figure of Matron bearing down on her. Matron hardly ever spoke to the lowly nursing assistants and Beth had only seen her once since the welcome speech they'd been given when she arrived. 'I want a word with you, please come to my office . . .'

'Yes, Matron.'

Beth's heart was thudding as she followed her along the corridor and into the office she'd never entered before. She must have done something terrible to be summoned to Matron's office, but she couldn't think what it was – unless someone had guessed her secret.

No, they couldn't have, Beth decided as they paused outside the holy of holies and Matron turned to look at her with what Beth could only think was sympathy.

'Please go in, Miss Court. Someone is waiting to see you . . .'

Beth's breath caught in her throat. Her first thought was that Mark had come at last, but it died instantly. Mark wouldn't have done that – he would have waited outside the door of the nurses' home. 'Is something wrong?'

'Yes, I believe so,' Matron said. 'Please go in. If there is anything I can do to assist you, please come to me in the morning . . .'

'Thank you . . .' Beth swallowed hard and then pushed open the door and went in to the office. All she noticed was the large mahogany desk and the shelves of books and files before her eyes came to rest on the man in uniform – the uniform of the Merchant Navy, she thought, and a high-ranking officer. Her throat tightened and she was suddenly short of breath. 'You wanted to see me, sir?'

'You are Miss Beth Court?' he asked and the grave look in his face made her gasp. 'Would you like to sit down, Miss Court?' He drew a chair for her. 'I'm afraid that what I have to tell you is rather distressing . . .'

'Is it Mark?' She couldn't have sat down to save her life, because her chest felt as if it was being crushed and the room had started to spin. 'Is he dead?'

'All we know for sure is that the vessel he was on was torpedoed by German U-boats,' he said and his voice seemed to come from a long way off. 'He may have been one of the lucky ones picked up by other ships in the area, but so far his name hasn't come up – we're classing him as missing in action, but of course there is always a chance . . .'

Beth missed the last few sentences because she couldn't breathe and the room seemed to be whirling round and round. A little cry of grief issued from her lips seconds before she fainted . . .

It wasn't until eight weeks after Harry had gone back to his unit that Lizzie began to feel sick in the mornings. She was a few weeks late with her monthlies and the sickness confirmed what she'd been fearing for a while; she was having Harry's baby, and it was a result of the rape, because he hadn't touched her after he'd abused her that night. Harry was too ashamed to approach her in bed and Lizzie wasn't sure she could have accepted him had he tried. It was getting easier to forget what he'd done, but she knew something was broken – a bond of trust that had existed between them.

It was almost as if he thought she didn't deserve his respect – and that hurt so much that she had to keep shutting it out of her mind or it would have destroyed her. She sometimes wished that she had never married him – but it was too late for regret.

She couldn't leave Harry, not when she knew what he was going through, but she no longer missed him or longed for him to come back on leave.

Lizzie hadn't told anyone that she was having a child. The only person she felt like telling was Beth, but her friend was in Cambridge and it wasn't the kind of secret she could divulge on the phone. Yet she needed to talk to her and so one evening she rang the number of the nurses' home in Cambridge and asked for Beth.

'Yes, she's here,' the disembodied voice at the other end sounded impatient. 'I'll call her . . .'

Beth came to the phone at last, sounding breathless. 'Who is it?' she asked.

'Lizzie, I wanted to talk, Beth. How are you? It seems ages since you were home on leave . . .'

'I'm coming home next week,' Beth said, a tremulous note in her voice. 'They're not keeping me on here . . .'

'Why not?' Lizzie demanded. 'I'm sure you would make a fine nurse. What reason did they give?'

'I'll tell you next week,' Beth said and Lizzie knew she was very upset. 'It's too public here to talk. Why did you ring me?'

'Oh, just feeling a bit low,' Lizzie said. 'I was sick this morning again. I think I'm pregnant . . .'

'You should be happy. Harry will be pleased, won't he?'

'I can't explain on the phone, Beth – but we're not getting on as well as we might . . .'

'You're so lucky to have someone who loves you,' Beth sounded angry now. 'You don't know what you've got . . .'

'Something is wrong, Beth. I knew it! Tell me now, please.'

'I've been told that Mark's ship went down,' Beth said and choked on a sob. 'He's reported missing in action – but they think he didn't survive because his name isn't on the list of men picked up by ships in the convoy . . .'

'Beth, no, I'm so sorry,' Lizzie said, gripping the phone. Her own worries seemed to fade into nothingness. 'Sorry isn't the word, love, but I am – and I'm glad you're coming home. It's where you should be – even though I don't understand why they're letting you go . . .'

'I'm in the same boat as you,' Beth said and Lizzie was shocked. It was bad enough for Lizzie that she'd become pregnant and her marriage was failing, but for Beth it was a huge tragedy.

'What will you do? Will your Mum take you in?'

'I doubt Dad will let her,' Beth said and Lizzie could hear the pain in her voice, raw and deep. 'I'll have to tell them – I fainted after I was told about Mark and Matron guessed. She demanded to know the truth and gave me two weeks' notice.'

'Couldn't she have let you stay on for a while longer?'

'She says not . . .' Beth gave a hollow laugh. 'Not a good example to her nurses . . .'

'You can stay with me for a while. Harry won't be back for weeks. You know I'd take you in, Beth, but when he's home . . .'

'It wouldn't work, but I'll come for a while if I get thrown out at home . . .' She made a sound that might have been a laugh or a sob. 'I suppose I'll find work of some kind, until it shows anyway . . .'

'Yes. I could have a word with Mr Oliver?'

'No, I'd rather go somewhere they don't know me. I'll see what is on offer when I get home – not that I have a home now . . .'

'We'll find you somewhere. I'll put my thinking cap on. You've still got me, love. You'll always be my friend.'

'Thanks, Liz,' Beth said. 'Don't be surprised if I turn up on your doorstep with all my worldly goods . . .'

'Just come. It isn't the end of the world – and Mark might turn up on a foreign ship. It has happened before.'

'Yes, I know. Matron said the same thing. She was amazingly kind really, but she's strict over things like this . . .' Beth lowered her voice. 'I can't talk anymore. I'll see you soon . . .'

Lizzie stared at the receiver as it went dead, replacing it with reluctance. The phone wasn't a good place to talk about secrets, but Beth's voice had made Lizzie open her heart and it had been the same for her – they needed each other more now than ever before . . .

CHAPTER 34

'Lizzie, that's wonderful news,' Ed said that morning. 'I expect Harry is over the moon?'

'I've written to tell him,' Lizzie forced a smile. 'His uncle was delighted. I've been told we need a boy to carry on the empire . . .'

'Trust Oliver to think of that,' Ed said scornfully. 'You'll stay on here until it gets too much for you?'

'Yes, of course – and I'll come back afterwards. Aunt Miriam has offered to look after the child when it's born. Uncle Bertie says I can work as many hours as I can manage and I'm not to worry about money. You'd think I'd suddenly sprouted angels' wings . . .'

Ed laughed good-naturedly. 'You'll come to supper with us this evening, Lizzie? Madge is feeling much better and she is preparing one of her delicious pies. It's the first time she's cooked since she lost our son . . .'

'Oh, Ed,' Lizzie said. 'I didn't think – this must remind you of your loss . . .'

'In a good way, only. I expect to be an honorary uncle and Madge will want her turn babysitting . . .'

'Yes, of course. We'd better get on if we want to

329

get those orders done on time. My angels' wings might fall off if I try his patience too much.'

Ed turned back to his bench. Lizzie picked up the pieces of an intricate hat she'd cut out and took it to Tilly with the tulle and silk flower she'd chosen. She lingered for a couple of minutes to explain what she needed and listen to Tilly's troubles with her mother and her daughter, and then went back to work.

It had been easier to tell the others after she'd spoken to Beth. With all the doubts and disappointment Lizzie felt over her own marriage, she knew she was a lot better off than Beth.

Despite what she'd said to Beth, Lizzie suspected that if Mark had been picked up it would have been reported before this – and yet it was the only hope of a decent life left to her friend. Young women with babies and no wedding ring didn't stand much chance in this critical world and Beth would find it hard to work and care for her child . . .

'Beth, what are you doing home?' Mrs Court's face lit up as Beth entered the kitchen. 'What a wonderful surprise?'

Beth hesitated, knowing that she had to be honest 'I'm home for good, Mum,' Beth said taking a deep breath. 'I've been dismissed.'

'Dismissed? Did you fail your exams or do your work badly? I thought you liked it there – were doing so well . . .'

'I was,' Beth said. Her insides felt twisted and she was curling up with shame as she went on, 'I'm having Mark Allen's baby – and he can't marry me because he's missing in action, presumed dead . . .'

'Beth!' The colour drained from her mother's face and she looked utterly shocked. 'Please tell me you're joking . . .'

'I wish I could, but it's true. I'm sorry. I know I've let you down – but please don't hate me, Mum. I can't bear it if you do . . .' Tears ran down her cheeks. 'I loved him – I loved him so much . . . he was going to marry me as soon as we could get permission, but now . . .'

Beth sat down on the old sofa, head bowed as the sobs burst from her. 'I don't know what to do . . .'

'Your father will be angry,' her mother said and the shock in her eyes had been replaced by a mixture of sorrow and anger. 'You've let him down, Beth. I know he expected so much of you – you were always his favourite . . .'

'Mark would have married me before he left but I knew Dad wouldn't let us – it's his fault. If he'd let me marry Tony this would never have happened . . .'

'I thought you said you loved this man? Why would it have helped if you'd married Tony?'

'Because I would never have met Mark or fallen in love with him,' Beth said bitterly. 'Oh, I don't regret it in my heart, but I can't be blamed for this, Mum – Mark was going away. I wanted him to be happy and he loved me . . .'

'You should have waited no matter how you both felt. We've warned you, Beth, brought you up to have proper values. I can't believe that you've let us down like this – and I know what Derek will say . . .'

'And what is that?'

Beth froze as she heard her father's voice and saw him in the hall doorway. He was wearing his old dressing gown and she could see that his nose was red. Beth had never known her father take a day off work for illness before, but it was obvious that he had done so today – and that he'd heard them talking.

'Derek, don't be too hard on her,' Beth's mother said, a look of alarm on her face. 'Her boyfriend is missing in action and she's lost her job – she's suffered enough . . .'

'For what she's done she deserves to be horse-whipped,' he said coldly. 'She's no daughter of mine – I don't want her in this house . . .'

'You can't just throw her out. Where would she go?'

'That's up to her – there are places for girls like her . . .'

'No, Derek! Whatever Beth has done she is still my daughter, I won't have her going to one of those places.'

'I won't have her here. She can stay tonight, but tomorrow she goes . . .'

'Please don't do this,' Beth's mother pleaded. 'I know she's done wrong – but I can't desert her.'

'I shan't stop you seeing her, but not here. I don't want to see her face again and that's final. I came down for a drink and now I'm going back to bed. I want her gone . . .'

Beth hid her face in her hands. She couldn't bear to see the scorn in her father's eyes and his words struck her like a bucket of ice water. For all her strictness, Matron had been kinder.

Feeling the touch of soft hands on her head, Beth looked up. 'He's hurt and angry,' her mother said. 'I'll talk to him and see if I can change his mind – but it may take a while, Beth.'

'You won't shut me out?'

'No, I won't. I'll visit you – and I can help with a little money, but that's all. Your father won't change his mind overnight.'

'I know . . .' Beth stood up wearily. 'I'd better go . . .'

'Do you have somewhere to stay?'

'Lizzie will take me in until I can find somewhere. I'll have to find a job, because I only have a couple of pounds left after my fare home . . .'

'I can give you ten shillings for now, but I'll get more. Your granny is in the hospital, Beth. She gave me all she had before they took her away and I know she wouldn't mind my lending you a few pounds. I'll pay it back of course . . .'

'What is the matter with Granny Shelly?'

'She had a nasty fall down the stairs two days

333

ago. It has shaken her up a bit and I'm not sure she'll ever be able to manage the stairs again. It will mean a bed in the front room if she comes out of hospital . . .'

'Poor Granny,' Beth said and her eyes were wet, but this time for her grandmother and not herself. 'We had some elderly women in the geriatric wards – they looked so hopeless and alone sometimes . . .'

'I shall look after her for as long as she lives,' Beth's mother said. 'But it means I can't openly defy your father, Beth. I don't agree with what he's done, but he's the boss of his own house . . .'

'Mum, I don't want you to quarrel with him,' Beth said. 'That would be worse than all the rest . . .'

'Here is your ten bob,' her mother said and pressed the money into her hands. 'I'll come and see you in a few days . . .'

Beth stood up and kissed her cheek and then left her standing there, knowing that she was crying. She went out into the hall, picked up her cases and went out of the front door . . .

'Oh, Beth, love,' Lizzie said as she saw her on the doorstep, her face wet with tears. She took one of Beth's cases. 'Come on up. You'll have to share my bed, but it will be like when I stayed with you . . .'

'Not quite,' Beth smiled wryly. 'I'm sorry to bring this to your door, Lizzie. I'll find somewhere else as soon as possible – and I've got to get a job. I've got a little money but it won't last long and I can't sponge off you.'

'I've got enough for us both. Uncle Bertie pays me more these days, and I'm getting a small share of the profits. I shan't charge you rent, Beth, so don't offer it. I'll be glad you're here.'

Beth sat down gratefully in an armchair. 'Have you told Harry you're expecting?'

'I've written but he hasn't replied. I'm not sure how he will feel. He wanted a child so much and now . . .' Lizzie caught back the words. She couldn't ever tell Beth what Harry had done, or that the child's conception was tainted with anger and hurt.

'What's wrong, Lizzie? You were a bit strange on the phone. You didn't quarrel with Harry?'

'He was in a bit of a mood that's all,' Lizzie said. 'Anyway, let's talk about you. What kind of a job are you after?'

'In an office if possible – but I'll take anything, even the munitions factory if I have to . . .'

'That's hard work and it wouldn't be good for the baby . . .'

'Beggars can't be choosers,' Beth shrugged. 'Are you staying on at work?'

'Yes. I've got two offers to look after the child so that I can go back to work, but I'm not sure how I'll manage here . . .'

'What do you mean?' Beth was puzzled. 'This is a lovely little flat.'

'It isn't easy to wash clothes in a flat. I send my

sheets and towels to the laundry, but nappies need frequent washing.'

'You won't give the flat up?'

'We always spoke of getting something bigger when the children came, but I thought I'd have longer . . .' Lizzie sighed.

'Nothing is ever easy, is it?'

Lizzie shook her head and poured more cocoa for them both. 'I hate the thought of sugar being rationed, don't you? I drink this all the time to save the sugar for tea . . .'

'Don't change the subject. Why aren't you happier? Are you worried about your work?'

'I can sell all the hats I can make, until we run out of material. After that – well, I don't know. Uncle Bertie talks vaguely of perhaps closing the wholesale side and taking on more government work . . .'

'It sounds as if you'll manage whatever happens.'

'Are you worried about when the baby comes, Beth?'

'A bit,' Beth admitted. 'I shall have to find child-minders and that is expensive and it's hard to find one you can trust . . .'

Lizzie hesitated, then, 'You haven't heard anything more – about Mark?'

'No. I suppose I have to accept he's gone. I cry myself to sleep sometimes, but it doesn't help. My child won't have a father and that hurts more than anything else.'

'Why don't you get in touch with Mark's parents? They might be pleased to hear about the baby?'

'I wouldn't be good enough for them – and I'm not going to tell them.'

'I just thought they might offer you some help.'

'I just want him to come back,' Beth said and a sob of grief escaped her. 'I want a proper home and a husband to love me . . .'

'I wish I had room for you to stay here, but Harry will be back on leave sometimes and there isn't room for two babies. I'm so sorry, Beth. I know it isn't easy to find a decent place, especially if . . .' she broke off and Beth looked at her, a defiant almost angry look in her eyes.

'If you're unmarried and pregnant,' she said. 'I know, Lizzie. It's going to be hard, but as my father told me, I've made my bed . . .'

Uncle Bertie had mixed feelings and showed them when Lizzie told them over Sunday lunch that her friend was staying for a while.

'Beth will find her own accommodation; she just needs a little time . . .'

'As long, as she doesn't take advantage.' Uncle Bertie said. 'Now then, back to business. I took that design of yours for a simple dress and the jacket to my contact and he thought it was just what they are looking for. It's going to be called the Utility brand and all clothing for women will have to conform more or less to that style. Until now there have been plenty of things in the shops for women to pick and choose, but in future there will be rules and regulations as to what they can buy new, but I feel that those big shoulders you came up with suit the mannish style women are looking for.'

'Ordinary girls like me won't mind too much, but rich women are soon going to get bored with that look.'

'Then they will have to make do with what's in their wardrobes or save their coupons and buy material to have made up – and that's another service I thought we might offer.'

'Do you think we shall be rationed for clothing as well as foodstuffs?'

'Certain of it,' Uncle Bertie said. 'If you need a new costume or coat, buy it now before it happens. Or better still, design something and we'll get it made up.'

'I can't believe women will accept being told what they can wear . . .'

'It's coming, believe me. You have no idea yet what a war is like, Lizzie. It was bad enough last time but . . .'

Everyone, said the same thing – no good complaining if you couldn't buy what you wanted because there was a war on, but apart from some shortages in the shops, rationing on butter, sugar, meat and bacon, and the sinking of British merchant ships, they were not suffering too badly at home.

Harry was still flying the missions he dreaded. He didn't say much in his infrequent letters and scarcely ever phoned now, because when he did neither of them had much to say after the first few words asking how they each were. Lizzie blamed herself but she hadn't been able to talk naturally despite trying to think of news that would interest him. She'd hoped he'd want to talk about the baby, but he didn't seem very interested. Lizzie was a little resentful, because it was his fault she was having the child and feeling so mixed up about it. Instead of joy, she couldn't help thinking that he'd just left her to get on with things – as if the child was nothing to do with him.

'Did you hear what I said, Lizzie?'

'About the clothing being rationed soon?'

'No, about where you're going to have the baby. Your aunt wants you to come to us. If you stay with us she can watch the child when you're working and do the washing herself . . .'

'I couldn't ask her to do all that,' Lizzie said. 'It is really kind of you both, but I'll have to think it over for a while – talk to Harry . . .'

'What does he know about things like that?' Uncle Bertie scoffed. 'No, your aunt is right; you'll come to us, Lizzie, and we'll look after you and the child until you can manage on your own.'

Lizzie knew that what he said made sense and she was being ridiculous to resist. Harry's aunt and uncle were the nearest to family she had, and yet she felt that she was being reeled in like a fish on a line, drawn into Uncle Bertie's net so tightly that she would never escape. He wanted her as part of his expanding business. She knew now that he'd often wanted to branch out into other things, but he'd needed Lizzie's talent to help him do that – and now he had her he had no intention of letting her go. Yet Lizzie valued her independence and there were moments when she lay in the dark and wondered what it would be like to work in the West End Store Sebastian had spoken of . . .

CHAPTER 35

Madge solved Beth's problem when Lizzie told her in confidence why Beth was staying with her at the flat. 'Ed is sleeping with me downstairs now,' she said. 'Which means the bed upstairs is empty. Bring Beth here for a visit, and if she's satisfied, she can stay for as long as she likes.'

'Madge, are you certain – would Ed mind?'

'Ed never minds anything if I'm happy. You should know I only have to ask and I get. Besides, she can help me in the house a little until the baby is born.'

'I'm sure Beth would help keep things nice,' Lizzie said. 'You are a darling, Madge. I know Beth will jump at the chance.'

'Good. Bring her round tomorrow before you go to work . . .'

'Yes, I will. I did tell you that she is starting work at the munitions factory next Monday, didn't I? She was lucky and got a job in the office there – and she likes the office manager. He told her to call him Bernie and he was glad to get her because most of the girls with qualifications are working in the services or other factories.'

'Does he know she's pregnant?'

'Yes, she told him.'

'And he still took her on?'

'Beth bought herself a cheap wedding ring and gave her name as Mrs Allen,' Lizzie said. 'I advised against it, but she said she can get away with being a widow for a while and she needs to earn some money even if he sacks her when he discovers the truth.'

'Oh dear, that was a foolish thing to do, but I suppose she isn't the first to lie in her situation,' Madge said. 'Never mind, it's done now – we'll just have to hope it doesn't come out too soon.'

'I'll go and tell her the good news. I know she's been worrying because all the rooms she's seen were awful and she turned them down.'

'Some of these landladies offer damp dirty rooms and charge the earth for them. Tell Beth I don't want rent. She can help with the chores and buy some food for us all to share sometimes and that is sufficient . . .'

'You must let her pay towards the food. Her mother charged her fifteen shillings; she can afford that while she's working.'

'Well, if you think so, Lizzie – but she will be company for me once she's home with the baby – and when she's ready to go back to work, I can look after the child . . .'

'You're so kind,' Lizzie said and bent to kiss her.

'You've been more than kind to me,' Madge told her. 'I would have done it just for your sake, Lizzie, but I'm sure Beth is a good girl. She has just been unfortunate . . .'

'It was unfortunate that she should fall for a child just like that – and to lose the man she loved as well . . .' She shook her head. 'It's happening to more and more women, Madge.'

'You worry about Harry?'

'He hasn't been home in months. He phones now and then and sends a card – but I know he's working too many shifts . . .'

'Well, perhaps he'll come soon. He ought to be home when you have the baby, Lizzie . . .'

'That's months away,' she said and laughed. 'I haven't even started to think about it yet.'

In April Hitler invaded Norway. At the end of the month, British troops were sent to key points to help the beleaguered Norwegian people and to push the Germans back in the north, but their hold on the south of the country was tight. It seemed to bring the war much closer to the British people and everyone wondered who was next. There was endless talk of the war and the papers were filled with pictures of fighting and destruction everywhere. More and more women were receiving the dreaded telegrams that told of loved ones missing or dead, and Beth was just one of thousands who waited for better news without much hope of it ever arriving. Lizzie had given up asking if she heard anything, because she knew it caused her friend grief.

'We kept moaning about the phoney war,' Beth said that morning of July 1940 and wriggled uncomfortably in her chair. Now nearly eight months gone, she'd grown very large recently and had finally been forced to give up work. Whenever she could, she came round to Lizzie for a coffee or a chat, helping her with anything that needed doing. 'I wish we could go back, Lizzie, forget all this horrid business. They say the Hun sticks babies on bayonets and roast them over a fire . . .'

'Don't have nightmares, love,' Lizzie said smiling at her; she was just over five months and showing little sign of her pregnancy. 'I don't believe that for a moment, besides, we're ready for them if they do try to invade – and our air force is doing a great job patrolling the skies . . . and the Army boys are just getting on with things, despite all the setbacks at Dunkirk last month.'

Beth sighed and pressed a hand to her back, the strain showing in her face. She'd been fine until the last couple of weeks, but now her ankles had swollen and she was feeling low.

'Are you in pain, love?' Lizzie asked, full of sympathy. 'It can't be much longer surely?'

'I don't know where I shall have the baby. I can't put all that on Madge because she couldn't cope. The hospitals are full of wounded soldiers these days. I was booked in at the London, but I'm not sure they're still taking maternity cases.'

'Don't worry, they will find room for you

somewhere,' Lizzie replied. 'I know you feel awful, Beth love, but it could be worse.'

'Yes, they'll start bombing us next,' Beth grumbled. 'Bernie says it's bound to happen.' She was still in touch with her boss at the munitions factory and he'd promised her her job back when she was ready.

'I suppose it will.'

'Sometimes I feel like running away . . .'

'Where would you go? Once they start bombing us they will be all over the country, so it won't make much difference,' Lizzie said. 'All the big towns and cities, especially where they have important factories, will catch it, Beth.'

'I know . . .' Beth sighed. 'It's just that I don't want to be a nuisance to Madge and Ed. You'll be all right, Lizzie. When you get near your time, you can go and stay with Harry's family – but I can't ask Madge to run up and down stairs for me, can I?'

'No, you can't. You will have to go into hospital, Beth . . .'

'Has Harry been home since last month?'

'I told you he came on a flying visit for a few hours but that was weeks ago.'

'We're a pair, aren't we?' Beth said. 'Neither of us is really happy – no, don't pretend, Lizzie. I don't know what happened between you and Harry but I know something did.'

'Yes. I wish it hadn't, but it did and things aren't the same. He was almost like a stranger when he came home . . .' Lizzie caught her breath. 'He did telephone last week; told me he'd been transferred to a new unit. He was flying special missions before but now he will be on bombers I think . . .' She shuddered, because even though she hadn't forgiven Harry for hurting her, she wanted him to come back safe. She often felt as if she were being racked by her conflicting emotions, because Harry was the father of her child and Lizzie was more and more aware of the new life within her. At first she'd felt resentment, but that was against her husband – she couldn't resent an innocent child. 'I can't bear to think of it, Beth. I really hate what's happening now.'

'Bernie asked me to marry him,' Beth said suddenly, bringing Lizzie's eyes to hers in shock. 'He says he's too old to have a child of his own and he would be happy to be a father to mine.'

'You told him the truth then?'

'He guessed and asked me straight out so I told him. I thought he might sack me, but there was no way I could keep on lying to him – and then he said he was glad. He was sorry that Mark had been lost at sea but he says he loves me and wants to make an honest woman of me.'

'Will you marry him, Beth? It would make your life so much easier – and you like him a lot, don't you?'

'No one could help liking Bernie,' Beth said. 'He's strict over work but he's fair and he's generous. I don't mind the limp – he got that from

346

the last war – and he isn't bad-looking, but I'm not sure I ought to marry him. Liking isn't the same as being in love, Lizzie.' She shook her head. 'Would it be fair if I can't love him the way he loves me, because I'm still in love with Mark. I think about him and I cry, even though I know he's gone – and, as for Bernie, when the baby is born, is he going to resent it?'

'Surely he wouldn't ask if he felt like that, Beth?'

'I think it might happen one day . . .' She sighed and heaved herself from the chair. 'I'd better go. Madge worries if I'm away too long.'

'Beth, if anything happens – if the baby starts, ring me and I'll come.'

'You're busy, and what could you do?' Beth said, leaning in to kiss her cheek. 'It will be a doctor I need. Don't worry, Lizzie. I dare say I'll have plenty of time to get to the hospital when the time comes. I just felt like a moan.'

'What does your mum say?'

'She says she'll be coming round all the time when the birth is imminent and that there's nothing to worry about.'

'Well, I suppose she's had four children . . .'

'Yes.' Beth's throat caught and she struggled to hold in the emotion. 'Mum has been a brick. I know she won't let me down – even though Dad hasn't forgiven me.'

Saying her farewells to Lizzie, Beth went downstairs and out of the side door. She looked back at her friend and waved, feeling the uncertainty and loneliness sweep over her. It was so much better when she was with Lizzie or her mother. Madge and Ed were kind and treated her as family; she was grateful, but she dreaded the times when she was alone in her small room and had nothing to do but think of Mark.

Beth shook her head as she walked slowly back to Madge and Ed's home. If she married Bernie she would have to leave their house, but she really didn't know if she wanted to be his wife. How could she sleep next to him at night and accept his kisses, the touch of his hands on her body, when she still longed for Mark? It wouldn't be fair to Bernie or her. Sometimes she thought it would be worth it to be safe and comfortable, to have someone take care of her – and then she thought again and realised she wasn't ready to marry anyone but Mark yet, perhaps she never would be.

Her throat was tight and she struggled to keep the tears back. Why did Mark have to die? She still loved him so much . . . still longed to see his face and touch him. Yet she knew he was lost to her.

'Oh Mum,' she whispered as the tears trickled slowly down her cheeks. 'Mum, I want to come home . . .'

Beth was feeling very sorry for herself, and Lizzie could understand why. It must be awful to be in her position. Lizzie sometimes felt fed up because Harry's aunt and uncle fussed over her too much, reminding her to keep her appointments at the clinic and asking if she was eating properly. Lizzie was working harder than ever. She'd thought their supplies of material might have started to run out by now, but Uncle Bertie seemed to have plenty. She was finding that most women were going for plainer hats at the moment. They admired the frivolous ones but then put them back and said there was a war on and they mustn't be wasteful. She felt wistful sometimes as she added just a ribbon or a feather, missing the yards of tulle, net and silk flowers she'd used on most of her special designs. She could still sell a cloche with a ribbon and a single flower, but the fussy big-brimmed hats were not as popular at the moment.

Sebastian's manager had not been to see her for three months. She sometimes thought it wasn't worth keeping the bespoke business going. Uncle Bertie would love it if she just concentrated on his end of the business. Well, did it matter if she no longer had the freedom to design beautiful hats? With men dying and the news from abroad looking grimmer all the time, silk hats seemed less important than they once had. She would have a child in a few months and perhaps Harry would come home for the birth and things would be better. They could never be the same as they were once, but perhaps they could find a way to be at least friends . . .

It was her fault he didn't come home much, Lizzie knew, because when he'd tried to take her in his arms and kiss her she'd held back. Seeing the hurt in his eyes, she'd felt sorry and tried to overcome her feelings but she couldn't help the shudder that went through her.

Harry had apologised more than once and she knew he'd been in a state that night. She sometimes lay and thought of him up there in the plane with the others, knowing that he was terrified and trying not to show it – not to be a coward. The least she could do was to be a loving wife when he came home – and yet she couldn't. Harry should not have taken his anger and resentment out on her, and even though she wanted to forgive him it wasn't possible to forget.

Thinking about her own problems wouldn't help anyone, Lizzie knew – but perhaps she might be able to help Beth. At least it was worth a try . . .

'I don't know if you're aware of how Beth is living, Mr Court,' Lizzie said. She heard Beth's mother's indrawn breath. 'The lady she lives with is a semi-invalid and if the baby starts Madge wouldn't be able to do much – or even run for the doctor . . .'

'In that case she should look for somewhere else to live,' Beth's father said harshly. 'There must be plenty of lodging houses in London.'

'Not all of them want a young baby,' Lizzie said. 'Beth's manager at work asked her to marry him but I don't think she will.'

'More fool him. She doesn't deserve to be a decent man's wife after the way she behaved.'

'No!' Mrs Court cried. 'I won't let you say such things about your own daughter. Beth isn't wicked; she just made a mistake. Is that any reason she should be punished forever? She ought to be here with her family . . .'

'I told you I won't have her here, bringing shame on me.'

'She's my baby, my youngest, and I want to look after her.' Mrs Court looked at Lizzie. 'If Lizzie hadn't come here and told us, I wouldn't have done anything but I can't leave her there with that poor woman at a time like this . . .'

'She doesn't come into my house . . .'

'Then I shall move out and find somewhere for us to live until the baby is born,' Mrs Court said defiantly.

Lizzie felt awful as she realised she'd caused a tremendous row. 'I'm sorry,' she apologised as Beth's father stared furiously at his wife. 'I shouldn't have come round, but I'm worried for Beth . . . I thought if you understood that both she and the baby might be in danger . . .'

'So am I worried,' Mrs Court said. 'I'm glad you did come, Lizzie. It's been on my mind, but I was too much of a coward to say. Now, I'm not going to keep quiet. Beth needs my help and I'm going to be with her.'

'All right, you win,' her husband said, capitulating to the amazement of both of them. 'You can bring Beth here until she's over the birth – but after that she can find somewhere to live. And I

351

don't want to see her. She can stay in her room while I'm in the house; those are my terms.'

Mrs Court met his angry gaze. 'Thank you, Derek,' she said. 'It's all I ask of you – just until she's well enough to go back to work.'

He turned his dark gaze on Lizzie. 'You are a good friend to my daughter, Mrs Oliver. Her mother will bring her here until after the birth, but don't ask me to be responsible for her bastard.'

With that he turned and slammed out of the kitchen.

'I'm sorry. I didn't mean to cause a row, but Beth is really miserable, even though she pretends not to be – and she's worried about having the baby and causing Madge a lot of worry. I don't think Madge thought things through before she offered – and it was my fault for letting her ask. If Beth is here I know she will be all right.'

'My husband is right about one thing. You are a good friend to Beth – you said the things I wanted to say and dared not.'

'Beth wouldn't want to cause trouble between you – but now she's really nervous and I think she needs your help. There's no one like a mother.'

Mrs Court smiled at her. 'When it's your turn, I'll be glad to do whatever I can, Lizzie.'

'I've already got people worrying about me,' Lizzie said. 'At least now, I can stop worrying about Beth for a while . . .'

★　★　★

It was Lizzie's afternoon off and she spent most of it wandering around the marketplace, looking for things she could use to make baby clothes and nappies. Lizzie's resentment had gone now and sometimes now she looked forward to holding the child in her arms.

'Lizzie, that basket looks heavy,' a voice said and she turned in surprise as Tilly came to stand beside her. 'Let me carry it home for you. I wanted to have a chat. We never can at work, without Mr Oliver havin' a go at us.'

Lizzie handed over her burden with a sigh of relief. 'I've got ages to go yet, but my back is aching like mad.'

'Tell me about it. I had it for ages when I was carrying my daughter,' Tilly said as their bus arrived. They found a seat at the front, Tilly sitting by the window with Lizzie's basket on her knees. 'Mind you, I'd go through it all again like a shot to have another child, but I don't seem to be able to get pregnant again.'

'I didn't realise you were trying for another baby?'

'We can't really afford it,' Tilly said with a shrug. 'I suppose it's just as well I haven't fallen again – but I get broody when I see other women with babies.'

'We couldn't do without you at the workshops.'

'Oh, Oliver would soon replace me,' Tilly said. 'I'm just another seamstress to him.'

'Well, you're not to me,' Lizzie said. 'If I ever

have my own business I'd employ you as a stylist . . .'

'You won't leave Oliver, will you?' Tilly looked shocked.

'No, I don't suppose I shall,' Lizzie said. 'Sometimes, I wish I could please myself what I make, that's all . . .'

Tilly laughed and shook her head. 'You wait for another few months and then you'll have too much to think about to worry about designing hats . . .'

CHAPTER 36

'What did you think you were doing, going to my parents behind my back?' Beth demanded as she came barging into Lizzie's flat that afternoon. 'I would never have begged him . . .'

'Don't be such a fool. I just told him the truth, and even though he wouldn't admit it, he realised he couldn't leave you exposed to danger. If Ed was at work, Madge couldn't cope. Go home for now and have the baby, and then you can look for a house somewhere. It is silly to stay with Madge when your father has given permission.'

'It's not just that – how can I leave Madge when she's been so kind?'

'And you've repaid her. Look at how much better the house looks since you took over the cleaning.'

'Madge's back hurts more again and she won't tell Ed . . . so I've been doing all the cooking and washing.'

'She isn't your responsibility, Beth. You should think of yourself and the child – you can still visit Madge and so shall I, but I think you should be with your mother for the birth.'

'I'll think about it,' Beth said. 'I've told Mum I shan't go for a few days anyway. I have to get Madge used to the idea gradually. It would be cruel to just leave like that . . .'

'Yes, I agree, but don't leave it too long, Beth.'

'No . . .' Beth smiled ruefully. 'I really want to be with Mum for the birth. Afterwards, I'll manage somehow – but I feel nervous sometimes and I do want my mum.'

'Of course you do. I'd feel the same if I had a mother like yours. You tell Madge that your mum needs you home she won't make a fuss then.'

'I don't want to lie to her,' Beth smiled oddly. 'I'm fond of Madge – but I do know she couldn't cope if I suddenly gave birth and Ed wasn't around.'

'Well then what alternative do you have? I didn't mean to go behind your back, Beth. I was just trying to help you.'

'I know . . .' Beth sighed and arched her back. 'It's just that I don't want my father thinking I'm crawling . . .'

'Forgive me?'

'Of course,' Beth said. 'I'd better go then . . .'

Leaving Lizzie, Beth was sunk in thought as she walked back to Madge's house. She knew it would distress Madge more than Lizzie realised if Beth left her, and she didn't want to hurt her feelings.

She stopped walking as she realised something was going on. Seeing the fire engines and police vans, people milling around, she suddenly noticed that the smoke was rising from a house near the end of the road. Beth's heart jerked. Had there been a bomb? Everyone was certain it had to start soon. Yet surely they would have heard something before this . . . She hadn't heard the sirens, but perhaps it had just been this area . . . and then she saw it was Madge's house that was on fire and she began to run.

'What happened?' she asked a woman who was standing watching all the activity. 'Is Madge all right?'

'They say it was a gas explosion. Probably a leak or something. I don't know if anyone was hurt, I only just got here . . .'

Beth ran towards the house. Everything she owned was inside and the house was almost demolished and what was left of it was burning, but all she could think about was Madge.

'You can't go in there, missus.' The policeman held her arm, preventing Beth from rushing into the burning house.

'I live there – my friend, was she hurt? Was anyone still inside?'

'It's your house?'

'It belongs to Madge and Ed. I'm their lodger.'

'There was a woman inside. She was lying at the foot of the stairs and they think she'd had a fall. She was unconscious when they brought her out and they've taken her to the infirmary.'

The tears trickled down Beth's cheeks. She had no choice but to follow Lizzie's suggestion now, but it wasn't so much her own predicament that haunted her it was Madge and Ed. She couldn't imagine why Madge should have tried to go upstairs, but she wished she'd been there when Madge needed her, because she knew how much Ed cared for his wife and if she died it would devastate the kindly man.

'Beth has nothing left,' Lizzie said to Aunt Miriam. 'And it's even worse for Madge and Ed; they've lost their home, furniture, photos, all their memories.'

'That is a terrible shame,' Aunt Miriam said. 'We'll raid my wardrobe and see what we can use. Some of my dresses can be made to fit Beth for now. As for Madge and Ed . . .' she shook her head sorrowfully. 'I'm sure Bertie will find something that fits Ed . . .'

'Ed doesn't care about anything but Madge,' Lizzie said. 'He's sitting up the hospital and won't budge even to come home and shave or rest – and I don't think he's eaten a thing.'

'When she does come out of it, he can home here for a while, just until he gets on his feet again,' Aunt Miriam said. 'I know Bertie would say that was right. We have to look after him . . .'

'If he'll let us . . .' Lizzie was worried. 'Madge hasn't come round yet. After all she's suffered, I'm frightened she's hurt too badly . . .'

'Do we know what actually happened yet?'

'The doctors think she fell before the gas explosion. Perhaps she slipped or fainted . . .'

'She was probably unconscious and knew nothing about it, Lizzie.'

'I hope that was the case. Have the police said what caused the gas leak?'

'They think it was due to some faulty work on the pipes when workmen were doing repairs in the road a few weeks back.'

Lizzie nodded. 'I'm going to take a clean nightie up to the infirmary for Madge and some things for Ed and then I shall go round to Beth's home. I'm going to give her some of the baby things I've prepared.'

'I'd offer her a bed here, but you said she'd gone to her mother's house. Will her father object?'

'He will let her stay until the baby is born and then she has to find her own place . . .'

'Well, you know we have more than enough room, Lizzie. Beth is your friend and I'm happy to help if she's stuck. It's entirely your choice, my dear. Our house is your house; you know that . . .'

'You're so kind,' Lizzie said. 'We'll see how Beth gets on at home. She was going to the infirmary to see Madge today.'

'I am so very sorry for all of them . . .'

'I can hardly believe it has happened – and caused by careless workmanship. They ought to lock those workmen up . . .'

'But they won't, because there's no way to prove they caused the problem, and they need all the skilled men they have. It might have been a cracked pipe in Madge's house. Didn't anyone notice the smell of gas?'

'Beth never mentioned it and she would have . . .' Lizzie shook her head. 'It was just an accident I suppose, but why did it have to happen to two of the nicest people I know?'

'There's no answer to that, Lizzie.' Aunt Miriam looked sad. 'I suppose you haven't heard from Harry recently? It seems a long time since he came home on leave.'

'No, I haven't heard,' Lizzie said. 'He's busy . . .'

'You two haven't fallen out, have you?'

'No, of course not,' she lied, but she couldn't look at Aunt Miriam, because to be honest she had no idea how things stood between her and Harry . . .

Her visit to the Infirmary left Lizzie feeling close to tears. She'd given the nurse the things she'd brought for Madge and asked how she was, but the answer was the same. It was touch and go and even if Madge recovered consciousness they didn't know if she would ever walk again; her spine had been cracked in the fall and she would probably never use her legs again.

Lizzie hadn't known how to hold back the tears. Madge had already suffered so much and if she was a permanent invalid, it would break both her and Ed's hearts.

She'd found Ed sitting in the dark corridor outside the ward; everywhere smelled of strong disinfectant and the small windows were high up, letting in very little daylight, the faded linoleum on the floor looking in need of a good polish. She'd given him a cup of tea, but talking to him elicited only a nod or a shake of the head. It was impossible to reach the silent stranger he'd become and Lizzie left the infirmary feeling close to breaking point. Whatever happened, she would find a way to help them. Lizzie didn't have much spare money, though she was comfortable in her little flat and never went short of the necessities, but Ed was going to need a lot more than that to get back on his feet. His house was a write-off and he would need to look for new lodgings for them – if Madge came out of hospital. Lizzie couldn't even imagine what he would do if his wife died . . .

Forcing back her desire to weep, Lizzie caught the bus to Beth's home. At least she was safe and with her family. She might have been caught in the explosion too had she not been drinking tea at Lizzie's home . . .

'Are you settling in all right?' Lizzie looked around Beth's room. 'I've brought you a dress and hat for after you've had the baby, and Aunt Miriam sent a couple of her dresses to wear for now. They're big and shapeless, but you can alter them to fit just until the baby comes, can't you?'

'Yes, of course, thanks. That's a lovely hat, Lizzie. I've always liked it.'

'Good, because you'll enjoy wearing it. I've brought a few things for the baby, too.'

'Mum's going to give me all her old baby things,' Beth said. 'I hadn't bought much because I was afraid that something would go wrong with the birth if I did . . .' She laughed. 'Silly, isn't it? I'm glad now, because what money I'd saved was in the Post Office and I had the book with me in my bag.'

'It's still rotten luck – and there's no insurance either. Ed didn't believe in it . . .'

'He probably couldn't afford it, and I didn't think of it,' Beth said. 'I'm more worried about Madge than my situation, to be honest. At least I've got a home for the time being.'

'Aunt Miriam has offered them a bed,' Lizzie said. 'Ed will probably manage with second-hand things for a while and I'll make Madge some dresses when she comes out – if she does . . .' She caught her breath. 'I visited them at the infirmary. She's still unconscious and Ed looks like death warmed up.'

'All we can do is pray for her,' Beth said. 'Mum says she's got some things that Madge can have – and Ed is more my dad's size than Oliver's. Don't worry, Lizzie. We'll all help them – but we can't give Madge her health back.'

'No and that's the awful thing,' Lizzie said. 'She was getting a little better. I can't think why she went upstairs – she never does . . .'

'She said something about giving me the clothes

she'd bought for her son – the baby who died and left her an invalid – I think they were upstairs. Ed told her he would bring them down for her when he had time.'

'And she couldn't wait, so she went after them herself and fell on the way back . . .'

'Yes, probably,' Beth looked miserable. 'I feel guilty, as if I caused it all . . .'

'Of course you didn't,' Lizzie told her. 'Madge made her own decision – and the gas leak wasn't your fault or hers. You never smelled gas when you were there?'

'No, not once,' Beth gasped suddenly. 'Oh, it's the baby kicking again. He's so restless now.'

'You haven't got much longer to go, have you?'

'Any day now . . .' Beth gave another cry and then doubled over. 'Oh, hell, Lizzie! That one really hurt . . .'

'Shall I run down and get your mother?'

'I've got my bag packed,' Beth said. 'Here's the number for the taxi and the hospital. Can you tell them I'm coming in and then . . .'? She let out a little scream. 'Hurry, Lizzie. I need to get there fast . . .'

'Yes, I know. I'll be as quick as I can,' Lizzie said and took the number from her. As she ran downstairs, Mrs Court came into the hall. 'I'm phoning for a taxi to take Beth to the hospital – she's starting the baby . . .'

'I thought I heard her call out. You get off, Lizzie. I'll go up to her now.'

Lizzie rushed out of the house and ran down the lane to the phone box. She fumbled with her change in her haste and rang through to the hospital and then the ambulance. When she returned to the house, she discovered that Mrs Court had got her daughter down into the hall.

'The taxi will be here soon. You'll be all right, Beth. These things take hours. You'll be in bed soon with a nurse to look after you . . .'

'I hope it won't take hours,' Beth said between gritted teeth. 'It hurts too damned much.'

Lizzie sat in the corridor and waited through the long night. Beth's mother had been allowed inside the delivery ward with her daughter but Lizzie had been asked to stay outside. She could hear the screams coming from inside; they seemed to go on and on for ages. Beth was having a terrible time and Lizzie felt as if her own baby moved in sympathy.

It was getting on for four in the morning when Beth's father came along the corridor. He looked down at Lizzie and then sat on the seat next to her, twisting his hat in his hands and looking miserable.

'Is that Beth?' he asked as they heard a particularly loud scream.

'Yes. We've been here since seven last evening. I didn't know how to let you know.'

'One of the neighbours saw you leave in a taxi. I knew it had to be the infirmary. Beth was so close to her time.'

'Yes. I don't know how much longer it can go on for . . .'

'Her mother was twelve hours with the twins. I thought I was going to lose her . . .' his eyes reflected his fear. 'Beth's just like her mother . . .'

'Beth's strong. She'll be all right.'

'Yes.' He looked awkward. 'I just wanted to know if she was all right . . .'

Suddenly they heard the sound of a baby crying and a moment or two later the door opened and the doctor came out. He walked up to Beth's father and smiled at him.

'Are you Mr Allen? Your wife has given birth to beautiful twins, sir.'

'She's my daughter.' He looked pale and shaken. 'Her mother had twins – I suppose that's why . . .' he shook his head as if to clear it. 'The children's father is dead . . .'

'I'm sorry to hear that,' the doctor said. 'Well, she's lucky to have such devoted friends and family. You'll be able to see her soon.'

Mr Court waited until the doctor had walked off and then stood up.

'I'll be off then. There's no need to tell anyone that I was here.'

'Won't you wait and see Beth and the twins?'

'No, I shall not see them – and I would prefer you didn't tell her I was here. I just wanted to know she was all right . . .'

★　　★　　★

365

'Oh, they are beautiful, and you've got a boy and a girl, Beth,' Lizzie said when she bent over the cots. 'I can't believe that you were in such pain. It must have been awful for you.'

'It was pretty awful, but the midwife said I was lucky, because she's never seen twins born so quickly.' Beth laughed. 'I must have been in labour all day, but worrying over Madge, well, I didn't realise it.'

'Yes, you're very lucky. When will they let you bring them home?'

'Probably in a day or so if I'm fit, but it's going to make a lot of work for mum looking after me and doing all the washing, especially with two of them. I'm going to get up as soon as I can.'

'You must have a rest for a bit. We don't want you getting ill so you can't feed the twins, do we?'

'No, I suppose not . . .' she sighed.

'What's wrong?'

'I've been thinking about Bernie. He sent me a gorgeous bunch of flowers, some chocolates and a lovely letter – I think he really wants to marry me, Lizzie – and I might . . .'

'Are you sure, Beth? Don't rush into anything just yet. You're in no fit state to be making a big decision right now. I'll help as much as I can – we all will.'

'I know, but I can't expect you or Mum to cope with my twins as well as your own lives. If I married Bernie, he would provide a home and I wouldn't

366

need to work until they're at school – though I'd like to go back to work one day.'

'What about Tony?'

Beth looked down at her children. 'Tony told me once not to come crying to him, Lizzie. Bernie says all I have to do is say the word.'

'Well, I still think you should wait a bit,' Lizzie cautioned.

'I just wish Mark had lived long enough to know . . .'

'Yes, of course you do, love,' Lizzie squeezed her hand, knowing nothing she said could ease that pain. 'I wish I could make it happen for you.'

'I wish my father had come,' Beth said and the sadness in her eyes tempted Lizzie to tell her that he'd been there in the corridor and known she was safe, but she'd been asked not to and perhaps it was best. Mr Court still hadn't forgiven his daughter for getting pregnant without a husband.

'Give him time,' she said and squeezed Beth's hand. 'I shall have to go, love, because it will be dark soon and I don't like being out in the blackout – even though I've got one of those new shaded torches.'

'You'll come and see me again soon?'

'Of course I shall,' Lizzie said and bent to kiss her and then touched the babies' soft cheeks. Seeing Beth's twins had made her realise how much she really wanted to hold her own baby. 'They are really gorgeous, Beth. Think about them and don't worry, love.'

She was anxious as she left her friend. Life was so precarious at the moment and people died suddenly. Beth had no hope of marrying the man she loved, but Lizzie still had a chance to make her marriage work. It was ridiculous to still care about what had happened one night when Harry had had too much to drink. Lizzie should make the most of her life while she could. She would write to Harry and tell him she loved him and was looking forward to seeing him, even if she wasn't sure in her heart that it was true. Yet for the sake of their child, she had to try to heal the breach between them.

CHAPTER 37

All through the summer the news had been dire as the Germans continued their relentless progress through Holland and Belgium. At the end of May, the British troops had been driven back to the beaches of Dunkirk, and the marvellous evacuation by the little ships and pleasure boats saved thousands of men that would have otherwise perished. The papers had been full of praise for the bravery of ordinary seamen who had put to sea to help in the evacuation of the trapped men, ferrying them from the shore out to the bigger ships that would transport them home to a heroes' welcome. Even though it had been a defeat for the Allies, the marvellous rescue seemed to make victory of what might have been despair. In everyone's mind the thought was the same: had those brave seamen not got the men out, we should have been finished as an independent country; few people said it out loud, because it was unthinkable that Britain had come so near to utter and complete defeat, but most thought it in private. The hospitals were overflowing with wounded men and the war was suddenly a painful reality in every home.

Now the Germans were parading through the streets of Paris and the French had been forced to sign a humiliating armistice in the coach used for the German surrender in 1918. Everyone was looking over their shoulders; wondering and thinking *are we next?*

It was a low point for the nation and people were gloomy, only a few still able to joke and laugh. Lizzie thought it was as if everyone knew things had gone badly wrong and they'd moved on to a new stage; they were waiting for the worst to happen.

As if on cue they received the news that Madge was dead. She'd gone in her sleep, so perhaps that was a mercy, but Ed wouldn't take the loss of his wife easily and Lizzie was worried for him. Beth was upset and cried, saying she shouldn't have left her alone that day; Madge had been well liked and everyone was upset by her death.

'It wasn't your fault,' Lizzie told her. 'Ed must feel the same – but Madge did what she did and the gas explosion was a tragedy no one could have foreseen. I went with Uncle Bertie and fetched Ed home, because the hospital said he was just sitting there staring at the wall. He didn't want to come, but in the end he allowed us to take him away. I don't know what he'll do . . .'

'He will either break down and cry or he'll just give up,' Beth said. 'Mum says she's heard of people like that . . . one can't survive without the other and they fade away . . .' She gave a little sob. 'I can't bear to think of her, Lizzie.'

Lizzie found it difficult too. She'd tried sitting with Ed, talking to him, trying to persuade him to eat, but he stared straight through her, and she wasn't sure anything got through to him.

However, on the morning of Madge's funeral, Ed was washed, shaved and dressed in the clothes he'd been given by friends and neighbours. The church was packed with people that Lizzie didn't know, as well as customers that she'd seen in Uncle Bertie's workshops. Ed was obviously well liked and there were lots of small wreathes and bunches of flowers for Madge.

Lizzie stood by Ed's side during the church service and when she realised he was crying she reached for his hand. He held on to it throughout the vicar's sermon and the hymns, not letting go until they all followed the coffin out to the churchyard.

Ed threw a single red rose into the open grave instead of earth, and both Beth and Lizzie followed with posies of their own. Ed nodded to the people who had come out to see his wife laid to rest but didn't speak before turning and walking away.

That afternoon, the flat seemed lonely, perhaps because she'd come back from a funeral and death was so final. Uncle Bertie had actually closed the workshop for the day as a mark of respect, and Lizzie didn't feel like trying to design anything.

She was just thinking of going shopping, even though there wasn't much to buy in the shops, when the bell on the front of the house rang. Lizzie went downstairs as quickly as she could, opening it and saying, 'Yes, can I help you . . .' She stared at the man in uniform on her doorstep. 'Sebastian?'

'Lizzie Larch, how are you?'

Shocked, Lizzie felt her heart give a kicking surge.

'Where did you come from?' she asked. 'I thought you were away somewhere on . . . well, war work?'

'I was but now I'm home for a few days. I wanted to see how things were going – but I hadn't realised. You're having a baby . . . congratulations. Your husband must be over the moon?'

'Yes . . .' Lizzie felt the lump in her throat. 'I don't really know what he thinks. I haven't heard from him for ages. I don't even know if he'll come home for our wedding anniversary next month . . .' Stupid tears stung her eyes and she blinked hard. 'Sorry, I've just come from a funeral and I'm feeling a bit down . . .'

'Oh, I am sorry.' Sebastian stepped into the hallway. 'Somebody close?'

'Ed's wife Madge, she had a terrible accident. There was a gas explosion and . . .' Lizzie lifted her chin. 'You don't want to hear this . . . I'm afraid the workshop is closed for the day – and I haven't made anything special myself, because materials are too scarce to waste on experiments now . . .'

'I didn't particularly come for hats, my manager does all that – I wanted to see how you were, Lizzie.'

'I'm all right really . . .'

'Why don't you let me take you out for tea somewhere nice?' he asked. 'You need cheering up – and I'm just the man to do it . . .'

Why shouldn't she? She did need cheering up and Sebastian was both a good customer and a friend.

'Yes, thank you, I'd like that. I'll just put my coat on – it's upstairs . . . if you'd like to come up for a minute while I get ready.'

'I should like to see where you live so I can picture you at home, Lizzie.' He followed her upstairs, wandering about the kitchen and sitting room while she fetched her coat from the bedroom. His eyes lit up as she returned. 'You look lovely – and I like your home. It shows your taste, but it will be a bit small when the baby comes, won't it?'

'Yes, perhaps. I'll have to see how things go . . .' Lizzie made the effort to smile. 'I have a friend, Beth – you remember her?' Sebastian nodded. 'She was going steady with Mark Allen and he was killed and – she's had his twins. Beth will need her own place and she might like this flat.'

'Yes, I was sorry to learn of Mark's loss at sea. He was a good friend. Unfortunately, quite a few young women will lose their men in this war . . .' He frowned, then, 'Has she written to Mark's family to tell them about his children? I can give her the address if she doesn't have it.'

'Mark told her they wouldn't be pleased that he'd chosen a girl out of his class, so I don't suppose she would consider it, but I'll give it to her just in case . . .'

'Still, they have the right to know of their grand-children, don't they?'

'It must be Beth's decision,' Lizzie said deter-minedly. 'I'm looking forward to our tea. Let's go, we can talk on the way.'

'I have my car outside, Lizzie.'

'How do you manage to get petrol?'

'Oh, it seems that I'm considered important enough by certain people,' he said and laughed softly. Lizzie felt warmth spread through her, the clouds of the day dispersing as they went outside and he held the door of his car open. 'Unfair, of course, but I can get hold of most things I want.' He hesitated, then, 'In fact the only thing I've wanted recently that eluded me was you, Lizzie Larch . . .'

'Now, I know you're talking nonsense,' she said. Lizzie looked at him in amusement as they drove away. She hadn't felt this carefree in an age. 'I was only ever a talent in the making that you rather fancied encouraging, Sebastian. I never thought it more than that . . .'

'I know and that was your mistake, but you're happy and I'm not a man to come between husband and wife, even though you broke my heart, Lizzie Larch.' His bantering tone made her smile; she was never certain whether to take him seriously, because he seemed to laugh at her.

'I've been going over and over it in my mind until I don't know where I'm at,' Beth said as Lizzie welcomed her into the flat. 'Mum says I should wait for a while but I can't find a decent place to rent anywhere, Lizzie.'

'How many have you seen so far?'

'About a dozen I think. They stink of other people's cooking or they're damp – and I can't afford the rent for a better place. It looks as if I don't have much choice but to take Bernie's offer . . . doesn't it?'

'I don't know, but I don't want you to do something you'll regret . . .'

'Do you regret what you did?'

'Sometimes . . .' Lizzie caught back a sob. 'I know I shouldn't, but Harry hasn't written for weeks now and . . .' she shook her head because she couldn't tell even Beth the way her thoughts had gone recently. Since Sebastian took her to tea he'd been in her thoughts more and more, and that was wrong. She was Harry's wife and she'd had no right to feel the way she did when Sebastian kissed her softly on the lips when he brought her home.

'I love you, Lizzie Larch,' he'd told her in a low voice. 'No, don't say anything. I don't expect you to love me, and I know you're happily married – but

I wanted you to know if I didn't come back this time . . .'

Lizzie caught something in his voice that made her stare at him, but she'd known she must not ask, because his work was secret and he couldn't tell her. Clearly, he was concerned about this next mission, whatever it was, which is why he'd come to see her. Her throat tightened and she hardly knew what to say, but she managed at last, 'You must come back, Sebastian . . . I'm not particularly happy . . .'

'Lizzie,' he said, and there was a note of concern in his voice. 'I sensed something – can't you tell me?'

'No,' Lizzie whispered. 'I may have made a mistake, but I can't run away now. Harry's my husband and I'm having his child – that's all there is to it.'

Sebastian took a gentle hold of her arms, looking into her face, 'Tell me, Lizzie, is there hope for me one day?'

'Perhaps . . . I don't know,' she whispered. 'I shouldn't even say that . . .'

'But you have and it will keep me going,' he said and smiled in his old confident way. 'I'm going to come back, Lizzie Larch, and when I do – you'll be mine . . .'

Lizzie hadn't answered; she couldn't because she felt choked. Harry was her husband and she ought to remain faithful to him despite what had happened.

'Take care of yourself,' she whispered as he walked back to his car, but she knew he hadn't heard the words.

'Come back to me, Lizzie,' Beth said. 'You were miles away.'

'Sorry. I was thinking – but don't marry for anything but love, Beth, or you will regret it. Please promise not to do it out of desperation. We'll work something out. I promise you.'

'All right, I'll wait until Dad throws me out,' Beth said and laughed. 'But if I turn up on your doorstep with the twins and all my clobber you've only got yourself to blame.'

CHAPTER 38

Lizzie looked at the registered letter that had come through the post for her. She knew the writing instantly and was reluctant to open it, but curiosity overcame her and she slit the seal, taking out the contents. Inside was a thin piece of writing paper and a bundle of five-pound notes. She didn't count them but guessed there was well over a hundred pounds. Pushing the money back inside the envelope, she took out the sheet of paper.

Please do not be offended my dearest Lizzie. I wanted you to have this just in case. I promised to return to you, but in war promises are sometimes broken from no fault of one's own. I want you to know I've made provision for you in my will if I die. You are a talented and wonderful person, Lizzie Larch, and you deserve your chance in life.

If things become too awful for you, you should use this money to escape – and one day, pray God, I shall be home and you can tell me why you're so unhappy. I love you and nothing can change that, my darling girl. I know you've never trusted me, Lizzie, though I'm not sure why – but trust me now. Make a life of your own if I never return . . .

Ever yours, Sebastian.

Lizzie felt the sting of tears. She couldn't accept Sebastian's generosity, of course she couldn't, but she would keep his money until he returned because she wanted to give it to him in person and explain why she couldn't accept. She could only pray that he came safely home so that she could thank him for his kindness.

The post girl had delivered an ordinary letter as well as the registered one. Picking it up, she realised that it was from her husband. She opened it and stared at the words Harry had written:

My dearest Lizzie,

You've no idea how much I have regretted what happened on my last leave. I love you so much, darling, and your generous letter gave me hope that you really mean to forgive me. Because of that, I've asked for leave and though it can't be just yet, I shall come home as soon as they can spare me, I hope in time for our anniversary. Things are still difficult here. I shan't say more, because I know you understand.

Please go on loving me, Lizzie. Your devoted Harry XXX

Lizzie felt wretched as she looked at the letter, reading it over and over again. He hadn't written all this time – and now such a loving letter that it tugged at her heart and made her remorseful that she'd allowed Sebastian to take her to tea and kiss her afterwards.

She was Harry's wife and she had no right to encourage another man – even if Sebastian's kiss had made her heart sing. Her mind was like a crazy pattern of pictures, colourful, jagged, none of them making sense – and yet she knew that she'd been too young to marry when she did.

However, it was done and much too late to think of running out on him. She would tell Sebastian next time that though she liked him very much she could never leave her husband for his sake . . . and yet the very thought of seeing the hurt in his eyes dimmed the day.

She put both the letters and the money away in a drawer and went to work. Ed had returned to work the day after the funeral; he'd been at his bench cutting out felt when Lizzie arrived that morning. She'd hesitated, wondering what to say, but he'd just nodded to her, so she'd taken his lead and started talking about their latest orders. It seemed that Ed was working longer hour He'd gone out and got himself a room in a lodging house, refusing to impose on Aunt Miriam's good nature for more than one night.

Lizzie believed he was shutting his grief out of

his mind, perhaps in a similar way to what she'd done after she'd been raped, but Ed hadn't lost his memory. He was working because he had to and it was the only way he could face life without Madge.

The Luftwaffe were attacking ships in the Channel and any neutral ship heading for Britain had been warned that they were liable to be attacked; the German High Command had, it seemed, determined to starve Britain into submission. Churchill said we were alone but would not be defeated and the mood of the people was angry, refusing to give into the bully Hitler.

By the middle of August, the German planes had started to attack Britain's airfields.

Towards the end of August, the first bombs fell in Surat Street in Bethnal Green, one directly on a house where two members of the family were trapped, and the other in the park behind the Anderson shelter, where the rest of the family had taken refuge.

It was early September and Lizzie was getting close to her time when a letter came from Harry to tell her he was coming home. He would in fact be home for their wedding anniversary on the 19th, because he was due some leave and intended to spend it with her. She told his uncle at work and that evening called in on Aunt Miriam on her way back to the flat.

'I thought you would want to know that Harry

is coming home next weekend. His letter said to expect him on Saturday evening.'

Aunt Miriam smiled at her. 'That's wonderful news. I can't remember how long it is since we've seen him. You must both come to Sunday dinner . . . you should be resting as much as possible now, my dear.'

It was strange that Harry was getting leave when the aerodromes were under constant attack from the Luftwaffe. A couple of nights earlier the East India Docks had been heavily raided, destroying an engineering works and a garage as well as damaging many other buildings in the area, just part of the savage onslaught on London that had begun in the last few days. These past couple of weeks, bombs had rained on the Capital and many other cities and towns and because of that Churchill had retaliated by bombing Berlin and now they were getting the Germans' answer as London suffered terrible raids that left parts of the city devastated.

After the first bombs had fallen, people came out from the shelters and the underground feeling stunned and disbelieving. London seemed to be a sea of flames with fires everywhere. Woolwich Arsenal was hit, also a power station and a gas works, which had left hundreds of people without power. A shelter in the East End had taken a direct hit, killing and injuring people. Water mains had burst, making it difficult for the fire crews to get their hoses working, and sirens from ambulances, fire engines and the police could be heard all over the city.

So why was Harry being given leave at such a crucial time?

Had he disgraced himself? Somehow Lizzie felt that Harry would rather die than let his comrades know he was frightened – in fact, his shame was worse than his fear, because if he'd really been a coward he would surely have deserted or feigned illness?

She would just have to wait and see what sort of state he was in when he got home – and this time she was determined to respond to his kisses. Harry needed her and she mustn't let him down again – she must, and would, conquer her feelings of anger or resentment every time he touched her.

Lizzie had saved her rations so that she could give Harry a few decent meals when he came home on leave. She had bacon and eggs, which were almost like gold dust these days, but she'd queued for them at her favourite grocer and he'd produced two eggs from beneath the counter, winking at her as he slipped them into her basket.

On the Saturday evening, Lizzie had just changed into her prettiest dress and was brushing her hair when the front doorbell rang. She went downstairs, feeling a nervous flutter in her stomach as she anticipated seeing Harry again. However, when she opened the door she saw there was someone else standing there. He was wearing uniform and it was a moment or two before she realised it was Harry's friend; the one she'd met at the pub that evening – the one who had caused the row between them.

'Robbie,' she said in surprise.

'May I come in please?'

'Yes, of course. I was expecting Harry.'

'I know you were and that's why I came myself. I wanted you to hear it from me, Lizzie. You'll hear lots of versions of what I'm going to tell you, but they won't be the whole truth. Harry was my best mate. I really liked him and he wasn't a coward, even though he thought he was . . .'

'What do you mean?' Lizzie asked, her throat catching as they stood in the hall.

'Harry never refused a mission but three days ago he had so much to drink that he wasn't fit for duty.'

'What are you saying?' Lizzie went cold all over. Robbie was talking as if . . .

'The CO told him to go and sober up if he wanted to fly with us again and Harry went mad, said a lot of things he didn't mean and threw a punch at the old man. They locked him in the guardhouse and he was put on a charge of assaulting an officer – and some of the chaps are saying he's a coward, that he deliberately got drunk so that he couldn't go on a particularly dangerous mission.'

'No! He wouldn't!'

'No, I don't believe it and I told the CO he was just due a break.'

'So is he still locked up?'

'The CO dropped the charges and told him he was relieved from active duty until further notice – said he would arrange for him to go on ground duties for a spell. But he said he was just tired and wanted to fly with the rest of us. I saw him leave with his crew; he was quiet, Lizzie, but he grinned and gave me the thumbs up.'

'What happened?' Lizzie asked, feeling sick inside. 'Harry's dead, isn't he?'

'Yes,' Robbie hesitated, then, 'he came back from the mission with the others and went off by himself. Someone said it was absolute hell and they were lucky to have got back in one piece . . . I don't know all of it, Lizzie, but Harry got stinking drunk and took the CO's car without permission. He drove into a tree and the car burst into flames . . .' he sounded emotional as he went on, 'I'm so sorry; I can't believe it myself. They say the car was a twisted wreck and he must have died instantly . . .'

'No! My God, Harry was terrified of burning in the cockpit . . .' She swayed and Robbie caught her arm. 'I feel a bit faint . . .'

'Let me get you upstairs. You need a drink.'

Lizzie wasn't quite sure afterwards how she got up the stairs, but she thought Robbie might have carried her. When she came to her senses she was lying on a sofa and he was standing over her with a glass of whisky – from the half bottle of whisky she'd bought for Harry.

'Drink a few sips, it will steady you,' Robbie said as she sat up a little uncertainly. 'I'm sorry to be the one who told you, but I didn't want you hearing some garbled table of Harry being a coward. Whatever anyone says to you, Lizzie, he was a bloody hero; they all are.'

'Why does driving a car drunk make him a coward?'

'Because there were no skid marks. They think he might have done it deliberately, but I don't believe it – he was looking forward to his leave with you.'

'Not suicide. He couldn't have done that – he wouldn't, I don't believe it.'

'Neither do I, but I've heard talk and they might put it in the police report – I'm sorry, Lizzie. Harry loved you and I'm sure it was an accident . . .'

'It must have been.' Lizzie sipped her drink. 'If he were really a coward, he would have asked for a transfer.'

'Harry had a lot to lose,' Robbie said. 'Some of us don't have a wife like you to come home to. He was very proud of you, Lizzie . . . I think that's why he brooded such a lot.' Robbie hesitated, then, 'The only thing I don't understand is why he volunteered for every dirty mission they handed out . . . He didn't come home when he could – you hadn't quarrelled?'

Lizzie didn't answer, because she couldn't. Her throat was too tight and she felt as if she were choking, the misery sweeping through her as she thought of all the wasted time – of all the times Harry might have spent a few hours with her but had chosen not to.

'I'm sorry that isn't my business,' Robbie apologised. 'But he became more silent, less inclined to talk about you and home, and he pushed himself too hard.'

'It was just a silly misunderstanding.' Lizzie couldn't tell him that Harry had been jealous of him and it was his jealousy that had led to the trouble between them. His flirting had made Harry jealous and caused the drunken attack on her. 'I think he volunteered for those missions, because he was trying to prove that he was as brave as the rest of you.'

'Believe me, we're all shit-scared,' Robbie said. 'Sorry, I should mind my language, but it's how we feel.'

'Don't apologise. I'm just grateful to you for explaining.'

'You will get an official letter but they tell you only the bare facts. You had to know it all – for Harry's sake. I don't believe he meant to kill himself, Lizzie. I think something happened and the car went out of control.'

'Yes, it must have, thank you . . .' Lizzie felt a spasm of grief for a young life ended. Her child would never know its father and she would never see Harry again. In that moment she was remembering that she'd loved him at the start and a fierce regret swept over her. What had gone so terribly wrong for them – and what was she going to tell his aunt and uncle? Her hand trembled and for just one instant she felt as if she might fall, and then she steadied herself.

'Do you want me to stay for a while? Is there anyone you can call?'

'I'll go and see my friend,' Lizzie said, deciding that she needed to talk to Beth before she could face Uncle Bertie.

'Shall I fetch her for you?'

'No, thank you, Robbie. Beth has two children of her own. I'll go round myself on the bus . . .'

'I've got my car outside. At least let me take you where you want to go.'

'All right,' Lizzie agreed. 'It will save waiting for the bus. It's very kind of you, Robbie. I'll just get my coat.'

Lizzie pulled on her jacket and picked up her bag. As she was getting into Robbie's car she thought she saw a man lift his hand to her from the end of the street but it was too far to see properly and she was blowing her nose prior to powdering it, because she knew her tears would have left streaks.

Beth opened the door, looking at her in surprise. 'What's wrong?' she said. 'Was that Harry in the car? Where has he gone?'

'It was his friend; he gave me a lift . . .' Lizzie swallowed hard. 'May I come in, Beth?'

'Of course, love – what's wrong?'

'It's Harry . . . he – he's dead . . .'

'Oh, Lizzie,' Beth said and drew her quickly inside, her arms going round her in a loving embrace. 'And you were expecting him home – how did it happen?'

Beth tried to draw her into the kitchen, but Lizzie hung back. 'Can we talk in private, Beth? There's something I need to discuss and – where's your father?'

'He's working late,' Beth said. 'I saw the car pull up from my window and came down to meet you. Mum's in the kitchen . . .'

'I want to tell you, no one else . . .'

Mrs Court came out into the hall, looking at them in surprise. 'Lizzie's had some bad news, Mum. We're going upstairs.' Beth turned and went up the stairs, Lizzie climbing laboriously after her.

'You're nearly as bad as I was,' Beth said. 'And I had twins . . .'

Lizzie would normally have laughed, but felt as if all the laughter had drained out of her body, leaving an empty husk. She entered Beth's room and sat on the edge of the bed, still numb with misery.

Beth sat next to her and held her hand. 'Now tell me, love. What is so awful it's making you look like that?'

'It is awful, Beth. Not just his death but the way he died – he got drunk, stole his Commanding Officer's car and drove it into a tree. They think he might have done it on purpose . . .'

'No, I don't believe it,' Beth cried and looked

stunned. 'Why would he do such a thing? He wasn't unhappy; he had everything to live for. You and the baby and a good job to come back to after the war . . .'

'You mustn't think less of him, but Harry was afraid,' Lizzie said. 'All the dogfighting over the Channel, and the bombing of the airfields and the rest, well, that's only just started to hot up – but Harry and Robbie, well, they were flying secret missions over German territory for months before this. They were being shot at and they risked death over and over again . . . Harry was frightened but more frightened of being thought a coward than dying.'

'Then why did he take his own life?' Beth asked, looking puzzled. 'If he was afraid of death – it doesn't make sense . . .'

'I don't know what happened, Beth. He got drunk previously and when his CO told him to go home and sober up he threw a punch at him and said things – they put him in the lock-up overnight and were going to charge him, but his CO offered leave and a change of duty. Harry said he'd just been tired, and went on a mission, but when he came back he disappeared and then they found him – the car went up in flames.'

'Oh Lizzie, no, that's awful. I can understand him being upset – but surely he wouldn't have taken his own life?'

'I don't understand it either. Robbie said the mission Harry went on was hell, but he wasn't there to see whether something happened, or someone said something that made him ashamed . . .'

'It doesn't make sense still,' Beth said. 'Harry had everything . . .'

'No,' Lizzie said, her throat catching. 'Things weren't right between us – hadn't been since his last leave.'

Beth stared at her, and then inclined her head. 'I suspected something was wrong – but I didn't think it was more than a lover's tiff . . .'

'I married in a rush,' Lizzie said, knowing she was only telling Beth half the truth, because she just couldn't tell her about that night. 'Perhaps it was my fault – because I disappointed him. Something went wrong between us . . .'

'It's all right, you don't have to tell me,' Beth said and then Lizzie gasped.

She placed her hands to her belly. 'He's restless tonight, Beth. I think he's in a rush to be born.'

'You're sure it's a boy?' Beth gave her a faint smile.

'Miriam is,' Lizzie said. 'I just know I feel huge and I want it to be over.'

'I was exactly the same towards the end, but it's funny how soon you forget once the baby is here.' Beth gave a little sob, 'Oh, Lizzie, this is so awful for you. I wish I could help . . .'

'Beth, I do love you,' Lizzie hugged her. 'I'm so glad you're here with your mum and we've got each other. Sometimes, I feel so alone – I don't know what I'd do without you.'

'What are you going to tell Harry's uncle?'

'I'm not sure,' Lizzie said. 'I don't want him to feel ashamed of Harry or think he was a coward but . . .'

'Can't you just say there was an accident?'

'Do you think I could get away with that?'

'Why not? Any official letters will come to you. They don't have to know what actually happened.'

'I suppose . . .' Lizzie drew a sharp breath. 'Perhaps I can keep the worst of it from them somehow . . .'

'I shall tell Mum that Harry died in an accident. There's no need for her or anyone else to know all the details. Why should they?'

Lizzie nodded, feeling relief flood through her. Beth was right. It would be so much easier to tell Harry's uncle and aunt that he'd died in an accident, and keep the rest to herself.

'Yes, I think that's what I'll do. I'll just tell them he died in a car accident – say he was tired and overworked and had a fatal accident . . .'

'It will be better if no one knows the truth,' Beth asserted. 'People would gossip and point the finger and you don't want that, Lizzie. Harry wasn't a coward; he didn't run away or refuse his duty, that's what cowards do.'

Lizzie agreed. In her mind Harry wasn't a coward and she couldn't help wondering if a part of the reason he'd broken down was because he was worried about coming home and facing her . . .

CHAPTER 39

'I shall have to get home,' Lizzie said after she'd calmed down a little. 'I'm sorry to dump my bad news on you, Beth, but I didn't know what else to do . . .'

'I'll come with you. Mum will keep an eye on the twins. I can't let you go all that way on your own . . .'

Just as they were walking down the stairs together they heard the siren go off and looked at each other in dismay.

Mrs Court came out into the hall as they reached it. She was wiping her hands on a towel and looked at them enquiringly.

'Lizzie came to tell me her husband died,' Beth said and her mother gave a little gasp of distress. 'I was going to walk home with her, Mum. I can't let her go on her own . . .'

'Neither of you is going anywhere but under the stairs until we hear the all-clear,' Mrs Court said. 'After the last few nights, it just isn't safe to be on the streets once the siren goes . . .'

Lizzie was about to thank her when she felt the first pain strike her. She cried out and clutched at herself, swaying against the wall.

'Oh – I'm so sorry, I think I'm starting the baby,' Lizzie said, feeling oddly calm. 'I'd booked to go to the hospital. If someone could telephone for a taxi . . .'

'You'd never get one with a raid starting,' Beth's mother said firmly. 'No, you'll stay here with us, Lizzie, and if you have the baby we'll manage.'

'I'm so sorry to be a nuisance. I've got three weeks or so to go yet . . .'

'Well, I'm afraid your baby has other ideas,' Mrs Court said as Lizzie gasped and clutched at herself. 'We'll have to get you upstairs, air raid or no air raid,' she said and turned to her husband, who had just come into the hall and was frowning at his daughter. 'Don't just stand there and stare, love – get a doctor or Mrs Benson down at number forty-five. She has delivered a few in her time – ask her to come first and then go for the doctor.'

He looked at her for a moment and then turned and went into the kitchen, grabbing his coat. They heard the door slam after him. Lizzie clutched at Beth's arm as the pain came again.

'Is it supposed to come so often?'

'I think it's the shock of what you've been told,' Beth's mother said and put an arm about her. 'Hang on to me, love, and we'll get you upstairs. Beth's grandmother had all her babies at home, and I had my first one at home, but after that Derek said hospital for the others – he couldn't stand the sound of me screaming I suppose.'

'Dad was annoyed with me coming down.' Beth bit her lip. 'I'm sorry, Mum. I know I'm supposed to stay in my room and I would if Lizzie hadn't told me . . .'

'I'd had a few vague pains this afternoon,' Lizzie said. 'I didn't think it was anything . . .'

'Shock will do it sometimes. It was terrible news, Lizzie. I am so very sorry, my dear.'

'I think I can hear planes . . .' Beth said as they reached the top of the stairs. 'They sound close.'

'They will be going for the docks again,' her mother said warningly, but the look of anxiety on her face gave her away.

'They don't care where they drop them these days,' Beth said. They heard an explosion, but it seemed to come from a long way off.

'Just hang on for a moment while I strip the bed, Lizzie,' Mrs Court said and pulled back the covers in what had been Lizzie's room when she stayed here, throwing them carelessly over a chair. She took some sheets from the ottoman and folded them so that the thickness would prevent blood going through and spoiling the good sheets already on the bed. There wasn't time to do more, because Lizzie was writhing in pain. 'Come and lie down, love,' she beckoned and then pulled a top sheet over her when she obeyed. 'We'll cover you up for a moment. Just lie whichever way you're comfortable. Mrs Benson worked as a midwife until she had her family. She'll know how close you are. You can scream all you like, love.'

Lizzie lay on her back and planted her feet on the bed with her knees up. She'd taken off her knickers, which were soaked through when her waters broke halfway up the stairs, as was her dress. She hitched it up a bit so that her legs were free, bracing as the pain ripped up through her and she gritted her teeth.

Why had she ever let a man near her? This was unbearable! She'd never expected it to feel half as bad, never thought she would feel as if she were being ripped apart, but then she'd expected to give birth in hospital and be given gas and air to make it easier.

Someone knocked at the street door and then opened it. A voice called from the hall downstairs. 'It's Maggie Benson. Shall I come up, Mrs Court? I've sent Mr Court off to get the doctor. No sense in the men hanging around is there?'

Beth's mother left them and went to the top of the stairs, calling Mrs Benson to come on up. Lizzie tried to hold back the scream and pushed as she tried to rid her body of the source of the terrible pain. Just as Mrs Court and Mrs Benson entered the room, she heard a huge explosion, much nearer than the earlier ones and let the scream rip.

'That's it, love, scream away,' Maggie said. 'I'll take a quick look at you, Lizzie, and then I'll give my hands a wash in the sink. I brought some special disinfectant with me. I keep a bottle in just in case I'm called out.'

She lifted back the sheet that was still half covering Lizzie and looked at her. 'Yes, you're coming along nicely. I think you're going to be lucky, young lady; you won't have to go through hours of labour. Your baby is in a hurry to get here.'

'No one could stand this for hours,' Lizzie gritted her teeth as her body convulsed with agony.

'You'd be surprised, especially in the old days when there wasn't half the medical help there is around today.' Maggie chuckled. 'Why didn't you go to the hospital earlier? You must have had warning pains?'

'Nothing much,' Lizzie said. 'I was all right and then it just came on suddenly.'

'Lizzie's been told her husband was killed . . .'

'Oh, that's awful,' Maggie said. 'I'm so sorry, Lizzie. It's getting so you dread the sight of a telegraph boy.'

'Yes,' Beth's mother agreed. 'Do you want to hold my hand, Lizzie?'

'I'll tie a towel to the bed rail,' Maggie said. 'I'll wash my hands and come back. Hang on, love . . .'

Lizzie grimaced as the cheerful Maggie went back downstairs to scrub her hands. 'She seems to think it's fun . . .' she muttered. 'Damn – bugger . . .'

'Now then, language,' Mrs Court said, holding her hand and wincing as she squeezed hard. 'I know it hurts, I've been through it four times, remember – but it will pass soon. As Maggie says, it looks as if you're going to be lucky . . .'

Lizzie screamed again and a sudden urge to push made her bear down hard, gripping Mrs Court's hand until she tried to pull away. There was a whooshing feeling and then something came through just as Maggie returned.

'Ah, there we are,' she said triumphantly. 'What a clever girl you are, Lizzie – the head is out already. Now, have another go when you're ready and we'll soon be done.'

Lizzie felt like hitting her, but the sound of a huge explosion that must have been at least in the street if not next door shocked her and in the terror of the moment she pushed hard and the rest of the child came slithering out in a mess of slime and blood.

'What a brilliant way to have a baby,' Maggie said. 'I must recommend loud explosions to the medical team at the hospital. Good girl, Lizzie – and you've got a lovely little girl . . .'

'Not a boy?' Beth said. 'Lizzie's aunt was sure it was a boy . . .'

'Well, we can all make mistakes,' Maggie said and lifted the child away. 'What a beauty. I'll give her a nice wash and wrap her in a towel for now while I look after you . . .'

'You'll be all right now, love,' Beth said. 'I'd better go and feed the twins before they scream the place down.' She smiled, kissed Lizzie and left.

Lizzie lay back feeling exhausted, their words seeming a long way off. Just at this moment she wasn't interested in what sex the child was, as long as it was all right. Maggie was saying how lucky she was to get it over so quickly, but Lizzie just felt drained. Perhaps it was because Harry had seemingly taken his own life that she wished she'd died during childbirth. Perhaps if she'd got caught on the street while the bombs were dropping, it would have ended there and she wouldn't feel this aching emptiness inside. Her eyes were gritty and yet she couldn't cry; her tears were locked inside her, making her hurt. The pain of learning of Harry's death was worse than the pain of child-birth and she wished she could just go to sleep and never wake up again. Just at this moment she didn't want to think about the future she would have to face alone or even her baby.

The bombs were still dropping but further away now. Lizzie felt exhausted, drained. Maggie was cleaning her and disposing of the afterbirth. She slipped the bloody sheets from under Lizzie and Beth's mother took them away.

'I'll get you out of that dress and into a clean nightie,' Maggie said. 'You'll feel a lot better soon, Lizzie. You're a really lucky girl to have such a lovely baby and so easily too.'

Lizzie was feeling sore and her body ached. All she wanted to do was sleep, but Maggie insisted she hold the baby for a few moments.

'It's that special bonding,' she said, smiling as she placed the soft sweet bundle in Lizzie's arms. 'I'm going home now; I'll come back later and see how you're getting on.'

'Thank you. It was good of you to come – and in the middle of an air raid.'

'I reckon we just got the tail end of it. They probably had a couple left over from bombing the docks and thought they would give us the pleasure of a little visit.'

'Rotten devils,' Lizzie muttered. She looked down at the pink and delicate face of her baby and felt the weariness slip away as she saw her pout. Instead of the emptiness there was an enveloping warmth that held her and the child wrapped together. 'Yes, I know. It was mean of me to bring you here while that was going on, wasn't it?'

'What are you going to call her?' Maggie asked, lingering.

'Elizabeth, perhaps, or Betty for short.'

'Lovely names.'

'Yes, my mother was Elizabeth – and there's Beth, of course. I'll call her Betty, I think.'

'Righto,' Maggie said. 'I'll see you in a bit, little Betty – and Lizzie . . .'

Beth's mother came in carrying a tray with a slice of toast and marmalade and a cup of tea. She set it down on the chest beside the bed and looked at the baby.

'She's lovely. Let me put her in the spare cot. It's old but will do for now.'

'It's so good of you,' Lizzie said, reluctantly giving the baby into Mrs Court's arms. 'I feel awful causing all this extra work for you – you must have enough to do looking after the twins.'

'Beth does most of it herself. She'll miss that if she has to leave them to go to work.'

'Yes, she will . . .' Lizzie heard her baby whimpering. 'Maggie said to feed her as soon as I feel able . . .'

'You have a rest for a bit,' Beth's mother said. 'Eat this toast and drink your tea, Lizzie love. I'll see to the baby for a bit if she cries – and Beth will be back when she's finished feeding the twins.'

Mrs Court wouldn't hear of Lizzie leaving until she was over the birth. She fussed over her and the child. Lizzie and Beth spent ages talking and laughing, sharing the experience of two young mothers learning to look after their babies. Beth was ahead of Lizzie and was able to show her a few tricks, but she'd had to supplement her milk with a bottle for Matt, because he was always hungry and she couldn't satisfy both the twins.

'I feel guilty about giving your mum all this extra work.'

'Mum loves babies; besides, what would you have done on your own in that flat? Even if the doctor had been in time to help, which I doubt, and sent his nurse to help care for you, you'd have spent too much time alone. This way I help mum and don't feel guilty about being here. Dad has given me a few funny looks when he's caught me doing ironing and washing but he hasn't told me to leave and never darken his door again . . .'

'You haven't thought anymore about taking Bernie's offer of marriage then?'

'Mum says to be sure it's what I want.' Beth looked uncertain, then, 'I went to the workshop and told Harry's uncle you'd had the baby with us, but I didn't say anything about Harry.'

'Thank you.' Lizzie smothered a sigh. 'I'm not sure what to do about the funeral. Uncle Bertie would arrange it I know – but he'd find out the truth and . . .' Lizzie shook her head. 'Could you go round to my flat in the morning and see if there's a letter. Robbie told me there should be an official letter – perhaps it will tell me what to do . . .'

'Yes, of course I will. Don't worry about it, Lizzie. There's nothing you can do lying here, is there?'

'I don't know who to contact . . .' Lizzie plucked at the bedcovers. 'Why did it have to happen, Beth?'

'I don't know . . .' Beth sighed as they heard a knock at the door. 'Someone is at the door. Mum is out so I'll go down and answer it . . .'

She went down the stairs. Lizzie heard her talking to someone and then she came back, looking uncertain.

'It's Harry's uncle. He's brought you some flowers and asked if you were well enough to see him . . .'

Lizzie pulled her borrowed bed jacket to at the front and nodded. 'Ask him to come up, Beth – I might as well get it over . . .'

She closed her eyes, trying to think of what to say as she heard the exchange of voices and then the heavy tread of a man's steps coming upstairs.

'Well, then, Lizzie, that was a shock when I heard you were here and the baby was early . . .'

'Yes, by several weeks,' Lizzie whispered and then, gathering courage, 'she was born during an air raid – but I had some terrible news before then. I'm sorry, Uncle Bertie, but there's no other way I can tell you . . . Harry is dead . . .'

He stared in disbelief. 'Harry dead? What are you talking about? I thought he was coming home on a visit – your aunt said it was odd he didn't come to tell us the news himself . . .' For a moment he swayed as if he'd received a physical blow and then sat down on the nearest chair with a bump. She thought he was fighting for his breath and felt guilty that she hadn't broken it to him in a gentler way. 'That's terrible, Lizzie, terrible. No wonder you gave birth too early . . . I'm so sorry, my dear. This is a terrible blow for you . . .' He shook his head as if in disbelief.

'Yes, I was very shocked and upset . . .' Lizzie swallowed hard as he gave her a sympathetic look. 'It didn't happen on a mission – there was some kind of an accident . . .'

'What do you mean?'

'His friend just said it was a car accident. I expect I'll get something from the War Office soon.' Lizzie hesitated, then, 'He wanted to be buried not cremated. He told me that once – so I'll arrange it when I get up. I shall be out and about in a couple of days and I haven't heard about – when I can have his body . . .'

'It isn't fitting that a young woman in your circumstances should have to do such a thing,' Uncle Bertie said. 'I insist that you leave this to me. I'll arrange it for the next week or so and give you time to get well, Lizzie.'

'Thank you . . .' Lizzie said, frantically wondering how she was going to conceal the truth from him. 'I should be up by tomorrow . . .'

'Nonsense, you must stay in bed for a few days and when you leave here come to us. Your aunt will be glad to look after you both . . .'

CHAPTER 40

Beth was returning from Lizzie's home with several letters in the basket over her arm. Just as she turned the corner of the street, she saw a man in Army uniform standing outside her door. He seemed to be hesitating, turning away without knocking. She caught her breath as she saw his face . . . Tony!

Beth was undecided whether to walk quickly away or face him, but then she knew she couldn't avoid him forever.

'Tony . . .' she said and stopped as they reached each other. 'How are you? You haven't been hurt?'

'No, I'm fine. I've been training most of the time, sitting around waiting to see some action – this is embarkation leave.'

'Oh, well I wish you lots of luck,' Beth said, feeling oddly sad because they were talking as strangers. Despite her love for Mark, she'd never quite forgotten Tony. 'And I'm glad to see you, Tony. I've wondered how you were getting on.'

'I heard you had twins,' Tony's brow furrowed. 'I understand he died . . . the father . . .'

'Mark's ship was sunk and he was posted missing in action.'

'I'm sorry, Beth.'

'Yes, me too,' she said, 'but I'm lucky to have the twins. Matt looks like his father, I think . . .'

'Oh . . .' Tony seemed lost for words. 'It can't be easy living at home?'

'My mother doesn't mind, but my father thought I'd shamed him. He's letting me stay for the moment, but I shall have to leave one day . . .'

He hesitated then, 'Well, I'd better go. Got a lot of friends to catch up with – just wanted to know you were all right.' 'Glad you came, Tony . . .'

He walked off down the road. Beth watched him, wondering why her throat caught and her eyes pricked with sudden tears. What was there to cry about, just because Tony had come to see her?

She went into the house, taking her jacket off and hanging it on the hallstand. Halfway up the stairs, she saw Lizzie at the top, obviously preparing to come down.

'Should you be up yet? It's only been a few days.'

'I can't stay here forever. I want to go home and settle in,' Lizzie said. 'Aunt Miriam wants me to stay there, but I shan't. I need to be independent . . .'

'There are a few letters for you,' Beth said. 'One of them looks official – I expect it's from the RAF . . . and one smells of perfume.'

'Yes, from the RAF,' Lizzie said as she saw the heading and began to read it. 'It doesn't say anything about when I can have the funeral. I'm having a cremation, because I don't want Uncle Bertie to hear things – I told him it was an accident, as you suggested.' Lizzie sniffed the perfumed letter and smiled. She opened the envelope and discovered a cheque from Mrs Mabel Carmichael, and a note apologising. She would be in shortly to purchase more hats and hoped Lizzie would forgive her. 'That's one piece of good news at least.' She showed Beth the letter.

'Yes, but she got you into trouble, didn't she?' Beth pointed out, then, looking thoughtful. 'I hope that my advice to you about telling Mr Oliver it was an accident doesn't cause trouble . . .'

'I only wanted to spare him and Aunt Miriam pain,' Lizzie said. 'I see no reason for him to be angry.'

'He's a funny sort,' Beth said and frowned as she changed the subject, 'Bernie sent me another letter to tell me my job will be there for me when I'm ready to return.'

'Bernie sounds really nice, Beth?'

'I suppose he is. I keep thinking and wondering if I should accept his offer of marriage or try to get my own place.' She sighed, then, 'I just saw Tony. He's home on leave and then he's off overseas somewhere.'

'What did he want?'

'He just came to see how I was before he was posted abroad.'

'How did that make you feel?'

'I'm not sure – a little sad perhaps? I don't like to think of him perhaps being hurt . . .'

'No, of course not, but I'm afraid a lot of our men are in the thick of it somewhere,' Lizzie said. 'It was strange, as if the war wasn't really happening for ages, but it certainly is now . . .'

'It's really happening now,' Beth agreed. She glanced at Lizzie's pale face as she took her letters. 'Are you sure you're ready for this?'

'I think I can manage. I shan't go home today but by tomorrow or the following day.'

Lizzie pushed away the feeling of loneliness that overcame her as she contemplated returning to the flat where she'd hoped to be so happy with Harry Oliver. Her dreams had been shattered, but there was no point in looking back. She just had to get on the best she could.

'I shall feel all at sea once you've both gone,' Mrs Court said looking wistful as the three women sat drinking tea that afternoon. 'I do understand why you feel you ought to get home, Lizzie – but you don't have to go yet, Beth.'

'I think I ought to stand on my own two feet,' Beth smiled at her mother lovingly. 'It doesn't make you redundant, Mum. We'll both need you to babysit sometimes.'

'Well, you know I'll always help where I can.'

'Thanks Mum.'

'You too, Lizzie.'

'Yes, I know,' Lizzie smiled at her. 'I shall never

be able to thank you enough, Mrs Court. It was so generous of you to do what you did and I'm very grateful.'

'In the circumstances I wouldn't have dreamed of letting you go home alone,' Mrs Court said. 'You must think of this house as your second home, Lizzie. I stand in place of a mother to you – and if you need anything, come to me for help.'

'You're so kind,' Lizzie said. 'I wish my aunt had been more like you – but she didn't have a very happy life.'

'Have you heard from her recently, Lizzie?'

I wrote once but she didn't answer my letter. Perhaps she doesn't feel up to it.' Or perhaps she didn't want anything to do with Lizzie.

Someone was knocking at the door. Beth went through to the hall and opened the door. It was Harry's uncle and he looked grim.

'Is Lizzie here?'

'Yes, she's in the kitchen. Would you like to come in?'

'I've something to say to her in private.'

'Then perhaps you should go through to the parlour – at the end of the hall, Mr Oliver. I'll ask Lizzie to join you . . .'

He glared at her, and then walked past her to the door at the end of the passage. Beth went back to the kitchen, feeling uneasy.

'Mr Oliver wants to speak with you in private,' she said, giving Lizzie a warning look. 'He's in the parlour . . .'

'Oh . . . I'd better go and see what he wants.'

Lizzie got to her feet immediately and went out.

'What does he want?' Beth's mother asked as the door closed after Lizzie.

'I dare say it concerns the funeral,' Beth said. 'I did tell you that Tony called round, didn't I? I think he's being posted overseas . . .'

Lizzie carefully closed the parlour door behind her. Beth's warning glance had told her that Uncle Bertie wasn't in a good mood. Had he discovered the rumours about Harry's death? His eyes met hers with a glacial stare.

'Why did you lie to me, Lizzie? You left me to discover the truth from a stranger . . .'

'What have you been told?' Her heart was thumping wildly but she tried to appear calm.

'My nephew disgraced himself and our name – he stole a car when he was drunk and deliberately drove it into a tree. Suicide is the coward's way out . . .'

'No, that isn't fair.' Lizzie's nails dug into the palms of her hands. 'Yes, Harry was frightened of dying, but who isn't? He'd flown mission after mission over enemy installations, taking pictures that helped us to know what was going on with the German army and their capabilities – not once did he refuse to go.'

'Then why did he take his own life? Tell me that, if you can – or can I guess? Did he discover that you had other men? I've seen you leaving the flat with

410

different men twice. Is that why Harry didn't want to come home – why he didn't take his leave and finally felt he couldn't go on?'

How could he blame her – accuse her of being unfaithful to her husband? It was totally unfair of him and it made her angry – and yet he was partially right. She had let Sebastian kiss her and she had gone to tea with him, but that was very different to what Uncle Bertie was hinting at. 'I can't believe you just said that to me,' Lizzie said quietly. 'I went out to tea with Sebastian Winters once, but he's a client of the business, and the other time was when Robbie told me about Harry's accident . . .' Her head went up proudly. 'I'd like to know who told you about Harry. I'm Harry's next of kin and if I chose to keep it from you that was my privilege.'

'You're a cold bitch. I was right about you from the start. I warned Harry not to be a fool. I knew you were just out for what you could get – well, don't think you or your brat will be getting my business when I've gone, and any arrangements we had are finished. I don't want you back at the workshops – do I make myself clear?'

'I'm sorry you feel I've let you and Harry down, but for what's it's worth I don't believe Harry did kill himself,' she said quietly, keeping calm despite her emotion. 'As far as the business is concerned that is your privilege – and I do thank you for all you've done for me. I never asked to be left anything in your will – and I think you must leave now.'

'Bitch. You won't get a reference from me . . .'

As he threw open the door and strode out into the hall, Beth looked thunderstruck. She went to Lizzie as the door slammed after him.

'What has he been saying to you? You're as white as a ghost . . .'

'He thinks I'm to blame for what happened to Harry. He said that I was a cold bitch and had made Harry so miserable that . . .' Lizzie felt faint and ill after Harry's uncle's verbal attack on her and grabbed at the back of a chair to steady herself.

Lizzie sat down, her head spinning. She bent her head, covering her face with her hands as the tears started. Then Beth's arms went round her, holding her as she sobbed. She kissed the top of Lizzie's head and stroked the back of her neck, gradually easing her.

Lizzie looked up. 'Harry's uncle is severing all connection with me. He wants to ruin me, refuses to give me a reference, but I'll manage – I'll manage somehow.'

'Of course you will,' Beth said. 'You'll find another job somewhere . . .'

'Yes, I shall manage, Beth. I'll have to think about what I'm doing – but I'll survive.'

CHAPTER 41

The flat felt cold after being closed up for some days. Lizzie switched on the electric fire; the air would soon warm up and she was used to living alone so this feeling of isolation would go. It was very strange knowing that Harry would never come home – and she no longer had the support of his family.

It wouldn't be easy to find a new job in the trade, but did she really want to work for anyone else? Lizzie had been too shocked to think straight at first but now she was wondering if perhaps she could work for herself. She still had the money Sebastian had sent her and the address of someone he'd said might help her if she wanted to leave Oliver's.

Lizzie had been reluctant to take his money, but now it might be the only way for her to go on making the hats she loved. It was surely what Sebastian had intended and she could repay him if she made a success of her own business . . .

Betty had started to cry. Lizzie picked her up and cuddled her before putting her back in her cot. She was feeling warmer now and she turned the fire off. She had a small amount of her own money put by because she'd saved what Harry sent her from his wages, but she must keep it for emergencies, because she couldn't know what her daughter might need in the future.

When Betty settled, Lizzie went through the flat with a broom and duster, then made herself a cup of Bovril and drank it with some of the bread she'd bought on the way home. She picked up her sketchbook and flicked through some of the drawings, but didn't feel like working.

Lizzie was close to tears because she felt so alone. Yes, she had good friends, but they couldn't help her now.

Going into her bedroom, she searched for the letter that Sebastian had sent her and the bundle of notes. She took the envelope back to the sitting room and read the postscript at the end of the letter.

Arthur is a friend of mine. If you need help setting up your own business, go and see him, Lizzie. This is his address . . .

He'd enclosed a business card for a Mr Arthur Stockton, maker of fine hats, which made Lizzie smile, because it was so old-fashioned and yet it would stick in the mind.

Sebastian had thought she might need help, because he'd known things weren't right with her marriage. Starting her own business would be a huge step to take, but Lizzie knew it was what she wanted – what she'd always wanted.

She counted the money that Sebastian had sent her and caught her breath. There was nearly three hundred pounds in the envelope – enough to secure her the lease of a small shop and workshop behind, and enough materials to get started.

She would go and talk to Arthur Stockton, the man Sebastian had mentioned in his postscript. It would mean leaving Betty with Mrs Court, but she would go first thing in the morning, because this was the future for her and her child . . .

Lizzie caught the bus which would take her to the premises she was seeking. It was in an area close to where Beth's family lived and only a few blocks from the East India Docks. She could even see some of the cranes working against the skyline as her bus halted. It couldn't go any further because there was a crater in the road, left by a bomb a couple of days previously. Her stomach was tying itself in knots as she got out and walked down the street. After all, why should Mr Stockton help a woman he didn't even know; he might even think of her as a rival . . . but she didn't really have a choice. Lizzie had only herself to rely on now and she had to take care of Betty and her own future. She had to at least ask for his help . . .

When Lizzie approached the building, she was disappointed to see the shutters were down on the window and a little closed notice was tucked into one corner. She almost turned away, but then the thought struck her that perhaps someone was on the premises. She would ring the bell and enquire because it was worth a try. It had to work out, because otherwise she didn't have a clue where to start.

She rang twice and was about to leave when the sound of a key gave her hope. A small wiry man opened the door a crack and looked at her over his gold-rimmed glasses.

'We're closed for business, ma'am.'

'When will you be open? Sebastian Winters sent me . . .'

'Sebastian?' His eyes narrowed. 'Well, that's different. The business is closing down. I can't keep going without my best workers and my daughter wants me to pack up and go and live in the country with her . . .'

'I'm Lizzie Larch. I design hats and was hoping you might make some basic shapes up for me . . .'

'Lizzie Larch, yes, Sebastian did tell me about you – I think he intended to launch your work at one time . . .' he smiled sadly as he offered his hand.

'Yes, but it didn't happen. I was working for someone else at the time but that has fallen through. I can't contact Sebastian and I need help. I want to open my own shop and I need suppliers – I wondered if you could help me . . .'

'Starting up in times like these? I'm not sure that's a good idea, young woman. A lot of little workshops won't make it through; I'm afraid one of them is mine,' he sighed. 'I'm Arthur and 'I've been here on this site since I was a boy. My father made gentlemen's hats and my grandfather before him. I started the ladies' department. I shall be sorry to leave it . . .' He gestured to her to come in. 'I cleared most of my basic hats yesterday – a large department store came and took most of what I had – but you're welcome to look . . .'

Lizzie followed him into his workroom, feeling sad because it was almost empty and it seemed a shame that after years of family businesses here, there was almost nothing left. She saw about twelve basic felt hats and picked one up to examine it; the quality was good and she could make it look individual in a few minutes if she had the right trimmings.

'I'd like to take these if they're not too expensive please. I would have liked more, but these will help me to build up a basic stock for a start.'

'You can have the lot for two pounds . . .'

'All these? That's far too cheap. I ought to pay at least ten shillings for each of them.'

'I wish you'd been here before the best went,' Arthur said. He thought for a moment, then, 'I suppose you can't find a use for some rolls of straw, felt and satin grosgrain . . .?'

'Oh yes, please, that's exactly what I need.'

'Well, I was thinking of taking the stock with me . . . but I dare say once I've retired, most of it would go to waste. Have a look in here . . .'

Lizzie followed him to a door. He opened it and she saw the small room was filled with rolls of various materials and several boxes of ribbons and silk flowers, feathers and cottons, velvets, boxes of sequins and all kinds of things she would need to buy from the wholesalers.

'I would love to buy all of this if you want to sell. I could keep a shop going for ages with all this material . . .'

'How about thirty pounds for the lot – the felt shapes included?'

'Are you sure? It must be worth more . . .' Lizzie felt a pang of guilt, because it must be hard having to give up a business you loved, and she liked him.

'I suppose it may be, but Sebastian told me you had a rare talent. I haven't seen him for a while.' Arthur considered for a moment, then, 'Give me thirty pounds and I'll be happy. Oh, and if you want a list of the suppliers I use I'll give you my book – there are a few moulds and my old steamer is around somewhere. No one wanted it, but it still works.'

'It is so kind of you: anything you want to get rid of – patterns, scissors. I shall have to buy them all, but I must pay for them . . .' Lizzie felt over-whelmed by his generosity. 'I shall have to make several trips to fetch all this, but I can pay you now.'

'I'll get my lad Fred to bring everything in his van this afternoon. He's a good lad, Miss Larch. Can't join the Army; they turned him down on account of his gammy leg, but he's a good worker. If you ever have a use for a delivery lad, you ask young Fred.'

'Thank you, I shall,' Lizzie said and paid him the thirty pounds he'd asked for stock she knew was worth at least four times as much. 'You've been so kind to me, Mr Stockton.'

'It's Arthur to you, Lizzie – don't mind me calling you that I hope?'

'Not at all. I'm only sorry you're leaving London.'

'Well, I dare say it was time for me to retire. I have no one to take over from me when I go – and my daughter wants to look after me.'

'Then I hope you'll be very happy.'

He handed her a receipt for the thirty pounds. 'Fred will come at about four this afternoon, if that's all right?'

'Lovely,' Lizzie said, feeling the excitement bubble inside her as she wrote down her address.

'Got your own premises, have you?'

'Not yet, but I've only just started to think about it and I came here first, because Sebastian told me you could help.'

'Well, this place is going cheap,' he told her. 'I've got five years left on my lease – and the rent is twenty-five bob a week – and there's a small flat over the top. When my lease is finished they will double or treble the rent. Mind you, it isn't the safest place now, because a friend of mine in the next row lost everything last week in a raid – but that's a chance we all have to take these days.'

Lizzie felt a quiver of excitement because the rent wasn't much more than she was paying on her flat. If she moved in here she would be further away from Oliver's and all reminders of the past, but she would be close to her work and someone could come in to keep an eye on Betty for her.

'Could I have a look at the flat? Would you mind?'

'Come on up,' he invited. 'You'll find it untidy because I've been packing, but we've always kept things in good order . . .'

Lizzie discovered that the rooms were slightly larger than she had now, but the decoration left much to be desired, as did the kitchen and bathroom. If she lived here she would have to spend money on making it decent. Her heart sank and it was on the tip of her tongue to turn him down, because she wasn't sure she wanted to live there.

'Think about it and let me know. I leave at the end of the week . . .'

'What would you want for the lease?'

'Ten pounds,' he said. 'I can't charge more because most people want much longer leases – besides, I'd like to do you a good turn. I had a good business here and I could let you have my client list. They would soon come back once you're up and running.'

'Would you really? Oh, that is so kind of you and would help me no end.' She smiled at him in delight.

What did it matter that the bath had a rust mark and she would have to buy a new gas cooker?

Everything she needed to begin her new life was right here. Lizzie made up her mind all at once.

'Thank you,' she said. 'I can pay you the money now – and Fred won't need to bring the stock round, because I'll be moving in as soon as you leave.'

'I'll let the landlord know you've taken over from me, and I'll send you a letter to say that the lease is yours. They'll be glad to get you at a time like this, because a lot of folk are getting out,' Arthur said. 'Sebastian was right. There's something about you Lizzie Larch – I almost wish I was going to be here to watch you make a success of the business . . .'

CHAPTER 42

Lizzie was busy packing cardboard boxes when Beth came round that evening.

'Mum wanted to know if you needed help, so I said I'd call in on my way home. I've been to see that flat, Lizzie. It's a bit bigger than this with two bedrooms, and I've decided to take it, if they will let me . . .'

'Can you afford the rent?' Lizzie guessed her friend was both excited and nervous.

'Just about – or I shall if you'll give me a few hours serving in your showroom when you open. Bernie has promised some part-time office work but the wage wouldn't cover everything.'

'In time I'll have some bookwork for you as well. I'll pay you extra for that, Beth. I've been thinking that between us we can probably manage, babysitting for each other . . .' Lizzie drew her breath sharply. 'I had a telephone call this morning about Harry. I can have the funeral towards the end of next week, so I've arranged for his body to be taken to a chapel of rest near here and the service for next Friday . . . I've written to Uncle

Bertie of the arrangements but I doubt he'd want to do it for me now . . .'

'It will be a relief to have it over, Lizzie. They've kept you waiting ages for the coroner's verdict . . .'

'Yes, and then it was left open. Harry hasn't been branded a suicide, Beth, so I can have him buried in consecrated ground.'

'I'm glad,' Beth said. 'If there's anything I can do? Mum won't expect me back for a while . . .'

Betty had been grizzling all night. It was almost as if the child knew that the day of her father's funeral had come. Lizzie had been up and down, nursing her, and her eyes were gritty from lack of sleep.

'Don't cry, little one,' she whispered. 'Mummy has to get ready to say goodbye to Daddy.'

The reality of what she was about to do hit Lizzie then. She was burying her husband, a man she'd loved when she married him – perhaps she still did a little, despite their estrangement. Her throat caught and tears pricked her eyes. They'd started out with such high hopes but it had all turned to ashes – except that she had her darling Betty and now she had a chance of her own business. Harry would have wanted her to make a success of it and she would . . .

Beth and her mother arrived and Beth settled her children in the sitting room so that the babies were apart and would not start each other off if one cried. Betty seemed much quieter and Lizzie hoped she'd panicked for nothing, just as the nurse said. She bent and kissed her cheek. Betty was a little warm but didn't seem in distress, so she left her with just a light cover over her tiny body.

'She was crying all night, but I rang the nurse and she thinks it's just a tummy upset. I hope she isn't too much trouble for you.'

'I've come armed with gripe water – and some powdered milk if she's hungry,' Mrs Court said with a smile. 'Don't worry, Lizzie. I'm used to babies with tummy aches – Beth was the worst of the lot.'

That made the girls laugh and Lizzie went off to the funeral feeling better than she had for a while. She'd let Harry's family know about the funeral, but wasn't sure if anyone would be there. However, both his aunt, uncle and some cousins on his mother's side had turned up. The cousins and Aunt Miriam greeted Lizzie with sympathetic respect, but Uncle Bertie stared through her. It seemed he's decided to come even though he'd been so angry and ashamed when he accused her of being the cause of Harry's distress.

Lizzie's throat contracted as the simple ceremony commenced. Her eyes stung with tears but she wouldn't let them fall. If Uncle Bertie thought her a cold bitch, let him. She wanted nothing more to do with him. Lizzie placed her posy on the coffin and soon the brief service came to an end, and the casket disappeared behind the curtains to be taken for cremation.

'It's almost over,' Beth said. 'We have to leave now . . .'

Outside, Lizzie hesitated for a moment, hardly knowing what to do because it had all been so quick and it seemed ridiculous that what had once been a living, loving man had been so easily lost. Gone like snow in sunshine, to remain only as a memory.

The vicar came to shake hands with her and offer his condolences. Lizzie thanked him in a small voice and turned away, clinging to Beth's arm – and then Aunt Miriam approached her.

'We're having a little tea at home, Lizzie – if you and your friend would like to come?'

'I'm sorry. I need to get back to Betty – but thank you for asking.'

'I don't know why you've fallen out with Harry's family,' Aunt Miriam said, her eyes sad and reproachful, 'but I hope you will let me see the baby sometimes?'

'Of course—' she said. 'I can't come to you – ask your husband why. Ed will tell you where to find me, if you want to . . .'

'I have asked Bertie but he will not answer me,' Aunt Miriam said. 'If it's business, you shouldn't let it stand between Betty and her family . . .'

Lizzie felt Beth touch her arm, steadying her. 'You and Harry's cousins are welcome to visit me. Now, if you will excuse me, I must get home . . .'

★   ★   ★

425

To Lizzie's relief her daughter was looking much better when she got home. Beth's mother had given her some gripe water when she woke grizzling and told Lizzie the most likely cause of the trouble was, as the nurse said, wind.

'Babies get it all the time, Lizzie,' she said.

'Well, as long as it's nothing serious,' Lizzie said. 'Next time I'll come to you rather than bothering the nurse.'

'Yes, you do that,' Mrs Court said. 'I think you can call me Muriel my dear. I believe we're good friends and next to family, so I would much rather you didn't call me Mrs Court all the time.'

'Thank you; yes, I should like that, Muriel.'

'Oh, and before I forget, a letter came for you by the second post. It looks official, so I put it on the table in the sitting room.'

Lizzie picked up it up, slitting the sealed envelope. She scanned the message inside, finding it so shocking that she had to read it again before she could take it in.

'You look upset,' Beth said. 'Is something wrong?'

'The letter is from Uncle Jack's solicitor. My aunt died a month ago. He has sent me a cheque for the rent due on my house and he says the present tenants would like to purchase the property . . .'

'You didn't know your aunt had died, did you?'

'It seems she left no instructions that I should be informed. She was cremated without fuss and only a witness from the home she'd been living in was present.'

'Why on earth didn't she let people know that you were her next of kin? We could have gone to the funeral . . .'

'My aunt hated me, Beth.'

'She was an unpleasant woman, bitter and twisted. You shouldn't grieve for her, Lizzie.'

'I don't think I feel grief – just sadness that she lived the way she did, not giving or receiving love . . .'

'Bad news?' Beth's mother said. 'I've got the toast under the grill, Lizzie and I've grated the cheese for our tea . . .'

'I've left you to do all of it,' Lizzie said. 'I'll come and help . . .'

'Lizzie's aunt is dead,' Beth said. 'She never even told them to let Lizzie know about the funeral, Mum.'

'After the way she behaved on your wedding day, I dare say she thought you wouldn't want to know.'

'Yes, perhaps . . .' Lizzie nodded, 'It means Uncle's house comes to me now. It has been let to tenants and the lawyer says they've made an offer to buy it – and the cobbler's shop next door as well.'

'Does it say how much they've offered?' Beth asked.

'No, he wants me to go in and talk to him.'

'Well, take my advice and think about it,' Beth's mother said. 'Property like that can be worth a lot of money.'

CHAPTER 43

'Thank you for coming to see me, Mrs Oliver,' the lawyer shook hands. 'Please do sit down. I was very sorry to pass on the news of your aunt's death. Unfortunately, I did not receive notice in time to tell you before the funeral.'

'My aunt was a difficult woman, Mr Broad. It was her choice that I should not be told and we did not truly get on well. My uncle and I were very close . . .' She sighed. 'I still miss him . . .'

'In that case I have something you may well wish to have,' Mr Broad said and handed her a sealed envelope. 'This was found amongst your aunt's things – but it was addressed to you. I believe it is in your uncle's hand . . .'

Lizzie looked at the envelope. 'Yes, I think it is.' She opened her bag and put it inside, closing it with a snap. 'Was there anything else, sir?'

'Yes. It concerns the proposed sale of your property, Mrs Oliver. I have received an offer of twelve hundred pounds for the house and eight hundred for the smaller property on the side, presently let as a cobbler's shop with accommodation over the top.'

'It is just one bedroom and a sitting room over the top, and a kitchen behind the workshop,' Lizzie said uncertain whether it was a good price. 'Suitable only for a man living alone, or perhaps a couple. As you know, I get one pound a week for the rent – but that comes in useful . . .'

'You could get thirty shillings for the house or perhaps as much as two pounds if the present tenants moved out,' Mr Broad said, 'but it wasn't let on a proper lease and if the tenants wish to stay on I doubt you could get a rent rise just yet. Selling to a sitting tenant is not always the best, but it is difficult to get them out – unless you needed the house for yourself or a relative. In that case you could give them a month's notice . . .'

'You don't think I could get more for either the house or the workshop?'

'I think the man who wishes to purchase the workshop might go to nine hundred pounds at a push, but I doubt the sitting tenants in the house would offer more.'

'May I have a few days to think it over, sir?' Lizzie had no idea of property prices and thought it best to ask for a little independent advice.

'Yes, of course. Property is not perhaps the investment it might be, given that we are in the middle of a war. If the property was to be bombed, you could lose everything.'

'Yes, I had considered that,' Lizzie said. 'I believe I would sell the shop if you can get nine hundred for me – but I might keep the house . . .' She was just beginning to get an idea but she'd need to talk to Beth before she decided . . .

Lizzie caught her bus to Beth's house. If Beth had already taken the flat she'd spoken of, Lizzie couldn't afford to live in her uncle's house on her own. Together, they could make it work and it would be better for both of them if they shared a house.

Beth welcomed her in, one of the twins in her arms. 'Matt is asleep in his cot but Jenny has been fractious all morning. How did you get on, Lizzie?'

'Oh, I've been offered twelve hundred for the house and eight hundred for the shop. I've told him I'll sell the shop if I can get nine hundred – but I've had an idea about the house . . .'

'You've got tenants there, haven't you?'

'Yes, but if I want the house for myself or a relative I can give them a month's notice . . .'

'I thought you hated it after your uncle died?'

'It seemed big and empty and my aunt made it feel like a morgue – but with two women and three children it would be very different . . .'

Beth stared. 'What are you saying? We could share the house – you and me, Lizzie?'

'The house is in good condition. We might want to decorate, but most of it is good and I'll be able to do whatever needs doing. There's a garden for the kids. We can put the prams out there and when they're older – but if you've taken the flat it's too late . . .'

'Oh, Lizzie, it's a wonderful idea. I went after the flat but they wouldn't let it to me because I'm a woman on my own with two kids and they thought I might not pay the rent. I could give you the same as they were charging – fifteen shillings a week . . .'

'I don't want rent from you. We'll share all the expenses, electric and all the rest – and it will make things easier for both of us . . .'

'Oh, Lizzie! I don't know what to say . . .'

'You could say yes . . .' Lizzie laughed because Beth threw herself at her and hugged her, her baby squeezed between them.

'But what about the flat over the workshop?'

'I think I know someone who might like to rent it,' Lizzie said. 'I'll go round later and speak to him – as long as you're happy with our arrangement?'

'When can we move in?'

'I'll telephone my uncle's lawyer and tell him to serve notice and as soon as he says the house is empty we'll go. It's a good thing I hadn't given notice on my flat just yet.'

'I can't wait,' Beth said. 'I'm glad I didn't say yes when Bernie asked me to marry him, Lizzie. I was in love with Mark, I still do love him, but I've accepted that he's gone, Lizzie. but you were right. I'm going to wait for the right man – a man I can love as I loved Mark.'

Lizzie telephoned the lawyer with her decision and he agreed that she had made a sensible choice.

'I'm able to tell you that my client has accepted your terms on the cobbler's shop, Mrs Oliver. He is anxious to go ahead and I believe you will receive your money in about six weeks.'

'Thank you. You will let me know when I can move into my house.'

'Yes, of course.'

Lizzie's mind was busy as she made herself poached egg on toast. Ed was not happy in his lodgings and she believed he might be ready for a place of his own again, but she wasn't quite sure how to put the suggestion to him. It would mean a bus ride every morning and evening for him to get to Oliver's but she would charge him no more than ten shillings for the rent and she happened to know he was paying twice that for a room, breakfast and evening meal . . .

After the dishes were finished, Lizzie looked about her. She had half her stuff in boxes but she couldn't be bothered to unpack it all again, just the things she would need to see her through another month or so . . .

Remembering the letter her lawyer had given her, Lizzie took a cup of tea through to the sitting room and slit the envelope. *My very dear Lizzie,* Uncle Jack had written.

I've wanted to tell you the truth for a long time, but the doctor thought it best that you should remember in your own way or not at all.

Lizzie closed her eyes, uncertain that she wanted to go on because her aunt had already told her in a way that had brought great distress. She wished that she'd been told everything years before, but it hardly mattered now. She was about to fold the letter and replace it in the envelope when the next sentence caught her eye.

It was my fault, Lizzie. I sent you for those wretched cigarettes, but you were gone so long. I became worried when you didn't return, and I went to the police. They told me a nurse had found you, and I was so upset, guilty because of what I'd done . . . You were attacked and abused, Lizzie, and because of that you were ill for a long time – and I blame myself for sending you out that night.

I hope in time you will forgive me for ruining your life. I loved you so much and I've done what little I can to make up for what happened . . .
Your contrite and loving uncle.

Lizzie sat by the fire in the front room and picked up her sketchbook, but her eyes were moist and she didn't feel like working, because she just wished she could talk to her uncle tell him how grateful she was – how much she loved him. She was staring into space, half asleep when her front doorbell rang.

Who could that be at this hour? She was

reluctant to answer, because it was getting dark and nearly nine in the evening, but it might be important . . . Reluctantly, she got to her feet and ran down the stairs, opening the door just as the man was turning away. She recognised him instantly and called to him, 'Ed, is that you?'

He turned with a smile. 'Forgive me for disturbing you at this hour, but I've only just learned what Oliver did to you . . .'

'Come up into the flat, Ed,' Lizzie invited and made sure her blackout was in place before putting the light on. 'I wanted to see you, but when you didn't come to see me I thought perhaps . . . you might blame me too.'

'He ordered me not to, said you didn't want to see anyone. Then I found out he's finishing with the special hats and I demanded the truth. I told him he's a damned fool and I've left Oliver's,' he said, turning to her as she locked the door behind them. 'It's obvious why you didn't tell him, because you wanted to spare them pain – and I don't believe for one moment that you would have cheated on your husband.'

'I didn't,' Lizzie said. 'Something happened – a quarrel that may have contributed to Harry's distress, but I had written to tell him I wanted him home so that we could start again.'

'If you quarrelled it was his fault; the lad always had a jealous streak and a temper like his father and his uncle. I know you, Lizzie, and I would trust you with my life.'

'Oh, Ed, thank you,' she said, her throat catching with emotion. 'It makes me feel so much better.'

'What are you going to do now?'

'Carry on as best I can,' she said. 'I've bought some rolls of material from Arthur Stockton; he's gone to the country to be with his daughter – and I've taken over his lease. It's only for five years, but long enough to discover whether I can make a go of my own millinery business.'

'At one time I thought of working with him – and I would have if you hadn't started designing for us . . . it's a pity he's gone.'

'Yes, his hats were good quality.'

'Better than some of Oliver's,' Ed said. 'I'm going to work in a boot factory – but over the years I've acquired things I need for the hat making, which I kept in the shed outside. They weren't burned, Lizzie, and you can have them if they're of any use – and I'd be glad to help you on Saturdays and Sundays too, if that doesn't bother you – we could produce more of your special styles.'

'Oh, Ed, that is the best news I've had in ages,' Lizzie said. 'It would help me so much if you could produce a few new shapes each week for me to work on. I don't know how long my stock will last but . . .'

'I might be able to help there,' Ed said. 'I've made contacts over the years – with suppliers that Oliver wouldn't give a contract to because he said they were too dear – but their stock was the best, Lizzie. He's always bought overseas when he could, but I like local suppliers and I bought a few rolls of good quality velvet last year from a young lad just started up as a salesman. He told me that if ever I needed more supplies to come to him. Of course the velvet was lost in the fire but . . .' Ed paused for a moment, and then went on in a firm tone, 'I can give him a ring and he will call to see you here. I know we have to comply with certain regulations, but that should be easy enough to work out – there isn't anything about Oliver's business I don't know, which is why he tried to hang on to me.'

'Oh, Ed,' Lizzie said. 'I bought a bit of velvet too. I've done some new shapes, tam-o'-shanters, caps and a soft turban which clings softly to the back of the head – it's the softer line a lot of women like at the moment.'

'I think we'll find most of what we want right here in this country. Local factories making simple, good quality materials we don't have to import. Maybe we shan't find all the exotic bits and pieces we've been used to – but we probably don't need them.' His eyes twinkled. 'They tell me there's a war on . . .'

Lizzie's eyes stung with tears because she'd been given fresh hope for the future. 'You are so very kind . . .'

'I like working for you and that's the truth. Bert Oliver treats his workers like he owns them; you treat us as individuals, Lizzie. I'll be glad to do what I can for you.'

Lizzie gave a scream of delight and hugged the older man. His plain, homely face broke into a smile and he gave her a quick bear hug back.

'I was going to come round and ask if you'd like to take the flat over Stockton's workshops. I'm going to live in my uncle's house with Beth and the children – and I could let you have the flat for ten shillings a week.'

'Offer it to me? That's really nice of you.' Ed looked pleased, and then a flicker of excitement showed in his eyes. 'It's worth more than that, Lizzie. I'll give you fifteen. I've been looking for a place I can afford and that would be ideal, because I could work for you when I'm not at the boot factory.'

'As soon as we start to get some customers for the workshop, you can work full-time if you want. If we can keep going long enough, you can be my partner and we'll make beautiful hats that everyone will want . . .'

'That we will, Lizzie,' he said. 'I've often thought of having my own workshops – and if you'd really have me as your partner, I'll put in a bit of my savings to buy us more stock.'

'Of course I meant it,' Lizzie said, and suddenly her future seemed to be glowing. Somehow she and Ed would make it through the dark days of war; they would keep going for as long as they could buy stock and sell hats . . . Women loved Lizzie's hats, particularly the different and unusual styles she could produce with Ed's skill and her flair, and she knew she could sell them to her special customers. 'What shall we call the new business?'

'We'll use your name, Lizzie,' Ed told her firmly. 'I'm a sleeping partner and we'll have a lawyer do it right, keep it fair, because you're the senior partner, Lizzie, and you should have the bigger share – but I promise you, I'll do everything I can to make this work for you.'

'For us, Ed,' she said and smiled. 'Life hurts, Ed, and we've both suffered, but together we'll get through somehow . . .'

AFTERWORD

'**I** found this emulsion paint in the shed,' Mrs Court said, handing the half-empty tin to Lizzie and looking about with interest. 'You've almost finished the showroom, but this might do out the back somewhere.'

'Oh, good, it's white,' Lizzie said as she took the tin. 'Ed could do with this for the ceilings in the flat . . .'

'Well, I'll get off now. Beth said to tell you she would be coming round later to help you finish getting things straight – Do you think you'll have the showroom open for Christmas week?'

'Yes, I'm hoping . . .' Lizzie broke off, her breath catching in her throat as the showroom door opened and someone walked in. 'Sebastian . . .' her heart missed a beat and sudden tears stung her eyes.

'I was told I might find you here,' Sebastian said. 'I've got a couple of days' leave and thought I might give you a hand . . .'

'Well, I'll be going, Lizzie,' Mrs Court said, looking curiously at Sebastian as he lifted his hat to her. 'Don't forget we're expecting you for lunch on Sunday, love . . . unless you have other plans . . .'

Lizzie's heart was racing so fast that she could hardly speak. 'Sebastian, I wasn't sure when I'd see you again . . . who told you I was here?'

'I think her name was Tilly,' Sebastian said. 'She was just leaving Oliver's and I asked her if she knew where I could find you. I went to the flat first but someone else is living there . . .'

'Yes, I've moved into a house with Beth and her children,' Lizzie said. 'A lot has happened since I last saw you . . .'

'I was sorry to hear about Harry's accident . . .' Sebastian frowned. 'I don't know if you've been told, Lizzie, but the brakes on that car were faulty, and the steering rod broke – it was a flaming liability and shouldn't have been on the road.'

Lizzie didn't need to ask how Sebastian knew. She simply took it for granted that he was telling her the truth, because he was Sebastian and he would make it his business to know – just as he'd known how to find her.

Tears slipped down her cheeks. 'I never believed it was suicide but there was a lot of talk – and Bert Oliver blamed me.'

'Then he is a fool and I'll tell him so . . .' Sebastian glanced about him. 'Are you going to be all right here, Lizzie? If you need money . . .?'

'I used the money you sent me, and Arthur was very generous to me, letting me have the lease here cheap; besides, I have some money my uncle left me.' Lizzie hesitated shyly. 'I wanted to thank you – and I'll pay you back one day, Sebastian.'

'That money was a gift because I wanted to make sure that you were all right. I don't want any talk of paying me back or gratitude'. Sebastian moved towards her and then stopped, as if afraid of overstepping the line. 'I heard you had a daughter?'

'Yes. Beth is looking after her this morning, and then her mother will take over this afternoon – that was Mrs Court you just met.'

A smile lit his eyes. 'Ah, the curious lady – I'm not sure she approves of me visiting you, Lizzie.'

'She's always been protective of me,' Lizzie smiled as she saw the mischief in his eyes. 'She wouldn't want me to be hurt, you see . . .'

Sebastian took a few steps closer. 'Do you think it's my intention to hurt you, Lizzie Larch?'

'No, I don't,' she whispered. 'I used to think you were a flirt, Sebastian – but I know you better now.'

'Do you?' he asked softly, looking down into her eyes. 'I might hurt you by disappearing and never coming back, or I might hurt you by being killed, because I shan't pretend that what I do isn't dangerous – but I promise I'll never hurt you because I don't care for you, my lovely Lizzie.'

'None of us can promise that we'll be safe these days,' she said. 'We've had bombs nearby and gas explosions. It's a case of taking what we can from life while we can . . . don't you think?'

441

'Then will you come to dinner with me this evening? Will you take a chance on me, Lizzie Larch – even though I can only promise you two days?'

She looked up into his eyes and liked what she saw there, because mixed with the mischief and the challenge was love.

'Yes, I'll take a chance on you, Sebastian Winters,' she whispered. 'If two days is all you can give me for now, I'll take it – but don't think that's all I want. I know you can't tell me what you do, and I shall never ask – but remember I'm waiting and you come back to me. Do you hear me, Sebastian? You damned well come back, because I'll be waiting.'

'Oh, I'll come back,' he murmured as he closed the distance between them, drawing her close. 'Don't you know what they say about bad pennies – they always turn up . . .'